I0688050

Henry Jones

Browning as a Philosopher and Religious Teacher

Henry Jones

Browning as a Philosopher and Religious Teacher

ISBN/EAN: 9783337075842

Printed in Europe, USA, Canada, Australia, Japan

Cover: Foto ©Raphael Reischuk / pixelio.de

More available books at **www.hansebooks.com**

BROWNING

AS A

PHILOSOPHICAL AND RELIGIOUS TEACHER

BY

SIR HENRY JONES

LL.D., D.Litt.

FELLOW OF THE BRITISH ACADEMY
PROFESSOR OF MORAL PHILOSOPHY IN THE UNIVERSITY OF GLASGOW

GLASGOW
JAMES MACLEHOSE & SONS
Publishers to the University
1912

First Edition 1891.   Second Edition 1892.
Reprinted 1896, 1899, 1902, 1912.

GLASGOW: PRINTED AT THE UNIVERSITY PRESS
BY ROBERT MACLEHOSE AND CO. LTD.

This Book is Dedicated

TO MY DEAR FRIENDS

MISS HARRIET MACARTHUR

AND

MISS JANE MACARTHUR

PREFACE TO THE FIRST EDITION.

THE purpose of this book is to deal with Browning, not simply as a poet, but rather as the exponent of a system of ideas on moral and religious subjects, which may fairly be called a philosophy. I am conscious that it is a wrong to a poet to neglect, or even to subordinate, the artistic aspect of his work. At least, it would be a wrong, if our final judgment on his poetry were to be determined on such a method. But there is a place for everything; and, even in the case of a great poet, there is sometimes an advantage in attempting to estimate the value of what he has said, apart from the form in which he has said it. And of all modern poets, Browning is the one who most obviously invites and justifies such a method of treatment. For, in the first place, he is clearly one of that class of poets who are also prophets. He was never merely 'the idle singer of an empty day,' but one for whom poetic enthusiasm was intimately bound up with religious faith, and who spoke 'in numbers,' not merely 'because the numbers came,' but because they were for him the necessary vehicle of an inspiring thought. If it is the business of philosophy to analyze and interpret all the great intellectual forces that mould the thought of an age, it cannot neglect the works of one who has exercised, and is exercising so powerful an influence on the moral and religious life of the present generation.

In the second place, as will be seen in the sequel, Browning has himself led the way towards such a philosophical interpretation of his work. For, even in his earlier poems, he not seldom crossed the line that divides the poet from the philosopher, and all but broke through the strict limits of art in the effort to express—and we might even say to preach —his own idealistic faith. In his later works he did this almost without any disguise, raising philosophical problems, and discussing all the *pros* and *cons* of their solution, with no little subtlety and dialectical skill. In some of these poems we might even seem to be receiving a philosophical lesson, in place of poetic inspiration, if it were not for those powerful imaginative utterances, those winged words, which Browning has always in reserve, to close the ranks of his argument. If the question is stated in a prosaic form, the final answer, as in the ancient oracle, is in the poetic language of the gods.

From this point of view I have endeavoured to give a connected account of Browning's ideas, especially of his ideas on religion and morality, and to estimate their value. In order to do so, it was necessary to discuss the philosophical validity of the principles on which his doctrine is more or less consciously based. The more immediately philosophical chapters are the second, seventh, and ninth ; but they will not be found unintelligible by those who have reflected on the difficulties of the moral and religious life, even although they may be unacquainted with the methods and language of the schools.

I have received much valuable help in preparing this work for the press from my colleague, Professor G. B. Mathews, and still more from Professor Edward Caird. I owe them both a deep debt of gratitude.

H. J.

UNIVERSITY COLLEGE OF NORTH WALES,
BANGOR, *May*, 1891.

PREFACE TO THE SECOND EDITION.

THE changes introduced into this edition are merely verbal. But one of my friends has supplied an Index of the references to the poems of Browning mentioned in the book, and has helped me in making an analysis of the argument.

Some of my critics have made suggestions by which I should have been glad to profit had the duties of my present office given me more leisure. I take this unexpected opportunity of expressing my gratitude to them.

THE UNIVERSITY OF ST. ANDREWS,
January 27th, 1892.

CONTENTS

CHAPTER I

INTRODUCTION

CHAPTER II

ON THE NEED OF A PHILOSOPHY OF LIFE

CHAPTER III

BROWNING'S PLACE IN ENGLISH POETRY

CHAPTER IV

BROWNING'S OPTIMISM

CHAPTER V

OPTIMISM AND ETHICS: THEIR CONTRADICTION

CHAPTER VI

BROWNING'S TREATMENT OF THE PRINCIPLE OF LOVE

CHAPTER VII

BROWNING'S IDEALISM, AND ITS PHILOSOPHICAL JUSTIFICATION

CHAPTER VIII

BROWNING'S SOLUTION OF THE PROBLEM OF EVIL

CHAPTER IX

A CRITICISM OF BROWNING'S VIEW OF THE FAILURE OF KNOWLEDGE

CHAPTER X

THE HEART AND THE HEAD—LOVE AND REASON

CHAPTER XI

CONCLUSION

ROBERT BROWNING

CHAPTER I

INTRODUCTION

"Grau, theurer Freund, ist alle Theorie,
Und grün des Lebens goldner Baum." (*Faust.*)

THERE is a saying of Hegel's, frequently quoted, that "a great man condemns the world to the task of explaining him." This condemnation is a double one, falling upon the great man who has to submit to explanation, no less than upon the world; and it falls with peculiar weight upon the great man who is also an artist. In proceeding to expound a poet I, therefore, think it meet to begin with an apology; and to acknowledge at the outset that no commentator on art has any right to be heard, if he is not aware of the subordinate and temporary nature of his office. His function, at its highest, is merely to guide others to the beautiful object; so soon as he has led his company into its presence, he must fall back in silence. He may, perhaps, suggest 'the line of vision,' or fix the point of view from which the intention of the artist may be best appreciated and his central idea understood ; but if he seeks to serve the ends of art, he will not attempt to do anything more.

In order to do even this in a successful manner, it is essential that every judgment that he passes should be exclusively based upon the principles which govern art. "Fine art is not real art till it is free." Its worth must be recognized as lying wholly within itself. So far from enhancing the value of a poet's work by enumerating the utilities that attend it—by showing that it gives pleasure, or refinement, or moral culture, we only degrade it into mere means and subordinate it to foreign uses which are antagonistic to its perfection as fine art. There is no doubt that great poetry has all these uses, but the reader can enjoy them only on condition of forgetting them ; for they are effects that *follow* the sense of its beauty. It is, unfortunately, still necessary to insist that art is, within its own sphere, supreme; that the beautiful is not more beautiful because it is also moral, and that a painting is not great because its subject happens to be religious. It is true that the spheres of art, morality and religion, overlap. Art is never at its best except when it is a beautiful representation of that which is good ; nevertheless, the points of view of the artist and of the ethical teacher are quite different, and even when they deal with the same subject they do not in all respects reveal the same truths.

On this account, I cannot pretend that this

attempt to discover Browning's philosophy of life
can be an adequate treatment of him as a writer.
Browning was, first of all, a poet; it is only as a
poet that he can be finally judged; and the value
of his contribution to English literature must be
primarily estimated by the extent to which his
writings are a revelation of that which is beautiful.

This task, however, I have not undertaken:
mine is a much humbler one. I am conscious
of its limitations, and aware that I can hardly
avoid doing some violence to the artist. What I
shall seek in the poet's writings is not beauty but
truth; and although truth is beautiful, and beauty
is truth, still the poetic and philosophic interpretation of life are not to be confused. Philosophy
must separate the matter from the form. Its
synthesis comes through analysis, and analysis is
destructive of beauty, as it is of all life. Art, therefore, resists the violence of the critical methods of
philosophy, and the feud of which Plato speaks,
between these 'two civilizing inspirations,' will last
through all time. The beauty of form and the
music of speech which criticism destroys, and to
which philosophy is, at the best, indifferent, are
elements essential to poetry. When we leave these
out of account we miss its ultimate secret, for
they cling to the meaning and penetrate it with
their charm. Thought and its expression are inseparable in poetry as they never are in philosophy;
hence, in the former, the loss of the expression is
the loss of truth. The pure idea that dwells in
a poem is suffused in the poetic utterance, as
sunshine breaks into beauty in the mist, as life

beats and blushes in the flesh, **or as an** impassioned thought breathes in a thinker's face.

But, although **art** and philosophy are supreme, **each** in its own realm, and neither can **be** subordinated to the uses of the other, they may help each other. They are independent, but not rival powers of the world of mind. Not only is the interchange of truth possible between them, but each may show and give to the other all its treasures and be none the poorer itself. "It is in works of art that some nations have deposited the profoundest intuitions and ideas of their hearts." Job **and** Isaiah, Æschylus and Sophocles, Shakespeare and Goethe, were **first of all** poets. Mankind **is** indebted to them **in the** first place for revealing beauty; **but it** also **owes to** them much insight into the facts and principles of **the** moral world. It would be an unutterable loss **to** the ethical thinker **and** the philosopher if the **region** of **art** were closed against them, so that they could no longer seek in the poets the inspiration and light that lead to goodness and truth. In our own day, **almost** above all others, we need the poets for these **ethical** and religious purposes. For the utterances **of the** dogmatic teacher of religion have been divested of much of their ancient authority; and **the** moral philosopher is often regarded either as **a** vendor of commonplaces or as the votary of a science so discredited that its primary principles are matter of doubt and debate. There are not a few educated Englishmen who find in the poets, and in the **poets** alone, the expression of their deepest convictions concerning the profoundest interests of life. They read the poets for fresh inspiration, partly, **no doubt,** because the passion and rapture of poetry lull **criticism** and soothe the questioning **spirit into acquiescence,** but partly also **for** weightier **reasons.** The poets of England **are greater than its moral** philosophers; and it **is of the nature** of the poetic art that, while eschewing **system, it** presents the strife between right **and wrong** in **concrete** character, **and** therefore **with a** fulness and truth impossible to the **abstract** thought **of a** moral science.

> **"A poet** never dreams :
> We prose folk do : we miss the proper duct
> **For** thoughts on things unseen." [1]

It is true that philosophy endeavours to correct the fragmentariness of science by starting from the unity of **the whole. But it can** never quite get **rid of** an element of abstraction and reach down **to** the concrete individual.

The making of character is so complex a process that the poetic representation of it, with its subtle suggestiveness, is always more complete and realistic than any possible philosophic analysis. Science can deal only with aspects and abstractions even in the case of simple natural objects ; and, as its matter grows more complex and concrete, its method be**comes more and more** inadequate. The true method is that which proceeds from the unity in which all the aspects are held together. In the case of **life,** and still more so in that of human conduct, the whole must precede the part, and the moral science

---

[1] *Fifine at the Fair,* lxxxviii.

should, therefore, **more** than any other, partake of the nature of poetry ; for it must start from living spirit, go from the heart outwards, in order to detect the meaning **of the actions of man.**

On this account poetry **is** peculiarly helpful to **the** ethical investigator, because it always treats the particular thing **as a** microcosm. **It** is the great corrective **of** the one-sidedness of science with its **harsh** method **of** analysis and distinction. It is a witness to the unity of man and the world. Every object which **art touches** into **beauty,** becomes in **the very act a whole. The** thing **that is beautiful is always** complete, **the** embodiment of something **absolutely** valuable, the product and the source of love ; and the beloved object is **all** the world for the lover—beyond all praise, because it is above all comparison.

> "**Then** why not witness, calmly gazing,
> **If earth** holds aught—speak truth—above her?
> Above this tress, and this, I touch
> But cannot praise, I love so much !"[1]

This characteristic of the work of art brings with it an important practical consequence, because, being complete, it appeals to the whole man.

"Poetry," it has been well said, is "the idealized and monumental utterance of the deepest feelings." And poetic feelings, it must not be forgotten, *are* deepest ; that is, they **are** the afterglow of the fullest activity of a complete soul, and not shallow titillations, or **surface** pleasures, such as the palate **knows.** Led by poetry, the intellect so sees truth

[1] *Song* (Dramatic Lyrics).

that it feels it, and the will is stirred to deeds of heroism. What truth it is, matters little; for there is hardly any fact so mean, but that when intensified by emotion, it grows poetic; as there is hardly any man so unimaginative, but that when struck with a great sorrow, or moved by a great passion, he is endowed for a moment with the poet's speech. A poetic fact, one may almost say, is any fact at its best. Art, it is true, looks at its object through a medium, but it always sees its inmost meaning. In Lear, Othello, Hamlet, in Falstaff and Touchstone, there is a revelation of the inner truth of human life beyond the power of moral science to bestow. We do well to seek philosophy in the poets, for though they teach only by hints and parables, they nevertheless reflect the concrete truth of life as it is half revealed and half concealed in facts.

On the other hand, the reflective process of philosophy may help poetry; for, as we shall show, there is a near kinship between them. Even the critical analyst, while severing element from element, may help art and serve the poet's ends, provided he does not in his analysis of parts forget the whole. His function, though humble and merely preliminary to full poetic enjoyment, is not unimportant. To appreciate the grandeur of the unity of the work of art there must be knowledge of the parts combined. It is quite true that the guide in the gallery is prone to be too talkative, and there are many who can afford to turn the commentator out of doors, especially if he moralizes. But, after all, man is not pure sensibility, any more than he

is pure **reason. And** the æsthete will not lose if
he occasionally allows those **whom he** may think
less sensitive than himself to the charm **of** rhythmic
phrase, **to** direct sober attention to the principles
which lie embedded **in** all great poetry. **At the
worst, to seek** for **truth in poetry** is a **protest
against the constant** tendency to read **it for** the
sake of the emotions which it **stirs,** the tendency
to make it a **refined** amusement and nothing **more.**
That is a **deeper** wrong to art than any which the
theoretical **moralist** can inflict. Of the two, it **is
better to read** poetry for **ethical** doctrines than **for
fine sensations;** for poetry purifies the passions only
when it lifts the reader **into the** sphere **of** truths
that are universal.

The task of interpreting a poet **may be** undertaken in different ways. One of **these,** with which
we **have** been **made familiar by** critics **of** Shakespeare **and of** Browning himself, is to analyze each
poem by itself and regard it as the artistic embodiment of some central idea; the other is to
attempt, without dealing separately with each poem,
to reach the poet's own point of view, and to reveal
the sovereign truths which rule his mind. It is the
latter way that I shall try to follow.

Such dominant, or even despotic, thoughts it is
possible to discover in all our great poets, except
perhaps Shakespeare, whose universality baffles every
classifier. As a **rule the English** poets have **been**
caught up and inspired by the exceeding grandeur
of some single idea, in whose service they spend
themselves with that prodigal thrift which grows
rich in giving. Such an idea gives them a fresh

way of looking at the world, **so** that **it** grows young again in the light of their new interpretation. In the highest instances, poets may become makers of epochs; they may reform as well as reveal; for ideas are never dead things, 'but grow in the hand that grasps them.' The energy of a nation's life **lies** in its thinkers, and we comprehend that life only when we make clear to ourselves the ideas which inspire it. **It is** thus true, in the deepest sense, that those who make the songs of a people make its history; and, consequently, there are, **in** all true poets, hints for a larger philosophy of life. But, in order to discover it, we must know the truths which dominate them and break into music **in their poems.**

Whether it is always possible, and whether it is at any time fair to **a poet to** define the idea which inspires him, I shall not inquire **at present.** No doubt, the interpretation of a poet from first principles carries us beyond the limits of art; and by insisting on the unity of his work, more may be attributed to him, or demanded **from** him, than he properly owns. To make such a demand is **to** require that poetry should be philosophy **as well,** which, owing to its method of intuition, poetry can **never be.** Nevertheless, among English poets there is no one who lends himself so easily, or so justly, to this way of treatment as Browning. Much **of** his poetry trembles on the verge of **the abyss** which is supposed to separate art from philosophy; and, as I shall try to show, there was in the poet a growing tendency to turn the power of dialectic **on** the presuppositions **of his art.** Yet, **even**

Browning puts great difficulties **in** the **way** of a critic who seeks **to** draw a philosophy of life from his poems. It is **not by any** means **an easy task** to lift the truths he utters **under the stress of poetic** emotion into the region of placid contemplation, or to connect **them** into a system by means of the principle from which he makes his departure.

The first of these difficulties arises from the extent and variety of his work. He was prodigal of poetic ideas, and wrote for fifty years on nature, art, and man, like a magnificent spendthrift of spiritual treasures. So great a store of knowledge **lay** at his hand, so real **and** informed with sympathy, that **we** can scarcely find any great literature which he has **not** ransacked, **or any** phase **of** life which is not represented in his poems. All kinds of men and women, in every **station of** life, **and** at every stage of evil and goodness, crowd **his** pages. There are few forms of human character he has not studied, and he has so caught each individual at the supreme moment of his life and in the hardest stress of circumstance, **that** the inmost working of his nature **is** revealed. The wealth is bewildering, and it is **hard to** follow the central thought, "the imperial **chord,** which steadily underlies the accidental mists of music springing thence."[1]

A second and still graver difficulty lies in the fact that his poetry, as he repeatedly insisted, is "always dramatic in principle, **and so** many utterances of so many imaginary persons, not **mine."**[2] In his earlier works, especially, Browning is creative rather than reflective, a Maker rather than a Seer; and

---

[1] *Fifine at the Fair.*   [2] Pref. to *Pauline*, 1888.

his creations stand aloof from him, working out their fate in an outer world. We often lose the poet in the imaginative characters, into whom he penetrates with his keen artistic intuition, and within whom he lies as a necessity revealing itself in their actions and words. It is not easy anywhere to separate the elements, so that we can say with certainty, 'Here I catch the poet, **there lies** his material.' **The** identification of the work and worker **is** too intimate, and the realization of **the** imaginary personage is too complete.

In regard to the dramatic interpretation **of his** poetry, Browning has manifested a peculiar sensitiveness. In his Preface to *Pauline* and in several of his poems—notably *The Mermaid*, *The House*, and *The Shop*—he explicitly cuts himself free from his work. He knew that direct self-revealment on the part of the poet violates the spirit of the drama. "With this same key Shakespeare unlocked his heart," said Wordsworth; "Did Shakespeare?" characteristically answers Browning, "If so, the less Shakespeare he!" **And of himself he asks:**

> "Which of you did I enable
>   Once to slip inside my breast,
>   There to catalogue and label
>   What I like least, what love best,
> **Hope and** fear, believe and doubt of,
>   Seek and shun, respect—deride?
>   Who has right to make a rout of
>   Rarities he found inside?"[1]

He repudiates all kinship with Byron and his subjective ways, and refuses to be made king by the

---

[1] *At the Mermaid.*

hands which anointed him. 'He will not give his woes an airing, and has no plague that claims respect.' Both as man and poet, in virtue of the native, sunny, outer-air healthiness of his character, every kind of subjectivity is repulsive to him. He hands to his readers 'his work, his scroll, theirs to take or leave : his soul he proffers not.' For him 'shop was shop only'; and though he dealt in gems, and threw

> "You choice of jewels, every one,
> Good, better, best, star, moon and sun,"[1]

he still *lived* elsewhere, and had 'stray thoughts and fancies fugitive' not meant for the open market. The poems in which Browning has spoken without the disguise of another character are very few. There are hardly more than two or three of much importance which can be considered as directly reflecting his own ideas, namely, *Christmas Eve* and *Easter Day*, *La Saisiaz*, and *One Word More* —unless, spite of the poet's warning, we add *Pauline*.

But, although the dramatic element in Browning's poetry renders it difficult to construct his character from his works—while this is comparatively easy in the case of Wordsworth or Byron—and although it throws a shade of uncertainty on every conclusion we might draw as to any specific doctrine held by him, still Browning lives in a certain atmosphere, and looks at his characters through a medium, whose subtle influence makes all his work indis- putably *his*. The light he throws on his men and

---

[1] *Shop.*

women is not the unobtrusive light of day, which reveals objects but not itself. Though a true dramatist, he is not objective like Shakespeare and Scott, whose characters seem never to have had an author. The reader feels, rather, that Browning himself attends him through all the sights and wonders of the world of man; he never escapes the sense of the presence of the poet's powerful personality, or of the great convictions on which his life was based. Browning has, at bottom, only one way of looking at the world and one way of treating his objects; one point of view and one artistic method. Nay, further, he has one supreme interest, which he pursues everywhere with a constancy shown by hardly any other poet; and, in consequence, his works have a unity and a certain originality, which make them in many ways a unique contribution to English literature.

This characteristic, which no critic has missed, and which generally goes by the name of "the metaphysical element" in his poetry, makes it the more imperative to form a clear view of his ruling conceptions. No poet, least of all a dramatic poet, goes about seeking concrete vehicles for ready-made ideas, or attempts to dress a philosophy in metaphors; and Browning, as an artist, is interested first of all in the object which he renders beautiful for its own sole sake, and not in any abstract idea it illustrates. Still, it is true in a peculiar degree in his case, that the eye of the poet brings with it what it sees. He is, as a rule, conscious of no theory, and does not construct a poem for its explication; he rather strikes his ideas out of his material, as the sculptor reveals the breathing life in the stone. Nevertheless, it may be shown that a theory rules him from behind, and that profound convictions arise in the heart and rush along the blood at the moment of creation, using his soul as an instrument of expression to his age and people.

Of no English poet, except Shakespeare, can we say with approximate truth that he is the poet of all times. The subjective breath of their own epoch dims the mirror which they hold up to nature. Missing by their limitation the highest universality, they can only be understood in their setting. It adds but little to our knowledge of Shakespeare's work to regard him as the great Elizabethan; there is nothing temporary in his dramas, except petty incidents and external trappings—so truly did he dwell amidst the permanent elements that constitute man in every age and clime. But this cannot be said of any other poet, not even of Chaucer or Spenser, far less of Milton, or Pope, or Wordsworth. In their case, the artistic form and the material, the idea and its expression, the beauty and the truth, are to some extent separable. We can distinguish in Milton between the Puritanic theology which is perishable, and the art whose beauty can never pass away. The former fixes his kinship with his own age, gives him a definite place in the evolution of English life; the latter is independent of time, a thing which has supreme worth in itself.

Nor can it be doubted that the same holds good of Browning. He also is ruled by the ideas of his own age. It may not be altogether possible for us, 'who are partners of his motion and mixed up with his career,' to allow for the influence of these ideas, and to distinguish between that which is evanescent and that which is permanent in his work : still I must try to do so ; for it is the condition of comprehending him, and of appropriating the truth and beauty he came to reveal. And if his nearness to ourselves makes this more difficult, it also makes it more imperative. For there is no doubt that, with Carlyle, he is the interpreter of our time, reflecting its confused strength and chaotic wealth. He is the high priest of our age, standing at the altar for us, and giving utterance to our needs and aspirations, our fears and faith. By understanding him we shall, to some degree, understand ourselves, and the power which is silently moulding us to its purposes.

It is because I thus regard Browning as not merely a poet but a prophet, that I think I am entitled to seek in him, as in Isaiah or Æschylus, a solution, or a help to the solution, of the problems that press upon us when we reflect upon man, his place in the world and his destiny. He has given us indirectly, and as a poet gives, a philosophy of life ; he has interpreted the world anew in the light of a dominant idea ; and it will be no little gain if we can make clear to ourselves those constitutive principles on which his view of the world rests.

CHAPTER II

ON THE NEED OF A PHILOSOPHY OF LIFE

"Art,—which I may style the love of loving, rage
Of knowing, seeing, feeling the absolute truth of things
For truth's sake, whole and sole, not any good truth brings
The knower, seer, feeler, beside,—instinctive Art
Must fumble for the whole, once fixing on a part
However poor, surpass the fragment, and aspire
To reconstruct thereby the ultimate entire."[1]

NO English poet has spoken more impressively than Browning on the weightier matters of morality and religion, or sought with more earnestness to meet the difficulties which arise when we try to penetrate to their ultimate principles. His way of poetry is, I think, fundamentally different from that of any other of our great writers. He often seems to be roused into speech rather by the intensity of his spiritual convictions than by the subtle incitements of poetic sensibility. His convictions catch fire, and truth becomes beauty for him ; not beauty, truth, as with Keats or Shelley. He is swayed by ideas, rather than by sublime

[1] *Fifine at the Fair*, xliv.

moods. Beneath the endless variety of his poems there are permanent principles, or 'colligating conceptions,' as science calls them ; and although these are expressed by the way of emotion, they are held by him with all the resources of his reason.

His work, though intuitive and perceptive as to form, 'gaining God by first leap,' as all true art must do, leaves the impression, when regarded as a whole, of an articulated system. It is a view of man's life and destiny that can be maintained, not only during the impassioned moods of poetry, but in the very presence of criticism and doubt. His faith, like Pompilia's, is held fast 'despite the plucking fiend.' He has given to us something more than intuitive glimpses into the mysteries of man's character. Throughout his life he held up the steady light of an optimistic conception of the world, and by its means injected new vigour into English ethical thought. In his case, therefore, it is not an irrelevant question, but one almost forced upon us, whether we are to take his ethical doctrine and inspiring optimism as valid truths, or to regard them merely as subjective opinions held by a religious poet. Are they creations of a powerful imagination, and nothing more? Do they give to the hopes and aspirations that rise so irrepressibly in the heart of man anything better than an appearance of validity, which will prove illusory the moment the cold light of critical inquiry is turned upon them?

It is to the systematic unity of his work that I would attribute, in the main, the impressiveness of his deliverances on morality and religion. And this unity justifies us, I think, in applying to Browning's view of life methods of criticism that would be out of place with any other English poet. It is one of his unique characteristics, as already hinted, that **he has** endeavoured to give us a complete and reasoned view of the ethical nature of man and of his relation to the world—has sought, in fact, to establish a philosophy of life. In his case, not without injustice, it is true, but with less injustice than in the case of any other **poet, we** may disregard, *for our purposes*, the artistic method of his thought, and lay stress on its content only. He has a right to a place amongst philosophers, as Plato has to a place amongst poets. There is such deliberate earnestness and systematic consistency in his teaching, that Hegel can scarcely be said to have maintained that 'the Rational is the Real' with greater intellectual tenacity than Browning held to his view of life. He sought, in fact, to establish an Idealism ; and that Idealism, like Kant's and Fichte's, has its last basis in the moral consciousness.

But, even if it be considered that it is not altogether just to apply these critical tests to the poet's teaching, and to make him pay the penalty for assuming a place amongst philosophers, it is certain that what he says of man's spiritual life cannot be rightly valued till it is regarded in the light of his guiding principles. We shall miss much of what is best in him, even as a poet, if, for instance, we regard his treatment of love merely as the expression of elevated passion, or his optimism as based upon mere hope. Love was to him rather an indwelling element in the world, present, like power, in everything.

> " From the first, Power was—I knew.
>   Life has made clear to me
>   That, strive but for closer view,
>   Love were as plain to see." [1]

Love yielded to him, as Reason did to Hegel, a fundamental explanation of the nature of things. Or, to express the same thing in another way, it was a deliberate hypothesis, which he sought to apply to facts and to test by their means, almost in the same manner as that in which natural science applies and tests its principles.

That Browning's ethical and religious ideas were for him something different from, and perhaps more than, mere poetic sentiments, will scarcely, I believe, be denied. That he held a deliberate theory, and held it with greater and greater difficulty as he became older, and as his dialectical tendencies grew and threatened to wreck his artistic freedom, is evident to any one who regards his work as a whole. But it will not be admitted so readily that anything other than harm can issue from an attempt to deal with him as if he were a philosopher. Even if it be true that he held and expressed a definite theory, will it retain any value if we take it out of the region of poetry and impassioned religious faith, into the frigid zone of philosophical inquiry? Could any one maintain, apart from the intoxication of religious and poetic sentiment, that the essence of existence is love? So long as we

---

[1] *Reverie—Asolando.*

remain within the realm of imagination, it may be argued, we may find in our poet's great sayings both solacement and strength, both rest and an impulse towards higher moral endeavour ; but if we seek to treat them as theories of facts, and turn upon them the light of the understanding, will they not inevitably prove to be hallucinations ? Poetry, we think, has its own proper place and function. It is an invaluable anodyne to the cark and care of reflective thought : an opiate which, by steeping the critical intellect in slumber, sets the soul free to rise on the wings of religious faith. But reason breaks the spell ; and the world of poetry and religion—a world which for them is always beautiful and good with God's presence —becomes for reason a system of inexorable laws, dead, mechanical, explicable as a mere equipoise of constantly changing forms of energy.

There is, at the present time, a widespread belief that we had better keep poetry and religion beyond the reach of critical investigation, if we set any store by them. Faith and reason are thought to be finally divorced. It is an article of the common creed that every attempt which the world has made to bring them together has resulted in denial, or, at the best, in doubt, regarding all supersensuous facts. The one condition of leading a full life, of maintaining a living relation between ourselves and both the spiritual and material elements of our existence, is to make our lives an alternating rhythm of the head and heart, to distinguish with absolute clearness between the realm of reason and that of faith.

Now, such an assumption would be fatal to any

attempt like the present, to find truth in poetry; and I must, therefore, try to meet it before entering upon a statement and criticism of Browning's view of life. I cannot admit that the difficulties of placing the facts of man's spiritual life on a rational basis are so great as to justify the assertion that there is no such basis, or that it is not discoverable by man. Surely it is unreasonable to make intellectual death the condition of spiritual life. If such a condition were imposed on man, it must inevitably defeat its own purpose; for man cannot possibly continue to live a divided life, and persist in believing that for which his reason knows no defence. We must, in the long run, either rationalize our faith in morality and religion, or reject it as illusory. And we should at least hesitate to deny that reason—in spite of its apparent failure in the past to justify our faith in the principles of spiritual life—may yet, as it becomes aware of its own nature and the might which dwells in it, find beauty and goodness, nay, God Himself, in the world. We should at least hesitate to condemn man to choose between irreflective ignorance and irreligion, or to lock the intellect and the highest emotions of our nature and principles of our life, in a mortal struggle. Poetry and religion may, after all, be truer than prose, and have something to tell the world that science, which is often ignorant of its own limits, cannot teach.

The failure of philosophy in the past, even if it were as complete as 'is believed by persons ignorant of its history, is no argument against its success in the future. Such persons have never known that the world of thought, like that of action, makes a

stepping stone **of its** dead self. He who presumes
to decide what passes the power of man's thought,
or to prescribe absolute limits to human knowledge,
is rash, to say the least ; and he has neither caught
the most important of the lessons of modern science,
nor been lifted to the level of its inspiration. **For**
science has done one thing greater than to unlock
the secrets of nature. It has revealed something
of the might of reason, and given new grounds for
the faith which in all **ages** has inspired the effort
to know,—the faith that the world is an intelligible
structure, meant to be penetrated by the thought of
man. Can it be that nature is an 'open secret,' but
that man, and he alone, must remain an enigma?
Or does he not rather bear within himself the **key**
to every problem which he solves, and is it not
his thought which penetrates **the** secrets of nature?
The success of science in reducing to law the most
varied and apparently unconnected facts, should
dispel any suspicion which attaches to the attempt
to gather these laws under still wider ones, and to
interpret the world in the light of the highest principles. And this is precisely what poetry and religion
and philosophy do, each in its own way. They carry
the work of the sciences into wider regions, and that,
as I shall try to show, by methods which, in spite of
many external differences, are fundamentally **at** one
with **those which** the sciences employ.

 There is only one way of giving the quietus to
the metaphysics of poets and philosophers, and of
showing the futility of a philosophy of life, or of any
scientific explanation of religion and morals. It is
to show that **there** is some radical absurdity in the

very attempt. Till this is done the human mind will not give up problems of such weighty import, however hard it **may be** to solve them. The world refused to believe Socrates when he pronounced a science of nature impossible, and centuries of failure did not break man's courage. Science, it is true, has given up some problems as insoluble; **it will not now** try to construct a perpetually moving machine, or to square the circle. But it has given these up, not because they are difficult, but because they are unreasonable tasks. The problems have a surd **or** irrational element in them; and to solve them would be to bring reason into collision with itself.

Now, whatever may be the difficulties of establishing a theory of life, or a philosophy, it has never been shown to be an unreasonable **task** to attempt it. One might, on the contrary, expect, *prima facie*, that in a world progressively proved to be intelligible to man, man himself would be no exception. It is impossible that the 'light in him should be darkness,' or that the thought which reveals the order of **the** world should be itself chaotic.

The need for philosophy is just the ultimate form of the **need** for knowledge; and the truths which philosophy brings to light are implied in every rational explanation of things. The only choice we can have is between a conscious metaphysics and an unconscious one, between hypotheses which we have examined and whose limitations we know, **and** hypotheses which rule us from behind, as pure prejudices do. It is because of this that the empiric is so dogmatic, and the ignorant man so certain of the truth of his opinion. They do not

know their postulates, nor are they aware that
there is no interpretation of an object which does
not finally point to a theory of being. We understand no joint or ligament, except in relation to
the whole organism, nor any fact, or event, except
by finding a place for it in the context of our
experience. The history of the pebble can be
given only in the light of the story of the earth,
as it is told by the whole of geology. We must
begin very far back, and bring our widest principles
to bear upon the particular thing, if we wish really
to know what it is. It is a law that explains,
and laws are always universal. All our knowledge,
even the most broken and inconsistent, streams
from some fundamental conception, in virtue of
which all the variety of objects constitutes one
world, one orderly kosmos, even to the meanest
mind. It is true that the central thought, be it
rich or poor, must, like the sun's light, be broken
against particular facts. But there is no need of
forgetting the real source of knowledge, or of
deeming that its progress is a synthesis without
law, or an addition of fact to fact without any
guiding principles.

Now, it is the characteristic of poetry and philosophy that they keep alive our consciousness of
these primary, uniting principles. They always
dwell in the presence of the idea which makes
their object *one*. To them the world is always,
and necessarily, a harmonious whole, as it is also
to the religious spirit. It is because of this that
the universe is a thing of beauty for the poet, a
revelation of God's goodness to the devout soul,

and a manifestation of absolute reason to the philosopher. Art, religion, and philosophy fail or flourish together. The age of prose and scepticism appears when the sense of the presence of the whole in the particular facts of the world and of life has been dulled. And there is a necessity in this; for if the conception of the world as a whole is held to be impossible, if philosophy is a futility, then poetry will be a vain sentiment and religion a delusion.

Nor will the failure of thought, when once demonstrated in these upper regions, be confined to them. On the contrary, it will spread downwards to science and ordinary knowledge, as mountain mists blot out the valleys. For every synthesis of fact to fact, every attempt to know, however humble and limited, is inspired by a secret faith in the unity of the whole world. Each of the sciences works within its own region, and colligates its details in the light of its own hypothesis; and all the sciences taken together presuppose the presence in the world of a principle that binds it into an orderly totality. Scientific explorers know that they are all working towards the same centre. And, ever and anon, as the isolated thinker presses home his own hypothesis, he finds his thought beating on the limits of his science, and suggesting some wider hypothesis. The walls that separate the sciences are wearing thin, and at times light penetrates from one to the other. So that to their votaries, at least, the faith is progressively justified, that there is a meeting point for the sciences, a central truth in which the dispersed rays will again be gathered together. In fact, all the sciences are working together under the guidance of a principle common to them all, although it may not be consciously known and no attempt is made to define **it**. In science, as in philosophy and art and **religion, there is** a principle of unity, which, though latent, is really prior **to all explanation of** particular matters of fact.

In **truth,** man has only one way of knowing. There is no fundamental difference between scientific and philosophic procedure. We always light **up** facts by means of general laws. The fall of **the stone was a** perfect enigma, a universally unintelligible bit of experience, till the majestic imagination of Newton conceived the idea of universal gravitation. Wherever mind successfully invades · the realm of chaos, poetry, the sense of the whole, has come first. There **is the** intuitive flash, the penetrative glimpse, got no one knows exactly whence—though we do know that it comes neither from the dead facts nor from the vacant region of *a priori* thought, but somehow from the interaction of both these elements of knowledge. **After** the intuitive flash comes the slow labour of proof, the application of the principle to details. And that application transforms both the principle and the details, so that the former is enriched with content and the latter are made intelligible— a veritable **conquest** and valid possession for mankind. And **in this labour of proof, science and** philosophy alike **take their** share.

Philosophy may be said to come midway between **poetry** and science, and to partake of the nature of both. **On the** one side, it deals, like poetry, with ideals of knowledge, and announces truths which it does **not** completely verify ; on the other, it leaves to science the task of articulating its principles in facts, though it begins the articulation itself. Philosophy reveals subsidiary principles, and **is, at** the same time, a witness for the unity of the categories of science. We may say, if we **wish,** that its principles **are mere** hypotheses. **But so** are the ideas which underlie the most practical of the sciences ; so is every forecast of genius by virtue of which knowledge is extended ; **so** is every principle of knowledge not completely worked out. And there is none worked out. **To** say that philosophy is hypothetical implies no charge, other than that which can be levelled in the same sense against the most solid body of scientific knowledge in the world. The fruitful question in each case alike is, How far **does the** hypothesis enable us to understand particular facts ?

The more careful of our scientific thinkers are well aware of the limits under which they work and of the hypothetical character of their results. " I take Euclidean space, and the existence of material particles and elemental energy for granted," says the physicist ; " deny them, and I am helpless ; grant them, and I shall establish quantitative relations between the different forms of this elemental energy, and make it tractable and tame to man's uses. All I teach depends upon my hypothesis. **In it is** the secret of all the power I wield. I do **not** pretend to say what this elemental energy is. I make no declaration regarding the actual nature of things ; **and all** questions as to the ultimate origin or final destination of the world are beyond **the** scope of my inquiry. I **am ruled** by my hypothesis ; I regard phenomena, *from **my** point of view* ; and my right to do so I substantiate by **the** practical and theoretical results which follow." The language of geology, chemistry, zoology, **and even** of mathematics is **the** same. **They all start from a** hypothesis ; they **are** all based **on an imaginative conception, and in** this sense **their** votaries are poets, who see the unity of being throb **in the** particular fact.

Now, so far as the particular sciences are con- cerned, **I presume** that no one will deny the supreme power of these colligating ideas. The sciences do not grow by a process of empiricism, which rambles tentatively and **blindly from fact to fact,** unguided **of any** hypothesis. But if **they do not, if, on the** contrary, each science **is ruled by its own hypo-** thesis, and uses that hypothesis **to bind** its facts **together, then** the question arises, Are there no **wider** colligating principles amongst these hypo- thesis themselves ? Are the sciences independent **of each other, or** is their independence only surface **appearance ?** This is the question which philosophy **asks, and the** sciences themselves, by their **progress,** suggest a positive answer to it.

The knowledge of the world which the sciences are building **is not a chaotic** structure. By their apparently independent efforts, the outer kosmos is gradually reproduced in the mind of man, **and** the temple of truth is silently rising. We may not, **as yet,** be able to connect wing with **wing, or to** declare definitely the law of the whole. The logical order of the hypotheses of the various sciences, the true connection of these categories of constructive thought, may still be uncertain. But yet there *is* such an order and connection : the whole building has its plan, which becomes more and more intelligible as it approaches to its completion. Beneath all the differences there are fundamental principles which give to human thought a definite unity of movement and direction. There are architectonic conceptions which are guiding, not only the different sciences, but all the modes of thought of an age. There are intellectual media, ' working hypotheses,' by means of which successive centuries observe all that they see ; and these far-reaching constructive principles divide the history of mankind into distinct stages. In a word, there are dynasties of great ideas, such as the idea of development in our own day ; and these successively ascend the throne of mind, and hold a sway over human thought which is well-nigh absolute.

Now, if this is so, is it certain that all *knowledge* of these ruling conceptions is impossible ? In other words, is the attempt to construct a philosophy absurd ? To say that it is, to deny the possibility of catching any glimpse of those regulative ideas which determine the main tendencies of human thought, is to place the supreme directorate of the human intelligence in the hands of a necessity which, *for us*, is blind. For, an order that is hidden is for us equivalent to chance. If in that case we believed order to exist, we would be doing so in the face of the fact that all we see, and all we *can* see, is the opposite of order, namely, lawlessness. Human knowledge, on this view, would be subjected to law in its details and compartments, but to disorder as a whole. Thinking men would be organized into regiments ; but the regiments would not constitute an army, nor would there be any unity of movement in the attack on the realm of ignorance.

But such is not the conclusion to which the study of human history leads, especially when we observe its movements on a large scale. On the contrary, it is found that history falls into great epochs, each of which has its own peculiar characteristics. Ages, as well as nations and individuals, have features of their own, special and definite modes of thinking and acting. The movement of thought in each age has its own direction, which is determined by some characteristic and fundamental idea, that does for it what a working hypothesis does for a particular science. It is the prerogative of the greatest leaders of thought in an age to catch a glimpse of this ruling idea when it first makes its appearance ; and it is their function, not only to discover it, but also to reveal it to others. And, in this way, they are at once the exponents and the prophets of their time. They reveal that which is already a latent but active power—' a tendency ' ; but they reveal it to a generation which will see the truth for itself, only after the potency which lies in it has manifested itself in national institutions and habits of thought and action. *After* the prophets have left us, we believe what they have said ; as long as they **are with us, they are** voices crying in the wilderness.

Now, these great ideas, these harmonies of the world of mind, first strike upon the ear of the poet. They seem to break into the consciousness of man by the way of emotion. They possess the seer ; he is divinely mad, and he utters words whose meaning passes his **own** calmer comprehension. What we find **in** Goethe, we find also in a manner in Browning—an insight which is **also** foresight, a dim **and** partial consciousness of the truth about **to be,** sending its light before it, and anticipating all systematic reflection. It is an insight which appears to be independent of all method; **but it** is **in** nature, though not in sweep and expanse, akin to the intuitive leap by which the scientific explorer lights upon his **new** hypothesis. We can **find no other** law for it than that sensitiveness to the beauty and truth hidden in facts, which much reflection **on** them generates for genius. For these great minds the 'muddy vesture' is **worn** thin by thought, and they hear the immortal music.

The poet soon passes his glowing torch into the hands of the philosopher. After Æschylus and Sophocles, come Plato and Aristotle. The intuitive flash grows into **a** fixed light, which rules the day. The great idea, when reflected upon, becomes **a** system. When the light of such **an** idea is steadily held on human affairs, it breaks into endless forms of beauty and truth. The **content** of the idea is gradually evolved ; hypotheses spring out of it which are accepted as principles, rule the mind of **an** age, and give it its work and its character.   In this way Hobbes and Locke laid down, **or at least** defined, the boundaries within which moved the thought of the eighteenth century; and no one acquainted with the poetic and philosophic thought of Germany, from Lessing to Goethe and from Kant to Hegel, **can** fail to find therein the source and spring of the constitutive principles of our own intellectual, social, political, and religious life.   The virtues and the vices of the aristocracy of the world of mind penetrate downwards.   **The works** of the poets and philosophers, so far from being filled with impracticable dreams, are repositories of great suggestions which the world adopts for its guidance.   The poets and philosophers lay no railroads and **invent no** telephones; but they, nevertheless, bring about that attitude towards nature, man, and God, and **generate those** moods of the general mind from which issue, not only the scientific, but also the social, political, and religious forces of the age.

It is mainly on this account that I cannot treat **the** supreme utterances of Browning lightly, or **think** it an idle task to try to connect them **into a** philosophy of life.   In his optimism of love, in his supreme confidence in man's destiny, **in** his sense of the infinite height of the moral horizon of humanity, in his courageous faith in the good, and **his** profound conviction of the evanescence **of** evil, there lies **a** vital energy whose inspiring power we are yet destined to feel.   Until a spirit kindred to his own arises, able to push the battle further into the same region, much of the practical task **of** the age that is coming will consist in living out in detail the ideas to which Browning has given expression.

I contend, then, not merely for a larger charity, but for a truer view of the facts of history than is evinced by those who set aside the poets and philosophers as mere dreamers, and who conceive that the sciences alone occupy the region of valid thought in all its extent. There is, rather, a universal brotherhood of which all who think are members. Not only do all thinkers contribute to man's victory over his environment and himself, but they contribute in a manner which is substantially the same. There are many points of superficial distinction between the processes of philosophy and science, and between both and the method of poetry ; but the inner movement, if one may so express it, is identical in all. It is time to have done with the notion that philosophers occupy a transcendent region beyond experience, or spin spiritual cocoons by *a priori* methods ; and with the view that scientific men are mere empirics, building their structures from below by an *a posteriori* way of thought, without the help of any ruling conceptions. All alike endeavour to interpret experience, but none of them get their principles from it.

<blockquote>
" But, friends,
Truth is within ourselves ; it takes no rise
From outward things, whate'er you may believe."
</blockquote>

There is room and need for the higher synthesis of philosophy and poetry, as well as for the more palpable and, at the same time, more narrow colligating conceptions of the systematic sciences

The quantitative relations between material objects, which are investigated by mathematics and physics, do not exhaust the realm of the knowable, so as to leave no place for the poet's or the philosopher's view of the world. The scientific investigator who, like Mr. Tyndall, so far forgets the limitations of his province as to use his natural data as premises for religious or irreligious conclusions, is as illogical as the popular preacher who attacks scientific conclusions because they are not consistent with his theological presuppositions. Looking only at their primary aspects, we cannot say that religious presuppositions and the scientific interpretation of facts are either consistent or inconsistent : they are simply different. Their harmony or discord can come only when the higher principles of philosophy have been fully developed, and when the departmental ideas of the various sciences are organized into a view of the world as a whole. And this is a task which has not as yet been accomplished. The forces from above and below have not met. When they do meet, they will assuredly find that they are friends and not foes. For philosophy can articulate its supreme conception only by interaction with the sciences ; and, on the other hand, the progress of science, and the effectiveness of its division of labour, are ultimately conditioned by its sensitiveness to the hints, given by poets and philosophers, of those wider principles in virtue of which the world is conceived as a unity. There are many, indeed, who cannot see the wood for the trees, as there are others who cannot see the trees for the wood. Carlyle cared nothing though science were able to turn a sunbeam on its axis; Ruskin sees little in the advance of invention except more slag-hills. And scientific men have not been slow to return with interest the scorn of the moralists. But a more comprehensive view of the movement of human knowledge will show that none labour in vain; for its movement is that of a thing which *grows*; and growth is a process towards *both* unity and difference. Science, in pursuing truth into greater and greater detail, is constrained by its growing consciousness of the unlimited wealth of its material, to divide and isolate its interests more and more; and on this account, the need for the poets and philosophers is growing deeper, while their task is becoming more difficult of achievement, and their triumph greater in so far as it is achieved. Both science and philosophy are working towards a more concrete view of the world as an articulated whole. If we cannot quite say with Browning that 'poets never dream,' we may yet admit with gratitude that their dreams are an inspiration.

"Sorrow is hard to bear, and doubt is slow to clear.
  Each sufferer says his say, his scheme of the weal and woe
But God has a few of us whom He whispers in the ear;
  The rest may reason and welcome: 'tis we musicians know."[1]

And side by side with the poetry that grasps the truth in immediate intuition, there is also the uniting activity of philosophy, which, catching up the poet's hints, carries "back our scattered knowledge of the facts and laws of nature to the principle upon

[1] *Abt Vogler.*

which they **rest** ; and, **on** the other hand, develops
that principle so as to fill **all the** details of knowledge with **a** significance which **they cannot** have
in themselves, but only as seen *sub specie æternitatis.*"[1]

So far we have spoken of the function of philosophy **in** the interpretation of **the phenomena of**
the outer world. It **bears** witness to the **unity of
knowledge** and strives by the constructive criticism
of the categories of science to render that **unity**
explicit.   Its function is, no doubt, valid and
important, for it is evident **that man cannot rest**
content with fragmentary knowledge. But still, it
might be objected that it is premature at present
to endeavour to formulate that unity.   Physics,
chemistry, biology, and **the** other sciences, while
they necessarily presuppose **the** unity **of** knowledge,
and attempt in their **own way and in** their own
sphere to discover it, are making **very** satisfactory
progress without raising any **of** the desperate questions of metaphysics as to the nature of the ultimate
reality.   For them it is not likely to matter **for a**
long time to come whether Optimism or **Pessimism,
Materialism or** Idealism, or none of them, be **true.
In any case the** principles they establish are **valid.**
Physical relations always remain true; " ginger
will **be** hot i' the mouth, **and** there will **be more
cakes and** ale."   It is only when the sciences
break down beneath **the weight of** knowledge
and prove themselves inadequate, that it becomes
necessary or advantageous to seek **for** more comprehensive principles.   **At present** is it not better

----

[1] *The Problem of Philosophy at the Present Time,* by Pro-
fessor Caird.

to persevere in the way of science, than to be seduced from it by the desire to solve ultimate problems, which, however reasonable and pressing, seem to be beyond our power to answer?

Such reasonings are not convincing, still, so far as natural science is concerned, they seem to indicate that there might be no great harm in ignoring, for a time, its dependence on the wider aspects of human thought. There is no department of nature so limited but that it may more than satisfy the largest ambition of the individual for knowledge. But this attitude of indifference to ultimate questions is liable at any moment to be disturbed.

> "Just when we are safest, there's a sunset-touch,
>   A fancy from a flower-bell, some one's death,
>   A chorus-ending from Euripides,—
> And that's enough for fifty hopes and fears
> As old and new at once as nature's self,
> To rap and knock and enter in our soul,
> Take hands and dance there, a fantastic ring,
> Round the ancient idol, on his base again,—
> The grand Perhaps! We look on helplessly.
> There the old misgivings, crooked questions are."[1]

Amongst the facts of our experience which cry most loudly for some kind of solution, are those of our own inner life. We are in pressing need of a 'working hypothesis' wherewith to understand ourselves, as well as of a theory which will explain the revolution of the planets or the structure of an oyster. And this self of ours intrudes everywhere. It is only by resolutely shutting

[1] *Bishop Blougram's Apology.*

our eyes, that we can forget the part it plays
even in the outer world of natural science. So
active is it in the constitution of things, so dependent is their nature on the nature of our knowing
faculties, that scientific men themselves admit that
their surest results are only hypothetical. Their
truth depends on laws of thought which natural
science does not investigate.

But quite apart from this doctrine of the
relativity of knowledge, which is generally first
acknowledged and then ignored, every man, the
worst and the best alike, is constrained to take
some *practical* attitude towards his fellows. Man
is never alone with nature, and the connections
with his fellows which sustain his intelligent life,
are liable to bring him into trouble, if they are
not to some degree understood.

> "There's power in me," said Bishop Blougram, "and will
>   to dominate
> Which I must exercise, they hurt me else."

The impulse to know is only a phase of the more
general impulse to act and to be. The specialist's
devotion to his science is his answer to a demand,
springing from his practical need, that he realize
himself through action. He does not construct his
edifice of knowledge, as the bird is supposed to
build its nest, without any consciousness of an end
to be attained thereby. Even if, like Lessing, he
values the pursuit of truth for its own sake, still
what stings him into effort is the sense that in
truth only can he find the means of satisfying and
realizing himself. Beneath all man's activities, as

their very spring and source, there lies **some** dim conception of an end to be attained. This is his moral consciousness, which no neglect will utterly suppress. All human effort, the effort to know like every other, conceals within it a reference to some good, conceived at the time as supreme and complete ; and this, in turn, contains a theory both of man's self and of the universe on which he must impress his image. Every man must have his philosophy of life, simply because **he** must act ; though in many cases that philosophy may be latent and unconscious, or, at least, not a definite object of reflection. The most elementary question directed at his moral consciousness will at once elicit the universal element. We cannot ask whether an action be right or wrong without awakening all **the** echoes of metaphysics. As there is no object on the earth's surface whose equilibrium **is** not fixed by its relation to the earth's centre, so the most elementary moral judgment, the simplest choice, the most irrational vagaries of **a** will calling itself free and revelling **in its supposed** lawlessness, are dominated by the conception of a universal **good. Everything that a man** does is an attempt to articulate his view of this good with a particular content. Hence, man as a moral agent is always the centre of his own horizon, and **stands** right beneath the zenith. Little as he may be **aware** of it, his relation between himself and his supreme good is direct. And he orders his **whole** world from his point of view, just as **he** regards east and west as meeting at the spot on which he stands. Whether he will or not, he cannot but regard the universe of men and objects as the instrument of his purposes. He extracts all its interest and meaning from himself. His own shadow falls upon it all. If he is selfish, that is, if he interprets the self that is in him as vulturous, then the whole outer world and his fellow-men fall for him into the category of carrion, or not-carrion. If he knows himself as spirit, as the energy of love or reason, if the prime necessity he recognizes within himself is the necessity to be good, then the universe becomes for him an instrument wherewith moral character is evolved. In all cases alike, his life-work is an effort to rob the world of its alien character, and to translate it into terms of himself.

We are in the habit of fixing a chasm between a man's deeds and his metaphysical, moral, and religious creed; and even of thinking that he can get on 'in a sufficiently prosperous manner,' without any such creed. Can we not digest without a theory of peptics, or do justice without constructing an ideal state? The truest answer, though it is an answer easily misunderstood, is that we cannot. In the sphere of morality, at least, action depends on knowledge: Socrates was right in saying that virtuous conduct ignorant of its end is accidental. Man's action, so far as it is good or evil, is shot through and through with his intelligence. And once we clearly distinguish between belief and profession, between the motives which really impel our actions and the psychological account of them with which we may deceive ourselves and others, we shall be obliged to confess that we always act our creed. A man's conduct, just because he is man, is generated by his view of himself and his world. He who cheats his neighbour believes in tortuosity, and, as Carlyle says, has the Supreme Quack for his God. No one ever acted without some dim, though perhaps foolish enough, half-belief that the world was at his back; whether he plots good or evil he always has God for his accomplice. And this is why character cannot be really bettered by any peddling process. Moralists and preachers are right in insisting on the need of a new life, that is, of a new principle, as the basis of any real improvement; and such a principle necessarily carries in it a new attitude towards men, and a new interpretation of the moral agent himself and of his world.

Thus, wherever we touch the practical life of man, we are at once referred to a metaphysic. His creed is the heart of his character, and it beats as a pulse in every action. Hence, when we deal with moral life, we *must* start from the centre. In our intellectual life, it is not obviously unreasonable to suppose that there is no need of endeavouring to reach upward to a constructive idea which makes the universe one, but when we act, such self-deception is not possible. As a moral agent, and a moral agent man always is, he not only may, but must have his working hypothesis, and that hypothesis must be all-inclusive. As there are natural laws which connect man's physical movements with the whole system of nature, so there are spiritual relations which connect him with the whole spiritual universe; and spiritual relations are always direct.

Now it follows from this, that, whenever we consider man as a moral agent, that is, as an agent who converts ideas into actual things, the need of a philosophy becomes evident. Instead of condemning ideal interpretations of the universe as useless dreams, the foolish products of an ambition of thought which refuses to respect the limits of the human intellect, we shall understand that philosophers and poets are really striving with greater clearness of vision, and in a more sustained manner, to perform the task which all men are obliged to perform in some way or other. Man subsists as a natural being only on condition of comprehending, to some degree, the conditions of his natural life, and the laws of his natural environment. From earliest youth upwards he is learning that fire will burn and water drown, and that he can play with the elements with safety only within the sphere lit up by his intelligence. Nature will not pardon the blunders of ignorance, nor tamely submit to every hasty construction. And this truth is still more obvious in relation to man's moral life. Here, too, and in a pre-eminent degree, conduct waits on intelligence. Deep will only answer unto deep; and great characters only come with much meditation on the things that are highest. And, on the other hand, the misconstruction of life's meaning flings man back upon himself, and makes his action nugatory. Byronism was driven 'howling home again,' says the poet. The universe will not be interpreted in terms of sense, nor be treated as carrion, as Carlyle said. There is no rest in the 'Everlasting No,' because it is a wrong view of man and of the world. Or rather, the negative is not everlasting; and man is driven onwards by despair, through the 'Centre of Indifference,' till he finds a 'Universal Yea'—a true view of his relation to the universe.

There is given to men the largest choice to do or to let alone, at every step in life. But there is one necessity which they cannot escape, because they carry it within them. They absolutely must try to make the world their home, find some kind of reconciling idea between themselves and the forces amidst which they move, have some kind of working hypotheses of life. Nor is it possible to admit that they will find rest till they discover a *true* hypothesis. If they do not seek it by reflection—if, in their ardour to penetrate into the secrets of nature, they forget themselves; if they allow the supreme facts of their moral life to remain in the confusion of tradition, and seek to compromise the demands of their spirit by sacrificing to the idols of their childhood's faith; if they fortify themselves in the indifference of agnosticism—they must reap the harvest of their irreflection. Ignorance is not harmless in matters of character any more than in the concerns of our outer life. There are in national and in individual history seasons of despair, and that despair, when it is deepest, is ever found to be the shadow of moral failure—the result of going out into action with a false view of the purpose of human life, and a wrong conception of man's destiny. At such times the people have not understood themselves or their environment, and, in consequence,

they come into collision with their own welfare.
There is no experiment so dangerous to an age
or people as that of relegating to the common
ignorance of unreasoning faith the deep concerns
of moral conduct ; and there is no attitude more
pitiable than that which leads it to turn a deaf
ear and the lip of contempt towards those philosophers who carry the spirit of scientific inquiry
into these higher regions, and endeavour to establish
for mankind, by the irrefragable processes of reason,
those principles on which rest all the great elements
of man's destiny.　We cannot act without a theory
of life ; and to whom shall we look for such a
theory, except to those who, undaunted by the
difficulties, ask once more, and strive to answer,
those problems which man cannot entirely escape
as long as he continues to think and act?

CHAPTER III

BROWNING'S PLACE IN ENGLISH POETRY

"But there's a great contrast between him and me. He seems very content with life, and takes much satisfaction in the world. It's a very strange and curious spectacle to behold a man in these days so confidently cheerful." (*Carlyle.*)

IT has been said of Carlyle, who may for many reasons be considered as our poet's twin figure, that he laid the foundations of his world of thought in *Sartor Resartus*, and never enlarged them. His *Orientirung* was over before he was forty years old —as is, indeed, the case with most men. After that period there was no fundamental change in his view of the world; nothing which can be called a new idea disturbed his outline sketch of the universe. He lived afterwards only to fill it in, showing with ever greater detail the relations of man to man in history, and emphasizing with greater grimness the war of good and evil in human action. There is evidence, it is true, that the formulæ from which he more or less consciously set forth, ultimately proved too narrow for him, and we find him beating himself in vain against their limitations; still, on the whole,

Carlyle speculated within the range and influence of principles adopted early in life, and never abandoned for higher or richer ideas, or substantially changed.

In these respects there is considerable resemblance between Carlyle and Browning. Browning, indeed, fixed his point of view and chose his battleground still earlier; and he held it resolutely to his life's close. In his *Pauline* and in his Epilogue to *Asolando*, we catch the triumphant tone of a single idea, which, during all the long interval, had never sunk into silence. Like

> "The wise thrush, he sings each song twice over,
>   Lest you should think he never could recapture
>   The first fine careless rapture!"[1]

Moreover, these two poets, if I may be permitted to call Carlyle a poet, taught the same truth. They were both witnesses to the presence of God in the spirit of man, and looked at this life in the light of another and a higher; or rather, they penetrated through the husk of time and saw that eternity is even here, a tranquil element underlying the noisy antagonisms of man's earthly life. Both of them, like Plato's philosopher, made their home in the sunlight of ideal truth: they were not denizens of the cave, taking the things of sense for those of thought, shadows for realities, echoes for the voices of men.

But, while Carlyle fought his way into this region, Browning found himself in it from the first; while Carlyle bought his freedom with a great sum, the poet 'was free born.' Carlyle saw the old world

[1] *Home Thoughts from Abroad.*

faith break up around him, and its fragments never ceased to embarrass his path. He was *at* the point of transition, present at the collision of the old and new, and in the midst of the confusion. He, more than any other English writer, was the instrument of the change from the Deism of the eighteenth century, and the despair which followed it, into the larger faith of our own. But, for Browning, there was a new heaven and a new earth, and old things had passed away. This notable contrast between the two men, arising at once from their disposition and their moral environment, had far-reaching effects on their lives and their writings. But their affinity was deeper than the difference, for they are essentially heirs and exponents of the same movement in English thought.

The main characteristic of that movement is that it is both moral and religious, a devotion to God and the active service of man, a recognition at once of the rights of nature and of spirit. It does not, on the one hand, raise the individual as a natural being to the throne of the universe, and make all forces, social, political, and spiritual, stoop to his rights; nor does it, on the other hand, deny these rights, or make the individual a mere instrument of society. It at least attempts to reconcile the fundamental facts of human nature, without compromising any of them. It cannot be called either individualistic or socialistic, but it strives to be both at once; so that both man and society mean more to this age than they ever did before. The narrow formulæ that cramped the thought of the period which preceded ours have been broken through. No one can pass from the hedonists and individualists to **Carlyle** and Browning without feeling that these two men are representatives of new forces in politics, in religion, and in literature—forces which will undoubtedly effect momentous changes before they are caught again and fixed in creeds.

That a new epoch in English thought was **veritably opened by** them is indicated by the **surprise and bewilderment they** occasioned at their first appearance. Carlyle had Emerson to break his loneliness and Browning had Rossetti; but, **to** most other men at that day, *Sartor* and *Pauline* were all but unintelligible. The general English reader could make little of the strange figures that had broken into the realm **of literature**; and the value and significance **of their** work, as well as its originality, will be recognized better by ourselves if we take a hurried glance at the times which lay behind them. Its main worth will be found to lie in the fact that they strove to bring together again certain fundamental elements, on which the **moral** life of man must always rest, and which had fallen asunder in the ages that preceded their own.

The whole-hearted, instinctive life of the Elizabethan age was narrowed and deepened into the severe one-sidedness of Puritanism, which cast on the bright earth the sombre shadow of a life to come. England was given up for a long time to a magnificent half-truth. It did not

> "Wait
> The slow and sober uprise all around
> O' the building,"

but

> "Ran up right to roof
> A sudden marvel, piece of perfectness."[1]

After Puritanism came Charles the Second and the rights of the flesh, which rights were gradually sublimated till they contradicted themselves in the benevolent self-seeking of altruistic hedonism. David Hume led the world out of the shadow of eternity, and showed that it was only an object of the five senses; or of six, if we add that of 'hunger.' The divine element was explained away, and the proper study of mankind was, not man, as that age thought but man reduced to his beggarly elements——a being animated solely by the sensuous springs of pleasure and pain, who should properly, as Carlyle thought, go on all fours, and not lay claim to the dignity of being moral. All things were reduced to what they seemed, robbed of their suggestiveness, changed into definite, sharp-edged, mutually exclusive particulars. The world was an aggregate of isolated facts, or, at the best, a mechanism into which particulars were fitted by force; and society was a gathering of mere individuals, repelling each other by their needs and greed, with a ring of natural necessity to bind them together. It was a fit time for political economy to supplant ethics. There was nowhere an ideal which could lift man above his natural self, and teach him, by losing it, to find a higher life. And, as a necessary consequence, religion gave way to naturalism, and poetry to prose.

After this age of prose came our own day. The new light first flushed the modern world in the writings of the philosopher-poets of Germany:

[1] *Prince Hohenstiel-Schwangau.*

D

Kant and Lessing, Fichte and Schiller, Goethe and Hegel. They brought about the Copernican change. For them this world of the five senses, of space and time and natural cause, instead of being the fixed centre around which all things revolved, was explicable only in its relation to a system which was spiritual; and man found his meaning in his connection with society, the life of which stretched endlessly far back into the past and forward into the future. Psychology gave way to metaphysics. The universal element in the thought of man was revealed. Instead of mechanism there was life. A new spirit of poetry and philosophy brought God back into the world, revealed His incarnation in the mind of man, and changed nature into a pellucid garment within which throbbed the love divine. The antagonism of hard alternatives was at an end; the universe was spirit-woven and every smallest object was "filled full of magical music, as they freight a star with light." There were no longer two worlds, but one; for 'the other' world penetrated this, and was revealed in it: thought and sense, spirit and nature, were re-conciled. These thinkers made room for man, as against the Puritans, and for God, as against their successors. Instead of the hopeless struggle of ascetic morality, which divides man against himself, they awakened him to that sense of his reconcilia-tion with his ideal which religion gives: 'Psyche drinks its stream and forgets her sorrows.'

Now, this is just the soil where art blooms. For what is beauty but the harmony of thought and sense, a universal meaning caught and tamed in the particular? To the poet each little flower that blooms has endless worth, and is regarded as perfect and complete; for he sees that the spirit of the whole dwells in it. It whispers to him the mystery of the infinite; it is a pulse in which beats the universal heart. The true poet finds God everywhere; for the ideal is actual wherever beauty dwells. And there is the closest affinity between art and religion, as its history proves, from Job and Isaiah, Homer and Æschylus, to our own poet; for both art and religion lift us, each in its own way, above one-sidedness and limitation, to the region of the universal. The one draws God to man, brings perfection *here*, and reaches its highest form in the joyous life of Greece, where the natural world was clothed with almost supernatural beauty; the other lifts man to God, and finds this life good because it reflects and suggests the greater life that is to be. Both poetry and religion are a reconciliation and a satisfaction; both lift man above the contradictions of limited existence, and place him in the region of peace—where,

> " with an eye made quiet by the power
> Of harmony, and the deep power of joy,
> He sees into the life of things."[1]

In this sense, it will be always true of the poet, as it is of the religious man, that

> " the world,
> The beauty and the wonder and the power,
> The shapes of things, their colours, lights and shades,
> Changes, surprises,"[2]

[1] *Tintern Abbey.*   [2] *Fra Lippo Lippi.*

lead him back to **God**, who **made it** all.   He **is** essentially **a** witness to the divine element in the world.

It is the re-discovery of this **divine** element, after its expulsion by the age of Deism and doubt, that **has given** to this century its poetic grandeur. **Unless** we regard Burke as the herald of the new **era, we** may say that England first felt **the** breath **of the** returning spirit in the poems of Shelley and Wordsworth.

> "The One remains, the many change and pass;
>   Heaven's light for ever shines, earth's shadows **fly:**
>   Life, like a dome of many-coloured glass,
>   Stains the white radiance **of eternity,**
>   Until death tramples it to fragments."[1]

"And I have felt," **says Wordsworth,**

> "A presence that disturbs me with **the joy**
>   Of elevated thoughts; a sense sublime
>   Of something far more deeply interfused,
>   Whose dwelling is the light of setting suns,
>   And the round ocean and the living air,
>   **And** the blue sky, and in the mind of man :
>   **A motion and** a spirit, that impels
>   **All** thinking things, all objects of all thought,
>   **And** rolls through all things."[2]

Such notes as these **could** not **be** struck by Pope, nor be understood by the age of prose.   Still they are only the prelude of the fuller song of Browning. Whether he be a greater poet than these **or** not— **a** question whose answer can benefit nothing, **for** each poet has his own worth, and reflects by his own facet the universal truth—his poetry contains

---

[1] *Adonais.*   [2] *Tintern Abbey.*

in it larger elements, and the promise of a deeper harmony from the harsher discords of his more stubborn material.   Even where their spheres touch, Browning held **by** the artistic truth in a manner different from theirs.   To Shelley, perhaps the most intensely **spiritual of all our poets,**

> "That light whose smile kindles the **universe,**
>   That beauty in which all things work and **move,**"

was an impassioned sentiment, a glorious intoxication ; to Browning **it was** a conviction, reasoned and willed, possessing the **whole man, and held in** the sober moments when the heart **is silent.** ' The heavy and the weary weight of all this unintelligible world ' was lightened for Wordsworth, only when he **was far** from the haunts of men, and free from the ' dreary intercourse of daily life '; but Browning weaved his song of hope right amidst the wail and woe of man's sin and wretchedness.   **For** Wordsworth ' sensations sweet, felt in **the blood and** felt along the heart, passed into his **purer** mind with tranquil restoration,' **and** issued ' **in a** serene and blessed mood ' ; but Browning's poetry is not **merely the poetry of the emotions** however sublimated.   **He starts** with **the hard** repellent fact, crushes by sheer force of thought its stubborn rind, presses into **it,** and brings forth the truth **at** its heart.   The greatness of Browning's poetry **is in its** perceptive grip; **and in** nothing is he more original than in the **manner in** which he takes up his task, and assumes his artistic function. In his postponement of feeling to thought we **recognize a new** poetic method, the significance of which we cannot estimate as yet. But, although we may fail to apprehend the meaning of the new method he employs, we cannot fail to perceive the fact, which is not less striking, that the region from which he quarries his material is new.

And yet he does not break away abruptly from his predecessors. His kinship with them, in that he recognizes the presence of God in nature, is everywhere evident. We quote one passage, scarcely to be surpassed by any of our poets, as indicative of his power of dealing with the supernaturalism of nature.

> " The centre-fire heaves underneath the earth,
> And the earth changes like a human face;
> The molten ore bursts up among the rocks,
> Winds into the stone's heart, outbranches bright
> In hidden mines, spots barren river-beds,
> Crumbles into fine sand where sunbeams bask—
> God joys therein. The wroth sea's waves are edged
> With foam, white as the bitter lip of hate,
> When, in the solitary waste, strange groups
> Of young volcanos come up, cyclops-like,
> Staring together with their eyes on flame—
> God tastes a pleasure in their uncouth pride.
> Then all is still; earth is a wintry clod:
> But spring-wind, like a dancing psaltress, passes
> Over its breast to waken it, rare verdure
> Buds tenderly upon rough banks, between
> The withered tree-roots and the cracks of frost,
> Like a smile striving with a wrinkled face.
>
> .   .   .   .   .   .
>
> Above, birds fly in merry flocks, the lark
> Soars up and up, shivering for very joy;
> Afar the ocean sleeps; white fishing gulls
> Flit where the strand is purple with its tribe
> Of nested limpets; savage creatures seek

> Their loves in wood and plain—and God renews
> His ancient rapture. Thus He dwells in all,
> From life's minute beginnings, up at last
> To man—the consummation of this scheme
> Of being, the completion of this sphere of life."[1]

Such passages as these contain neither the rapt, reflective calm of Wordsworth's solemn tones, nor the ethereal intoxication of Shelley's spirit-music; but there is in them the same consciousness of the infinite meaning of natural facts. And beyond this, there is also, in the closing lines, a hint of a new region for art. Shelley and Wordsworth were the poets of nature, as all men truly say; Browning was the poet of the human soul. For Shelley, the beauty in which all things work and move was well-nigh 'quenched by the eclipsing curse of the birth of man'; and Wordsworth lived beneath the habitual sway of fountains, meadows, hills, and groves, while he kept grave watch o'er man's mortality, and saw the shades of the prison-house gather round him. From the life of man they garnered little but mad indignation, or mellowed sadness. It was a foolish and furious strife, with unknown powers fought in the dark, from which the poet kept aloof, for he could not see that God dwelt amidst the chaos. But Browning found 'harmony in immortal souls, spite of the muddy vesture of decay.' He saw that nature was crowned in man, though man was mean and miserable. At the heart of the most wretched abortion of wickedness there was the mark of the loving touch of God. Shelley turned

---

[1] *Paracelsus.*

away from man ; Wordsworth paid him rare visits, like those of a being from a strange world, made wise and sad with looking at him from afar ; Browning dwelt with him. He was a comrade in the fight, and ever in the van of man's endeavour, bidding him be of good cheer. He was a witness for God in the midmost dark, where meet in deathless struggle the elemental powers of right and wrong. For God is present for him, not only in the order and beauty of nature, but in the world of will and thought. Beneath the caprice and wilful lawlessness of individual action, he saw a beneficent purpose which cannot fail, but 'has its way with man, not he with it.'

Now this was a new world for poetry to enter into ; a new depth to penetrate with hope ; and Browning was the first of modern poets to

> " Stoop
> Into the vast and unexplored abyss,
> Strenuously beating
> The silent boundless regions of the sky."[1]

It is also a new world for religion and morality ; and to understand it demands a deeper insight into the fundamental elements of human life.

To show this in a proximately adequate manner we should be obliged, as already hinted, to connect the poet's work, not merely with that of his English predecessors, but with the deeper and more comprehensive movement of the thought of Germany since the time of Kant. It would be necessary to indicate how, by breaking a way

[1] *Paracelsus*

through the narrow creeds and equally narrow scepticism of the previous age, the new spirit extended the horizon of man's active and contemplative life, and made him free of the universe, and the repository of the past conquests of his race. It proposed to man the great task of solving the problem of humanity; but it strengthened him with its past achievement, and inspired him with the conviction of its boundless progress. It is not that the significance of the individual or the meaning of his endeavour is lost. Under this new view man has still to fight for his own hand, and it is still recognized that spirit is always burdened with its own fate, and cannot share its responsibility. Morality does not give way to religion or pass into it, and there is a sense in which the individual is always alone in the sphere of duty.

But from this new point of view the individual is re-explained for us, and we begin to understand that he is the focus of a light which is universal, 'one more incarnation of the mind of God.' His moral task is no longer to seek his own in the old sense, but to elevate humanity; for it is only by taking this circuit that he can come to his own. Such a task as this is a sufficiently great one to occupy all time; but it is to humanity in him that the task belongs, and it will therefore be achieved. This is no new one-sidedness. It does not mean, to those who comprehend it, the supplanting of the individual thought by the collective thought, or the substitution of humanity for man. The universal is *in* the particular, the fact *is* the law. There is no collision between the whole and the part, for the whole lives in the part. As each individual plant has its own life and beauty and worth, although the universe has conspired to bring it into being ; so also, and in a far higher degree, man has his own duty and his own dignity, although he is but the embodiment of forces, natural and spiritual, which have come from the endless past. Like a letter in a word, or a word in a sentence, he gets his meaning from his context ; *but the sentence is meaningless without him.* 'Rays from all round converge in him,' and he has no power except that which has been lent to him ; but all the same, nay, all the more, he must

> "Think as if man never thought before !
>   Act as if all creation hung attent
>   On the acting of such faculty as his."[1]

His responsibility, his individuality, is not less, but greater, in that he can, in his thought and moral action, command the forces that the race has stored for him. The great man speaks the thought of his people, and his invocations as their priest are just the expression of their dumb yearnings. And even the mean and insignificant man is what he is, in virtue of the humanity which is blurred and distorted within him; and he can shed his insignificance and meanness only by becoming a truer vehicle for that humanity.

Thus, when spirit is spiritually discerned, it is seen that man is bound to man in a union closer than any physical organism can show ; while 'the individual,' in the old sense of a being *opposed* to

[1] *Prince Hohenstiel-Schwangau.*

society and *opposed* to the world, is found to be a
fiction of abstract thought, not discoverable anywhere, because not real.   And, on the other hand,
society is no longer 'collective,' but so organic that
the whole is potentially in every part—an organism
of organisms.

The influence of this organic idea in every department of thought which concerns itself with man
is not to be measured.   It is already fast changing
all the practical sciences of man—economics, politics,
ethics, and religion.   The material, being newly
interpreted, is wrought into a new purpose, and
revelation is once more bringing about a reformation.
But human action in its ethical aspect is, above all,
charged with a new significance.   The idea of duty
has received an expansion almost illimitable, and
man himself has thereby attained new worth and
dignity—for what is duty except a dignity and
opportunity, man's chance of being good?   When
we contrast this view of the life of man, as the life
of humanity in him, with the old individualism, we
may say that morality also has at last, in Bacon's
phrase, passed from the narrow seas into the open
ocean.   And, after all, the greatest achievement of
our age may be, not that it has established the
sciences of nature, but that it has made possible
the science of man.   We have at length reached
a point of view from which we may hope to understand ourselves.   Law, order, continuity, in human
action—the essential pre-conditions of a moral
science—were beyond the reach of an individualistic
theory.   It left to ethical writers no choice but that
of either sacrificing man to law, or law to man ;

of denying either the particular or the universal element in his nature. Naturalism did the first. Intuitionism, the second. The former made human action the *re*action of a natural agent on the incitement of natural forces. It made man a mere object, a *thing* capable of being affected by other things through his faculty of being pained or pleased ; an object acting in obedience to motives that had an external origin, just like any other object. The latter theory cut man free from the world and his fellows, endowed him with a will that had no law, and a conscience that was dogmatic ; and thereby succeeded in stultifying both law and morality.

But this new consciousness of the relation of man to mankind and the world takes him out of his isolation, and still leaves him free. It relates men to one another in a humanity, which is incarnated anew in each of them. It elevates the individual above the distinctions of time ; it treasures up the past in him as the active energy of his knowledge and morality in the present, and also as the potency of the ideal life of the future. On this view, the individual and the race are possible only through each other.

This fundamental change in our way of looking at the life of man is bound to abolish the ancient landmarks, and to bring confusion for a time. Out of the new conception, *i.e.* out of the idea of evolution, has sprung the tumult as well as the strength of our time. The present age is moved with thoughts beyond the reach of its powers : great aspirations for the well-being of the people and high ideals of social welfare flash across its mind, to be followed again by thicker darkness. There is hardly any limit to its despair or hope. It has a far larger faith in the destiny of man than any of its predecessors, and yet it is *sure* of hardly anything—except that the ancient rules of human life are false. Individualism is now detected as scepticism and moral chaos in disguise. We know that the old methods are no longer of use. We cannot now cut ourselves free of the fate of others. The confused cries for help that are heard on every hand are recognized as the voices of our brethren; and we now know that our fate is involved in theirs, and that the problem of their welfare is also ours. We grapple with social questions at last, and recognize that the issues of life and death lie in the solution of these enigmas. Legislators and economists, teachers of religion and socialists, are all alike social reformers. Philanthropy has taken a deeper meaning; and all sects bear its banner.

But their forces are beaten back by the social wretchedness, for they have not found the sovereign remedy of a great idea; and the result is in many ways sad enough. Our social remedies often work mischief; for we degrade those whom we would elevate, and in our charity forget justice. We insist on the rights of the people and the duties of the privileged classes, and thereby tend to teach greed to those for whom we labour, and goodness to those whom we condemn. The task that lies before us is plain: we want the welfare of the people as a whole. But we fail to grasp the complex social elements together, and our very

remedies tend to sunder them. We know that the
public good will not be obtained by separating man
from man, securing each unit in a charmed circle
of personal rights, and protecting it from others by
isolation. We must find a place for the individual
within the social organism, and we know now that
this organism has not, as our fathers seemed to
think, the simple constitution of a wooden doll
Society is not put together mechanically, and the
individual cannot be outwardly attached to it if
he is to be helped. He must rather share its life,
be the heir of the wealth it has stored for him in
the past, and participate in its onward movement.
Between this new social ideal and our attainment,
between the magnitude of our social duties and the
resources of intellect and will at our command, there
lies a chasm which we despair of bridging over.

The characteristics of this epoch faithfully reflect
themselves in the pages of Carlyle, with whose
thoughts those of Browning are immediately connected. It was Carlyle who first effectively revealed
to England the continuity of human life, and the
magnitude of the issues of individual action. Seeing
the infinite in the finite, living under a continued
sense of the mystery that surrounds man, he flung
explosive negations amidst the narrow formulæ of
the social and religious orthodoxy of his day, blew
down the blinding walls of ethical individualism,
and, amidst much smoke and din, showed his
English readers something of the greatness of the
moral world. He gave us a philosophy of clothes,
penetrated through symbols to the immortal ideas,
condemned all shibboleths, and revealed the soul

of humanity behind the external modes of man's activity. He showed us, in a word, that the world is spiritual, that loyalty to duty is the foundation of all human good, and that national welfare rests on character. After reading him it is impossible, for any one who reflects on the nature of duty, to ask, "Am I my brother's keeper?" He not only imagined, but knew, how "all things the minutest that man does, minutely influence all men, and the very look of his face blesses or curses whom-so it lights on, and so generates ever new blessing or new cursing. I say, there is not a red Indian, hunting by Lake Winnipeg, can quarrel with his squaw, but the whole world must smart for it; will not the price of beaver rise? It is a mathematical fact that the casting of this pebble from my hand alters the centre of gravity of the universe." Carlyle dealt the deathblow to the 'laissez-faire' theory rampant in his day, and made each individual responsible for the race. He demonstrated that the sphere of duty does not terminate with ourselves and our next-door neighbours. There will be no pure air for the correctest Levite to breathe, till the laws of sanitation have been applied to the moral slums. "Ye are my brethren," said he, and he adds, as if conscious of his too denunciatory way of dealing with them, "hence my rage and sorrow."

But his consciousness of brotherhood with all men brought only despair for him. He saw clearly the responsibility of man, but not the dignity which that implies; he felt the weight of the burden of humanity upon his own soul, and it crushed him, for he forgot that all the good of the world was there to help him **bear** it, and that " One with God is a majority." He taught only the half-truth, that all men are united on the side of duty, and that the spiritual life of each is conditional on striving **to save all.** But he neglected the complement of **this truth, and** forgot the greatness of the beings **on whom** so great a duty could be laid. He therefore dignifies humanity only to degrade it again. The ' twenty millions ' each must try to **save ' are** mostly fools.' But how fools, when they can have such a task ? **Is it** not true, **on** the contrary, that no man ever **saw a** duty beyond his strength, and that ' man can because he ought,' **and** ought only because **he can ?** The evils **an** individual cannot overcome are the moral opportunities of his fellows. **The** good are not lone workers of God's purposes, and there is no need of despair. But Carlyle, like the ancient prophet, was too conscious of his own mission, and too forgetful **of that of others. "I** have been very jealous for the Lord God **of hosts ;** because the children of Israel have forgotten **Thy** covenant, thrown down Thine altars, and slain Thy prophets, and I, even I only, am left ; and they seek my life to take it away." He needed, beside the consciousness of his prophetic function, a con**sciousness of** brotherhood with humbler workers. " **Yet I have** left **Me seven thousand in** Israel, all the knees which have **not** bowed unto Baal, and every mouth which **hath not** kissed him." It would have helped him had he remembered, that there **were on** all sides other workers engaged on the temple not made with hands, although he could

not hear the sound of their hammers for the din
he made himself.   It would have changed his
despair into joy, and his pity into a higher moral
quality, had he been able to believe that, amidst all
the millions against whom he hurls his anathemas,
there is no one who, let him do what he will,
is not constrained to illustrate either the folly and
wretchedness of sin, or the glory of goodness.   It
is not given to any one, least of all to the wicked,
to hold back the onward movement of the race, or
to destroy the impulse for good which is planted
within it.

But Carlyle saw only one side of the truth about
man's moral nature and destiny.   He knew, as the
ancient prophets did, that evil is potential wreck;
and he taxed the power of metaphor to the utmost
to indicate how wrong gradually takes root and
ripens into putrescence and self-combustion, in
obedience to a necessity which is absolute.   That
morality is the essence of things, that wrong *must*
prove its weakness, that right is the only might,
is reiterated and illustrated on all his pages; they
are now commonplaces of speculation on matters
of history, if not conscious practical principles
which guide its makers.   But Carlyle never in-
quired into the character of this moral necessity,
and he overlooked the beneficence which places
death at the heart of sin.   He never saw wrong
except on its way to execution, or in the death-
throes; but he did not look in the face of the
gentle power that led it on to death.   He saw
the necessity which rules history, but not the
beneficent character of that necessity.

The same limitations marred his view of duty, which was his greatest revelation to his age. He felt its categorical authority and its binding force. But the power which imposed the duty was an alien power, awful in majesty, infinite in might, a 'great task-master'; and the duty itself was an outer law, written in letters of flame across the high heavens, in comparison with which man's action at its best sank into failure. His only virtue is obedience, and his last rendering even of himself is 'unprofitable servant.' In this he has much of the combined strength and weakness of the old Scottish Calvinism. "He stands between the individual and the Infinite without hope or guide. He has a constant disposition to crush the human being by comparing him with God," said Mazzini, with marvellous penetration. "From his lips, at times so daring, we seem to hear every instant the cry of the Breton Mariner—'My God protect me! My bark is so small, and Thy ocean so vast.'" His reconciliation of God and man was incomplete : God seemed to him to have manifested Himself *to* man but not *in* man. He did not see that the 'Eternity which is before and behind us is also within us.'

But the moral law which commands is just the reflection of the aspirations of progressive man, who always creates his own horizon. The extension of duty is the objective counterpart of man's growth; a proof of victory and not of failure, a sign that man is mounting upwards. And, if so, it is irrational to infer the impossibility of success from the magnitude of the demands of a moral law, which is itself the promise of a better future. The hard problems set for us by our social environment are recognized as set by ourselves; for, in matters of morality, the eye sees only what the heart prompts. The very statement of the difficulty contains the potency of its solution; for evil, when understood, is on the way towards being overcome, and the good, when seen, contains the promise of its own fulfilment. It is ignorance which is ruinous, as when the cries of humanity beat against a deaf ear; and we can take a comfort, denied to Carlyle, from the fact that he has made us awake to our social duties. He has let loose the confusion upon us, and it is only natural that we should at first be overcome by a sense of bewildered helplessness. But this very sense contains the germ of hope, and England is struggling to its feet to wrestle with its wrongs. Carlyle has brought us within sight of our future, and we are now taking a step into it. He has been our guide in the wilderness; but he died there, and was even denied the view from Pisgah.

But this view was given to Robert Browning, and he broke out into a song of victory, whose strains will give strength and comfort to many in the coming time. That his solution of the evils of life is not final may at once be admitted. There are elements in the problem of which he has taken no account, and which will force those who seek light on the deeper mysteries of man's moral nature to go beyond anything that the poet has to say. Even the poet himself becomes, at least in some directions, less confident of the completeness of his triumph as he grows older. His faith in the good does not fail, but it is the faith of one who confesses to ignorance, and links himself to his finitude. Still, so thorough is his conviction of the moral purpose of life, of the certainty of the good towards which man is moving, and of the beneficence of the power which is at work everywhere in the world, that many of his poems ring like the triumphant songs of Luther.

CHAPTER IV

BROWNING'S OPTIMISM

> " Gladness be with thee, Helper of the World !
>   I think this is the authentic sign and seal
>   Of Godship, that it ever waxes **glad**,
>   And more glad, until gladness **blossoms, bursts**
>   **Into a rage to** suffer for mankind,
>   And recommence at sorrow." [1]

I HAVE tried to show that one of the distinctive features of the present era is the stress it lays on the worth of the moral life of man, and the new significance it has given to that life by its view of the continuity of history. This view finds expression, on its social and ethical side, in the pages of Carlyle and Browning, both of whom are interested exclusively, one may almost say, in the evolution of human character; and both of whom, too, regard that evolution as the realization by man of the purposes, greater than man's, which rule in the world. And although neither of them developed the organic view of humanity, which is implied in their doctrines, into an explicit philo-

[1] *Balaustion's Adventure.*

sophy, still the moral life of the individual is for each of them the infinite life in the finite. The meaning of the universe is moral, its last might is rightness; and the task of man is to catch up that meaning, convert it into his own motive, and thereby make it the source of his actions, the inmost principle of his life. This, fully grasped, will bring the finite and the infinite, morality and religion together, and reconcile them.

But the reconciliation which Carlyle sought to effect was incomplete on every side—even within the sphere of duty, with which alone, as moralist, he specially concerned himself. The moral law was imposed upon man by a higher power, in the presence of whom man was awed and crushed; for that power had stinted man's endowment, and set him to fight a hopeless battle against endless evil. God was everywhere around man, and the universe was merely the expression of His will—a will inexorably bent on the good, so that evil could not prevail; but God was not *within* man, except as a voice of conscience issuing imperatives and threats. An infinite duty was laid upon a finite being, and its weight made him break out into a cry of despair.

Browning, however, not only sought to bring about the reconciliation, but succeeded, in so far as that is possible *in terms of mere feeling*. His poetry contains suggestions that the moral will without is also a force within man; that the power which makes for righteousness in the world has penetrated into, or rather manifests itself *as*, man. Intelligence and will, the reason which apprehends the nature of things, and the original impulse of self-conscious life which issues in action, are God's power in man ; so that God is realizing Himself in the deeds of man, and human history is just His return to Himself. Outer law and inner motive are, for the poet, manifestations of the same beneficent purpose ; and instead of duty in the sense of an autocratic imperative, or beneficent tyranny, he finds, deep beneath man's foolishness and sin, a constant tendency towards the good which is bound up with the very nature of man's reason and will. If man could only understand himself he would find without him no limiting necessity, but the manifestation of a law which is one with his own essential being. A beneficent power has loaded the dice, according to the epigram, so that the chances of failure and victory are not even ; for man's nature is itself a divine endowment, one with the power that rules his life, and man must finally reach through error to truth, and through sin to holiness. In the language of theology, it may be said that the moral process is the spiritual incarnation of God ; it is God's goodness as love effecting itself in human action. Hence Carlyle's cry of despair is turned by Browning into a song of victory. While the former regards the struggle between good and evil as a fixed battle in which the forces are immovably interlocked, the latter has the consciousness of battling against a retreating foe ; and the conviction of coming triumph gives joyous vigour to every stroke. Browning lifted morality into an optimism, and translated its battle into song. This was the distinctive mark and mission which give to him such power of moral inspiration.

In order, however, to estimate the value of this feature of the poet's work, it is necessary to look more closely into the character of his faith in the good. Merely to attribute to him an optimistic creed is to say very little; for the worth, or worthlessness, of such a creed depends upon its content—upon its fidelity to the facts of human life, the clearness of its consciousness of the evils it confronts, and the intensity of its realism.

There is a sense, and that a true one, in which it may be said that all men are optimists; for such a faith is implied in every conscious and deliberate action of man. There is no deed which is not an attempt to realize an ideal; whenever man acts he seeks a good, however ruinously he may misunderstand its nature. Final and absolute disbelief in an ultimate good in the sphere of morals, like absolute scepticism in the sphere of knowledge, is a disguised self-contradiction, and therefore an impossibility in fact. The one stultifies action, and asserts an effect without any cause, or even contrary to the cause; the other stultifies intellectual activity: and both views imply that the critic has so escaped the conditions of human life, as to be able to pass a condemnatory judgment upon them. The belief that a harmonious relation between the self-conscious agent and the supreme good is possible, underlies the practical activity of man; just as the belief in the unity of thought and being underlies his intellectual activity. A moral order—that is, an order of rational ends—

is postulated in all human actions, and we act **at
all only in virtue** of it—just as truly as we move
and work only in virtue of the forces which **make**
the spheres revolve, or think by help of the meaning
which presses upon **us** from the thought-woven
world, through all the pores of sense. **A true**
ethics, like a true psychology, **or a true science
of** nature, must **lean** upon metaphysics, **and it**
cannot pretend to start *ab initio.* **We live in the**
Copernican age, which puts the individual in a
system, in obedience to whose laws he finds **his**
welfare. And this is simply the assertion of **an**
optimistic creed, for it implies a harmonious world.

But, though this is true, it must be remembered
that this faith is a prophetic anticipation, rather
than acquired knowledge. We are only on the **way**
towards reconstructing in thought the fact which we
are, or towards bringing into clear knowledge the
elemental power which manifests itself within **us**
as thought, desire, and deed. And, until this **is**
achieved, we have no full right to an optimistic
creed. The revelation of the unity which pervades
all things, even in the natural world, will be the
last attainment of science ; and the reconciliation
of nature and man and God is still further in the
future, and will be the last triumph of philosophy.
During all the interval the world will be a scene of
warring elements ; and poetry, religion, and philosophy can only hold forth a promise, and give **to**
man a foretaste of ultimate victory. And in this
state of things even *their* assurance often falters.
Faith lapses into doubt, poetry becomes a wail for a
lost god, and its votary exhibits, ' through Europe

to the Ætolian shore, the pageant of his bleeding heart.' The optimistic faith is, as a rule, only a hope and a desire, a 'Grand Perhaps,' which knows no defence against the critical understanding, and sinks dumb when questioned. If, in the form of a religious conviction, its assurance is more confident, then, too often, it rests upon the treacherous foundations of authoritative ignorance, which crumble into dust beneath the blows of awakened and liberated reason. Nay, if by the aid of philosophy we turn our optimism into a faith held by reason, a fact before which the intellect as well as the heart worships and grows glad, it still is for most of us only a general hypothesis, a mere leap to God which spurns the intermediate steps, a universal without content, a bare form that lacks reality.

Such an optimism, such a plunge into the pure blue and away from facts, was Emerson's. Caroline Fox tells a story of him and Carlyle which reveals this very pointedly. It seems that Carlyle once led the serene philosopher through the abominations of the streets of London at midnight, asking him with grim humour at every few steps, 'Do you believe in the devil *now?*' Emerson replied that the more he saw of the English people the greater and better he thought them. This little incident lays bare the limits of both these great men. Where the one saw, the other was blind. To the one there was the misery and the universal mirk; to the other, the pure white beam was scarcely broken. Carlyle believed in the good, beyond all doubt: he fought his great battle in its strength and won, but 'he was sorely wounded.' Emerson was Sir Galahad, blind to all but the Holy Grail ; his armour spotless-white, his virtue cloistered and unbreathed, his race won without the dust and heat. But his optimism was too easy to be satisfactory. His victory was not won in the enemy's citadel, where sin sits throned amidst the chaos, but in the placid upper air of poetic imagination. And, in consequence, Emerson can only convince the converted ; and his song is not heard in the dark, nor does it cheer the wayfarer on the muddy highway, along which burthened humanity meanly toils.

But Browning's optimism is more earnest and real than any pious hope, or dogmatic belief, or benevolent theory held by a placid philosopher, protected against contact with the sins and sorrows of man as by an invisible garment of contemplative holiness. It is a conviction which has sustained the shocks of criticism and the test of facts ; and it therefore, both for the poet and his readers, fulfils a mission beyond the reach of any easy trust in a mystic good. Its power will be felt and its value recognized by those who have themselves confronted the contradictions of human life and known something of their depth.

No lover of Browning's poetry can miss the vigorous manliness of the poet's own bearing, or fail to recognize the strength that flows from his joyous, fearless personality and the might of his intellect and heart. "When British literature," said Carlyle of Scott and Cobbett, "lay all puking and sprawling in Wertherism, Byronism and other Sentimentalisms, nature was kind enough to send us two healthy men." And he breaks out into a eulogy of mere health, of " the just balance of faculties that radiates a glad light outwards, enlightening and embellishing all things." But he finds it easy to account for the health of these men : they had never faced the mystery of existence. Such healthiness we find in Browning, although he wrote with Carlyle at his side, and within earshot of the infinite wail of this moral fatalist. And yet, the word health is inadequate to convey the depth of the joyous meaning which the poet found in the world. His optimism was not a constitutional and irreflective hopefulness, to be accounted for on the ground that "the great mystery of existence was not great to him : did not drive him into rocky solitudes to wrestle with it for an answer, to be answered or to perish." There are, indeed, certain rash and foolish persons who pretend to trace Browning's optimism to his mixed descent ; but there is a 'pause in the leading and the light' of those wiseacres who pretend to trace moral and mental characteristics to physiological antecedents. They cannot quite catch a great man in the making, nor, even by the help of evolution, say anything wiser about genius than that 'the wind bloweth where it listeth.' No doubt the poet's optimism indicates a native sturdiness of head and heart. He had the invaluable endowment of a predisposition to see the sunny side of life, and a native tendency to revolt against that subjectivity, which is the root of our misery in all its forms. He had little respect for the *Welt-schmerz*, and can scarcely be civil to the hero of the bleeding heart.

> " Sinning, sorrowing, despairing,
>   Body-ruined, spirit-wrecked—
> Should I give my woes an airing,—
>   Where's one plague that claims respect?
>
> " Have you found your life distasteful?
>   My life did, and does, smack sweet.
> Was your youth of pleasure wasteful?
>   Mine I saved and hold complete.
> Do your joys with **age diminish?**
>   When mine fail me I'll complain.
> Must in death your daylight finish?
>   My sun sets to rise again.
>
>   .   .   .   .
>
> " I find earth not grey but rosy,
>   Heaven not grim but fair of hue.
> Do I stoop? I pluck a posy.
>   Do I stand and stare? All's blue." [1]

Browning was no doubt least of all men inclined to pout at his 'plain bun'; on the contrary, he was awake to **the** grandeur of his inheritance, and valued most highly 'his life-rent of God's universe with the tasks it offered and the tools to do them with.' But his optimism sent its roots deeper than any 'disposition'; it penetrated beyond mere health of body and mind, as it did beyond a mere sentiment of God's goodness. Optimisms resting on these bases are always weak; for the former leaves man naked and sensitive to the evils that crowd round him when the powers of body and mind decay, and the latter is, at best, useful only for the individual who possesses it, and it breaks down under the stress of criticism and doubt. Browning's optimism is a great element in English literature,

[1] *At the Mermaid.*

because it opposes with such strength the shocks
that come from both these quarters. His joyous-
ness is the reflection *in feeling* of a conviction as
to the nature of things, which he had verified in
the darkest details of human life, and established
for himself in the face of the gravest objections
that his intellect was able to call forth. In fact,
its value lies, above all, in this,—that it comes after
criticism, after the condemnation which Byron and
Carlyle had passed, each from his own point of
view, on the world and on man.

The need of an optimism is one of the penalties
which reflection brings. Natural life takes the goodness of things for granted ; but reflection disturbs
the placid contentment and sets man at variance
with his world. The fruit of the tree of knowledge
always reveals his nakedness to man ; he is turned
out of the paradise of unconsciousness and doomed
to force Nature, now conceived as a step-dame, to
satisfy needs which are now first felt. Optimism
is the expression of man's new reconciliation with
his world ; as the opposite doctrine of pessimism is
the consciousness of an unresolved contradiction.
Both are a judgment passed upon the world, from
the point of view of its adequacy or inadequacy
to meet demands, arising from needs which the
individual has discovered in himself.

Now, as I have tried to show, one of the main
characteristics of the opening years of the present
era was its deeper intuition of the significance of
human life, and, therefore, by implication, of its
wants and claims. The spiritual nature of man,
lost sight of during the preceding age, was re-dis-

covered ; and the first and immediate consequence was that man, as man, attained infinite worth. "Man was born free," cried Rousseau, with a conviction which swept all before it ; 'he has original, inalienable, and supreme rights against all things which can set themselves against him.' And Rousseau's countrymen believed him. There was not a *Sans-culotte* amongst them all but held his head high, being creation's lord ; and history can scarcely show a parallel to their great burst of joy and hope, as they ran riot in their new-found inheritance, from which they had so long been excluded. They flung themselves upon the world, as if they would 'glut their sense' upon it.

> "Expend
> Eternity upon its shows,
> Flung them as freely as one rose
> Out of a summer's opulence."[1]

But the very discovery that man is spirit, which is the source of all his rights, is also an implicit discovery that he has outgrown the resources of the natural world. The infinite hunger of a soul cannot be satisfied with the things of sense. The natural world is too limited even for Carlyle's shoe-black ; nor is it surprising that Byron should find it a waste, and dolefully proclaim his disappointment to much-admiring mankind. Now, both Carlyle and Browning apprehended the cause of the discontent, and both endured the Byronic utterance of it with considerable impatience. "Art thou nothing other than a vulture, then," asks the former, "that fliest

---

[1] *Easter Day.*

through the universe seeking after somewhat *to eat*, and shrieking dolefully because carrion enough is not given thee? Close thy Byron, open thy Goethe."

"Huntsman Common Sense
Came to the rescue, bade prompt thwack of thong dispense
Quiet i' the kennel : taught that ocean might be blue,
And rolling and much more, and yet the soul have, too,
Its touch of God's own flame, which He may so expand
'Who measured the waters i' the hollow of His hand'
That ocean's self shall dry, turn dew-drop in respect
Of all-triumphant fire, matter with intellect
Once fairly matched."[1]

But Carlyle was always more able to detect the disease than to suggest the remedy. He had, indeed, 'a glimpse of it.' "There is in man a Higher than love of Happiness : he can do without Happiness, and instead thereof find Blessedness." But the glimpse was misleading, for it penetrated no further than the first negative step. The 'Everlasting Yea,' was, after all, only a deeper 'No!' only *Entsagung*, renunciation : "the fraction of life can be increased in value not so much by increasing your numerator as by lessening your denominator." Blessed alone is he that expecteth nothing. The holy of holies where man hears whispered the mystery of life, is "the sanctuary of sorrow." "What Act of Legislature was there that *thou* shouldst be Happy? A little while ago thou hadst no right to *be* at all. What if thou wert born and predestined not to be Happy, but to be Unhappy? Nay, is not 'life itself a disease,

[1] *Fifine at the Fair*, lxvii.

knowledge the symptom of derangement'? Have not the poets sung 'Hymns to the Night' as if Night were nobler than Day ; as if Day were but a small motley-coloured veil spread transiently over the infinite bosom of Night, and did but deform and hide from us its pure transparent eternal deeps." "We, the whole species of Mankind, and our whole existence and history, are but a floating speck in the illimitable ocean of the All . . . borne this way and that way by its deep-swelling tides, and grand ocean currents, of which what faintest chance is there that we should ever exhaust the significance, ascertain the goings and comings ? A region of Doubt, therefore, hovers for ever in the background. . . . Only on a canvas of Darkness, such is man's way of being, could the many-coloured picture of our Life paint itself and shine."

In such passages as these there is far deeper pessimism than in anything which Byron could experience or express. Scepticism is directed by Carlyle, not against the natural elements of life —the mere sensuous outworks—but against the citadel of thought itself. Self-consciousness, or the reflecting interpretation by man of himself and his world, the very activity that lifts him above animal existence and makes him man, instead of being a divine endowment, is declared to be a disease, a poisonous subjectivity destructive of all good. The discovery that man is spirit and no vulture, which was due to Carlyle himself more than to any other English writer of his age, seemed, after all, to be a great calamity ; for it led to the renunciation of happiness, and filled **man with** yearnings after a better than happiness, but **left him** nothing wherewith these could be satisfied, except 'the duty next to hand.' And **the duty next to hand, as** interpreted by Carlyle, **is a** means of suppressing by action, **not** idle speech only, but thought itself. But, **if** this be true, the highest in man **is set** against itself. For what kind of action remains possible to a 'speck **on the** illimitable ocean, borne this way **and** that way by its deep-swelling tides'? "Here on **earth we** are soldiers, fighting in a foreign land; that understand not the plan of the campaign, and have no need to understand **it,** seeing what **is at** our hand to be done." And **there** is one element of still deeper gloom in **this** blind fighting; it is fought for a foreign **cause. It is** God's cause, and not ours, **or ours** only **in so far as it** has been despotically imposed **upon us; and** it is hard **to** discover from Carlyle what interest we can **have** in **the** victory. Duty is to him a menace—like the duty of a slave, were that possible. **It lacks** the element which alone can make it imperative to a **free** being, namely, that it be recognized **as** *his* good, **and that** the outer law become his inner motive. The **moral** law is rarely looked at by Carlyle as a beneficent revelation, and still more rarely as the condition which, if fulfilled, will reconcile **man with nature and** with God. And, consequently, **he can draw** little strength from religion; **for it is** only **love that** can cast out fear.

To sum up all in a word, Carlyle regarded evil as having penetrated into the inmost recesses of man's being. **Thought** was disease; morality was **blind** obedience to a foreign authority; religion was awe of an Unknowable with whom man can claim no kinship. Man's nature **was** discovered to be spiritual only **on the** side **of its** Wants. It **was an endowment of** a hunger **which** nothing **could satisfy**—not **the** infinite, because it **is too** great; **not the finite,** because it is **too little; not** God, because He is too far above man; not nature, because it is **too far** beneath him. We are unable **to** satisfy ourselves with the things of sense, and are also 'shut **out of the** heaven of spirit.' What have been called 'the three great terms of thought' —the World, Self, and **God—have** fallen asunder in his teaching. It is **the** difficulty of reconciling these which brings despair; while **optimism is** evidently **the** consciousness of their **harmony.**

Now, these evils which reflection has revealed, **and which are so** much deeper than those of mere **sensuous** disappointment, can only be removed by deeper reflection. The **harmony** of the world of man's experience, which has been broken by 'the comprehensive curse of sceptical despair,' **can,** as Goethe teaches us, be **restored** only by thought—

> "In thine own soul, build it **up** again."

The complete refutation of Carlyle's pessimistic view can only **come** by reinterpreting each of the contradicting **terms** in the light of **a higher conception.** We must have a new view and a deeper grasp of the Self, the World, and God. And such a view **can** be adequately **given only by** philosophy.

Reason alone can justify the faith that has been disturbed by reflection, and re-establish its authority.

How, then, it may be asked, can a poet be expected to turn back the forces of a scepticism, which have been thus armed with the weapons of dialectic? Can anything avail in this region except explicit demonstration? A poet never demonstrates, but perceives; art is not a process, but a result; truth for it is immediate, and it neither admits nor demands any logical connection of ideas. The standard-bearers and the trumpeters may be necessary to kindle the courage of the army and to lead it on to victory, but the fight must be won by the thrust of sword and pike. Man needs more than the intuitions of the great poets if he is to maintain solid possession of the truth.

Now, I am prepared to admit the force of this objection, and I shall endeavour in the sequel to prove that, in order to establish optimism, more is needed than Browning can give, even when interpreted in the most sympathetic way. His doctrine is offered in terms of art, and it cannot have any demonstrative force without violating the limits of art. In some of his poems, however,—for instance, in *La Saisiaz*, *Ferishtah's Fancies* and the *Parleyings*, Browning sought to advance definite proofs of the theories which he held. He appears before us at times armed *cap-a-pie*, like a philosopher. Still, it is not when he argues that Browning proves: it is when he sees, as a poet sees. It is not by means of logical demonstrations that he helps us to meet the despair of Carlyle, or contributes to the establishment of a better faith. Browning's proofs are least convincing when he is most aware of his philosophical presuppositions ; and a philosophical critic could well afford to agree with the critic of art, in relegating the demonstrating portions of his poems to the chaotic limbo lying between philosophy and poetry.

When, however, he forgets his philosophy, and speaks as poet and religious man, when he is dominated by that sovereign thought which gave unity to his life-work, and which, therefore, seemed to lie deeper in him than the necessities of his art and to determine his poetic function, his utterances have a far higher significance. For he so lifts the artistic object into the region of pure thought, and makes sense and reason so to interpenetrate, that the old metaphors of 'the noble lie' and 'the truth beneath the veil' seem no longer to help. He seems to show us the truth so vividly and simply, that we are less willing to make art and philosophy mutually exclusive, although their methods differ Like some of the greatest philosophers, and notably Plato and Hegel, he constrains us to doubt whether the distinction penetrates low beneath the surface ; for philosophy, too, when at its best, is a thinking of things together. In the light of their teaching we begin to ask, whether it is not possible that the interpretation of the world in terms of spirit, which is the common feature of both Hegel's philosophy and Browning's poetry, does not necessarily bring with it a settlement of the ancient feud between these two modes of thought.

But, in any case, Browning's utterances, especially those which he makes when he is most poet and least philosopher, have something of the convincing impressiveness of a reasoned system of optimism. And this comes, as already suggested, from his loyalty to a single idea, which gives unity to all his work. That idea we may, in the end, be obliged to treat not only as a hypothesis—for all principles of reconciliation, even those of the sciences, so long as knowledge is incomplete, must be regarded as hypothesis—but also as a hypothesis which he had no right to assume. It may be that in the end we shall be obliged to say of him, as of so many others—

> " See the sage, with the hunger for the truth,
> And see his system that's all true, except
> The one weak place, that's stanchioned by a lie !"[1]

It may be that the religious form, through which he generally reaches his convictions, is not freed from a dogmatic element which so penetrates his thoughts as to vitiate it as a philosophy. Nevertheless, it answered for the poet all the uses of a philosophy, and it may do the same for many who are distrustful of the systems of the schools, and who are 'neither able to find a faith nor to do without one.' It contains far-reaching hints of a reconciliation of the elements of discord in our lives, and a suggestion of a way in which it may be demonstrated, that an optimistic theory is truer to facts than any scepticism or agnosticism, with the despair that they necessarily bring.

For Browning not only advanced a principle, whereby, as he conceived, man might again be

---

[1] *Prince Hohenstiel-Schwangau.*

reconciled to the world and God, and all things be viewed as the manifestation of a power that is benevolent ; he also sought to apply his principle to the facts of life. He illustrates his fundamental hypothesis by means of these facts ; and he tests its validity with the persistence and impressive candour of a scientific investigator. His optimism is not that of an eclectic, who can ignore inconvenient difficulties. It is not an attempt to justify the whole by neglecting details, or to make wrong seem right by reference to a far-off result, in which the steps of the process are forgotten. He stakes the value of his view of life on its power to meet *all* facts : one fact, ultimately irreconcilable with his hypothesis, will, he knows, destroy it.

> "All the same,
> Of absolute and irretrievable black,—black's soul of black
> Beyond white's power to disintensify,—
> Of that I saw no sample : such may wreck
> My life and ruin my philosophy
> To-morrow, doubtless."[1]

He knew that, to justify God, he had to justify *all* His ways to man ; that if the good rules at all, it rules absolutely ; and that a single exception would confute his optimism.

> "So, gazing up, in my youth, at love
>   As seen through power, ever above
>   All modes which make it manifest,
>   My soul brought all to a single test—
>   That He, the Eternal First and Last,
>   Who, in His power, had so surpassed

[1] *A Bean Stripe—Ferishtah's Fancies.*

> All man conceives of what is might,—
> Whose wisdom, too, showed infinite,
> —Would prove as infinitely good ;
> Would never, (my soul understood,)
> With power to work all love desires,
> Bestow e'en less than man requires."[1]

> " No : love which, on earth, amid all the shows of it,
> Has ever been seen the sole good of life in it,
> The love, ever growing there, spite of the strife in it,
> Shall arise, made perfect, from death's repose of it.
> And I shall behold Thee, face to face,
> O God, and in Thy light retrace
> How in all I loved here, still wast Thou !"[2]

We can scarcely miss the emphasis of the poet's own conviction in these passages, or in the assertion that—

> " The acknowledgment of God in Christ
> Accepted by thy reason, solves for thee
> All questions in the earth and out of it,
> And has so far advanced thee to be wise."[3]

Consequently, there is a defiant and aggressive element in his attitude. Strengthened with an unfaltering faith in the supreme Good, this knight of the Holy Spirit goes forth over all the world seeking out wrongs. "He has," said Dr. Westcott, "dared to look on the darkest and meanest forms of action and passion, from which we commonly and rightly turn our eyes, and he has brought back for us from this universal survey a conviction of hope." I believe, further, that it was in order to justify this conviction that he set out on his

[1] *Christmas Eve.*　　[2] *Ibid.*　　[3] *A Death in the Desert.*

quest. His interest in vice—in malice, cruelty, ignorance, brutishness, meanness, the irrational perversity of a corrupt disposition, and the subtleties of philosophic and æsthetic falsehood—was no morbid curiosity. Browning was no 'painter of dirt'; no artist can portray filth for filth's sake, and remain an artist. He crowds his pages with criminals because he sees deeper than their crimes. He describes evil without 'palliation or reserve,' and allows it to put forth all its might, in order that he may, in the end, show it to be subjected to God's purposes. He confronts evil in order to force it to give up the good, which is all the reality that is in it. He conceives it as his mission to prove that evil is 'stuff for transmuting,' and that there is nought in the world

> "But, touched aright, prompt yields each particle its tongue
> Of elemental flame—no matter whence flame sprung,
> From gums and spice, or else from straw and rottenness."

All we want is—

> "The power to make them burn, express
> What lights and warms henceforth, leaves only ash behind,
> Howe'er the chance."[1]

He had Pompilia's faith.

> "And still, as the day wore, the trouble grew,
> Whereby I guessed there would be born a star."

He goes forth in the might of his faith in the power of good, as if he wished once for all to try the resources of evil at their uttermost, and pass upon it a complete and final condemnation. With

[1] *Fifine at the Fair.*

this view, he seeks evil in its own haunts. He creates Guido, the subtlest and most powerful compound of vice in our literature—except Iago, perhaps—merely in order that we may see evil at its worst; and he places him in an environment suited to his nature, as if he was carrying out an *experimentum crucis.* The

> " Midmost blotch of black
> Discernible in the group of clustered crimes
> Huddling together in the cave they call
> Their palace." [1]

Beside him are his brothers, each with his own ' tint of hell '; his mistress on whose face even Pompilia saw the glow of the nether pit ' flash and fade '; and his mother—

> "The gaunt grey nightmare in the furthest smoke,
> The hag that gave these three abortions birth,
> Unmotherly mother and unwomanly
> Woman, that near turns motherhood to shame,
> Womanliness to loathing." [2]

Such ' denizens o' the cave now cluster round Pompilia and heat the furnace sevenfold.'   While she

> " Sent prayer like incense up
> To God the strong, God the beneficent,
> God ever mindful in all strife and strait,
> Who for our own good, makes the need extreme,
> Till at the last He puts forth might and saves." [3]

In these lines we feel the poet's purpose, constant throughout the whole poem. We know all the

---

[1] *The Ring and the Book—The Pope*, 869-872.
[2] *Ibid.* 911-915.
[3] *The Ring and the Book—Pompilia*, 1384-1388.

while that with him at our side we can travel safely through the depths of the Inferno—for the flames bend back from him; and it is only what we expect as the result of it all, that there should come

> "A bolt from heaven to cleave roof and clear place,
>   . . . . then flood
> And purify the scene with outside day—
> Which yet, in the absolutest drench of dark,
> Ne'er wants its witness, some stray beauty-beam
> To the despair of hell."[1]

The superabundant strength of Browning's conviction in the supremacy of the good, which led him in *The Ring and the Book* to depict criminals at their worst, forced him later on in his life to exhibit evil in another form. The real meaning and value of such poems as *Fifine at the Fair*, *Prince Hohenstiel-Schwangau*, *Red Cotton Nightcap Country*, *Ferishtah's Fancies*, and others, can only be determined by a careful and complete analysis of each of them. But they have one characteristic so prominent, and so new in poetry, that the most careless reader cannot fail to detect it. Action and its dramatic treatment give place to a discussion which is metaphysical; instead of the conflict of motives within a character, the stress and strain of passion and will in collision with circumstances, there is reflection on action after it has passed, and the conflict of subtle arguments on the ethical value of motives and ways of conduct, which the ordinary moral consciousness condemns without hesitation. All agree that these poems represent a

---

[1] *The Ring and the Book—The Pope*, 996-1003.

new departure in poetry, and some consider that
in them the poet, in thus dealing with metaphysical
abstractions, has overleapt the boundaries of the
poetic art.   To such critics this later period seems
the period of his decadence, in which the casuistical
tendencies, which had already appeared in *Bishop
Blougram's Apology, Mr. Sludge the Medium*, and
other poems, have overwhelmed his art, and in
which his intellect, in its pride of strength, has
grown wanton.   *Fifine at the Fair* is said to be
" a defence of inconstancy, or of the right of
experiment in love."   Its hero, who is " a modern
gentleman, a refined, cultured, musical, artistic and
philosophic person, of high attainments, lofty aspirations, strong emotions, and capricious will," produces
arguments ' wide in range, of profound significance
and infinite ingenuity,' to defend and justify immoral
intercourse with a gipsy trull.   The poem consists
of the speculations of a libertine, who coerces into
his service truth and sophistry, and ' a superabound-
ing wealth of thought and imagery,' with no further
purpose on the poet's part than the dramatic de-
lineation of character.   *Prince Hohenstiel-Schwangau*
is spoken of in a similar manner as the justification,
by reference to the deepest principles of morality,
of compromise, hypocrisy, lying, and a selfishness
that betrays every cause to the individual's meanest
welfare.   The object of the poet is " by no means
to prove black white, or white black, or to make
the worse appear the better reason, but to bring
a seeming monster and perplexing anomaly under
the common laws of nature, by showing how it
has grown to be what it is, and how it can

with more or less self-delusion reconcile itself to itself."

I am not able to accept this as a complete explanation of the intention of the poet, except with reference to *Prince Hohenstiel-Schwangau*. The *Prince* is a psychological study, like *Mr. Sludge the Medium* and *Bishop Blougram*. No doubt Browning had the interest of a dramatist in the hero of *Fifine at the Fair*, and of *Red Cotton Nightcap Country*; but, in these poems, his dramatic interest is itself determined by an ethical purpose, which is still more profound. His meeting with the gipsy at Pornic, and the spectacle of her unscrupulous audacity in vice, not only 'sent his fancy roaming,' but opened out before him the fundamental problems of life. What I would find, therefore, in *Fifine at the Fair*, is not the casuistic defence of an artistic and speculative libertine, but an earnest attempt on the part of the poet to prove,

> "That, through the outward sign, the inward grace allures,
> And sparks from heaven transpierce earth's coarsest cover-
> tures,—
> All by demonstrating the value of Fifine." [1]

Within his scheme of the universal good he seeks to find a place even for this gipsy creature, who traffics 'in just what we most pique us that we keep.' Having, in *The Ring and the Book*, challenged evil at its worst as it manifests itself practically in concrete characters and external action, and having wrung from it the victory of

[1] *Fifine at the Fair*, xxviii.

the good, in *Fifine* and his other later poems he
meets it again in the region of dialectic. In this
sphere of metaphysical ethics, evil has assumed a
more dangerous form, especially for an artist. His
optimistic faith has driven the poet into a realm
into which poetry never ventured before. His
battle is now, not with flesh and blood, but with
the subtler powers of darkness grown vocal and
argumentative, and threatening to turn the poet's
faith in good into a defence of immorality, and to
justify the worst evil by what is highest of all.
Having indicated in outward fact 'the need,' as
well as the 'transiency of sin and death,' he seeks
here to prove that need ; and, in doing so, he
seems to degrade the highest truth of religion into
a defence of the worst wickedness.

No doubt the result is sufficiently repulsive to
the abstract moralist, who is apt to find in *Fifine*
nothing but a casuistical and shameless justification
of evil, which is blasphemy against goodness itself.
We are made to 'discover,' for instance, that

> "There was just
> Enough and not too much of hate, love, greed and lust,
> Could one discerningly but hold the balance, shift
> The weight from scale to scale, do justice to the drift
> Of nature, and explain the glories by the shames
> Mixed up in man, one stuff miscalled by different names."[1]

We are told that—

> "Force, guile were arms which earned
> My praise, not blame at all."

Confronted with such utterances as these, it is
only natural that, rather than entangle the poet in

[1] *Fifine at the Fair*, cviii.

them, we should regard them as the sophistries of a philosophical Don Juan, powerful enough, under the stress of self-defence, to confuse the distinctions of right and wrong. But, as we shall try to show in the next chapter, such an apparent justification of evil cannot be avoided by a reflective optimist; and it is implicitly contained even in those religious utterances of *Rabbi Ben Ezra*, *Christmas Eve*, and *A Death in the Desert*, with which we identify not only the poet but ourselves, in so far as we share his faith that

> "God's in His heaven,—
> All's right with the world."

The poet had far too much speculative acumen to be ignorant of this, and too much boldness and strength of conviction in the might of the good to refuse to confront the issues that sprang from his faith. In his later poems, as in his earlier ones, he is endeavouring to justify the ways of God to man; and the difficulties which surround him are not those of a casuist, but the stubborn questionings of a spirit whose religious faith is thoroughly earnest and fearless. To a spirit so loyal to the truth, and so bold to follow its leading, the suppression of such problems is impossible; and, consequently, it was inevitable that he should use the whole strength of his dialectic to try those fundamental principles on which the moral life of man is based. It is this, I believe, which we find in *Fifine*, as in *Ferishtah's Fancies* and the *Parleyings*; and not an exhibition of the argumentive subtlety of a mind whose strength has become lawless, and which spends itself in intellectual gymnastics that have no place within the realm of either the beautiful or the true.

CHAPTER V

OPTIMISM AND ETHICS: THEIR CONTRADICTION

> " Our remedies oft in ourselves do lie,
>   Which we ascribe to heaven. The fated sky
>   Gives us free scope ; only doth backward pull
>   Our slow designs, when we ourselves are dull.
>
>   .   .   .   .   .   .
>
> But most it is presumption in us, when
> The help of heaven we count the act of men."[1]

I HAVE tried to show that one of the ruling
conceptions of Browning's view of life is that
the Good is absolute, and that it reveals itself in
all the events of human life. By means of this
conception, he endeavoured to bring together the
elements which had fallen asunder in the sensational
and moral pessimism of Byron and Carlyle. In
other words, through the re-interpreting power which
lies in this fundamental thought when it is soberly
held and fearlessly applied, he sought to reconcile
man with the world and with God, and thereby
with himself. And the governing motive, whether

[1] *All's Well that Ends Well.*

the conscious motive or not, of Browning's poetry,
the secret impulse which led him to dramatize the
conflicts and antagonisms of human life, **was the**
necessity of finding in them evidence of the presence
of this absolute Good.

Browning's optimism was deep and comprehensive
enough to reject all compromise. His faith in the
good seemed to rise with the demands that were
made upon it by the misery and wickedness of man,
and the apparently purposeless waste of life and its
resources. There was in it a deliberate earnestness
which led him to grapple, not only with the concrete
difficulties of individual life, but with those also that
spring from reflection and theory.

The test of a philosophic optimism, as of any
optimism which is more than a pious sentiment,
must finally lie in its power to reveal the presence
of the good in actual individual evils. But there
are difficulties still nearer than those presented by
concrete facts, difficulties arising **out of** the very
suggestion that evil is a form of good. Such
speculative difficulties must be met by a reflective
mind, before it can follow out the application of
an optimistic theory to particular facts. **Now,**
Browning's creed, at least as he held it in his later
years, was not merely the allowable exaggeration
of an ecstatic religious sentiment, the impassioned
conviction of a God-intoxicated man. It **was**
deliberately presented as a solution of moral **pro-**
blems, and was intended to serve as a theory of the
spiritual nature of things. It is therefore justly
open to the same kind of criticism as that to which
a philosophic doctrine is exposed. The poet

deprived himself of the refuge, legitimate enough to the intuitive method of art, when, in his later works, he not only offered a dramatic solution of the problem of life, but definitely attempted to meet the difficulties of speculative ethics.

In this chapter I shall point out some of these difficulties, and then proceed to show how the poet proposed to solve them.

A thorough-going optimism, in that it subdues all things to the idea of the supreme Good, and denies to evil the right even to dispute the absoluteness of its sway, naturally seems to imply a pantheistic theory of the world. And Browning's insistence on the presence of the highest in all things may easily be regarded as a mere revival of the oldest and crudest attempt at finding their unity in God. For if *all*, as he says, is for the best, there seems to be no room left for the differences apparent in the world, and the variety which gives it beauty and worth. Particular existences would seem to be illusory and evanescent phenomena, the creations of human imagination, itself a delusive appearance. The infinite, on this view, stands over against the finite, and it overpowers and consumes it ; and the optimism, implied in the phrase that "God is all," turns at once into a pessimism. For, as soon as we inquire into the meaning of this 'all,' we find that it is only a negation of everything we can know or be. Such a pantheism as this is self-contradictory ; for, while seeming to level all things upwards to a manifestation of the divine, it really levels all downwards to the level of mere unqualified being, a stagnant and empty unknowable. It leaves only a choice between **akosmism and atheism**, and, at the same time, it makes each of the alternatives impossible. For, in explaining the world it abolishes it, and in abolishing the world it empties itself of all significance ; so that the Godhood which it attempts to establish throughout the whole realm of being is found to mean nothing. " It is the night, in which all cows are black."

The optimistic **creed** which the poet strove **to** teach must, therefore, not only establish the immanence of God, but **show** in some way how such immanence is consistent with the existence of particular things. **His** doctrine that there is no failure, or folly, or wickedness, or misery, but conceals within it, at its heart, a divine element ; that there **is** no incident in human history **which is** not **a** pulsation of the life **of** the highest, and which has not its place in **a scheme of universal** good, must leave room for the moral **life of man,** and all **the** risks which morality brings with it. Otherwise, optimism is impossible. For a God who, in filling the universe with His presence, encroaches on the freedom and extinguishes the independence of man, precludes the possibility of all that is best for man —namely, moral achievement. Life, deprived **of its** moral purpose, is worthless to the poet, and so, in consequence, is all that exists in order to maintain that life. Optimism and ethics seem **thus to come** into immediate collision. **The former, finding the** presence of God in all things, seems to leave no room for man ; and the latter seems to set man to work out his own destiny in solitude, and to give

him supreme and absolute authority over his own
life ; so that any character which he forms, be it
good or bad, is entirely the product of his own
activity. So far **as** his life is culpable or praise-
worthy, in other words, so far as we pass any moral
judgment upon it, we necessarily think of it as the
revelation of a self, that is, of an independent will,
which **cannot divide** its responsibility. There may
be, **and indeed there** always is for every individual,
a hereditary predisposition and a soliciting environment, tendencies which are his inheritance from a
remote past, and which rise to the surface in his
own life ; in other words, the life of the individual
is always led within the larger **sweep** of the life of
humanity. He is part of a whole, and has his place
fixed, and his function predetermined, by a **power**
which **is** greater than his own. But if we are to
call him good or evil, if he is to aspire and repent
and strive, in a word, if he **is to** have any *moral*
character, he cannot be merely a part of a system ;
there must be something within him which is
superior to circumstances, and which makes him
master of his own fate. His natural history may
begin with the grey dawn of primal being, but his
moral history begins with himself, from **the time**
when he **first** reacted upon the world in which he **is**
placed, and transformed his natural relations into
will and character. For who can be responsible
for what he did not will ? What could a moral
imperative mean, what could an 'ought' signify, to
a being who was only a temporary embodiment of
forces that are prior to and independent of himself?
It would seem, therefore, as if morality were irre-

concilable with optimism. The moral life of man cannot be the manifestation of a divine benevolence whose purpose is necessary ; it is a trust laid upon himself, which he may either violate or keep. It surpasses divine goodness, 'tho' matched with equal power' to *make* man good, as it has made the flowers beautiful. From this point of view, spiritual attainment, whether intellectual or moral, is man's own, a spontaneous product. Just as God is conceived as all in all in the universe, so man is all in all within the sphere of duty ; for the kingdom of heaven is within. In both cases alike there is absolute exclusion of external interference.

For this reason, it has often seemed both to philosophers and theologians, as if the world were too confined to hold within it both God and man. In the East, the consciousness of the infinite seemed at times to leave no room for the finite ; and in the West, where the consciousness of the finite and interest therein is strongest, where man strives and aspires, a Deism arose which set God at a distance, and allowed Him to interfere in the fate of man only by a benevolent miracle. Nor is this collision of pantheism and freedom, nay, of religion and morality, confined to the theoretical region. This difficulty is not merely the punishment of an over-bold and over-ambitious philosophy, which pries too curiously into the mystery of being. It lies at the very threshold of all reflection on the facts of the moral life. Even children feel the mystery of God's permitting sin, and embarrass their helpless parents with the contradiction between absolute benevolence and the miseries and cruelties

of life. "A vain interminable controversy," says
Teufelsdröckh, "which arises in every soul since the
beginning of the world: and in every soul, that
would pass from idle suffering into actual endeavouring, must be put an end to. The most, in our
own time, have to go content with a simple, incomplete enough Suppression of this controversy: to a
few Solution of it is indispensable."

Solution, and **not** Suppression, is what Browning
sought; he did, in fact, propound a solution, which,
whether finally **satisfactory** or not, at least carries
us beyond the easy compromises of ordinary religious and ethical teaching. He does not deny
the universality of God's beneficence or power, and
divide the realm of being between Him and the
adversary: nor, on the other hand, does he limit
man's freedom, and stultify ethics by extracting
the sting **of reality** from sin. To limit God, he
knew, was to deny Him; and, whatever the difficulties he felt in regarding the absolute Spirit as
realizing itself in man, he could not be content to
reduce man into a temporary phantom, an evanescent embodiment of 'spiritual' or natural forces,
that take a fleeting form in him as they pursue their
onward way.

Browning held with equal tenacity to the idea
of a universal benevolent order, and to the idea
of the moral freedom of man within it. He was
driven in opposite directions by two beliefs, both
of which he knew to be essential to the life of
man as spirit, and both of which he illustrates
throughout his poems with an endless variety of
poetic expression. He endeavoured to find God in

man and still to leave man free. His optimistic faith sought reconciliation with morality. The vigour of his ethical doctrine is as pre-eminent as the fulness of his conviction of the absolute sway of the Good. Side by side with his doctrine that there is no failure, no wretchedness of corruption that does not conceal within it a germ of goodness, is his sense of the evil of sin, of the infinite earnestness of man's moral warfare, and of the surpassing magnitude of the issues at stake for each individual soul. So powerful is his interest in man as a moral agent, that he sees nought else in the world of any deep concern. "My stress lay," he said in his preface to *Sordello* (1863), "on the incidents in the development of a soul: little else is worth study. I, at least, always thought so—you, with many known and unknown to me, think so—others may one day think so." And this development of a soul is not at any time regarded by the poet as a peaceful process, like the growth of a plant or animal. Although he thinks of the life of man as the gradual realization of a divine purpose within him, he does not suppose it to take place in obedience to a tranquil necessity. Man advances morally by fighting his way inch by inch, and he gains nothing except through conflict. He does not become good as the plant grows into maturity. "The kingdom of heaven suffereth violence, and the violent take it by force."

> "No, when the fight begins within himself,
>   A man's worth something. God stoops o'er his head,
>   Satan looks up between his feet,—both tug—

> He's left, himself, i' the middle : the soul awakes
> And grows. Prolong that battle through this life !
> Never leave growing till the life to come."[1]

Man is no idle spectator of the conflict of the forces of right and wrong ; Browning never loses the individual in the throng, or sinks him into his age or race. And although the poet ever bears within him the certainty of victory for the good, he calls his fellows to the fight as if the fate of all hung on the valour of each. The struggle is always personal, individual, like the duels of the Homeric heroes.

It is under the guise of warfare that morality always presents itself to Browning. It is not a mere equilibrium of qualities—the measured, self-contained, statuesque ethics of the Greeks, nor the asceticism and self-restraint of Puritanism, nor the peaceful evolution of Goethe's artistic morality : it is valour in the battle of life. His code contains no negative commandments, and no limitations ; but he bids each man let out all the power that is within him, and throw himself upon life with the whole energy of his being. It is better even to seek evil with one's whole mind, than to be lukewarm in goodness. Whether you seek good or evil, play for the counter or the coin, stake it boldly !

> "Let a man contend to the uttermost
> For his life's set prize, be it what it will !

> "The counter our lovers staked was lost
> As surely as if it were lawful coin :
> And the sin I impute to each frustrate ghost

[1] *Bishop Blougram.*

> "Is, the unlit lamp and the ungirt loin
>   Though the end in sight was a vice, I say.
>   You, of the virtue (we issue join)
>   How strive you?—'*De te fabula!*'"[1]

Indifference and spiritual lassitude are, to the poet, the worst of sins. "Go!" says the Pope to Pompilia's pseudo-parents,

> "Never again elude the choice of tints!
>   White shall not neutralize the black, nor good
>   Compensate bad in man, absolve him so:
>   Life's business being just the terrible choice."[2]

In all the greater characters of *The Ring and the Book*, this intensity of vigour in good and evil flashes out upon us. Even Pompilia, the most gentle of all his creations, at the first prompting of the instinct of motherhood, rises to the law demanding resistance, and casts off the old passivity.

> "Dutiful to the foolish parents first,
>   Submissive next to the bad husband,—nay,
>   Tolerant of those meaner miserable
>   That did his hests, eked out the dole of pain,"[3]

she is found

> "Sublime in new impatience with the foe."

> "I did for once see right, do right, give tongue
>   The adequate protest: for a worm must turn
>   If it would have its wrong observed by God.
>   I did spring up, attempt to thrust aside

---

[1] *The Statue and the Bust.*
[2] *The Ring and the Book—The Pope*, 1235-1238.
[3] *Ibid.* 1052-1055.

> That ice-block 'twixt the sun and me, lay low
> The neutralizer of all good and truth."[1]

> "Yet, shame thus rank and patent, I struck, bare,
> At foe from head to foot in magic mail,
> And off it withered, cobweb armoury
> Against the lightning ! 'Twas truth singed the lies
> And saved me."[2]

Beneath the mature wisdom of the Pope, amidst the ashes of old age, there sleeps the same fire. He is as truly a warrior priest as Caponsacchi himself, and his matured experience only muffles his vigour. Wearied with his life-long labour, we see him gather himself together " in God's name," to do His will on earth once more with concentrated might :

> "I smite
> With my whole strength once more, ere end my part,
> Ending, so far as man may, this offence."[3]

Nor, spite of doubts, the promptings of mercy, the friends plucking his sleeve to stay his arm, does he fear 'to handle a lie roughly'; or shrink from sending the criminal to his account, though it be but one day before he himself is called before the judgment seat. The same energy, the same spirit of bold conflict, animates Guido's adoption of evil for his good. At all but the last moment of his life of monstrous crime, just before he hears the echo of the feet of the priests, who descend the stair to lead him to his death, " he repeats his evil deed in will."

---

[1] *The Ring and the Book—Pompilia*, 1591-1596.
[2] *Ibid.* 1637-1641.
[3] *The Ring and the Book—The Pope*, 1958-1960.

> "Nor is it in me to unhate my hates,—
> I use up my last strength to strike once more
> Old Pietro in the wine-house-gossip-face,
> To trample underfoot the whine and wile
> Of beast Violante,—and I grow one gorge
> To loathingly reject Pompilia's pale
> Poison my hasty hunger took for food."[1]

If there be any concrete form of evil with which the poet's optimism is not able to cope, any irretrievable black "beyond white's power to disintensify," it is the refusal to take a definite and resolute stand for either virtue or vice; the hesitancy and compromise of a life that is loyal to nothing, not even to its own selfishness. The cool self-love of the old English moralists, which "reduced the game of life to principles," and weighed good and evil in the scales of prudence, is to our poet the deepest damnation.

> "Saint Eldobert—I much approve his mode;
> With sinner Vertgalant I sympathize;
> But histrionic Sganarelle, who prompts
> While pulling back, refuses yet concedes—
> .   .   .   .
> Surely, one should bid pack that mountebank!"

In him, even,

> "thickheads ought to recognize
> The Devil, that old stager, at his trick
> Of general utility, who leads
> Downward, perhaps, but fiddles all the way!"[2]

For the bold sinner, who chooses and sustains his part to the end, the poet has hope. Indeed,

---

[1] *The Ring and the Book—Guido*, 2400-2406.
[2] *Red Cotton Nightcap Country*.

the resolute choice is itself the beginning of hope, for, let a man only give *himself* to anything, wreak *himself* on the world in the intensity of his hate, set all sail before the gusts of passion and 'range from Helen to Elvire, frenetic to be free'; let him rise into a decisive self-assertion against the stable order of the moral world, and he cannot fail to discover the nature of the task he has undertaken, and the meaning of the power without, against which he has set himself. If there be sufficient strength in a man to vent himself in action, and 'try conclusions with the world,' he will then learn that it has another destiny than to be the instrument of evil. Self-assertion taken by itself is good; indeed, it is the very law of all life, human and other.

> "Each lie
> Redounded to the praise of man, was victory
> Man's nature had both right to get and might to gain."[1]

But it leads to the revelation of a higher law than that of selfishness. The very assertion of the self which leads into evil, ultimately leaves the self-assertion futile. There is the disappointment of utter failure; the sinner is thrown back upon himself empty-handed. He finds himself subjected, even when sinning,

> "To the reign
> Of other quite as real a nature, that saw fit
> To have its way with man, not man his way with it."[2]

> "Poor pabulum for pride when the first love is found
> Last also! and, so far from realizing gain,
> Each step aside just proves divergency in vain.

---

[1] *Fifine at the Fair*, cxxviii.   [2] *Ibid.*

> The **wanderer** brings home no profit from his quest
> Beyond the sad surmise that keeping house **were best**
> Could life begin anew."[1]

The impossibility of living **a divided** life, of enjoying **at** once the sweets of **the** flesh on the 'Turf,' **and** the security of the 'Towers,' is the **text of** *Red Cotton Nightcap Country.* The sordid **hero** of the poem is gradually driven to choose between the alternatives. The **best of** his luck, **the** poet thinks, was the

> "Rough but wholesome shock,
>   An accident which comes to kill or **cure,**
>   **A jerk which mends a dislocated joint !**"[2]

The **continuance of** disguise and subterfuge, and the **retention of** "**the** first falsehood," are ultimately **made impossible to** Léonce Miranda :

> "Thus by a rude in seeming—rightlier judged
>   Beneficent surprise, publicity
>   Stopped further fear and trembling, and what **tale**
>   Cowardice thinks a covert : one bold splash
>   Into the mid-shame, and the shiver ends,
>   **Though** cramp **and drowning may** begin perhaps."[3]

In the same spirit **he** finds Miranda's suicidal leap the best deed possible for *him.*

> " 'Mad !' 'No ! sane, I say.
> **Such being the conditions of** his life,
> Such end of life was not irrational.
> Hold a belief, you only half-believe,
> With all-momentous issues **either** way,—

[1] *Fifine at the Fair,* cxxix.
[2] *Red Cotton Nightcap Country.*   [3] *Ibid.*

> And I advise you imitate this leap,
> Put faith to proof, be cured or killed at once !'"[1]

Thus it is the decisive deed that gains the poet's approval.   He finds the universe a great plot against a pied morality.   Even Guido claims some kind of regard from him, since " hate," as Pompilia said, " was the truth of him."   In that very hate we find, beneath his endless subterfuges, something real at last.   And since, through his hate, he is frankly measuring his powers against the good at work in the world, there cannot remain any doubt of the issue.   To bring the rival forces face to face is just what is wanted.

> "I felt quite sure that God had set
> Himself to Satan: who would spend
> A minute's mistrust on the end?"[2]

It is the same respect for strenuous action and dislike of compromise, that inspired the pathetic lines in which he condemns the Lost Leader, who broke 'From the van and the free-men, and sunk to the rear and the slaves': for the good pursues its work without him.

> "We shall march prospering,—not thro' his presence ;
>   Songs may inspirit us,—not from his lyre ;
> Deeds will be done,—while he boasts his quiescence,
>   Still bidding crouch whom the rest bade aspire :
> *Blot out his name*, then, record one lost soul more,
>   One task more declined, one more footpath untrod,
> One more devil's triumph and sorrow for angels,
>   One wrong more to man, one more insult to God !"[3]

[1] *Red Cotton Nightcap Country.*   [2] *Count Gismond.*
[3] *The Lost Leader.*

Everywhere, Browning's ethical teaching has this characteristic feature of vigorous decisiveness. As Dr. Westcott has said, "No room is left for indifference or neutrality. There is no surrender to an idle optimism. A part must be taken and maintained. The spirit in which Luther said '*Pecca fortiter*' finds in him powerful expression." Browning is emphatically the poet-militant, and the prophet of struggling manhood. His words are like trumpet-calls sounded in the van of man's struggle, wafted back by the winds, and heard through all the din of conflict by his meaner brethren, who are obscurely fighting for the good in the throng and crush of life. We catch the tones of this heart-strengthening music in the earliest poems he sung: nor did his courage fail, or vigour wane, as the shades of night gathered round him. In the latest of all his poems, he still speaks of

"One who never turned his back but marched breast forward,
        Never doubted clouds would break,
Never dreamed, though right were worsted, wrong would triumph,
        Held we fall to rise, are baffled to fight better,
        Sleep to wake.

"No, at noon-day in the bustle of man's work-time
        Greet the unseen with a cheer!
Bid him forward, breast and back as either should be,
        'Strive and thrive!' cry 'Speed!—fight on, fare ever
        There as here.'"[1]

These are fit words to close such a life. His last act is a kind of re-enlistment in the service of the good —the joyous venturing forth on a new war under

[1] Epilogue to *Asolando*.

new conditions and in lands unknown, by a heroic man who is sure of himself and sure of his cause.

But now comes the great difficulty. How can the poet combine such earnestness in the moral struggle with so deep a conviction of the ultimate nothingness of evil, and of the complete victory of the good? Again and again we have found him pronounce such victory to be absolutely necessary and inevitable. His belief in God, his trust in His love and might, will brook no limit anywhere. His conviction is invincible that the power of the good subjects evil itself to its authority.

> "My own hope is, a sun will pierce
> The thickest cloud earth ever stretched;
>   That, after Last, returns the First,
> Though a wide compass round be fetched;
>   That what began best, can't end worst,
> Nor what God blest once, prove accurst."[1]

It is the poet himself and not merely the sophistic æsthete of *Fifine* that speaks:

> "Partake my confidence! No creature's made so mean
>   But that, some way, it boasts, could we investigate,
>   Its supreme worth: fulfils, by ordinance of fate,
>   Its momentary task, gets glory all its own,
>   Tastes triumph in the world, pre-eminent, alone.
>
>   .   .   .   .
>
> "As firm is my belief, quick sense perceives the same
>   Self-vindicating flash illustrate every man
>   And woman of our mass, and prove, throughout the plan,
>   No detail but, in place allotted it, was prime
>   And perfect."[2]

[1] *Apparent Failure.*   [2] *Fifine at the Fair,* xxix.

But if so,—if Helen, Fifine, **Guido**, find themselves within the plan, fulfilling, after all, the task allotted to them in the universal scheme, how can **we** condemn them. Must we not plainly either modify our optimism and keep **our** faith in God within bounds, or, on the other hand, make every failure "apparent" only, sin a phantom, and **the** distinction between right and wrong a helpful illusion that **stings** man to effort—but an illusion all the same?

> "What but the weakness in a Faith supplies
> The incentive to humanity, no strength
> Absolute, irresistible, comports.
> How can man love but what he yearns to help?"[1]

Where **is the need**, nay, the possibility, of self-sacrifice, except where there is misery? How can **good, the** good which is highest, find itself **and give utterance** and actuality to the power that slumbers within it, except as resisting evil? Are **not** good and evil relative? Is not every criminal, when really known, working out in his own **way the** salvation of himself and **the** world? Why **cannot** he, then, **take** his stand on his right to move towards the **good** by any path **that** best pleases himself: **since move he** must. It is easy for the religious conscience to admit with Pippa that

> "All service ranks the same with God—
> With God, whose puppets, best **and worst,**
> Are we: there is **no last or first.**"[2]

But, if so, why do we admire her sweet pre-eminence

---

[1] *The Ring and the Book—The Pope,* 1649-1652.
[2] *Pippa Passes.*

in moral beauty, and in what is she really better than
Ottima?   The doctrine that

> "God's in His heaven—
> All's right with the world!"[1]

finds its echo in every devout spirit from the beginning of the world; it is of the very essence of
religion.   But what of its moral consequences?
Religion, when fully manifested, is the triumphant
reconciliation of all contradictions.   It is optimism,
the justification of things as the process of evolving
the good; and its peace and joy are just the out-
come of the conviction, won by faith, that the ideal
is actual, and that every detail of life is, in its own
place, illumined with divine goodness.   But morality
is the condemnation of things as they are, by reference to a conception of a good which ought to be.
The absolute identification of the actual and ideal
extinguishes morality, either in something lower or
in something higher.   But the moral ideal, when
reached, turns at once into a stepping-stone a dead
self; and the good formulates itself anew as an ideal
in the future.   So that morality is the sphere of
discrepancy, and the moral life a progressive realization of a good that can never be complete.   It
would thus seem to be irreconcilably different from
religion, which must, in some way or other, find the
good to be present, actual, absolute, without shadow
of change, or hint of limit or imperfection.

   How, then, does the poet deal with the apparently
fundamental discrepancy between religion, which
postulates the absolute and universal supremacy

[1] *Pippa Passes.*

of God, and morality, which postulates the absolute supremacy of man within the sphere of his own action, in so far as it is called right or wrong?

This difficulty, in one or other of its forms, is, perhaps, the most pressing in modern philosophy. It is the problem of the possibility of rising above the "Either, Or" of discrepant conceptions, to a position which grasps the alternatives together in a higher idea. It is at bottom the question, whether we can have a philosophy at all; or whether we must fall back once more into compromise, and the scepticism and despair which it always brings with it.

It is just because Browning does not compromise between the contending truths that he is instructive. The value of his solution of the problem corresponds accurately to the degree in which he holds both the absoluteness of God's presence in history, and the complete independence of the moral consciousness. He refused to degrade either God or man. In the name of religion, he refuses to say that "a purpose of reason is visible in the social and legal structures of mankind"—*only* "on the whole"; and in the name of morality, he refuses to "assert the perfection of the actual world" as it is, and by implication to stultify all human endeavour. He knew the vice of compromising, and strove to hold both the truths in their fulness.

That he did not compromise God's love or power and make it dominant merely "on the whole," leaving within His realm, which is universal, a limbo for the "lost," is evident to the most casual reader.

> "This doctrine, which one healthy view of things,
> One sane sight of the general ordinance—
> Nature,—and its particular object,—man,—
> Which one mere eyecast at the character
> Of Who made these and gave man sense to boot,
> Had dissipated once and evermore,—
> This doctrine I have dosed our flock withal.
> Why? Because none believed it."[1]

"O'er-punished wrong grows right," Browning says. Hell is, for him, the consciousness of opportunities neglected, arrested growth ; and even that, in turn, is the beginning of a better life.

> "However near I stand in His regard,
> So much the nearer had I stood by steps
> Offered the feet which rashly spurned their help.
> That I call Hell ; why further punishment?"[2]

Another ordinary view, according to which evil is self-destructive, and ends with the annihilation of its servant, he does not so decisively reject. At least, in a passage of wonderful poetic and philosophic power, which he puts into the mouth of Caponsacchi, he describes Guido as gradually lapsing towards the chaos, which is lower than created existence. He observes him

> "Not to die so much as slide out of life,
> Pushed by the general horror and common hate
> Low, lower,—left o' the very ledge of things,
> I seem to see him catch convulsively,
> One by one at all honest forms of life,
> At reason, order, decency and use,
> To cramp him and get foothold by at least ;
> And still they disengage them from his clutch.

.   .   .   .

[1] *The Inn Album.*   [2] *A Camel Driver.*

> And thus I see him slowly and surely edged
> Off all the table-land whence life upsprings
> **Aspiring to** be immortality."

There he loses him in the loneliness, silence, and dusk—

> "**At** the horizontal line, creation's verge,
> From what just is to absolute nothingness."[1]

But the matchless moral insight of the Pope leads to
a different conclusion, and the poet again retrieves
his faith.   The Pope puts his first trust 'in **the**
suddenness of Guido's fate,' and hopes that the truth
may be 'flashed out by the blow of death, and Guido
see one instant and be saved.'   Nor is his trust vain.
"The end comes," said Dr. Westcott.   "The minis-
ters of death claim him.   In his agony he summons
every helper whom he has known or heard of—

> 'Abate,—Cardinal,—Christ,—Maria,—God—'

and **then** the light breaks through the blackest
gloom :

> 'Pompilia ! will you let them murder **me?**'

In this supreme moment he has known what love
is, and, knowing it, has begun to feel it.   The cry,
like the intercession of the rich man in Hades, is a
promise of a far-off deliverance."

But **even** beyond this hope, which **is the** last for
most men, the Pope has still **another.**

> "Else I avert my face, nor follow **him**
> Into that sad obscure sequestered **state**

[1] *The Ring and the Book—Giuseppe Caponsacchi*, 1911-1931.

> Where God unmakes but to remake the soul
> He else made first in vain : *which must not be.*" [1]

This phrase, "which must not be," seems to me to carry in it the irrefragable conviction of the poet himself. The same faith in the future appears in the words in which Pompilia addresses her priest—

> "O lover of my life, O soldier-saint,
> No work begun shall ever pause for death !
> Love will be helpful to me more and more
> I' the coming course, the new path I must tread,
> My weak hand in thy strong hand, strong for that !" [2]

For the poet, the death of man brings no change in the purpose of God ; nor does it, or aught else, fix a limit to His power, or stultify by failure the end implied in all God's work, in nature no less than in man himself—to wit, that every soul shall learn the lesson of goodness, and reflect the divine life in desire, intelligence, and will.

Equally emphatic, on some sides at least, is Browning's rejection of those compromises, with which the one-sided religious consciousness threatens the existence of the moral life. At times, indeed, he seems to teach, as man's best and highest, a passive acquiescence in the divine benevolence; and he uses the dangerous metaphor of the clay and potter's wheel. *Rabbi Ben Ezra* bids us feel

> "Why time spins fast, why passive lies our clay";

and his prayer is,

[1] *The Ring and the Book—The Pope*, 2129-2132.
[2] *The Ring and the Book—Pompilia*, 1786-1790.

"So, take and use Thy work :
  Amend what flaws may lurk,
  What strain o' the stuff, what warpings past the aim !
  My times be in Thy hand !
  Perfect the cup as planned !
  Let age approve of youth, and death complete the same !"[1]

But this attitude of quiescent trust, which is so characteristic of religion, is known by the poet to be only a phase of man's best life. It is a temporary resting-place for the pilgrim : "the country of Beulah, whose air is very sweet and pleasant, where he may solace himself for a season." But, "the way lies directly through it," and the pilgrim, "being a little strengthened and better able to bear his sickness," has to go forward on his journey. Browning's characteristic doctrine on this matter is not acquiescence and resignation. "Leave God the way" has, in his view, its counterpart and condition —"Have you the will !"

"For a worm must turn
If it would have its wrong observed by God."[2]

The root of Browning's joy is in the need of progress towards an infinitely high goal. He rejoices

"that man is hurled
From change to change unceasingly,
His soul's wings never furled."

The bliss of endeavour, the infinite worth of the consciousness of failure, with its evidence of coming triumph, "the spark which disturbs our clod," these are the essence of his optimistic interpretation of

---

[1] *Rabbi Ben Ezra.*
[2] *The Ring and the Book—Pompilia*, 1592, 1593.

human life, and also of his robust ethical doctrine.

> "Then, welcome each rebuff
>   That turns earth's smoothness rough,
>   Each sting that bids nor sit nor stand but go:
>   Be our joys three-parts pain!
>   Strive, and hold cheap the strain;
>   Learn, nor account the pang; dare, never grudge the
>   throe!"[1]

And he prolongs the battle beyond time; for the
battle is the moral life, and man's best, and therefore
God's best in man. The struggle upward from the
brute may, indeed, end with death. But this only
means that man "has learned the uses of the flesh,"
and there are in him other potencies to evolve:

> "Other heights in other lives, God willing."[2]

Death is the summing up of this life's meaning—
stored strength for new adventure.

"The future I may face now I have proved the
past"; and, in view of it, Browning is

> "Fearless and unperplexed
>   When I wage battle next,
>   What weapons to select, what armour to indue."

He is sure that it will be a battle, and a winning
one. There is no limiting here of man's possibility,
or confining of man's endeavour after goodness.

> "Strive and Thrive! cry 'Speed,' fight on, fare ever
>   There as here,"

are the last words which came from his pen.

Now, it may fairly be argued that these allusions

---

[1] *Rabbi Ben Ezra.*   [2] *One Word More.*

to what death may mean, and what may lie beyond death, valuable as they may be as poetry, cannot help in philosophy. They do not solve the problem of the relation between morality and religion, but merely continue the antagonism between them into a life beyond, of which we have no experience. If the problem is to be solved, it must be solved as it is stated for us in the present world.

This objection is valid, so far as it goes. But Browning's treatment is valuable all the same, in so far as it indicates his unwillingness to limit or compromise the conflicting truths. He, by implication, rejects the view, ordinarily held without being examined, that the moral life is preliminary to the joy and rest of religion ; a brief struggle, to be followed by a sudden lift out of it into some serene sphere, where man will lead an angel's life which knows no imperfection and therefore no growth. He refuses to make morality an accident in man's history, and "to put man in the place of God," by identifying the process with the ideal ; he also refuses to make man's struggle, and God's achievement within man, mutually exclusive alternatives. As I shall show in the sequel, movement towards an ideal, actualizing but never actualized, is for the poet the very nature of man. And to speak about either God or man (or even the absolute philosopher) as "the last term of a development" has no meaning to him. We are not first moral and then religious, first struggling with evil and then conscious of overcoming it. God is with us in the battle, and the victory is in every blow.

But there lies a deeper difficulty than this in the

way of reconciling morality and religion, *i.e.* in proving the presence of both God and man in human action. Morality, in so far as it is achievement, might conceivably be immediately identified with the process of an absolute good ; but morality is always a consciousness of failure as well. Its very essence and verve is the conviction that the ideal is not actual. And the higher a man's spiritual attainments, the more profound is his sense of the evil of the world, and of the greatness of the work pressing to be done. "Say not ye, there are yet four months, and then cometh harvest? Behold I say unto you, 'Lift up your eyes and look on the fields ; for they are white already to harvest.'" It looks like blasphemy against morality to say "that God lives in eternity and has, therefore, plenty of time." Morality destroys one's contentment with the world ; and its language seems to be, 'God is not here, but there ; the kingdom is still to come.'

Nor does it rest with condemning the world. It finds flaws also in its own highest achievement ; so that we seem ever 'To mock ourselves in all that's best of us.' The beginning of the spiritual life seems just to consist in a consciousness of complete failure, and that consciousness ever grows deeper.

This is well illustrated in Browning's account of Caponsacchi ; from the time when Pompilia's smile first 'glowed' upon him, and set him—

> "Thinking how my life
> Had shaken under me—broken short indeed
> And showed the gap 'twixt what is, what should be—
> And into what abysm the soul may slip"—[1]

[1] *The Ring and the Book—Giuseppe Caponsacchi*, 485-488.

up to the time when his pure love for her revealed
to him something of the grandeur of goodness, and
led him to define his ideal and also to express his
despair.

> "To have to do with nothing but the true,
>   The good, the eternal—and these, not alone
> In the main current of the general life,
> But small experiences of every day,
> Concerns of the particular hearth and home :
> To learn not only by a comet's rush
> But a rose's birth—not by the grandeur, God,
> But the comfort, Christ. *All this how far away!*
> Mere delectation, meet for a minute's dream !"[1]

So illimitably beyond his strength is such a life
that he finds himself like the drudging student who

> "Trims his lamp,
> Opens his Plutarch, puts him in the place
> Of Roman, Grecian ; draws the patched gown close,
> Dreams, 'Thus should I fight, save or rule the world !'—
> Then smilingly, contentedly, awakes
> To the old solitary nothingness."[2]

The moral world with its illimitable horizon had
opened out around him, the voice of the new com-
mandment bidding him "be perfect as his Father
in heaven is perfect " had destroyed his peace, and
made imperative a well nigh hopeless struggle ; and
as he compares himself at his best with the new
ideal, he breaks out into the cry,

> "O great, just, good God ! Miserable Me !"

This humility and contrition, this discontent verging

[1] *The Ring and the Book—Giuseppe Caponsacchi*, 2089-2097.
[2] *Ibid.* 2098-2103.

on hopelessness, constituted, as we have seen, the characteristic attitude of Carlyle ; and it represents a true and, in fact, an indispensable element of man's moral life.

But this self-condemnation in the face of the moral law is nothing more than an element, and must not be taken either for the whole truth or for the most fundamental one. It is because it is taken as fundamental and final that the discrepancy between morality and religion is held to be absolute, and the consciousness of evil is turned against faith in the Good. It is an abstract way of thinking that makes us deduce, from the transcendent height of the moral ideal, the impossibility of attaining goodness, and the failure of God's purpose in man. And this is what Carlyle did. He stopped short at the consciousness of imperfection, and he made no attempt to account for it. He took it as a complete fact, and therefore drew a sharp line of distinction between the human and the divine. And, so far, he was right ; for, if we look no further than this negative side, it is emphatically absurd to identify man, be he 'philosopher' or not, with the Absolute. "Why callest thou Me good? there is none good save One, that is God." The 'ought' *must* stand above *all* human attainment, and declare that "whatever is, is wrong." But whence comes the ought itself, the ideal which condemns us? Is it not also immanent in the fact it condemns?

"Who is not acute enough," asks Hegel, "to see a great deal in his surroundings which is really far from being what it ought to be?" And who also, we may add, has not enough of the generalizing faculty, often mistaken for a philosophical one, to extend this condemnation over the whole of "this best of all possible worlds"? But what is this 'ought-to-be,' which has such potency in it that all things when confronted with it lose their worth?

The first answer is, that it is an idea which men, and particularly good men, carry with them. But a little consideration will show that it cannot be a mere idea. It must be something more valid than a capricious product of the individual's imagination. For we cannot wisely condemn things because they do not happen to answer to any casual conception which we may choose to elevate into a criterion. A criterion must have objective validity. It must be an idea *of* something and not an empty notion; and that something must, at the worst, be possible. Nay, when we consider all that is involved in it, it becomes obvious that a true ideal—an ideal which is a valid criterion—must be not only possible but real, and, indeed, more real than that which is condemned by reference to it. Absolute pessimism has in it the same contradiction that absolute scepticism has,—it is, in fact, its practical counterpart; for both scepticism and pessimism involve the assumption that it is possible to reach a position outside the realm of being, from which being may be condemned as a whole. But the rift between actual and ideal must fall within the real or intelligible world, do what the pessimists will; and a condemnation of man which is not based on a principle realized by humanity is a fiction of abstract thought, which lays stress on the actuality of the imperfect, and treats the perfect as if it were as good as nothing, which it cannot be. In other words, this way of regarding human life isolates the passing phenomenon, and does not look to that which reveals itself in it and causes it to pass away.

Confining ourselves, however, for the present, to the ideal in morality, we can easily see that, in this sphere at least, the actual and the ideal change places; and that the latter contrasts with the former as the real contrasts with the phenomenal. For, in the first place, the moral ideal is something more than a mere idea not yet realized. It is more even than a *true* idea; for no mere knowledge, however true, has such intimate relation to the self-consciousness of man as his moral ideal. A mathematical axiom, and the statement of a physical law, express what is true; but they do not occupy the place in our mind that a moral principle does. Such a principle is an ideal, as well as an idea. It is an idea which has causative potency in it. It supplies motives, it is an incentive to action, and, though in one sense a thing of the future, it is also the actual spring and source of present activity. In so far as the agent acts,—as Kant put it,—not according to laws, but according to an *idea* of law (and a responsible agent always acts in this manner), the ideal is as truly actualized in him as the physical law is actualized in the physical fact, or the vegetable life in the plant. In fact, the ideal of a moral being is his life. All his actions are its manifestations. And, just as the physical fact is not seen as it really is, nor its reality proved, till science has penetrated through the husk of the sensuous phenomenon, and grasped it in thought as an instance of a law; so an individual's actions are not understood, and can have no moral meaning whatsoever, except in the light of the purpose which gave them being. We know the man only when we know his creed. His reality is what he believes in; that is, it is his ideal.

It is the consciousness that the ideal is the real which explains the fact of contrition. To become morally awakened is to become conscious of the vanity and nothingness of the past life, as confronted with the new ideal implied in it. The past life is something to be cast aside as false show, just because the self that experienced it was not realized in it. It is for this reason that the moral agent sets himself against it, and desires to annihilate all its claims upon him by undergoing its punishment, and drinking to the dregs its cup of bitterness. Thus his true life lies in the realization of his ideal, and his advance towards it is his coming to himself. Only in attaining to it does he attain reality, and the only realization possible for him in the present is just the consciousness of the potency of .the ideal. To him to live is to realize his ideal. It is a power that irks, till it finds expression in moral habits that accord with its nature, *i.e.* till the spirit has, out of its environment, created a body adequate to itself.

The condemnation of self, which characterizes all moral life and is the condition of moral progress, must not, therefore, be regarded as a complete truth. For the very condemnation implies the actual presence of something better. Both of the terms—the criterion and the fact which is condemned by it—fall within the same individual life. Man cannot, therefore, without injustice, condemn himself in all that he is; for the condemnation is itself a witness to the activity of that good of which he despairs. Hence, the threatening majesty of the moral imperative is nothing but the shadow of man's own dignity; and moral contrition, and even the complete despair of the pessimistic theory, when rightly understood, are recognized as unwilling witnesses to the authority and the actuality of the highest good. And, on the other hand, the highest good cannot be regarded as a mere phantom, without nullifying all our condemnation of the self and of the world.

The legitimate deduction from the height of man's moral ideal is thus found to be, not, as Carlyle thought, the weakness and worthlessness of human nature, but its promise and native dignity: and in a healthy moral consciousness it produces, not despair, but faith and joy. For, as has been already suggested in a previous chapter, the authority of the moral law over man is rooted in man's endowment. Its imperative is nothing but the voice of the future self bidding the present self aspire, while its reproof is only the expression of a moral aspiration which has misunderstood itself. Contrition is not a bad moral state which should bring despair, but a good state, full of promise of one that is still better. It is, in fact, just the first step which the ideal takes in its process of self-realization: "the sting that bids nor sit, nor stand, but go!"

The moral ideal thus, like every other ideal, even that which we regard as present in natural life, contains a certain guarantee of its own fulfilment. It is essentially an active thing, an energy, a movement upwards. It may, indeed, be urged that the guarantee is imperfect. Ideals tend to self-realization, but the tendency may remain unfulfilled. Men have some ideals which they never reach, and others which, at first sight at least, it were better for them not to reach. The goal may never be attained, or it may prove "a ruin like the rest." And, as long as man is moral, the ideal is not, and cannot be, fully reached. Morality necessarily implies a rift within human nature, a contradiction between what is and what ought to be; although neither the rift nor the contradiction is absolute. There might seem for this reason to be no way of bringing optimism and ethics together, of reconciling what is and what ought to be.

My answer to these difficulties must at this stage be very brief and incomplete. That the moral good, if attained, should itself prove vain is a plain self-contradiction. For moral good has no meaning except in so far as it is conceived as the highest good. The question, "Why should I be moral," has no answer, because it is self-contradictory. The moral ideal contains its justification in itself, and requires to lean on nothing else.

But it is not easy to prove that it is attainable. In one sense it is not attainable, at least under the conditions of human life which fall within our experience, from which alone we have a right to speak. For, as I shall strive to show in a succeeding chapter, the essence of man's life as spiritual, that is, as intelligent and moral, is its self-realizing activity. Intellectual and moral life is progress, although it is the progress of an ideal which is real and complete, the **return of the** infinite to itself through the finite. The cessation of the progress of the ideal in man, whereby man interprets the world in terms of himself and makes it the instrument of his purposes, is intellectual and **moral** death. From one point of view, therefore, this **spiritual life, or moral and intellectual activity, is inspired at every** step by the consciousness of a 'beyond' not possessed, of an unsolved contradiction between the self and the not-self, of a good that ought to be and is not. **The last** word, or rather the last word *but one*, regarding man is 'failure.'

But failure *is* the last word but one, as the poet well knew. "What's come to perfection perishes," he tells us. From this point of view the fact that perfection is not reached, merely means that the **process** is not ended. " It seethes **with** the morrow for us and more." The recognition of failure implies more effort and higher progress, and contains a suggestion of an absolute good, and even a proof of its active presence. 'The beyond,' for knowledge and morality, is the Land of Promise. And **the** promise is not **a** false one; for the 'land' is possessed. The recognition of the fact to be known, **the statement of** the problem, is the first step in its solution ; and **the consciousness** of the moral ideal not attained, is the first step in its self-actualizing progress. Had man not come so far, he would not have known the further difficulty, or recognized the higher good. To say that the moral ideal is never attained, is thus only a half-truth. We must add to it the fact that it is always being attained; nay, that it is always present as an active reality, attaining itself, evolving its own content. Or, to return to the previous metaphor, the land of promise is possessed, although the possession always reveals a still better beyond, which is again a ' land of promise.'

While, therefore, it must always remain true that knowledge does not reach absolute reality, nor morality absolute goodness, this cannot be used as an argument against optimism, except on the pre-supposition that mental and moral activity are a disease. And this is a contradiction in terms. If the ideal is in itself good, the process whereby it is attained is good ; if the process in itself is evil, the ideal it seeks is evil, and therefore the condemnation of the actual by reference to it is absurd. And, on the other hand, to postulate as best the identity of ideal and actual, so that no process is necessary, is to assume a point of view where both optimism and pessimism are meaningless, for there is no criterion. As Aristotle teaches us, we have no right either to praise or to blame the highest. A process, such as morality is, which is not the self-manifestation of an actual ideal, and an ideal which does not reveal its potencies in its passing forms, are both fictions of one-sided thought. The process is not the ideal, but its manifestation ; and the ideal is not the process, but the principle which is its source and guide.

But if the process cannot be thus immediately

indentified with **the ideal, or** "man take the place
of God," or "human self-consciousness be confused
with the absolute self-consciousness," far less can
they be separated. **The** infinitely high ideal of
perfect knowledge and perfect goodness, implied in
the Christian command, "Be ye perfect as your
Father in heaven is perfect," is an ideal, just because
the unity of what is and what ought to be is deeper
than their **difference.** The recognition **of the limit
of our** knowledge, or the imperfection of our moral
character, is a direct witness to the fact that there
is more to be known and a better to be achieved.
The negative implies the affirmative, and is its effect.
Man's confession of the limitation of his knowledge
is made on the supposition that **the** universe of facts,
in all its infinitely rich complexity, is meant to be
known ; and his confession of moral imperfection is
made by reference to a good which is absolute, and
which yet may be and ought to be his. The good
in morality is necessarily supreme and perfect. **A**
good that is " merely human," " relative to man's
nature," in the sense of not being true goodness,
is a phantom of confused thinking. Morality
demands "*the* good," and not a simulacrum or
makeshift. The distinction between **right and**
wrong, and with it all moral aspiration, contrition,
and repentance would otherwise become meaningless. What can a seeming good avail to a moral
agent ? There is no better or worse among merely
apparent excellencies, and of phantoms it matters
not which is chosen. And in a similar way, the
distinction between **true and** false in knowledge,
and the common condemnation of human know-

ledge—as merely of phenomena, imply the absolute unity of thought and being, and the knowledge of that unity as a fact. There is no true or false amongst merely apparent facts.

But, if the ideal of man as a spiritual being is conceived as perfect, then it follows not only that its attainment is possible, but that it is necessary. The guarantee of its own fulfilment which an ideal carries with it as an ideal, that is, as a potency in process of fulfilment, becomes complete when that ideal is absolute. "If God be for us, who can be against us?" The absolute good in the language of Emerson, is "too good not to be true." If such an ideal be latent in the nature of man, it brings the order of the universe over to his side. For it implies a kinship between him, as a spiritual being, and the whole of existence. The stars in their courses fight for him. In other words, the moral ideal means nothing, if it does not imply a law which is universal. It is a law which exists already, whether man recognizes it or not; it is the might in things, a law of which "no jot or tittle can in any wise pass away." The individual does not institute the moral law; he finds it to be written both within and without him. His part is to recognize, not to create it; to make it valid in his own life, and so to identify himself with it that his service of it may be perfect freedom.

We thus conclude that morality, and even the self-condemnation, contrition, and consciousness of failure which it brings with it as phases of its growth, are witnesses of the presence, and the actual product, of an absolute good in man. Morality, in other words, rests upon, and is the self-evolution of the religious principle in man.

A similar line of proof would show that religion implies morality. An absolute good is not conceivable, except in relation to the process whereby it manifests itself. In the language of theology, we may say that God must create and redeem the world in order to be God; or that creation and redemption,—the outflow of the universe from God as its source, and its return to Him through the salvation of mankind,—reveal to us the nature of God. Apart from this outgoing of the infinite to the finite and its return to itself through it, the name God would be an empty word signifying a something unintelligible, dwelling in the void beyond the realm of being. But religion, as we have seen, is the recognition, not of an unknown, but of the absolute good as real; the joyous consciousness of the presence of God in all things. And morality, in that it is the realization of an ideal which is perfect, is the process whereby the absolute good actualizes itself in man. It is true that the ideal cannot be identified with the process; for the ideal is the principle of the process, and therefore more than it. Man does not reach "the last term of development," for there is no last term to a being whose essence is progressive activity. He does not, therefore, take the place of God, and his self-consciousness is never the absolute self-consciousness. But still, in so far as his life is a progress towards the true and good, it is the process of truth and goodness within him. It is the activity of the ideal. It is God lifting man up to Himself, or, in

the language of philosophy, "returning to Himself
in history." And yet it is at the same time man's
effort after goodness. Man is not a mere "vessel
of divine grace," or a passive recipient of the highest
bounty. All man's goodness is necessarily man's
achievement. And the realization by the ideal of
itself is man's achievement of it. For it is *his*
ideal. The law without is also the law within.
It is the law within, because it is recognized as the
law without. Thus, the moral consciousness passes
into the religious consciousness. The performance
of duty is the willing service of the absolute good ;
and, as such, it involves also the recognition of a
purpose that cannot fail. It is both activity and
faith, both a struggle and a consciousness of victory,
both morality and religion. We cannot, therefore,
treat these as alternative phases of man's life. There
is not first the pain of the moral struggle, and then
the joy and rest of religion. The meat and drink
is "to do the will of Him that sent Me, to finish
His work." Heaven is the service of the good.
"There is nothing in the world or out of it that
can be called unconditionally good, except the good
will." The process of willing—the moral activity—
is its own reward ; 'the only jewel that shines in
its own light.'

It may seem to some to be presumptuous thus to
identify the divine and the human ; but to separate
them makes both morality and religion impossible.
It robs morality of its ideal, and makes God a
mere name for 'the unknown.' Those who think
that this identification degrades the divine, mis-
apprehend the nature of spirit ; and forget that

it is of its essence to communicate itself. And goodness and truth do not become less when shared ; they grow greater. Spiritual possessions imply community wherein there is no exclusion ; and to the Christian the glory of God is His communication of Himself. Hence the so-called religious humility, which makes God different in nature from His work, really degrades the object of its worship. It puts mere power above the gifts of spirit, and it indicates that the worshipper has not been emancipated from the slavishness which makes a fetish of its God. Such a religion is not free, and the development of man destroys it.

> " I never realized God's birth before—
> How He grew likest God in being born."[1]

The intense love of the young mother drew the divine and the human together, and set at nought the contrast which prose ever draws between them. This thought of the unity of God and man is one which gets frequent utterance from the poet when his religious spirit is most deeply moved ; for it is the characteristic of religious feeling that it abolishes all sense of separation. It removes all the limitations of finitude and lifts man into rapturous unity with the God he adores ; and it gives such completeness to his own life that it seems to him to be a joyous pulse of the life that is absolute. The feeling of unity may be an illusion. This we cannot discuss here ; but, in any case, it is a feeling essential to religion. And the philosophy which seeks to lift this feeling into clear con-

[1] *The Ring and the Book—Pompilia*, 1690, 1691.

sciousness and to account for its existence, cannot but recognize that it implies and presupposes the essential affinity of the divine nature with the nature of man.

Thus, both from the side of morality and from that of religion, we are brought to recognize the unity of God with man as a spiritual being. The moral ideal is man's idea of perfection, that is, his idea of God. Theology and philosophy are often occupied with the vain task of bridging an imaginary chasm between the finite and the infinite, while the supreme facts of the life of man as a spirit are ever resting upon their unity. In other words, morality and religion are but different manifestations of the same principle. The good that man effects is, at the same time, the working of God within him. The activity that man *is*,

> "tending up,
> Holds, is upheld by, God, and ends the man
> Upward in that dread point of intercourse,
> Nor needs a place, for it returns to Him."[1]

> "God, perchance,
> Grants each new man, by some as new a mode,
> Inter-communication with Himself,
> Wreaking on finiteness infinitude."[2]

And while man's moral endeavour is thus recognized as the activity of God within him, it is also implied that the divine being can be known only as revealed, and incarnated, if one may so say, in a perfect human character. It was a permanent conviction of Browning, that

[1] *A Death in the Desert.*
[2] *Prince Hohenstiel-Schwangau.*

> "the acknowledgment of God in Christ
> Accepted by thy reason, solves for thee
> All questions in the earth and out of it."

So far from regarding the Power in the world which makes for righteousness, as "not-ourselves," as Matthew Arnold did in his haste, that Power is known to be the man's true self and more; and morality is known as the gradual process whereby its content is evolved. Man's state of perfection, which is symbolized for the intelligent by the term **Heaven, is,** for Browning,

> "The equalizing, ever and anon,
>   In momentary rapture, great with small,
>   Omniscience with intelligency, God
>   With man—the thunder glow from pole to pole
>   Abolishing, a blissful moment-space,
>   Great cloud alike and small cloud, in one fire—
>   As sure to ebb as sure again to flow
>   When the new receptivity deserves
>   The new completion."[1]

Thus, therefore, does the poet wed the divine strength with human weakness; and the principle of unity, thus conceived, gives him at once his moral strenuousness and that ever present foretaste of victory, which we may call his religious optimism.

Whether this principle receives adequate expression from the poet, we shall inquire in the next chapter. For on this depends its worth as a solution of the enigma of man's moral life.

[1] *Prince Hohenstiel-Schwangau.*

CHAPTER VI

BROWNING'S TREATMENT OF THE PRINCIPLE OF LOVE

"God! Thou art Love! I build my faith on that!"[1]

IT may be well before going further to gather together the results so far reached.

Browning was aware of the conflict of the religious and moral consciousness, but he did not hesitate to give each of them its most uncompromising utterance. And it is on this account that he is instructive; for, whatever may be the value of compromise in practical affairs, there is no doubt that it has never done anything to advance human thought. His religion is an optimistic faith, a peaceful consciousness of the presence of the highest in man, and therefore in all other things. Yet he does not hesitate to represent the moral life as a struggle with evil, and a movement through error towards a highest good which is never finally realized. He sees that the contradiction is not an absolute one, but that a good man is always both moral and religious, and that

[1] *Paracelsus.*

in every good act he does he transcends their difference. He knew that the ideal apart from the process is nothing, and that "a God beyond the stars" is simply the unknowable. But he knew, too, that the ideal is not *merely* the process, but also that which starts the process, guides it, and comes to itself through it. God, emptied of human elements, is a mere name ; but, at the same time, the process of human evolution does not exhaust the idea of God. The process by itself, *i.e.* mere morality, is a conception of a fragment, a fiction of abstract thought ; it is a movement which has no beginning or end ; and in it neither the head nor the heart of man could find contentment. He is driven by ethics into philosophy, and by morality into religion.

It was in this way that Browning found himself compelled to trace back the moral process to its origin, and to identify the moral law with the nature of God. It is this that gives value to his view of moral progress as reaching beyond death to a higher stage of being, for which man's attainments in this life are only preliminary.

> "What's time? Leave Now for dogs and apes
> Man has Forever."[1]

There are other 'adventures brave and new' for man, 'more lives yet,' other ways of warfare, other depths of goodness and heights of love. The poet lifts the moral ideal into infinitude, and removes all limits to the possibility and necessity of being good. Nay, the process itself is good. Moral

[1] *Grammarian's Funeral.*

activity is its own bountiful reward ; for moral progress, which means struggle, is the best thing in the world or out of it. To end such a process, to stop that activity, were therefore evil. But it cannot end, for it is the self-manifestation of the divine life. There is plenty of way to make, for the ideal is *absolute* goodness. The process cannot exhaust the absolute, and it is impossible that man should be God. And yet this process is the process *of* the absolute, the working of the ideal, the presence of the highest in man as a living power realizing itself in his acts and in his thoughts. And the absolute cannot fail ;—not in man, for the process is the evolution of his essential nature ; and not in the world, for that is but the necessary instrument of the evolution. By lifting the moral ideal of man to infinitude, the poet has identified it with the nature of God, and made it the absolute law of things.

Now, this idea of the identity of the human and the divine is a perfectly familiar Christian idea.

> "Thence shall I pass, approved
>   A man, for aye removed
> From the developed brute ; a God though in the germ."[1]

This idea is involved in the ordinary expressions of religious thought. But, nevertheless, both theology and philosophy shrink from giving to it a clear and unembarrassed utterance. Instead of rising to the sublime boldness of the Nazarene Teacher, they set up prudential differences between God and man— differences not of degree only, but of nature ; and

[1] *Rabbi Ben Ezra.*

in consequence, God is reduced to an unknowable absolute, and man is made incapable not only of moral, but also of intellectual life. The poet himself has proved craven-hearted in this, as we shall see. He, too, sets up insurmountable barriers between the divine and the human, and thereby weakens both his religious and his moral convictions. His moral inspiration is greatest just where his religious enthusiasm is most intense. In *Rabbi Ben Ezra, The Death in the Desert*, and *The Ring and the Book*, there prevails a constant sense of the community of God and man within the realm of goodness; and the world itself, "with its dread machinery of sin and sorrow," is made to join the great conspiracy, whose purpose is at once the evolution of man's character, and the realization of the will of God.

> " So, the All-Great, were the All-Loving too—
> So, through the thunder comes a human voice
> Saying, 'O heart I made, a heart beats here !
> Face, my hands fashioned, see it in myself !
> Thou hast no power nor may'st conceive of mine,
> But love I gave thee, with myself to love,
> And thou must love Me who have died for thee.' "[1]

But, if we follow Browning's thoughts in his later and more reflective poems, such as *Ferishtah's Fancies* for instance, it will not be possible to hold that the poet altogether realized the importance, for both morality and religion alike, of the idea of the actual immanence of God in man. In these poems he seems to have abandoned that idea in

[1] *An Epistle from Karshish.*

favour of the hypotheses of a more timid philosophy. But, if his religious faith had not been embarrassed by certain dogmatic presuppositions of which he could not free himself, he might have met more successfully some of the difficulties which later reflection revealed to him, and might have been able to set a true value on that 'philosophy,' which betrayed his faith while appearing to support it.

But, before trying to criticize the principle by means of which Browning sought to reconcile the moral and religious elements of human life, it may be well to give it a more explicit and careful statement.

What, then, is that principle of unity between the divine and the human? How can we interpret the life of man as God's life in man, so that man, in attaining the moral ideal proper to his own nature, is at the same time fulfilling ends which may justly be called divine?

The poet, in early life and in late life alike, has one answer to this question—an answer given with the confidence of complete conviction. The meeting-point of God and man is love. Love, in other words, is, for the poet, the supreme principle both of morality and religion. Love, once for all, solves that contradiction between them which, both in theory and in practice, has embarrassed the world for so many ages. Love is the sublimest conception attainable by man ; a life inspired by it is the most perfect form of goodness he can conceive ; therefore, love is, at the same moment, man's moral ideal, and the very essence of Godhood. A life actuated by love is divine, whatever other limitations it may have. Such is the perfection and glory of this emotion, when it has been translated into a self-conscious motive, and become the energy of an intelligent will, that it lifts him who owns it to the sublimest height of being.

> " For the loving worm within its clod,
>   Were diviner than a loveless God
>   Amid his worlds, I will dare to say." [1]

So excellent is this emotion that, if man, who has this power to love, did not find the same power in God, then man would excel Him, and the creature and Creator change parts.

> " Do I find love so full in my nature, God's ultimate gift,
>   That I doubt His own love can compete with it? Here,
>   the parts shift?
>   Here, the creature surpass the Creator,—the end what
>   began?" [2]

Not so, says David, and with him no doubt the poet himself. God is Himself the source and fulness of love.

> " 'Tis Thou, God, that givest, 'tis I who receive:
> In the first is the last, in Thy will is my power to believe.
> All's one gift."
>
> .   .   .   .

> " Would I suffer for him that I love? So would'st Thou,
>   —so wilt Thou !
>   So shall crown Thee, the topmost, ineffablest, uttermost
>   crown—
>   And Thy love fill infinitude wholly, nor leave up nor down
>   One spot for the creature to stand in !" [3]

And this same love not only constitutes the nature

[1] *Christmas Eve.*   [2] *Saul.*   [3] *Ibid.*

of God and the moral ideal of man, but it is also the purpose and essence of all created being, both · animate and inanimate.

> "This world's no blot for us,
> Nor blank; it means intensely and means good."[1]

> "O world, as God has made it! All is beauty:
> And knowing this is love, and love is duty,
> What further may be sought for or declared?"[2]

In this world then "all's love, yet all's law." God permits nothing to break through its universal sway, even the very wickedness and misery of life are brought into the scheme of good, and, when rightly understood, reveal themselves as its means.

> "I can believe this dread machinery
> Of sin and sorrow, would confound me else,
> Devised—all pain, at most expenditure
> Of pain by Who devised pain—to evolve,
> By new machinery in counterpart,
> The moral qualities of man—how else?—
> To make him love in turn and be beloved,
> Creative and self-sacrificing too,
> And thus eventually Godlike."[3]

The poet thus brings the natural world, the history of man, and the nature of God, within the limits of the same conception. The idea of love solves for Browning all the enigmas of human life and thought.

> "The thing that seems
> Mere misery, under human schemes,
> Becomes, regarded by the light

[1] *Fra Lippo Lippi.*   [2] *The Guardian Angel.*
[3] *The Ring and the Book—The Pope,* 1375-1383.

> Of love, as very near, or quite
> As good a gift as joy before."[1]

Taking Browning's work as a whole, it is scarcely possible to deny that this is at once the supreme motive of his art, and the principle on which his moral and religious doctrine rests. He is always strong and convincing when he is dealing with this theme. It was evidently his own deepest conviction, and it gave him the courage to face the evils of the world, and the power as an artist to "contrive his music from its moans." It plays, in his philosophy of life, the part that Reason fills for Hegel, or the Blind Will for Schopenhauer; and he is as fearless as they are in reducing all phenomena into forms of the activity of his first principle. Love not only gave him firm footing amid the wash and welter of the present world, where time spins fast, life fleets, and all is change, but it made him look forward with joy to "the immortal course"; for, to him, all the universe is love-woven. All life is but treading the 'love-way,' and no wanderer can finally lose it. "The way-faring men, though fools, shall not err therein."

Since love has such an important place in Browning's theory of life, it is necessary to see what he means by it. For love has had for different individuals, ages and nations, a very different significance; and almost every great poet has given it a different interpretation. And this is not unnatural. For love is a passion which, beginning with youth and the hey-day of the blood, expands with the expanding life, and takes new forms of beauty and goodness

[1] *Easter Day.*

at every stage. And this is equally true, whether we speak of the individual or of the human race.

Love is no accident in man's history, nor a passing emotion. It is rather a constitutive element of man's nature, fundamental and necessary as his intelligence. And, like everything native and constitutive, it is obedient to the law of evolution, which is the law of man's being ; it passes, therefore, through ever varying forms. To it—if we may for the moment make a distinction between the theoretical and practical life, or between ideas and their causative potency—must be attributed the constructive power which has built the world of morality, with its intangible but most real relations, binding man to man and age to age. It is the author of the organic institutions which, standing between the individual and the rudeness of nature, awaken in him the need, and give him the desire and the faculty, of attaining higher things than physical satisfaction. Man is meant to act as well as to think, to be virtuous as well as to have knowledge. It is possible that reverence for the intellect may have led men, at times, to attribute the evolution of the race too exclusively to the theoretic consciousness, forgetting that, along with reason, there co-operates a twin power in all that is wisest and best in us, and that a heart which can love is as essential a pre-condition of all worthy attainment as an intellect which can see. Love and reason [1] are equally primal powers in man, and they

[1] It would be more correct to say the reason that is loving or the love that is rational ; for, though there is distinction, there is no dualism.

reflect might into each other: for love increases knowledge, and knowledge love. It is their combined power that gives interest and meaning to the facts of life, and transmutes them into a moral and intellectual order. They, together, are lifting man out of the isolation and chaos of subjectivity into membership in a spiritual kingdom, where collision and exclusion are impossible, and all are at once kings and subjects.

And, just as reason is present as a transmuting power in the sensational life of the infancy of the individual and race, so is love present amidst the confused and chaotic activity of the life that knows no law other than its own changing emotions. Both make for order, and both grow with it. Both love and reason have travelled a long way in the history of man. The patriot's passion for his country, the enthusiasm of pity and helpfulness towards all suffering which marks the man of God, are as far removed from the physical attraction of sex for sex, and the mere liking of the eye and ear, as is the intellectual power of the sage from the vulpine cunning of the savage. "For," as Emerson well said, "it is a fire that, kindling its first embers in the narrow nook of a private bosom, caught from a wandering spark out of another heart, glows and enlarges until it warms and beams upon multitudes of men and women, upon the universal heart of all, and so lights up the world and all nature with its generous flames." Both love and reason alike pass through stage after stage, always away from the particularity of selfishness and ignorance, into larger and larger cycles of common truth and goodness,

towards the full realization of knowledge and benevolence, which is the inheritance of emancipated
man. In this transition, the sensuous play of feeling
within man, and the sensitive responses to external
stimuli, are made more and more organic to ends
which are universal, that is, to spiritual ends. Love,
which in its earliest form seems to be the natural
yearning of brute for brute, appearing and dis-
appearing at the suggestion of physical needs, passes
into an idealized sentiment, into an emotion of the
soul, into a principle of moral activity which manifests itself in a permanent outflow of helpful deeds
for man. It represents, when thus sublimated, one
side at least of the expansion of the self, which
culminates when the world beats in the pulse of
the individual, and the joys and sorrows, the defeats
and victories of mankind are felt by him as his
own. It is no longer dependent merely on the
incitement of youth, grace, beauty, whether of body
or character; it transcends all limitations of sex
and age, and finds objects on which it can spend
itself in all that God has made, even in that which
has violated its own law of life, and become mean
and pitiful. It becomes a love of fallen humanity,
and an ardour to save it by becoming the conscious
and permanent motive of all men. The history of
this evolution of love has been written by the poets.
Every phase through which this ever-deepening
emotion has passed, every form which this primary
power has taken in its growth, has received from
them its own proper expression. They have made
even the grosser instincts lyric with beauty; and,
ascending with their theme, they have sung the

pure passion of soul for soul, its charm and its strength, its idealism and heroism, up to the point at which, in Browning, it transcends the limits of finite existence, sheds all its earthly vesture, and becomes a spiritual principle of religious aspiration and self-surrender to God.

Browning nowhere shows his native strength more clearly than in his treatment of love. He has touched this world-old theme—which almost every poet has handled, and handled in his highest manner—with that freshness and insight which is possible only to the inborn originality of genius. Other poets have, in some ways, given to love a more exquisite utterance, and rendered its sweetness, and tenderness, and charm with a lighter grace. It may even be admitted that there are poets whose verses have echoed more faithfully the fervour and intoxication of passion, and who have shown greater power of interpreting it in the light of a mystic idealism. But, in one thing, Browning stands alone. He has given to love a moral significance, a place and power amongst those substantial elements on which rest the dignity of man's being and the greatness of his destiny, in a way which is, I believe, without example in any other poet. And he has done this by means of that moral and religious earnestness which pervades all his poetry. The one object of supreme interest to him is the development of the soul, and his penetrative insight revealed to him the power to love as the paramount fact in that development. To love, he repeatedly tells us, is the sole and supreme object of man's life; it is the one lesson which he has to learn on earth;

and, love once learnt, in what way matters little,
"it leaves completion in the soul." Love we dare
not, and, indeed, cannot absolutely miss. No man
can be absolutely selfish and be man.

> "Beneath the veriest ash, there hides a spark of soul
> Which, quickened by love's breath, may yet pervade the
> whole
> O' the grey, and, free again, be fire; of worth the same,
> Howe'er produced, for, great or little, flame is flame."[1]

Love, once evoked, once admitted into the soul,

> "adds worth to worth,
> As wine enriches blood, and straightway sends it forth,
> Conquering and to conquer, through all eternity,
> That's battle without end."[2]

This view of the significance of love grew on
Browning as his knowledge of man's nature and
destiny became fuller and deeper, while, at the
same time, his trust in the intellect became less.
Even in *Paracelsus* he reveals love, not as a sentiment or intoxicating passion, as one might expect
from a youthful poet, but as one of the great
fundamental 'faculties' of man. Love, " blind,
oft-failing, half-enlightened, often-chequered trust,"
though it be, still makes man

> "The heir of hopes too fair to turn out false."[3]

In that poem love is definitely lifted by the
poet to the level of knowledge. Intellectual gain,
apart from love, is folly and futility, worthless for
the individual and worthless to the race. " Mind
is nothing but disease," Paracelsus cries in the

---

[1] *Fifine at the Fair*, xliii.   [2] *Ibid.* liv.   [3] *Paracelsus.*

bitterness of his disappointment, "and natural health is ignorance"; and he asks of the mad poet who "loved too rashly,"

> "Are we not halves of one dissevered world,
>   Whom this strange chance unites once more? Part?
>   Never !
>   Till thou the lover, know ; and I, the knower,
>   Love—until both are saved."[1]

And, at the end of the poem, Paracelsus, coming to an understanding with himself as to the gain and loss of life, proclaims with his last strength the truth he had missed throughout his great career, namely, the supreme worth of love.

> "I saw Aprile—my Aprile there !
>   And as the poor melodious wretch disburthened
>   His heart, and moaned his weakness in my ear,
>   I learned my own deep error ; love's undoing
>   Taught me the worth of love in man's estate,
>   And what proportion love should hold with power
>   In his right constitution ; love preceding
>   Power, and with much power, always much more love ;
>   Love still too straitened in his present means,
>   And earnest for new power to set love free."

As long as he hated men or, in his passionate pursuit of truth was indifferent to their concerns, it was not strange that he saw no good in men and failed to help them. Knowledge without love is not *true* knowledge, but falsehood and weakness. But, great as is the place given to love in *Paracelsus*, it is far less than that given to it in the poet's later works. In *Ferishtah's Fancies* and *La Saisiaz* it is no longer rivalled by knowledge ;

[1] *Paracelsus.*

nor even in *Easter Day*, where the voice beside the poet proclaiming that

> " Life is done,
> Time ends, Eternity's begun,"

gives a final pronouncement upon the purposes of the life of man. The world of sense—of beauty and art, of knowledge and truth, are given to man, but none of them satisfy his spirit ; they merely sting with hunger for something better. " Deficiency gapes every side," till love is known as the essence and worth of all things.

> "Is this thy final choice?
> Love is the best? 'Tis somewhat late !
> And all thou dost enumerate
> Of power and beauty in the world,
> The righteousness of love was curled
> Inextricably round about.
> Love lay within it and without,
> To clasp thee,—but in vain ! Thy soul
> Still shrunk from him who made the whole,
> Still set deliberate aside
> His love !—Now take love ! Well betide
> Thy tardy conscience !"[1]

In his later reflective poems, in which he deals with the problems of life in the spirit of a meta-physician seeking a definite answer to the questions of the intelligence, he declares the reason for his preference of love to knowledge. In *La Saisiaz* he states that man's love is God's too, a spark from His central fire ; but man's knowledge is man's only. Knowledge is finite, limited and tinged with sense. The truth we reach at best

[1] *Easter Day.*

is only truth *for us*, relative, distorted. We are
for ever kept from the fact which is supposed to
be given ; our intellects play about it ; sense and
even intellect itself are interposing media, which we
must use, and yet, in using them, we only fool ourselves with semblances. The poet has now grown
so cautious that he will not declare his own knowledge to be valid for any other man. David
Hume could scarcely be more suspicious of the
human intellect, nor Berkeley more surely persuaded
of the purely subjective nature of its attainments.
In fact, the latter relied on human knowledge in
a way impossible to Browning, for he regarded it
as the language of spirit speaking to spirit. Out
of his experience, Browning says,

> " There crowds conjecture manifold,
> But, as knowledge, this comes only,—things may be as I
>   behold
> Or may not be, but, without me and above me, things there are;
> I myself am what I know not—ignorance which proves no bar
> To the knowledge that I am, and, since I am, can recognize
> What to me is pain and pleasure : this is sure, the rest—
>   surmise." [1]

Thought itself, for aught he knows, may be afflicted
with a kind of colour-blindness ; and he knows no
appeal when one affirms " green as grass," and
another contradicts him with " red as grass." Under
such circumstances, it is not strange that Browning
should decline to speak except for himself, and that
he will

> "Nowise dare to play the spokesman for my brothers strong
>   or weak," [2]

[1] *La Saisiaz.*   [2] *Ibid.*

or that he will far less presume to pronounce for God, and pretend that the truth finds utterance from lips of clay—

"Pass off human lisp as echo of the sphere-song out of
    reach."

"Have I knowledge? Confounded it shrivels at Wisdom laid
    bare !
  Have I forethought? how purblind, how blank to the
    Infinite Care !

.   .   .   .

And thus looking within and around me, I ever renew
(With that stoop of the soul, which in bending upraises it too)
The submission of man's nothing-perfect to God's all-
    complete,
As by each new obeisance in spirit, I climb to His feet."[1]

But David finds in himself one faculty so supreme in worth that he keeps it in abeyance—

"Lest, insisting to claim and parade in it, wot ye, I worst
  E'en the Giver in one gift.—Behold I could love if I durst,
  But I sink the pretension as fearing a man may o'ertake
  God's own speed in the one way of love : I abstain for love's
    sake."[2]

This faculty of love, so far from being tainted with finitude, like knowledge ; so far from being mere man's, or a temporary and deceptive power given to man for temporary uses, by a Creator who has another ineffably higher way of loving, as He has of truth, is itself divine. In contrast with the activity of love, Omnipotence itself dwindles into insignificance, and creation sinks into a puny exercise of power. Love, in a word, is the highest

<hr>

[1] *Saul*, III.   [2] *Ibid.*

good : and, as such, it has all its worth in itself, and gives to all other things what worth they have. God Himself gains the " ineffable crown " by showing love and saving the weak. Love is the power divine, the central energy of God's being.

Browning never forgets this moral or religious quality of love. So pure is this emotion to the poet, " so perfect in whiteness, that it will not take pollution ; but, ermine-like, is armed from dishonour by its own soft snow." In the corruptest hearts, amidst the worst sensuality, love is still a power divine, making for all goodness. Even when it is kindled into flame by an illicit touch, and wars against the life of the family, which is its own product, its worth is supreme. He who has learned to love in any way, has " caught God's secret." How he has caught it, whom he loves, whether or not he is loved in return, all these things matter little. The paramount question on which hangs man's fate is, has he learned to love another, any other, Fifine or Elvire. " She has lost me," said the unloved lover ; " I have gained her. Her soul's mine."

The supreme worth of love, the mere emotion itself however called into activity, secures it against all taint. No one who understands Browning in the least, can accuse him of touching with a rash hand the sanctity of the family ; rather he places it on the basis of its own principle, and thereby makes for it the strongest defence. Such love as he speaks of, however irregular its manifestation or sensuous its setting, can never be confounded with lust—" hell's own blue tint." It is further removed from lust than even asceticism is. It has not even a negative attitude towards the flesh ; but finds the flesh to be "stuff for transmuting," and reduces it to the uses of the spirit. The love which is sung by Browning is more pure and free, and is set in a higher altitude than anything that can be reached by the way of negation. It is a consecration of the undivided self, so that "soul helps not flesh more, than flesh helps soul." It is not only a spiritual and divine emotion, but it also " shows a heart within, blood-tinctured with a veined humanity."

> "Be a God and hold me
>   With a charm !
> Be a man and hold me
>   With thine arm !
>
> "Teach me, only teach, Love !
>   As I ought
> I will speak thy speech, Love !
>   Think thy thought—
>
> "Meet, if thou require it,
>   Both demands,
> Laying flesh and spirit
>   In thy hands."[1]

True love is always an infinite giving, which holds nothing back. It is a spendthrift, magnificent in its recklessness, squandering the very essence of the self upon its object, and, by doing so, in the end enriching the self beyond all counting. For in loving, the individual becomes re-impersonated in another ; the distinction of Me

[1] *A Woman's Last Word.*

and Thee is swept away, and there pulses in two individuals one warm life.

> " If two lives join, there is oft a scar,
>   They are one and one with a shadowy third ;
> One near one is too far.

> " A moment after, and hands unseen
>   Were hanging the night around us fast ;
> But we knew that a bar was broken between
>   Life and life : we were mixed at last
> In spite of the mortal screen." [1]

The throwing down of the limits that wall a man within himself, the mingling of his own deepest interests with those of others, always marks love— be it love of man for maid, parent for child, or patriot for his country. It opens an outlet into the pure air of the world of objects, and enables man to escape from the stuffed and poisonous atmosphere of his narrow self. It is a streaming outwards of the inmost treasures of the spirit, a consecration of its best activities to the welfare of others. And when this is known to be the native quality and quintessence of love, no one can regard it anywhere, or at any time, as out of place. " Prize-lawful or prize-lawless " it is ever a flower, even though it grow, like the love of the hero of *Turf and Towers*, in slime. Lust, fleshly desire, which has been too often miscalled love, is its worst perversion. Love spends itself for another, and seeks satisfaction only in another's good. But lust uses up others for its own worst purposes, wastes its object, and turns the current

[1] *By the Fireside.*

of life back inwards, into the slush and filth of selfish pleasure. The distinction between love and its perversion, which is impossible in the naïve life of an animal, ought to be clear enough to all men, and probably is. Nor should the sexual impulse itself in human beings be confused with fleshly desire, and treated as if it were merely natural, " the mere lust of life " common to all living things,—" that strive," as Spinoza put it, " to persevere in existing." For there is no purely natural impulse in man ; all that he is, is transfused with spirit, whether he will or no. He cannot act as a mere animal, because he cannot leave his rational nature behind him. He cannot desire as an innocent brute desires : his desire is always love or lust. We have as little right to say that the wisdom of the sage is *nothing but* the purblind savagery of a Terra del Fuegian, as we have to assert that love is *nothing but* a sexual impulse. That impulse rather, when its potency is set free, will show itself, at first confusedly, but with more and more clearness as it expands, to be the yearning of soul for soul. It puts us " in training for a love which knows not sex, nor person, nor partiality ; but which seeks virtue and wisdom everywhere, to the end of increasing virtue and wisdom." The height to which this passion lifts man is just what makes possible the fall into a sensuality and excess of brutishness, in comparison with which animal life is a paradise of innocence.

If this is clearly recognized, many of the idle questions of casuistry that are sometimes raised regarding sexual love and marriage will cease to trouble. For these questions generally presuppose the lowest possible view of this passion. Browning shows us how to follow with serene security the pure light of the emotion of love, amidst all the confused lawlessness of lustful passion, and through all the intricacies of human character. Love, he thinks, is never illicit, never unwise, except when it is disloyal to itself; it never ruins, but always strives to enrich its object. Bacon quotes with approval a saying "That it is impossible to love, and to be wise." Browning asserts that it is impossible to love and *not* be wise. It is a power that, according to the Christian idea which the poet adopts, has infinite goodness for its source, and that, even in its meanest expression, is always feeling its way back to its origin, flowing again into the ocean whence it came.

So sparklingly pure is this passion that it could exorcise the evil and turn old to new, even in the case of Léonce Miranda. At least Browning, in this poem, strives to show that, being true love, though the love of an unclean man for an unclean woman, it was a power at war with the sordid elements of that sordid life. Love has always the same potency, flame is always flame,

> "no matter whence flame sprung,
> From gums and spice, or else from straw and rottenness."[1]

> "Let her but love you,
> All else you disregard! what else can be?
> You know how love is incompatible

[1] *Fifine at the Fair*, lv.

> With falsehood—purifies, assimilates
> All other passions to itself." [1]

> " Ne'er wrong yourself so far as quote the world
> And say, love can go unrequited here !
> You will have blessed him to his whole life's end—
> Low passions hindered, baser cares kept back,
> All goodness cherished where you dwelt—and dwell." [2]

But, while love is always a power lifting a man upwards to the level of its own origin from whatever depths of degradation, its greatest potency can reveal itself only in characters intrinsically pure, such as Pompilia and Caponsacchi. Like mercy and every other spiritual gift, it is mightiest in the mighty. In the good and great of the earth, love is veritably seen to be God's own energy ;

> "Who never is dishonoured in the spark
> He gave us from His fire of fires, and bade
> Remember whence it sprang, nor be afraid
> While that burns on, though all the rest grow dark." [3]

It were almost an endless task to recount the ways in which Browning exhibits the moralizing power of love : how it is for him the quintessence of all goodness ; the motive, and inspiring cause, of every act in the world that is completely right ; and how, on that account, it is the actual working in the man of the ideal of all perfection. This doctrine of love is, in my opinion, the richest vein of pure ore in Browning's poetry.

But it remains to follow briefly our poet's treatment of love in another direction—as a principle

---

[1] *Colombe's Birthday.*   [2] *Ibid.*
[3] *Any Wife to any Husband*, III.

present, not only in God as creative and redeeming Power, and in man as the highest motive and energy of the moral life, but also in the outer world, in the 'material' universe. In the view of the poet, the whole creation is nothing but love incarnate, a pulsation from the divine heart. Love is the source of all law and of all beauty. "Day unto day uttereth speech, and night unto night speaketh knowledge. There is no speech nor language where their voice is not heard." And our poet speaks as if he had caught the meaning of the language, and believes that all things speak of love—the love of God.

"I think," says the heroine of the *Inn Album*,

> "Womanliness means only motherhood ;
> All love begins and ends there,—roams enough,
> But, having run the circle, rests at home."

And Browning detects something of this motherhood everywhere. He finds it as

> "Some cause
> Such as is put into a tree, which turns
> Away from the north wind with what nest it holds."[1]

The Pope—who, if any one, speaks for Browning—declares that

> "Brute and bird, reptile and the fly,
> Ay and, I nothing doubt, even tree, shrub, plant
> And flower o' the field, [are] all in a common pact
> To worthily defend the trust of trusts,
> Life from the Ever Living."[2]

[1] *The Ring and the Book—Giuseppe Caponsacchi*, 1374-1376.
[2] *The Ring and the Book—The Pope*, 1076-1081.

" Because of motherhood," said the minor pope in
Iván Ivánovitch,

> "each male
> Yields to his partner place, sinks proudly in the scale :
> His strength owned weakness, wit—folly, and courage—fear,
> Beside the female proved male's mistress—only here.
> The fox-dam, hunger-pined, will slay the felon sire
> Who dares assault her whelp."

The betrayal of the mother's trust is the "un-
exampled sin," which scares the world and shames
God.

> " I hold that, failing human sense,
> The very earth had oped, sky fallen, to efface
> Humanity's new wrong, motherhood's first disgrace." [1]

This instinct of love, which binds brute-parent to
brute-offspring, is a kind of spiritual law in the
natural world : it, like all law, guarantees the continuity and unity of the world, and it is scarcely
akin to merely physical attraction.   No doubt its
basis is physical ; it has an organism of flesh and
blood for its vehicle and instrument : but mathematical physics cannot explain it, nor can it be
detected by chemical tests.   Rather, with the poet,
we are to regard brute affection as a kind of rude
outline of human love ; as a law in nature, which,
when understood by man and adopted as his rule
of conduct, becomes the essence and potency of his
moral life.

Thus Browning regards love as an omnipresent
good. There is nothing, he tells us in *Fifine*, which
cannot reflect it ; even moral putridity becomes

---

[1] *Iván Ivánovitch.*

phosphorescent, "and sparks from heaven transpierce earth's coarsest covertures."

> "There is no good of life but love—but love !
> What else looks good, is some shade flung from love,
> Love gilds it, gives it worth."[1]

There is no fact which, if seen to the heart, will not prove itself to have love for its purpose, and, therefore, for its substance. And it is on this account that everything finds its place in a kosmos, and that there is

> "No detail but, in place allotted it, was prime
> And perfect."[2]

Every event in the history of the world and of man is explicable, as the bursting into new form of this elemental, all-pervading power. The permanence in change of nature, the unity in variety, the strength which clothes itself in beauty, are all manifestations of love. Nature is not merely natural ; matter and life's minute beginnings are more than they seem. Paracelsus said that he knew and felt

> "What God is, what we are,
> What life is—how God tastes an infinite joy
> Infinite ways—one everlasting bliss,
> From whom all being emanates, all power
> Proceeds : in whom is life for evermore,
> Yet whom existence in its lowest form
> Includes."[3]

The scheme of love does not begin with man, he is rather its consummation.

[1] *In a Balcony.*   [2] *Fifine at the Fair*, xxxi.
[3] *Paracelsus.*

> "Whose attributes had here and there
> Been scattered o'er the visible world before,
> Asking to be combined, dim fragments meant
> To be united in some wondrous whole,
> Imperfect qualities throughout creation,
> Suggesting some one creature yet to make,
> Some point where all those scattered rays should meet
> Convergent in the faculties of man.
>
> .   .   .   .
>
> Hints and previsions of which faculties,
> Are strewn confusedly everywhere about
> The inferior natures, and all lead up higher,
> All shape out divinely the superior race,
> The heir of hopes too fair to turn out false,
> And man appears at last."[1]

Power, knowledge, love,—all these are found in the world, in which

> "All tended to mankind,
> And, man produced, all has its end thus far:
> But, in completed man begins anew
> A tendency to God."[2]

For man, being intelligent, flings back his light on all that went before—

> "Illustrates all the inferior grades, explains
> Each back step in the circle."[3]

He gives voice to the mute significance of Nature, and lets in the light on its blind groping:

> "Man, once descried, imprints for ever
> His presence on all lifeless things."[4]

And how is this interpretation achieved? By penetrating behind force, power, mechanism, and even intelligence, thinks the poet, to a purpose

---

[1] *Paracelsus.*   [2] *Ibid.*   [3] *Ibid.*   [4] *Ibid.*

which is benevolent, a reason which is all embracing and rooted in love. The magnificent failure of Paracelsus came from missing this last step. His transcendent hunger for knowledge was not satisfied, not because human knowledge is essentially an illusion or mind a disease, but because his knowledge did not reach the final truth of things, which is love. For love alone makes the heart wise, to know the secret of all being. Love is the ultimate hypothesis in the light of which alone man can catch a glimpse of the general direction and intent of the universal movement in the world and in man. Dying, Paracelsus, taught by Aprile, caught a glimpse of this elemental 'love-force,' in which alone lies the clue to every problem, and the promise of the final satisfaction of the human spirit. Failing in this knowledge, man may know many things, but nothing truly : all love-less knowledge stays with outward shows. It is love alone that puts man in the right relation to his fellows and to the world, and removes the distortion which fills life with sorrow, and makes it

> "Only a scene
> Of degradation, ugliness and tears,
> The record of disgraces best forgotten,
> A sullen page in human chronicles
> Fit to erase."[1]

But in the light of love, man " sees a good in evil, and a hope in ill success," and recognizes that mankind are

> "All with a touch of nobleness, despite
> Their error, upward tending all though weak ;

[1] *Paracelsus.*

> Like plants in mines which never saw the sun,
> But dream of him, and guess where he may be,
> And do their best to climb and get to him."[1]

" All this I knew not," adds Paracelsus, " and I failed. Let men take the lesson and press this lamp of love, ' God's lamp close to their breasts '; its splendour, soon or late, will pierce the gloom " and show that the universe is a transparent manifestation of His beneficence.

[1] *Paracelsus.*

CHAPTER VII

BROWNING'S IDEALISM, AND ITS PHILOSOPHICAL JUSTIFICATION

> " Master, explain this incongruity !
> When I dared question, ' It is beautiful,
> But is it true?' thy answer was, ' In truth
> Lives Beauty.' "[1]

WE have now seen how Browning sought to explain all things as manifestations of the principle of love; how he endeavoured to bring all the variety of finite existence, and even the deep discrepancies of good and evil, under the sway of one idea. I have already tried to show that all human thought is occupied with the same task: science, art, philosophy, and even the most ordinary common-sense, are all, in their different ways, seeking for constant laws amongst changing facts. Nay, we may even go so far as to say that all the activity of man, the practical as well as the theoretical, is an attempt to establish a *modus vivendi* between his environment and himself.

[1] *Shah Abbas.*

And such an attempt rests on the assumption that there is some ground common to both of the struggling powers within and without, some principle that manifests itself both in man and in nature. So that all men are philosophers to the extent of postulating a unity, which is deeper than all differences ; and all are alike trying to discover, in however limited or ignorant a way, what that unity is. If this fact were more constantly kept in view, the effort of philosophers to bring the ultimate colligating principles of thought into clear consciousness would not, at the outset at least, be regarded with so much suspicion. For the philosopher differs from the practical man of the world, not so much in the nature of the task which he is trying to accomplish, as in the distinct and conscious purpose with which he enters upon it.

Now, I think that those who, like Browning, offer an explicitly optimistic idea of the relation between man and the world, have a special right to a respectful hearing ; for it can scarcely be denied that their optimistic explanation is invaluable, *if it is true*—

> " So might we safely mock at what unnerves
>   Faith now, be spared the sapping fear's increase
>   That haply evil's strife with good shall cease
>   Never on earth."[1]

Despair is a great clog to good work for the world, and pessimists, as a rule, have shown much more readiness than optimists to let evil have its

[1] *Bernard de Mandeville.*

unimpeded way.   Having found, like Schopenhauer, that "Life is an awkward business," they
"determine to spend life in reflecting on it," or, at
least, in moaning about it.   The world's helpers
have been men of another mould ; and the contrast
between Fichte and Schopenhauer is suggestive of
a general truth :—" Fichte, in the bright triumphant
flight of his idealism, supported by faith in a moral
order of the world which works for righteousness,
turning his back on the darker ethics of self-torture
and mortification, and rushing into the political
and social fray, proclaiming the duties of patriotism,
idealizing the soldier, calling to and exercising an
active philanthropy, living with his nation, and
continually urging it upwards to higher levels of
self-realization—Schopenhauer recurring to the idea
of asceticism, preaching the blessedness of the
quiescence of all will, disparaging efforts to save
the nation or elevate the masses, and holding that
each has enough to do in raising his own self
from its dull engrossment in lower things to an
absorption in that pure, passionless being which
lies far beyond all, even the so-called highest,
pursuits of practical life." [1]

A pessimism, which is nothing more than
flippant fault-finding, frequently gains a cheap
reputation for wisdom ; and, on the other hand,
an optimism, which is really the result of much
reflection and experience, may be regarded as the
product of a superficial spirit that has never
known the deeper evils of life.   But, if pessimism
be true, it differs from other truths by its useless-

[1] *Schopenhauer*, by Prof. Wallace.

ness; for, even if it saves man from the bitterness of petty disappointments, it does so only by making the misery universal. There is no need to specify, when "*All* is vanity." The drowning man does not feel the discomfort of being wet. But yet, if we reflect on the problem of evil, we shall find that there is no neutral ground, and shall ultimately be driven to choose between pessimism and its opposite. Nor, on the other hand, is the suppression of the problem of evil possible, except at a great cost. It presents itself anew in the mind of every thinking man; and some kind of solution of it, or at least some definite way of meeting its difficulty, is involved in the attitude which every man assumes towards life and its tasks.

It is not impossible that there may be as much to be said for Browning's joy in life and his love of it, as there is for his predecessor's rage and sorrow. Browning certainly thought that there was; and he held his view consistently to the end. We cannot, therefore, do justice to the poet without dealing critically with the principle on which he has based his faith, and observing how far it is applicable to the facts of human life. As I have previously said, he strives hard to come into fair contact with the misery of man in all its sadness; and, after doing so, he claims, not as a matter of poetic sentiment, but as a matter of strict truth, that good is the heart and reality of it all. It is true that he cannot demonstrate the truth of his principle by reference to all the facts, any more than the scientific man can justify his hypothesis in every detail; but he holds it as a faith which reason can justify and experience establish, although not in every isolated phenomenon. The good may, he holds, be seen actually at work in the world, and its process will be more fully known as human life advances towards its goal.

> "Though Master keep aloof,
> Signs of His presence multiply from roof
> To basement of the building."[1]

Thus Browning bases his view upon experience, and finds firm footing for his faith in the present, although he acknowledges that the "profound of ignorance surges round his rockspit of self-knowledge."

> "Enough that now,
> Here where I stand, this moment's me and mine,
> Shows me what is, permits me to divine
> What shall be."[2]

"Since we know love we know enough"; for in love, he confidently thinks, we have the key to all the mystery of being.

Now, what is to be made of an optimism of this kind, which is based upon love and which professes to start from experience, or to be legitimately and rationally derived from it?

If such a view be taken seriously, as I propose doing, we must be prepared to meet at the outset some very grave difficulties. The first of these is that it is an interpretation of facts by a human emotion. To say that love blushes in the rose, or breaks into beauty in the clouds, that it shows

---

[1] *Francis Furini.*　　　　[2] *Ibid.*

its strength in the storm, and sets the stars in
the sky, and that it is in all things the source of
order and law, may imply a principle of supreme
worth both to poetry and religion; but when we are
asked to take it as a metaphysical explanation of
facts, we are prone, like the judges of Caponsacchi,
not to " levity, or to anything indecorous "—

> " Only—I think I apprehend the mood :
>   There was the blameless shrug, permissible smirk,
>   The pen's pretence at play with the pursed mouth,
>   The titter stifled in the hollow palm
>   Which rubbed the eye-brow and caressed the nose,
>   When I first told my tale ; they meant, you know—
>   'The sly one, all this we are bound believe !
>   Well, he can say no other than what he says.' "[1]

We are sufficiently willing to let the doctrine be
held as a pious opinion : the faith that "all's love
yet all's law," like many another illusion, if not
hugged too closely, may comfort man's nakedness.
But if we are asked to substitute this view for
that which the sciences suggest,—if we are asked
to put 'love' in the place of physical energy, and,
by assuming it as a principle, to regard as unreal
all the infinite misery of humanity and the degradation of intellect and character from which it
arises, common-sense seems at once to take the
side of the doleful sage of Chelsea. When the
optimist postulates that the state of the world, were
it rightly understood, is completely satisfactory,
reason seems to be brought to a stand ; and if
poetry and religion involve such a postulate, they

---

[1] *The Ring and the Book—Giuseppe Caponsacchi*, 14-20.

are taken to be ministering to the emotions at the expense of the intellect.

Browning, however, was not a mere sentimentalist who could satisfy his heart without answering the questions of his intellect. Nor is his view without support—at least, as regards the substance of it. The presence of an idealistic element in things is recognized even by ordinary thought. No man's world is so poor that it would not be poorer still for him if it were reduced by the abstract sciences of nature into a mere manifestation of physical force. Such a world Richter compares to an empty eye-socket.

The great result of speculation since the time of Kant is to teach us to recognize that objects are essentially related to mind, and that the principles which rule our thought enter, so to speak, into the constitution of the things we know. A very slight acquaintance with the history even of psychology, especially in modern times, shows that facts are more and more retracted into thought. This science, which began with a sufficiently common-sense view, not only of the reality and solidity of the things of the outer world, but of their opposition to, or independence of thought, is now thinning that world down into a mere shadow—a something which excites sensation. It shows that external things as we know them—and we cannot be concerned in any others—are, to a very great extent, the product of our thinking activities. No one will now subscribe to the Lockian or Humean view, of images impressed by objects on mind : the object which 'impresses' has first to be made by mind, out of the results of nervous excitation. In a word, modern psychology as well as modern metaphysics, is demonstrating more and more fully the dependence of the world, as it is known, on the nature and activity of man's mind. Every explanation of the world is found to be, in this sense, idealistic; and in this respect there is no difference whatsoever between the interpretation given by science and that of poetry, or religion, or philosophy. If we say that a thing is a 'substance,' or has 'a cause'; if, with the physicist, we assert the principle of the transmutation of energy, or make use of the idea of evolution with the biologist or geologist; nay, if we speak of time and space with the mathematician, we use principles of unity derived from self-consciousness, and interpret nature in terms of ourselves, just as truly as the poet or philosopher does, who makes love, or reason, the constitutive element in things. If the practical man of the world charges the poet and philosopher with living amidst phantoms, he can be answered with a " *Tu quoque.*" "How easy," said Emerson, "it is to show the materialist that he also is a phantom walking and working amid phantoms, and that he need only ask a question or two beyond his daily questions to find his solid universe proving dim and impalpable before his sense." "Sense," which seems to show directly that the world is a solid reality, not dependent in any way on thought, is found not to be reliable. All science is nothing but an appeal to thought from ordinary sensuous opinion. It is an attempt to find the reality of things by thinking about them; and this reality,

when it is found, turns out to be a law. But laws
are ideas ; though, if they are true ideas, they
represent not merely thoughts in the mind, but also
real principles, which manifest themselves in the
objects of the outer world, as well as in the thinker's
mind.

It is not possible in such a work as this, to give
a carefully reasoned proof of this view of the
relation of thought and things, or to repeat the
argument of Kant. I must be content with simply
referring to it, as showing that the principles in
virtue of which we think are the principles in virtue
of which objects as we know them exist ; and we
cannot be concerned with any other objects. The
laws which scientific investigation discovers are not
only ideas that can be written in books, but also
principles which explain the nature of things. In
other words, the hypotheses of the natural sciences,
or their categories, are points of view, in the light
of which the external world can be regarded as
governed by uniform laws. And these constructive
principles, which lift the otherwise disconnected world
into an intelligible system, are revelations of the
nature of intelligence, and only on that account
principles for explaining the world.

> "To know
> Rather consists in opening out a way
> Whence the imprisoned splendour may escape,
> Than in effecting entry for a light
> Supposed to be without." [1]

In this sense, it may be said that all knowledge is

[1] *Paracelsus.*

anthropomorphic; and in this respect there is no difference between the Physics, which speaks of energy as the essence of things, and the poetry, which speaks of love as the ultimate principle of reality. Between such scientific and idealistic explanations there is not even the difference that the one begins without, and the other within, or that the one is objective, and the other subjective. The true distinction is that the principles upon which the latter proceed are less abstract than those of science. 'Reason' and 'love' are higher principles for the explanation of the nature of things than 'substance' or 'cause': all are equally forms of the unity of thought. And if the latter seem to have nothing to do with the self, it is only because they are inadequate to express its full character. On the other hand, the higher categories, or ideas of reason, seem to be merely anthropomorphic, and, therefore, ill-suited to explain nature, only because the relation of nature to intelligence is habitually neglected by ordinary thought—which never presses its problems far enough to know that such higher categories can alone satisfy the demand for truth.

But natural science is gradually driven from the lower to the higher categories, or, in other words, it is learning to take a more and more idealistic view of nature. It is moving very slowly, because it is a long labour to exhaust the uses of an instrument of thought; and it is only at great intervals in the history of the human intellect that we find the need of a change of categories. But, as already hinted, there is no doubt that science is becoming increasingly aware of the conditions

under which alone its results may be held as valid.
At first, it drove 'mind' out of the realm of
nature, and offered to explain both it and man in
physical and mathematical terms. But, in our day,
the man of science has become too cautious to
make such rash extensions of the principles he
uses. He is more inclined to limit himself to his
special field, and he refuses to make any declaration
as to the ultimate nature of things. He holds
himself apart from materialism, as he does from
idealism. I think I may even go further, and say
that the fatal flaw of materialism has been finally
detected, and that the essential relativity of all
objects to thought is all but universally acknowledged.

The common notion that science gives a complete view of truth, to which we may appeal as
refuting idealism, is untenable. Science itself will
not support the appeal, but will direct the appellant
to another court. Perhaps, rather, it would be
truer to say that its attitude is one of doubt
whether or not any court, philosophical or other,
can give any valid decision on the matter. Confining themselves to the region of material phenomena, scientific men generally leave to common
ignorance, or to moral and theological tradition,
all the interests and activities of man, other than
those which are physical or physiological. And
some of them are even aware, that if they could
find the physical equation of man, or, through their
knowledge of physiology, actually produce in man
the sensations, thoughts, and notions now ascribed
to the intelligent life within him, the question of
the spiritual or material nature of man and the

world would remain precisely where it was. The explanation would still begin with mind and end there. The principles of the materialistic explanation of the world would still be derived from intelligence ; mind would still underlie all it explained, and completed science would still be, in this sense, anthropomorphic.

The charge of anthropomorphism thus falls to the ground, because it would prove too much. It is a weapon which cuts the hand that wields it. And, as directed against idealism, it only shows that he who uses it has inadequate notions both of the nature of the self and of the world, and is not aware that each of these has meaning, only as an exponent of the other.

On the whole, we may say that it is not men of science who now assail philosophy because it gives an idealistic explanation of the world, so much as unsystematic dabblers in matters of thought. The best men of science, rather, show a tendency to acquiesce in a kind of dualism of matter and spirit, and to leave morality and religion, art and philosophy to pursue their own ends undisturbed. Mr. Huxley, for instance, and some others, offer two philosophical solutions, one proceeding from the material world and the other from the sensations and other " facts of consciousness." They say that we may either explain man as a natural phenomenon, or the world as a mental one.

But it is a little difficult not to ask which of these explanations is true. Both of them cannot well be, seeing that they are different. And neither of them can be adopted without very serious consequences. It would require considerable hardihood to suggest that natural science should be swept away in favour of psychology, which would be done if the one view held by Mr. Huxley were true. And, in my opinion, it requires quite as much hardihood to suggest the adoption of a theory that makes morality and religion illusory, which would be done were the other view adopted.

As a matter of fact, however, such an attitude can scarcely be held by any one who is interested *both* in the success of natural science and in the spiritual development of mankind. We are constrained rather to say that, if these rival lines of thought lead us to deny either the outer world of things, or the world of thought and morality, then they must both be wrong. They are not 'explanations' but false theories, if they lead to such conclusions as these. And, instead of holding them up to the world as the final triumph of human thought, we should sweep them into the dust-bin, and seek for some better explanation from a new point of view.

And, indeed, a better explanation is sought, and sought not only by idealists, but by scientific men themselves,—did they only comprehend their own main tendency and method. The impulse towards unity, which is the very essence of thought, if it is baulked in one direction by a hopeless dualism, only breaks out in another. Subjective idealism, that is, the theory that things are nothing but phenomena of the individual's consciousness, that the world is really all inside the philosopher, is now known by most people to end in self-contradiction ; and materialism is also known to begin with it. And there are not many people sanguine enough to believe with Mr. Huxley and Mr. Herbert Spencer, that, if we add two self-contradictory theories together, or hold them alternately, we shall find the truth. Both modern science, that is, the science which does not philosophize, and modern philosophy deny, with tolerable unanimity, this absolute dualism. They do not know of any ' thought that is not of things, or of any things that are not for thought. It is necessarily assumed that, in some way or other, the gap between things and thought is got over by knowledge. How the connection is brought about may not be known ; but, that there is the connection between real things and true thoughts, no one can well deny. It is an ill-starred perversity which leads men to deny such a connection, merely because they have not found out how it is established.

A new category of thought has taken possession of the thought of our time—a category which is fatal to dualism. The idea of development is breaking down the division between mind and matter, as it is breaking down all other absolute divisions. Geology, astronomy, and physics at one extreme ; biology, psychology, and philosophy at the other, combine in asserting the idea of the universe as a unity which is always evolving its content, and bringing its secret potencies to the light. It is true that these sciences have not linked hands as yet. We cannot get from chemistry to biology without a leap, or from physiology to psychology without another. But no one will postulate a rift right through being. The whole tendency of modern science implies the opposite of such a conception. History is striving to trace continuity between the civilized man and the savage. Psychology is making towards a junction with physiology and general biology, biology with chemistry, and chemistry with physics. That there is an unbroken continuity in existence is becoming a postulate of modern science, almost as truly as the "universality of law" or "the uniformity of nature." Nor is the postulate held less firmly because the evidence for the continuity of nature is not yet complete. Chemistry has not yet quite lapsed into physics ; biology at present shows no sign of giving up its characteristic conception of life, and the former science is as yet quite unable to deal with that peculiar phenomenon. The facts of consciousness have not been resolved into nervous action, and, so far, mind has not been shown to be a secretion of brain. Nevertheless, all these sciences are beating against the limits which separate them, and new suggestions of connection between natural life and its inorganic environment are continually discovered. The sciences are boring towards each other, and the dividing strata are wearing thin ; so that it seems reasonable to expect that, with the growth of knowledge, an unbroken way upwards may be discovered, from the lowest and simplest stages of existence to the highest and most complex forms of self-conscious life.

Now, to those persons who are primarily interested in the ethical and religious phenomena of man's life, the idea of abolishing the chasm between spirit and nature is viewed with no little apprehension. It is supposed that if evolution were established as a universal law, and the unity of being were proved, the mental and moral life of man would be degraded into a complex manifestation of mere physical force. And we even find religious men rejoicing at the failure of science to bridge the gap between the inorganic and the organic, and between natural and self-conscious life ; as if the validity of religion depended upon the maintenance of these separating boundaries. But no religion that is free from superstitious elements has anything to gain from the failure of knowledge to relate things to each other. It is difficult to see how breaks in the continuity of being can be established, when every living plant confutes the absolute difference between the organic and inorganic, and, by the very fact of living, turns the latter into the former ; and it is difficult to deny the continuity of 'mind and matter,' when every human being is relating himself to the outer world in all his thoughts and actions. And religion is the very last form of thought which could profit from such a proof of absolute distinctions, were it possible. In fact, as we have seen, religion, in so far as it demands a perfect and absolute being as the object of worship, is vitally concerned in maintaining the unity of the world. It must assume that matter, in its degree, reveals the same principle as that which, in a higher form, manifests itself in spirit.

But closer investigation will show that the real

ground for such apprehension does not lie in the continuity of existence, which evolution implies ; for religion itself postulates the same thing. The apprehension springs, rather, from the idea that the continuity asserted by evolution is obtained by resolving the higher forms of existence into the lower. It is believed that, if the application of development to facts were successfully carried out, the organic would be shown to be nothing but complex inorganic forces, mental life nothing but a physiological process, and religion, morality, and art nothing but products of the highly complex motion of highly complex aggregates of physical atoms.

It seems to me quite natural that science should be regarded as tending towards such a materialistic conclusion. This is the view which many scientific investigators have themselves taken of their work ; and some of their philosophical exponents, notably Mr. Herbert Spencer, have, with more or less inconsistency, interpreted the idea of evolution in this manner. But, it may be well to bear in mind that science is generally far more successful in employing its constructive ideas, than it is in rendering an account of them. In fact, it is not its business to examine its categories : that task properly belongs to philosophy, and it is not a superfluous one. For, so long as the employment of the categories in the special province of a particular science yields valid results, scientific explorers and those who attach, and rightly attach, so much value to their discoveries, are very un-willing to believe that these categories are not valid universally. The warning voice of philosophy is not heeded, when it charges natural science with applying its conceptions to materials to which they are inadequate ; and its examination of the categories of thought is regarded as an innocent, but also a useless, activity. For, it is argued, what good can arise from the analysis of our working ideas? The world looked for causes, and found them, when it was very young ; but, up to the time of David Hume, no one had shown what causality meant, and the explanation which he offered is now rejected by modern science as definitely as it is rejected by philosophy. Meantime, while philosophy is still engaged in exposing the fallacies of the theory of association as held by Hume, science has gone beyond this category altogether ; it is now establishing a theory of the conservation of energy, which supplants the law of causality by tracing it to a deeper law of nature.

There is some force in this argument, but it cuts both ways. For, even if it be admitted that the category was successfully applied in the past, it is also admitted that it was applied without being understood ; and it cannot now be questioned that the philosophers were right in rejecting 'Cause' as the final explanation of the relation of objects to each other, and in pointing to other and higher connecting ideas. And this consideration should go some way towards convincing evolutionists that, though they may be able successfully to apply the idea of development to particular facts, this does not guarantee the soundness of their view of it as an instrument of thought, or of the nature of

the final results which it is destined to achieve.
Hence, without any disparagement to the new extension which science has received by the use of
this new idea, it may be maintained that the
ordinary view of its tendency and mission is
erroneous.

"The prevailing method of explaining the
world," says Professor Caird, "may be described
as an attempt to 'level downwards.' The doctrine
of development, interpreted as that idea usually is
interpreted, supports this view, as making it necessary to trace back higher and more complex to
lower or simpler forms of being ; for the most
obvious way of accomplishing this task is to show
analytically that there is really nothing more in
the former than in the latter."[1] "Divorced from
matter," asks Professor Tyndall, "where is life to
be found? Whatever our *faith* may say our
knowledge shows them to be indissolubly joined.
Every meal we eat, and every cup we drink,
illustrates the mysterious *control of Mind by
Matter*. Trace the line of life backwards and see
it approaching more and more to what we call
the *purely physical condition*."[2] And then, rising
to the height of his subject, or even above it, he
proclaims, "By an intellectual necessity I cross
the boundary of the experimental evidence, and
discern in that Matter which we, in our ignorance of its latent powers, and notwithstanding
our professed reverence for its Creator, have
hitherto covered with opprobrium, the promise

[1] *The Critical Philosophy of Kant*, Vol. I., p. 34.
[2] *Address to the British Association*, 1874, p. 54.

and potency of all terrestrial life."[1] A little further on, speaking in the name of science, and on behalf of his scientific fellow-workers (with what right is a little doubtful), he adds—" We claim, and we shall wrest, from theology, the entire domain of cosmological theory. All schemes and systems which thus infringe upon the domain of science, must, *in so far as they do this*, submit to its control, and relinquish all thought of controlling it." But if science is to control the knowable world, he generously leaves the remainder for religion. He will not deprive it of a faith in "a Power absolutely inscrutable to the intellect of man. As little in our days as in the days of Job can a man by searching find this Power out." And, now that he has left this empty sphere of the unknown to religion, he feels justified in adding, " There is, you will observe, no very rank materialism here."

'Yet they did not abolish the gods, but they sent them well
    out of the way,
  With the rarest of nectar to drink, and blue fields of nothing
    to sway."[2]

Now these declarations of Mr. Tyndall are, to say the least, somewhat ambiguous and shadowy. Yet, when he informs us that eating and drinking 'illustrate the control of mind by matter,' and 'that the line of life traced backwards leads towards a purely physical condition,' it is a little

---

[1] *Belfast Address*, 1874.

[2] Clerk Maxwell: "*Notes of the President's Address*," British Association, 1874.

difficult to avoid the conclusion that he regards science as destined

> "To tread the world
> Into a paste, and thereof make a smooth
> Uniform mound, whereon to plant its flag."[1]

For the conclusion of the whole argument seems to be, that all *we know as facts* are mere forms of matter—although the stubborn refusal of consciousness to be resolved into natural force, and its power of constructing for itself a world of symbols, gives science no little trouble, and forces it to acknowledge complete ignorance of the nature of the power from which all comes.

> "So roll things to the level which you love,
>   That you could stand at ease there and survey
>   The universal Nothing undisgraced
>   By pert obtrusion of some old church-spire
>   I' the distance!"[2]

Some writers on ethics and religion have adopted the same view of the goal of the idea of evolution. In consistency with this supposed tendency of science, to resolve all things into their simplest and earliest forms, religion has been traced back to the superstition and ghost-worship of savages ; and then it has been contended that it is, in essence, *nothing more* than superstition and ghost-worship. And, in like manner, morality, with its categorical imperative of duty, has been traced back, without a break, to the ignorant fear of the vengeance of a savage chief.   A similar process in the same direction reduces the love divine, of which our poet

---

[1] *Prince Hohenstiel-Schwangau.*   [2] *Ibid.*

speaks, into brute lust; somewhat sublimated, it
is true, in its highest forms, but not fundamentally
changed.

> "Philosophers, deduce you chastity
> Or shame, from just the fact that at the first
> Whoso embraced a woman in the field,
> Threw club down and forewent his brains beside;
> So, stood a ready victim in the reach
> Of any brother-savage, club in hand.
> Hence saw the use of going out of sight
> In wood or cave to prosecute his loves."[1]

And when the sacred things of life are treated
in this manner——when moral conduct is showed to
be evolved by a continuous process from 'conduct
in general,' the conduct of an 'infusorium or a
cephalopod,' or even of wind-mills or water-wheels,
it is not surprising if the authority of the moral
law seems to be undermined, and that 'devout
souls' are apprehensive of the results of science.
"Does law so analyzed coerce you much?" asks
Browning.

The derivation of spiritual from natural laws
thus appears to be fatal to the former; and
religious teachers naturally think that it is necessary for their cause to snap the links of the chain
of evolution, and, like Professor Drummond, to
establish absolute gaps, not only between the inorganic and the organic worlds, but also between
the self-conscious life of man and the mysterious,
spiritual life of Christ, or God. But it seems to
me that, in their antagonism to evolution, religious
teachers are showing the same incapacity to dis-

---

[1] *Bishop Blougram's Apology.*

tinguish between their friends and their foes, which they previously manifested in their acceptance of the Kantian doctrine of 'things in themselves,'— a doctrine which placed God and the soul beyond the power of speculative reason either to prove or disprove.   It is, however, already recognized that the attempt of Mansel and Hamilton to degrade human reason for the behoof of faith was really a veiled agnosticism ; and a little reflection must show that the idea of evolution, truly interpreted, in no wise threatens the degradation of man, or the overthrow of his spiritual interests. On the contrary, this idea is, in all the history of thought, the first constructive hypothesis which is adequate to the uses of ethics and religion.   By means of it we may hope to solve many of the problems, arising from the nature of knowledge and moral conduct, which the lower category of cause turned into pure enigmas.   It seems, indeed, to contain the promise of establishing the science of man, as intelligent, on a firm basis ; on which we may raise a superstructure, comparable in strength and superior in worth, to that of the science of nature.   And, even if the moral science must, like philosophy, always return to the beginning—must, that is, from the necessity of its nature, and not from any complete failure—it will still begin again at a higher level, now that the idea of evolution is in the field.

It now remains to show in what way the idea of evolution leaves room for religion and morality ; or, in other words, to show how, so far from degrading man to the level of the brute creation, and running life down into 'purely physical conditions,' it contains the promise of establishing that idealistic view of the world, which is maintained by art and religion.

In order to show this, it is necessary that the idea of evolution should be used fearlessly, and applied to all facts that can in any way come under it. It must, in other words, be used as a category of thought, whose application is universal ; so that, if it is valid at all as a theory, it is valid of all finite things. For the question we are dealing with is not the truth of the hypothesis of a particular science, but the truth of a hypothesis as to the relation of all objects in the world, including man himself. We must not be deterred from this universal application by the fact that we cannot, as yet, prove its truth in every detail. No scientific hypothesis ever has exhausted its details. I consider, therefore, that Mr. Tyndall had a complete right to "cross the boundary of the experimental evidence by an intellectual necessity" ; for the necessity comes from the assumption of a possible explanation by the aid of an hypothesis. It is no argument against such a procedure to insist that, as yet, there is no proof of the absolute continuity of matter and physical life, or that the dead begets the living. The hypothesis is not disproved by the absence of evidence ; it is only not proved. The connection may be there, although we have not, as yet, been able to find it. In the face of such difficulties as these the scientific investigator has always a right to claim more time ; and his attitude is impregnable so long as he remembers, as Mr. Tyndall did on the whole, that his hypothesis is a hypothesis.

But Mr. Tyndall has himself given up this right. He, like Mr. Huxley, has placed the phenomena of self-consciousness outside of the developing process, and confined the sphere in which evolution is applicable, to natural objects. Between objects and the subject, even when both subject and object are man himself, there lies 'an impassable gulf.' Even to try "to comprehend the connection between thought and thing is absurd, like the effort of a man trying to lift himself by his own waistband." Our states of self-consciousness are symbols only—symbols of an outside entity, whose real nature we can never know. We know only these states ; we only *infer* "that anything answering to our impressions exists outside of ourselves." And it is impossible to justify even that inference ; for, if we can only know states of consciousness, we cannot say that they are symbols of anything, or that there is anything to be symbolized. The external world, on this theory, ceases to exist even as an unknown entity. In triumphantly pointing out that, in virtue of this psychological view, " There is, you will observe, no very rank materialism here," Mr. Tyndall forgets that he has destroyed the basis of all natural science, and reduced evolution into a law of 'an outside entity,' of which we can never know anything, and any inference regarding which violates every law of thought.

It seems to me quite plain that either this psychological theory, which Mr. Tyndall has mistaken for a philosophy, is invalid ; or else it is useless to endeavour to propound any view regarding a "nature which is the phantom of the individual's mind." I prefer the science of Mr. Tyndall (and of Mr. Huxley, too) to his philosophy; and he would have escaped materialism more effectively, if he had remained faithful to his theory of evolution. It is disloyalty, not only to science, but to thought, to cast away our categories when they seem to imply inconvenient consequences. They must be valid universally, if they are valid at all.

Mr. Tyndall contends that nature makes man, and he finds evidence in the fact that we eat and drink, " of the control of mind by matter." Now, it seems to me, that *if* nature makes man, then nature makes man's thoughts also. His sensations, feelings, ideas, notions, being those of a naturally-evolved agent, are revelations of the potency of the primal matter, just as truly as are the buds, flowers, and fruits of a tree. No doubt, we cannot as yet 'comprehend the connection' between nervous action and sensation, any more than we can comprehend the connection between inorganic and organic existence. But, if the absence of ' experimental evidence ' does not disprove the hypothesis in the one case, it cannot disprove it in the other. All we can say is that there are two crucial points in which the theory has not been established.

But, in both cases alike, there is the same kind of evidence that the connection exists; although in neither case can we, as yet, discover what it is. Plants live by changing inorganic elements into organic structure ; and man is intelligent only in so far as he crosses over the boundary between subject and object, and knows the world that is without. There is no " impassable gulf separating the subject and object"; if there were, we could not know anything of either. There are not two worlds—the one of thoughts, the other of things— which are absolutely exclusive of each other, but one universe in which both thought and reality meet. Mr. Tyndall thinks that it is an inference (and an inference over an impassable gulf!) that anything answering to our impressions exists outside ourselves. "The question of the external world is the great battleground of metaphysics," he quotes approvingly from Mr. J. S. Mill. But the question of the external world is not whether that world exists ; it is, how we are to account for our knowledge that it does exist. The inference is not from thoughts to things, nor from things to thoughts, but from a partially known world to a systematic theory of that world. Philosophy is not engaged on the foolish enterprise of trying to discover whether the world exists, or whether we know that it exists ; its problem is how to account for our knowledge. It asks what must the nature of things be, seeing that they are known ; and what is the nature of thought, seeing that it knows facts.

There is no hope whatsoever for ethics, or religion, or philosophy—no hope even for science —in a theory which would apply evolution all the way up from inorganic matter to life, but which would postulate an absolute break at consciousness. The connection between thought and things is there to begin with, whether we can account for it or not; if it were not, then natural science would be impossible. It would be palpably irrational even to *try* to find out the nature of things by thinking. The only science would be psychology, and even that would be the science of 'symbols of an unknown entity.' What symbols of an unknown can signify, or how an unknown can produce symbols of itself across an impassable gulf—Mr. Spencer, Mr. Huxley, and Mr. Tyndall have yet to inform us.

It is the more necessary to insist on this, because the division between thought and matter, which is admitted by these writers, is often grasped at by their opponents, as a means of warding off the results which they draw from the theory of evolution. When science breaks its sword, religion assails it with the fragment. It is not at once evident that if this chasm were shown to exist, knowledge would be a chimera, seeing that there would be no outer world at all, not even a phenomenal one, to supply an object for it. We *must* postulate the ultimate unity of all beings with each other and with the mind that knows them, just because we are intellectual and moral beings; and to destroy this unity is to "kill reason itself, as it were, in the eye," as Milton said.

Now, evolution not only postulates unity, or the unbroken continuity of all existence, but it also negates all differences, except those which are expressions of that unity. It is not the mere assertion of a substratum under qualities; but it implies that the substratum penetrates into the qualities, and manifests itself in them. That which develops—be it plant, child, or biological kingdom —is, at every stage from lowest to highest, a concrete unity of all its differences; and in the whole history of its process its actual content is always the same. The environment of the plant evokes that content, but it adds nothing to it. No addition of anything absolutely new, no external aggregation, no insertion of anything alien into a growing thing, is possible. What it is now, it was in the beginning; and what it will be, it is now. Granting the hypothesis of evolution, there can be no quarrel with the view that the crude beginnings of things, matter in its most nebulous state, contains potentially all the rich variety of both natural and spiritual life.

But this continuity of all existence may be interpreted in two very different ways. It may lead us either to radically change our notions of mind and its activities, or "to radically change our notions of matter." We may take as the principle of explanation, either the beginning or the end of the process of development. We may say of the simple and the crass, 'There is all that your rich universe really means'; or we may say of the spiritual activities of man, 'This is what your crude beginning really was.' We may explain the complex by the simple, or the simple by the complex. We may analyze the highest back into the lowest, or we may follow the lowest, by a process of synthesis, up to the highest.

And one of the most important of all questions for morality and religion is the question, which of these two methods is valid. If out of crass matter is evolved all animal and spiritual life, does that prove life to be nothing but matter; or does it not rather show that what we, in our ignorance, took to be mere matter was really something much greater? If 'crass matter' contains all this promise and potency, by what right do we still call it 'crass'? It is manifestly impossible to treat the potencies, assumed to lie in a thing that grows, as if they were of no significance;—first, to assert that such potencies exist, in saying that the object develops, and then, to neglect them, and to regard the result as constituted *merely* of the simplest elements. Either these potencies are not in the object, or else the object has in it, and is, at the first, more than it appears to be. Either the object does not grow, or the lowest stage of its being is no explanation of its true nature.

If we wish to know what any particular living thing means, we look in vain to its primary state. We must watch the evolution and revelation of the secret hid in natural life, as it moves through the ascending cycles of the biological kingdom. The idea of evolution, when it is not muddled, is synthetic—not analytic; it explains the simplest in the light of the complex, the beginning in the light of the end, and not *vice versa*. In a word, it follows the ways of nature, the footsteps of fact, instead of inventing a wilful backward path of its own. And nature explains by gradually expanding. If we hearken to nature, and not to the voice of illusory preconceptions, we shall hear her proclaim at the *last* stage, "Here is the meaning of the seedling. Now it is clear what it really was; for the power which lay dormant has pushed itself into light, through bud and flower and leaf and fruit." The reality of a growing thing is its highest form of being. The last explains the first, but not the first the last. The first is abstract, incomplete, not yet actual, but mere potency; and we could never know even the potency, except in the light of its own actualization.

From this correction of the abstract view of development momentous consequences follow. If the universe is, as science pronounces, an organic totality, which is ever converting its promise and potency into actuality, then we must add "that the ultimate interpretation even of the lowest existence in the world cannot be given except on principles which are adequate to explain the highest. We must 'level up and not level down': we must not only deny that matter can explain spirit, but we must say that even matter itself cannot be fully understood, except as an element in a spiritual world."[1]

That the idea of evolution, even when applied in this consistent way, has difficulties of its own, it is scarcely necessary to say. But there is nothing in it which imperils the ethical and religious interests of humanity, or tends to reduce man into a natural phenomenon. Instead of degrading man, it lifts nature into a manifestation of spirit. If it were established, if every link of the endless chain were discovered and the continuity of existence were irrefragably proved, science would not overthrow idealism: it would rather vindicate it. It would

---

[1] Professor Caird, *The Critical Philosophy of Kant*, p. 35.

justify *in detail* the attempt of poetry and religion and philosophy, to interpret all being as the 'transparent vesture' of reason, or love, or whatever other power in the world is regarded as highest.

I have now arrived at the conclusion that was sought. I have tried to show, not only that the attempt to interpret nature in terms of man is not a superstitious anthropomorphism, but that such an interpretation is implied in all rational thought. In other words, self-consciousness is the key to all the problems of nature. Science, in its progress, is gradually substituting one category for the other, and every one of these categories is at once a law of thought and a law of things as known. Each category, successively adopted, lifts nature more to the level of man ; and the last category of modern thought, namely, development, constrains us so to modify our views of nature as to regard it as finally explicable only in the terms of spirit. Thus, the movement of science is towards idealism. Instead of lowering man, it elevates nature into a potency of that which is highest and best in man. It represents the life of man, in the language of philosophy, as the return of the highest to itself; or in the language of our poet and of religion, as a manifestation of infinite love. The explanation of nature from the principle of love, if it errs, errs "because it is not anthropomorphic enough," not because it is too anthropomorphic ; it is not too high and concrete a principle, but too low and abstract.

It now remains to show that the poet, in employing the idea of evolution, was aware of its upward direction. I have already quoted a few passages which indicate that he had detected the false use of it. I shall now quote a few others in which he shows a consciousness of its true meaning:

> "'Will you have why and wherefore, and the fact
>   Made plain as pike-staff?' modern Science asks.
> 'That mass man sprung from was a jelly-lump
>   Once on a time; he kept an after course
>   Through fish and insect, reptile, bird and beast,
>   Till he attained to be an ape at last,
>   Or last but one. And if this doctrine shock
>   In aught the natural pride—'"[1]

' Not at all,' the poet interrupts the man of science :
' Friend, banish fear!'

> "I like the thought He should have lodged me once
>   I' the hole, the cave, the hut, the tenement,
>   The mansion and the palace; made me learn
>   The feel o' the first, before I found myself
>   Loftier i' the last."[2]

This way upward from the lowest stage through every other to the highest, that is, the way of development, so far from lowering us to the brute level, is the only way for us to attain to the true highest, namely, the all-complete.

> "But grant me time, give me the management
>   And manufacture of a model me,
>   Me fifty-fold, a prince without a flaw,—
>   Why, there's no social grade, the sordidest,
>   My embryo potentate should blink and scape.
>   King, all the better he was cobbler once,
>   He should know, sitting on the throne, how tastes
>   Life to who sweeps the doorway."[3]

---

[1] *Prince Hohenstiel-Schwangau.*   [2] *Ibid.*   [3] *Ibid.*

But then, unfortunately, we have no time to make our kings in this way.

> "You cut probation short,
> And, being half-instructed, on the stage
> You shuffle through your part as best you can."[1]

God however, 'takes time.' He makes man pass his apprenticeship in all the forms of being. Nor does the poet

> "Refuse to follow farther yet
> I' the backwardness, repine if tree and flower,
> Mountain or streamlet were my dwelling-place
> Before I gained enlargement, grew mollusc."[2]

It is, indeed, only on the supposition of having been thus evolved from inanimate being, that he is able to account

> "For many a thrill
> Of kinship, I confess to, with the powers
> Called Nature ; animate, inanimate,
> In parts or in the whole, there's something there
> Man-like that somehow meets the man in me."[3]

These passages make it clear that the poet recognized that the idea of development 'levels up,' and that he makes an intelligent, and not a perverted and abstract use of this instrument of thought. He sees each higher stage carrying within it the lower, the present storing up the past ; he recognizes that the process is a self-enriching one. He knows it to be no degradation of the higher that it has been in the lower ; for he distinguishes between that life which is continuous amidst the

---

[1] *Prince Hohenstiel-Schwangau.*   [2] *Ibid.*   [3] *Ibid.*

fleeting forms, and the temporary tenements which it makes use of during the process of ascending.

> "From first to last of lodging, I was I,
> And not at all the place that harboured me."[1]

When nature is thus looked upon from the point of view of its final attainment, in the light of the self-consciousness into which it ultimately breaks, a new dignity is added to every preceding phase. The lowest ceases to be lowest, except in the sense that its promise is not fulfilled and its potency not actualized; for, throughout the whole process, the activity streams from the highest. It is that which is about to be, which guides the growing thing and gives it unity. The final cause is the efficient cause; the distant purpose is the ever-present energy; the last is always first.

Nor does the poet shrink from calling this highest, this last which is also first, by its highest name—God.

> "He dwells in all,
> From life's minute beginnings, up at last
> To man—the consummation of this scheme
> Of being, the completion of this sphere
> Of life."[2]

"All tended to mankind," he said, after reviewing the whole process of nature in *Paracelsus*,

> "And, man produced, all has its end thus far:
> But in completed man begins anew
> A tendency to God."[3]

There is nowhere a break in the continuity. God

[1] *Prince Hohenstiel-Schwangau.*
[2] *Paracelsus.*   [3] *Ibid.*

is at the beginning, His rapturous presence is seen in all the processes of nature, His power and knowledge and love work in the mind of man, and all history is His revelation of Himself.

The gap which yawns for ordinary thought between animate and inanimate, between nature and spirit, between man and God, does not baffle the poet. At the stage of human life, which is 'the grand result' of nature's blind process,

> "A supplementary reflux of light,
> Illustrates all the inferior grades, explains
> Each back step in the circle."[1]

Nature is retracted into thought, built again in mind.

> "Man, once descried, imprints for ever
> His presence on all lifeless things."[2]

The self-consciousness of man is the point where 'all the scattered rays meet'; and 'the dim fragments,' the otherwise meaningless manifold, the dispersed activities of nature, are lifted into a kosmos by the activity of intelligence. In its light, the forces of nature are found to be, not blind nor purposeless, but 'hints and previsions'

> "Strewn confusedly everywhere about
> The inferior natures, and all lead up higher,
> All shape out dimly the superior race,
> The heir of hopes too fair to turn out false,
> And man appears at last."[3]

In this way, and in strict accordance with the principle of evolution, the poet turns back at each higher stage to re-illumine in a broader light what

---

[1] *Paracelsus.*   [2] *Ibid.*   [3] *Ibid.*

went before,—just as we know the seedling after it is grown ; just as, with every advance in life, we interpret the past anew, and turn the mixed ore of action into pure metal by the reflection which draws the false from the true.

> "Youth ended, I shall try
> My gain or loss thereby ;
> Leave the fire ashes, what survives is gold :
> And I shall weigh the same,
> Give life its praise or blame :
> Young, all lay in dispute ; I shall know, being old." [1]

As youth attains its meaning in age, so does the unconscious process of nature come to its meaning in man.   And as old age,

> "Still within this life
> Though lifted o'er its strife,"

is able to

> "Discern, compare, pronounce at last,
> This rage was right i' the main,
> That acquiescence vain" ; [2]

so man is able to penetrate beneath the apparently chaotic play of phenomena, and find in them law, and beauty, and goodness. For the laws which he finds by thought are not his inventions, but his discoveries. The harmonies are in the organ, if the artist only knows how to elicit them. Nay, the connection is still more intimate. It is in the thought of man that silent nature finds its voice ; it blooms into 'meaning,' significance, thought, in him, as the plant shows its beauty in the flower.

[1] *Rabbi Ben Ezra.*   [2] *Ibid.*

Nature is making towards humanity, and in humanity it finds *itself*.

> "Striving to be man, the worm
> Mounts through all the spires of form."[1]

The geologist, physicist, chemist, by discovering the laws of nature, do not bind unconnected phenomena, but they refute the hasty conclusion of sensuous thought that the phenomena ever were unconnected. Men of science do not introduce order into chance and chaos, but show that there never was chance or chaos. The poet does not make the world beautiful, but finds the beauty that is dwelling there. Without him, indeed, the beauty would not be, any more than the life of the tree is beautiful until it has evolved its potencies into the outward form. Nevertheless, he is the expression of what was before, and the beauty was there in potency, awaiting its expression. "Only let his thoughts be of equal scope, and the frame will suit the picture," said Emerson.

> "The winds
> Are henceforth voices, wailing or a shout,
> A querulous mutter, or a quick gay laugh,
> Never a senseless gust now man is born.
> The herded pines commune and have deep thoughts,
> A secret they assemble to discuss
> When the sun drops behind their trunks.
>
> .   .   .   .
>
> The morn has enterprise, deep quiet droops
> With evening, triumph takes the sunset hour,
> Voluptuous transport ripens with the corn
> Beneath a warm moon like a happy face."[2]

[1] *Emerson.*   [2] *Paracelsus.*

Such is the transmuting power of imagination, that there is "nothing but doth suffer change into something rich and strange"; and yet the imagination, when loyal to itself, only sees more deeply into the truth of things, and gets a closer and fuller hold of facts.

But, although the human mind thus heals the breach between nature and spirit, and discovers the latter in the former, still it is not in this way that Browning finally establishes his idealism. For him, the principle working in all things is not reason, but love. It is from love that all being first flowed; into it all returns through man; and, in all "the wide compass which is fetched," through the infinite variety of forms of being, love is the permanent element and the true essence. Nature is on its way back to God, gathering treasure as it goes. The static view is not true to facts; it is development that for the poet explains the nature of things; and development is the evolution of love. Love is for Browning the highest, richest conception man can form. It is our idea of that which is perfect; we cannot even imagine anything better. And the idea of evolution necessarily explains the world as the return of the highest to itself. The universe is homeward bound.

Now, whether love is the highest principle or not, I shall not inquire at present. My task in this chapter has been to try to show that the idea of evolution drives us onward towards *some* highest conception, and then uses that conception as a principle to explain all things. If man is veritably higher as a physical organism than the bird or reptile, then biology, if it proceeds according to the principles of evolution, *must* seek the meaning of the latter in the former, and make the whole kingdom of life a process towards man. "Man is no upstart in the creation. His limbs are only a more exquisite organization— say rather the finish—of the rudimental forms that have already been sweeping the sea and creeping in the mud." And the same way of thought applies to man as a spiritual agent. If spirit be higher than matter, and if love be spirit at its best, then the principle of evolution leaves no option to the scientific thinker, but to regard all things as potentially spirit, and all the phenomena of the world as manifestations of love. Evolution necessarily combines all the objects to which it is applied into a unity. It knits all the infinite forms of natural life into an organism of organisms, so that it is a universal life which really lives in all animate beings. "Each animal or vegetable form remembers the next inferior and predicts the next higher. There is one animal, one plant, one matter, and one force." In its still wider application by poetry and philosophy, the idea of evolution gathers all being into one self-centred totality, and makes all finite existence a movement within, and a movement of that final perfection which, although last in order of time, is first in order of potency,—the *prius* of all things, the active energy *in* all things, and the *reality* of all things. It is the doctrine, of the immanence of God ; and it reveals "the effort of God, of the supreme intellect, in the extreme frontier of His universe."

In pronouncing, as Browning frequently does, that "after last comes first" and "what God once blessed cannot prove accursed"; in **the boldness of the faith** whereby he makes all the inferior grades of being into embodiments of the supreme good; in resolving the evils of human life, **the sorrow,** strife, and sin of man into means of man's **promotion,** he is only applying in a thorough manner the principle on which all modern speculation rests. His conclusions may shock common-sense; and they may seem to stultify not only our observation of facts, but the testimony of our moral consciousness. But I do not know of any principle of speculation which, **when** elevated into a universal principle, will not shock common-sense; and this **is** why the greatest poets and philosophers seem to be touched with a divine madness. Still, if this be madness, there is a method in it. We cannot escape from its logic, except by denying the idea of evolution—the hypothesis by means of which modern thought aims, and in the main successfully aims, at reducing the variety of existence, and the chaos of ordinary experience, into an order-ruled world and a kosmos of articulated knowledge.

The new idea of evolution differs from that of universal causation, to which even the ignorance of our own day has learnt to submit, in this mainly —it does not leave **things on the level** on which it finds them. Both cause and evolution assert **the unity of being,** which, indeed, every one must assume—even sceptics and pessimists; but development represents that unity as self-enriching; so that its true nature is revealed, only in the highest form of existence which man can conceive. The attempt of poets and philosophers to establish a universal synthesis by means of evolution differs from the work which is done by men of science, only in the extent of its range and the breadth of its results. It is not 'idealism,' but the scepticism which, in our day, conceals its real nature under the name of dualism or agnosticism, that is at war with the inner spirit of science. " Not only," —we may say of Browning, as it was said of Emerson by Professor Tyndall,—" is his religious sense entirely undaunted by the discoveries of science ; but all such discoveries he comprehends and assimilates. By him scientific conceptions are continually transmuted into the finer forms and warmer hues of an ideal world." And this he does without any distortion of the truth. For natural science, to one who understands its main tendency, does not militate against philosophy, art, and religion ; nor threaten to overturn a metaphysic whose principle is truth, or beauty, or goodness. Rather, it is gradually eliminating the discord of fragmentary existence, and making the harmony of the world more and more audible to mankind. It is progressively proving that the unity, of which we are all obscurely conscious from the first, actually holds in the whole region of its survey. The idea of evolution is reconciling science with art and religion, in an idealistic conception of the universe.

CHAPTER VIII

BROWNING'S SOLUTION OF THE PROBLEM OF EVIL

"Let him, therefore, who would arrive at knowledge of nature, train his moral sense, let him act and conceive in accordance with the noble essence of his soul; and, as if of herself, nature will become open to him. Moral action is that great and only experiment, in which all riddles of the most manifold appearances explain themselves." [1]

IN the last chapter, I tried to set forth some considerations that justify the attempt to interpret the world by a spiritual principle. The conception of development, which modern science and philosophy assume as a starting point for their investigation, was shown to imply that the lowest forms of existence can be explained, only as stages in the self-realization of that which is highest. This idea 'levels upwards,' and points to self-consciousness as the ultimate truth of all things. In other words, it involves that every interpretation of the world is anthropomorphic, in the sense that

[1] *Novalis.*

what constitutes thought constitutes things, and, **therefore**, that the key to nature is man.

In propounding this theory of love, and establishing an idealism, **Browning** is in agreement with the latest achievement of modern thought. For, if the principle of evolution be granted, love is a far more adequate hypothesis for the explanation of the nature of things than any purely physical principle. Nay, science itself, in so far as it presupposes evolution, tends towards an idealism of this type. Whether love be the best expression for that highest principle, which is conceived as the truth of being, and whether Browning's treatment of it is consistent and valid, I do not as yet inquire. Before attempting that task, it must be seen to what extent, and in what way, he applies the hypothesis of universal love to the particular facts of life. For the present, I take it as admitted that the hypothesis is legitimate, as an hypothesis; it remains to ask, with what success, if any, we may hope, by its means, to solve the contradictions of life, and to gather its conflicting phenomena into the unity of an intelligible system. This task cannot be accomplished within our limits, except in a very partial manner. I can attempt to meet only a few of the more evident and pressing difficulties that present themselves, and I can do that only in a very general way.

The first of these difficulties, or, rather, the main difficulty from which all others spring, is that the hypothesis of universal love is incompatible with the existence of any kind of evil, whether natural or moral. Of this Browning was well aware. He knew that he had brought upon himself the hard task of showing that pain, weakness, ignorance, failure, doubt, death, misery, and vice, in all their complex forms can find their legitimate place in a scheme of love.   And there is nothing more admirable in his attitude, or more inspiring in his teaching, than the manly frankness with which he endeavours to confront the manifold miseries of human life, and to constrain them to yield, as their ultimate meaning and reality, some spark of good.

But, as we have seen, there is a portion of this task in the discharge of which Browning is drawn beyond the strict limits of art. Neither the magnificent boldness of his religious faith, nor the penetration of his artistic insight, although they enabled him to deal successfully with the worst samples of human evil, as in *The Ring and the Book*, could dissipate the gloom which reflection gathers around the general problem. Art cannot answer the questions of philosophy. The difficulties that critical reason raises reason alone can lay. Nevertheless, the poet was forced by his reflective impulse, to meet that problem in the form in which it presents itself in the region of metaphysics. He was conscious of the presuppositions within which his art worked, and he sought to justify them. Into this region we must now follow him, so as to examine his theory of life, not merely as it is implied in the concrete creations of his art, but as it is expressed in those later poems, in which he attempts to deal directly with the speculative difficulties that crowd around the conception of evil.

To the critic of a philosophy, there is hardly more than one task of high importance. It is that of determining the precise point from which the theory he examines takes its departure ; for, when the central conception is clearly grasped, it will generally be found that it rules all the rest. The superstructure of philosophic edifices is usually put together in a sufficiently solid manner—it is the foundation that gives way. Hence Hegel, who, whatever may be thought of his own theory, was certainly the most profound critic of philosophy since Aristotle, generally concentrates his attack on the preliminary hypothesis. He brings down the erroneous system by removing its foundation-stone. His criticism of Spinoza, Kant, Fichte, and Schelling may almost be said to be gathered into a single sentence.

Browning has made no secret of his central conception. It is the idea of an immanent or 'immundate' love. And that love we have shown, is conceived by him as the supreme moral motive, the ultimate essence and end of all self-conscious activity, the veritable nature of both man and God.

> "Denn das Leben ist die Liebe,
> Und des Lebens Leben Geist."

His philosophy of human life rests on the idea that it is the realization of a moral purpose, which is a loving purpose. To him there is no supreme good, except good character ; and the formation of that character by man and in man is the ultimate purpose, and, therefore, the true meaning of all existence.

> "I search but cannot see
> What purpose serves the soul that strives, or world it tries
> Conclusions with, unless the fruit of victories
> Stay, one and all, stored up and guaranteed its own
> For ever, by some mode whereby shall be made known
> The gain of every life. Death reads the title clear—
> What each soul for itself conquered from out things here :
> Since, in the seeing soul, all worth lies, I assert."[1]

In this passage, Browning gives expression to an idea which continually reappears in his pages—the idea that human life, in its essence, is movement to moral goodness through opposition. His fundamental conception of the human spirit is that it is a process, and not a fixed fact. "Man," he says, "was made to grow not stop."

> "Getting increase of knowledge, since he learns
> Because he lives, which is to be a man,
> Set to instruct himself by his past self."[2]

> "By such confession straight he falls
> Into man's place, a thing nor God nor beast,
> Made to know that he can know and not more :
> Lower than God who knows all and can all,
> Higher than beasts which know and can so far
> As each beast's limit, perfect to an end,
> Nor conscious that they know, nor craving more ;
> While man knows partly but conceives beside,
> Creeps ever on from fancies to the fact,
> And in this striving, this converting air
> Into a solid he may grasp and use,
> Finds progress, man's distinctive mark alone,
> Not God's and not the beasts' : God is, they are,
> Man partly is and wholly hopes to be."[3]

[1] *Fifine at the Fair*, lv.
[2] *A Death in the Desert.*   [3] *Ibid.*

It were easy to multiply passages which show that his ultimate deliverance regarding man is, not that he is, nor that he is not, but that he is ever becoming. Man is ever at the point of contradiction between the actual and ideal, and moving from the latter to the former. Strife constitutes him. He is a war of elements; 'hurled from change to change unceasingly.' But rest is death; for it is the cessation of the spiritual activity, whose essence is acquirement, not mere possession, whether in knowledge or in goodness.

> "Man must pass from old to new,
> From vain to real, from mistake to fact,
> From what once seemed good, to what now proves best."[1]

Were the movement to stop, and the contradiction between the actual and ideal reconciled, man would leave man's estate, and pass under "angel's law."

> "Indulging every instinct of the soul
> There, where law, life, joy, impulse are one thing."[2]

But so long as he is man, he has

> "Somewhat to cast off, somewhat to become."

In *Paracelsus*, *Fifine at the Fair*, *Red Cotton Nightcap Country*, and many of his other poems, Browning deals with the problem of human life from the point of view of development. And it is this point of view, consistently held, which enables him to throw a new light on the whole subject of ethics. For, if man be veritably a being in process of evolution, if he be a permanent that always changes from earliest childhood to old age, if he be

---

[1] *A Death in the Desert.*   [2] *Ibid.*

a living thing, a potency in process of actualization, then no fixed distinctions made with reference to him can be true. If, for instance, it be asked whether man is rational or irrational, free or bound, good or evil, God or brute, the true answer, if he is veritably a being moving from ignorance to knowledge, from wickedness to virtue, from bondage to freedom, is, that he is at once neither of these alternatives and both. All hard terms of division, when applied to a subject which grows, are untrue. If the life of man is a self-enriching process, if he is *becoming* good, and rational, and free, then at no point in the movement is it possible to pass fixed and definite judgments upon him. He must be estimated by his direction and momentum, by the whence and whither of his life. There is a sense in which man is from the first and always good, rational, and free; for it is only by the exercise of reason and freedom that he exists as man. But there is also a sense in which he is none of these; for he is at the first only a potency not yet actualized. He is not rational, but becoming rational; not good, but becoming good; not free, but aspiring towards freedom. It is his prayer that "in His light he may see light truly, and in His service find perfect freedom."

In this frank assumption of the point of view of development, Browning suggests the question whether the endless debate regarding freedom, and necessity, and other moral terms, may not spring from the fact, that both of the opposing schools of ethics are fundamentally unfaithful to the subject of their inquiry. They are treating a developing reality from an abstract point of view, and taking for granted,—what cannot be true of man, if he grows in intellectual power and moral goodness— that he is *either* good or evil, *either* rational or irrational, *either* free or bond, at every moment in the process. They are treating man from a static, instead of from a kinetic point of view, and forgetting that it is his business to acquire the moral and intellectual freedom, which he has potentially from the first—

> " Some fitter way express
> Heart's satisfaction that the Past indeed
> Is past, gives way before Life's best and last,
> The all-including Future !"[1]

But, whether or not the new point of view renders some of the old disputations of ethics meaningless, it is certain that Browning viewed moral life as a growth through conflict.

> "What were life
> Did soul stand still therein, forego her strife
> Through the ambiguous Present to the goal
> Of some all-reconciling Future?"[2]

To become, to develop, to actualize by reaction against the natural and moral environment, is the meaning both of the self and of the world it works upon. 'We are here to learn the good of peace through strife, of love through hate, and reach knowledge by ignorance.'

Now, since the conception of development is a self-contradictory one, or, in other words, since it necessarily implies the conflict of the ideal and

---

[1] *Gerard de Lairesse.*　　　　　[2] *Ibid.*

actual in all life, and in every instant of its history, it remains for us to determine more fully what are the warring elements in human nature. What is the nature of this life of man which, like all life, is self-evolving ; and by conflict with what does the evolution take place? What is the ideal which condemns the actual, and yet realizes itself by means of it ; and what is the actual which wars against the ideal, and yet contains it in potency, and reaches towards it? That human life is conceived by Browning as a moral life, and not a more refined and complex form of the natural life of plants and animals—a view which finds its exponents in Herbert Spencer, and other so-called evolutionists—it is scarcely necessary to assert. It is a life which determines itself, and determines itself according to an idea of goodness. That idea, moreover, because it is a *moral ideal*, must be regarded as the conception of perfect and absolute goodness. Through the moral end, man is ideally identified with God, who, indeed, is necessarily conceived as man's moral ideal regarded as already and eternally real. 'God' and the 'moral ideal' are, in truth, expressions of the same idea ; they convey the conception of perfect goodness from different standpoints. And perfect goodness is, to Browning, limitless love. Pleasure, wisdom, power, and even the beauty which art discovers and reveals, together with every other inner quality and outer state of being, have only relative worth. "There is nothing either in the world or out of it, which is unconditionally good, except a good will," said Kant ; and a good will, according to Browning, is a will that wills lovingly. From love all other goodness is derived. There is earnest meaning, and not mere sentiment, in the poet's assertion that

> "There is no good of life but love—but love !
> What else looks good, is some shade flung from love
> Love gilds it, gives it worth. Be warned by me,
> Never you cheat yourself one instant ! Love,
> Give love, ask only love, and leave the rest."[1]

" Let man's life be true," he adds, "and love's the truth of mine." To attain this truth, that is, to constitute love into the inmost law of his being, and permanent source of all his activities, is the task of man. And Browning defines that love as

> " Yearning to dispense,
> Each soul, its own amount of gain thro' its own mode
> Of practising with life."[2]

There is no need of illustrating further the doctrine, so evident in Browning, that ' love ' is the ideal which in man's life makes through conflict for its own fulfilment. From what has been already said, it is abundantly plain that love is to him a divine element, which is at war with all that is lower in man and around him, and which by reaction against circumstance converts its own mere promise into fruition and fact. Through love man's nature reaches down to the permanent essence amid the fleeting phenomena of the world, and is at one with what is first and last. As loving he ranks with God. No words are too strong to represent the intimacy of the relation. For, however limited in range and tainted with alien qualities human love

---

[1] *In a Balcony.*   [2] *Fifine at the Fair*, lix.

may be, it is still "a pin-point rock of His boundless continent." It is not a semblance of the divine nature, an analogon, or verisimilitude, but the love of God Himself in man : so that man is in this sense an incarnation of the divine. The Godhood in him constitutes him, so that he cannot become himself, or attain his own ideal or true nature, except by becoming perfect as God is perfect.

But the emphasis thus laid on the divine worth and dignity of human love is balanced by the stress which the poet places on the frailty and finitude of every other human attribute. Having elevated the ideal, he degrades the actual. Knowledge and the intellectual energy which produces it ; art and the love of beauty from which it springs ; every power and every gift, physical and spiritual, other than love, has in it the fatal flaw of being merely human. All these are so tainted with creatureship, so limited and conditioned, that it is hardly too much to say that they are at their best, deceptive endowments. Thus, the life of man, regarded as a whole, is, in its last essence, a combination of utterly disparate elements. The distinction of the old moralists between divinity and dust ; the absolute dualism of the old ascetics between flesh and spirit, sense and reason, find their accurate parallel in Browning's teachings. But he is himself no ascetic, and the line of distinction he draws does not, like theirs, pass between the flesh and the spirit. It rather cleaves man's spiritual nature into two portions, which are absolutely different from each other. A chasm divides the head from the heart, the intellect from the motions, the moral and practical from the perceptive and reflective faculties.

It is **this absolute** cleavage that gives to Browning's teaching, both on ethics and religion, one of its **most peculiar** characteristics. By keeping it constantly in sight, we **may hope** to render intelligible to ourselves the solution he offers **of the** problem of evil, and of other fundamental difficulties in **the** life of man. For, while Browning's optimism has its original source in his conception of the unity of God and man, through the Godlike quality of love—even " the poorest love that was ever offered " —**he finds** himself **unable** to maintain it, except at the expense of degrading man's knowledge. Thus, his optimism and faith in God is finally based upon ignorance. If, on **the** side **of** love, he insists, almost **in the spirit of** a Spinozist, on God's communication of His own substance to man ; on the side of knowledge **he may** be called an agnostic, **in spite** of stray expressions which break through his deliberate theory. While " love gains God at first leap,"

> " Knowledge means
> Ever-renewed assurance by defeat
> That victory is somehow still to reach."[1]

A radical flaw runs through our knowing faculty. Human knowledge is not only incomplete—no **one** **can be so** foolish as to deny that—but it is, as regarded by Browning, essentially inadequate to the nature of fact, and we must " distrust it, even when it seems demonstrable." No professed agnostic can condemn the human intellect more utterly than he

---

[1] *A Pillar at Sebzevar.*

does. He pushes the limitedness of human knowledge into a disqualification of it to reach truth at all; and makes the conditions according to which we know, or seem to know, into a deceiving necessity, which makes us know wrongly.

> "To know of, think about,—
> Is all man's sum of faculty effects
> When exercised on earth's least atom, Son!
> What was, what is, what may such atom be?
> No answer!"[1]

Thought plays around facts, but never reaches them. Mind intervenes between itself and its objects, and throws its own shadow upon them ; nor can it penetrate through that shadow, but deals with it as if it were reality, though it knows all the time that it is not.

This theory of knowledge, or rather of nescience or no-knowledge, he gives in *La Saisiaz*, *Ferishtah's Fancies*, *The Parleyings*, and *Asolando*—in all his later and more reflective poems, in fact. It must, I think, be held to be his deliberate and final view— and all the more so, because, by a peculiar process, he gets from it his defence of his ethical and religious faith.

In the first of these poems, Browning, while discussing the problem of immortality in a purely speculative spirit, and without stipulating, " Provided answer suits my hopes, not fears," gives a tolerably full account of that which must be regarded as the principles of his theory of knowledge. Its importance to his ethical doctrine justifies a somewhat exhaustive examination of it.

[1] *A Bean-Stripe.*

He finds himself to be 'a midway point, between
a cause before and an effect behind—both blanks.'
Within that narrow space, of the self hemmed in
by two unknowns, all experience is crammed. Out
of that experience crowds all that he knows,
and all that he misknows. There issues from
experience—

> "Conjecture manifold,
> But, as knowledge, this comes only—things may be as I behold,
> Or may not be, but, without me and above me, things there are;
> I myself am what I know not—ignorance which proves no bar
> To the knowledge that I am, and, since I am, can recognize
> What to me is pain and pleasure ; that is sure, the rest—
>   surmise.
> If my fellows are or are not, what may please them and what
>   pain,—
> Mere surmise : my own experience—that is knowledge once
>   again." [1]

Experience, then, within which he (and every one
else) acknowledges that all his knowledge is confined, yields him as certain facts—the consciousness
that he is, but not what he is : the consciousness
that he is pleased or pained by things about him,
whose real nature is entirely hidden from him :
and, as he tells us just before, the assurance that
God is the thing the self perceives outside itself—

> "A force
> Actual e'er its own beginning, operative thro' its course,
> Unaffected by its end." [2]

But, even this knowledge, limited as it is to the
bare existence of unknown entities, has the further
defect of being merely subjective. The 'experi-

---

[1] *La Saisiaz.*   [2] *Ibid.*

ence' from which he draws his conclusions, is his own in an exclusive sense. His 'thinking thing' has, apparently, no elements in common with the 'thinking things' of other selves. He ignores the fact that there may be general laws of thought, according to which his mind must act in order to be a mind. Intelligence seems to have no nature, and may be anything. All questions regarding 'those apparent other mortals' are consequently unanswerable to the poet. 'Knowledge stands on my experience'; and this 'My' is totally unrelated to all other Mes.

> "All outside its narrow hem,
> Free surmise may sport and welcome! Pleasures, pains affect mankind
> Just as they affect myself? Why, here's my neighbour colour-blind,
> Eyes like mine to all appearance : 'green as grass' do I affirm?
> 'Red as grass' he contradicts me : which employs the proper term?"[1]

If there were only they two on earth as tenants, there would be no way of deciding between them ; for, according to his argument, the truth is apparently decided by majority of opinions. Each individual, equipped with his own particular kind of senses and reason, gets his own particular experience, and draws his own particular conclusions from it. If it be asked whether these conclusions are true or not, the only answer is that the question is absurd ; for, under such conditions, there cannot be either truth or error. Every one's opinion is its own criterion. Each man is the

---

[1] *La Saisiaz.*

measure of all things: "His own world for every mortal," as the poet puts it.

> "To each mortal peradventure earth becomes a new machine,
>   Pain and pleasure no more tally in our sense than red and
>   green."[1]

The first result of this subjective view of knowledge is clearly enough seen by the poet. He is well aware that his convictions regarding the high matters of human destiny are valid only for himself.

> "Only for myself I speak,
> Nowise dare to play the spokesman for my brothers strong
>   and weak."[2]

Experience, as he interprets it, that is, present consciousness, "this moment's me and mine," is too narrow a basis for any universal or objective conclusion. So far as his own inner experience of pain and pleasure goes,

> "All—for myself—seems ordered wise and well
>   Inside it,—what reigns outside, who can tell?"[3]

But as to the actual world, he can have no opinion nor from the good and evil that apparently play around him, can he deduce either

> "Praise or blame of its contriver, shown a niggard or profuse
>   In each good or evil issue."[4]

The moral government of the world is a subject regarding which we are doomed to absolute ignorance. A theory that it is ruled by the "prince of the power of the air" has just as much, and

---

[1] *La Saisiaz.*   [2] *Ibid.*   [3] *Francis Furini.*
[4] *La Saisiaz.*

just as little, validity as the more ordinary view held by religious people. Who needs be told

> "The space
> Which yields thee knowledge—do its bounds embrace
> Well-willing and wise-working, each at height?
> Enough: beyond thee lies the infinite—
> Back to thy circumscription!"[1]

And our ignorance of God, and the world, and ourselves is matched by a similar ignorance regarding moral matters.

> "Ignorance overwraps his moral sense,
> Winds him about, relaxing, as it wraps,
> So much and no more than lets through perhaps
> The murmured knowledge—' Ignorance exists.'"[2]

We cannot be certain even of the distinction and conflict of good and evil in the world. They, too, and the apparent choice between them to which man is continually constrained, may be mere illusions—phenomena of the individual consciousness. What remains, then? Nothing but to " wait."

> "Take the joys and bear the sorrows—neither with extreme
>   concern !
> Living here means nescience simply . 'tis next life that
>   helps to learn."[3]

It is hardly necessary to enter upon any detailed criticism of such a theory of knowledge as this which is proffered by the poet. It is well known by all those who are in some degree acquainted with the history of philosophy—and it will be easily seen by all who have any critical acumen—

<hr>

[1] *Francis Furini.*   [2] *Ibid.*   [3] *La Saisiaz.*

that it leads directly into absolute scepticism. And absolute scepticism is easily shown to be self-contradictory. For a theory of nescience, in condemning all knowledge and the faculty of knowledge, condemns itself. If nothing is true, or if nothing is known, then this theory itself is not true, or its truth cannot be known. And if this theory is true, then nothing is true ; for this theory, like all others, is the product of a defective intelligence. In whatsoever way the matter is put, there is left no standing-ground for the human critic who condemns human thought. And he cannot well pretend to a footing in a sphere above man's, or below it. There is thus one pre-supposition which every one must make, if he is to propound any doctrine whatsoever, even if that doctrine be that no doctrine can be valid ; it is the presupposition that knowledge is possible, and that truth can be known. And this presupposition fills, for modern philosophy, the place of the *Cogito ergo sum* of Descartes. It is the starting-point and criterion of all knowledge.

It is, at first sight, a somewhat difficult task to account for the fact that so keen an intellect as the poet's did not perceive the conclusion to which his theory of knowledge so directly and necessarily leads. It is probable, however, that he never criti-cally examined it, but simply accepted it as equivalent to the common doctrine of the relativity of knowledge, which, in some form or other, all the schools of philosophy adopt. But the main reason will be found to lie in the fact that know-ledge was not, to Browning, its own criterion or end. The primary fact of his philosophy is that human life is a moral process. His interest in the evolution of character was his deepest interest, as he informs us; he was an ethical teacher rather than a metaphysician. He is ever willing to asperse man's intelligence. But that man is a moral agent he will in no wise doubt. This is his

> "Solid standing-place amid
> The wash and welter, whence all doubts are bid
> Back to the ledge they break against in foam."[1]

His practical maxim was

> "Wholly distrust thy knowledge then, and trust
> As wholly love allied to ignorance!
> There lies thy truth and safety."[2]

All phenomena must, in some way or other, be reconciled by the poet with the fundamental and indubitable fact of the progressive moral life of man. For the fundamental presupposition which a man makes, is necessarily his criterion of knowledge, and it determines the truth or illusoriness of all other opinions whatsoever.

Now, Browning held, not only that no certain knowledge is attainable by man, but also that such certainty is incompatible with moral life. Absolute knowledge would, he contends, lift man above the need and the possibility of making the moral choice, which is our supreme business on earth. Man can be good or evil, only on condition of being in absolute uncertainty regarding the true meaning of the facts of nature and the phenomena of life.

---

[1] *Francis Furini.* [2] *A Pillar at Sebzevar.*

This somewhat strange doctrine finds the most explicit and full expression in *La Saisiaz*. 'Fancy,' amongst the concessions it demands from 'Reason,' claims that man should *know*—not merely surmise or fear—that every action done in this life awaits its proper and necessary meed in the next.

> "I also will that man become aware
> Life has worth incalculable, every moment that he spends
> So much gain or loss for that next life which on this life
>   depends."[1]

But Reason refuses the concession, upon the ground that such sure knowledge would be destructive of the very distinction between right and wrong, which the demand implies. The " promulgation of this decree," by Fancy, " makes both good and evil to cease." Prior to it "earth was man's probation-place"; but under this decree man is no longer free; for certain knowledge makes man's action necessary action.

> "Once lay down the law, with Nature's simple 'Such effects
>   succeed
>   Causes such, and heaven or hell depends upon man's
>   earthly deed
>   Just as surely as depends the straight or else the crooked
>   line
>   On his making point meet point or with or else without
>   incline,'
>   Thenceforth neither good nor evil does man, doing what
>   he must."[2]

If we presuppose that " man, addressed this mode, be sound and sane " (and we must stipulate sanity, if his actions are to be morally judged at

---

[1] *La Saisiaz.*   [2] *Ibid.* 195.

all)—then **a law** which binds punishment and reward **to action in a necessary** manner, and is known so to bind them, would "obtain prompt and absolute obedience." There are some "edicts, now styled God's, now nature's," "which to hear means to obey." All the laws relating to the preservation of life are of this **character.** And, if the law—"Would'st thou live again, be just "— were in all ways as stringent as the other law—

"Would'st thou live now, regularly draw thy breath!
 For, suspend the operation, straight law's breach results in
     death "—[1]

then no one would disobey it, nor could. "It is the liberty of doing evil that gives the doing good a grace." And that liberty would be taken away by complete assurance that effects follow actions in the moral world with the necessity seen in the natural sphere. Since, therefore, man is made to grow, and earth is the place wherein he is to pass probation and prove his powers, there must remain a certain doubt as to the issues of his actions ; conviction must not be so strong as to carry with it man's whole nature, "The best I both see and praise, the worst I follow," is the adage rife in man's mouth regarding his moral conduct. But, spite of his seeing and praising,

"he disbelieves
In the heart of him that edict which for truth his head receives."[2]

He has a dim consciousness of ways whereby he may elude the consequences of his wickedness, and of the possibility of making amends to law.

[1] *La Saisiaz.*   [2] *Ibid.*

> " And now, auld Cloots, I ken ye're thinkin',
> A certain Bardie's rantin', drinkin',
> Some luckless hour will send him linkin'
>   To your black pit ;
> But, faith he'll turn a corner jinkin',
>   And cheat you yet."

The more orthodox and less generous individual is prone to agree, as regards himself, with Burns ; but, he sees, most probably, that such an escape is impossible to others. He has secret solacement in a latent belief that he himself is an exception. There will be a special method of dealing with him. He is a 'chosen sample'; and 'God will think twice before he damns a man of his quality.' It is just because there is such doubt as to the universality and necessity of the law which connects actions and consequences in the moral sphere, that man's deeds have an ethical character ; while, to disperse doubt and ignorance by the assurance of complete knowledge, would take the good from goodness and the ill from evil.

In this ingenious manner, the poet turns the imperfect intellect and delusive knowledge of man to a moral use. Ordinarily, the intellectual impotence of man is regarded as carrying with it moral incapacity as well, and the delusiveness of knowledge is one of the strongest arguments for pessimism. To persons pledged to the support of no theory, and to those who have the *naïveté*, so hard to maintain side by side with strong doctrinal convictions, it seems amongst the worst of evils that man should be endowed with fallacious faculties, and cursed with a futile desire for true knowledge which is so strong that it cannot be quenched even in those who believe that truth can never be attained. It is the very best men of the world who cry

> "Oh, this false for real,
> This emptiness which feigns solidity,—
> Ever some grey that's white, and dun that's black,—
> When shall we rest upon the thing itself,
> Not on its semblance? Soul—too weak, forsooth,
> To cope with fact—wants fiction everywhere!
> Mine tires of falsehood: truth at any cost!"[1]

The poet himself was burdened in no small degree with this vain desire for knowing the truth; and he recognized, too, that he was placed in a world which seems both real and beautiful, and well worth knowing. Yet, it is this very failure of knowledge—a failure which, be it remembered, is complete and absolute, because, as he thinks, all facts must turn into phantoms by mere contact with our 'relative intelligences,'—which he constitutes into the basis of his optimistic faith.

So high is the dignity and worth of the moral life to Browning, that no sacrifice is too great to secure it. And, indeed, if it were once clearly recognized that there is no good thing but goodness, nothing of supreme worth except the realization of a loving will, then doubt, ignorance, and every other form of apparent evil would be fully justified—provided they were conditions whereby this highest good is attained. And, to Browning, ignorance was one of the conditions. And, consequently, the dread pause in the music which

[1] *A Bean-Stripe.*

agnosticism brings, is only 'silence implying sound'; and the vain cry for truth, arising from the heart of the earth's best men, is only a discord moving towards resolution into the more rapturous harmony of moral goodness.

I do not stay here to inquire whether sure knowledge would really have this disastrous effect of destroying morality, or whether its failure does not rather imply the impossibility of a moral life. I return to the question asked at the beginning of this chapter, and which it is now possible to answer. That question was: How does Browning reconcile his hypothesis of universal love with the natural and moral evils existing in the world?

His answer is quite explicit. The poet solves the problem by casting doubt upon the facts which threaten his hypothesis. He reduces them into phenomena, in the sense of phantoms begotten by the human intellect upon unknown and unknowable realities.

> "Thus much at least is clearly understood—
> Of power does Man possess no particle:
> Of knowledge—just so much as shows that still
> It ends in ignorance on every side."[1]

He is aware of the phenomena of his own consciousness,

> "My soul, and my soul's home,
> This body";

but he knows not whether 'things outside are fact or feigning.' And he heeds little, for in either case they

[1] *Francis Furini.*

> "Teach
> What good is and what evil,—just the same,
> Be feigning or be fact the teacher."[1]

It is the mixture, or rather the apparent mixture, of shade and light in life, the conflict of seeming good with seeming evil in the world, that constitutes the world a probation-place. The world is a kind of moral gymnasium, crowded with phantoms, wherein by exercise man makes moral muscle. And the vigour of the athlete's struggle is not in the least abated by the consciousness that all he deals with are phantoms.

> "I have lived, then, done and suffered, loved and hated, learnt
>   and taught
> This—there is no reconciling wisdom with a world distraught,
> Goodness with triumphant evil, power with failure in the aim,
> If—(to my own sense, remember! though none other feel the
>   same!)
> If you bar me from assuming earth to be a pupil's place,
> And life, time—with all their chances, changes,—just pro-
>   bation-space,
> Mine, for me."[2]

And the world would not be such a probation-space did we once penetrate into its inmost secret, and know its phenomena as veritably either good or evil. There is the need of playing something perilously like a trick on the human intellect, if man is to strive and grow.

> "Here and there a touch
> Taught me, betimes, the artifice of things—
> That all about, external to myself,
> Was meant to be suspected,—not revealed
> Demonstrably a cheat—but half seen through."[3]

[1] *Francis Furini.*　　　[2] *La Saisiaz.*　　　[3] *A Bean-Stripe.*

To know objects as they veritably are, might reveal
all things as locked together in a scheme of universal good, so that "white would rule unchecked
along the line." But this would be the greatest of
disasters ; for, as moral agents, we cannot do
without

> "the constant shade
> Cast on life's shine,—the tremor that intrudes
> When firmest seems my faith in white."[1]

The intellectual insight that would penetrate through
the vari-colour of events into the actual presence
of the incandescent white of love, which glows, as
hope tells us, in all things, would stultify itself,
and lose its knowledge even of the good.

> "Think !
> Could I see plain, be somehow certified
> All was illusion—-evil far and wide
> Was good disguised,—why, out with one huge wipe
> Goes knowledge from me. Type needs antitype :
> As night needs day, as shine needs shade, so good
> Needs evil : how were pity understood
> Unless by pain ?"[2]

Good and evil are relative to each other, and each
is known only through its contrary.

> "For me
> (Patience, beseech you !) Knowledge can but be
> Of good by knowledge of good's opposite—
> Evil."[3]

The extinction of one of the terms would be the
extinction of the other. And, in a similar manner,
clear knowledge that evil is illusion and that all

---

[1] *A Bean-Stripe.*　　　[2] *Francis Furini.*　　　[3] *Ibid.*

things have their place in an infinite divine order would paralyze all moral effort, as well as stultify itself.

> "Make evident that pain
> Permissibly masks pleasure—you abstain
> From out-stretch of the finger-tip that saves
> A drowning fly."[1]

Certainty on either side, either that evil is evil for evermore, irredeemable and absolute, a drench of utter dark not illuminable by white; or that it is but mere show and semblance, which the good takes upon itself, would alike be ruinous to man. For both alternatives would render all striving folly. The right attitude for man is that of ignorance, complete uncertainty, the equipoise of conflicting alternatives. He must take his stand on the contradiction. Hope he may have that all things work together for good. It is right that he should nourish the faith that the antagonism of evil with good in the world is only an illusion; but that faith must stop short of the complete conviction that knowledge would bring. When, therefore, the hypothesis of universal love is confronted with the evils of life, and we ask how it can be maintained in the face of the manifold miseries everywhere apparent, the poet answers, 'You do not know, and cannot know, whether they are evils or not. Your knowledge remains at the surface of things. You cannot fit them into their true place, or pronounce upon their true purpose and character; for you see only a small

[1] *Francis Furini.*

arc of the complete circle of being. Wait till you see more, and, in the meantime, hope!'

> "Why faith—but to lift the load,
>   To leaven the lump, where lies
>   Mind prostrate through knowledge owed
>   To the loveless Power it tries
>   **To withstand, how** vain!"[1]

And, if we reply in turn, that **this** necessary ignorance leaves **as** little room for his scheme of love as it does for its opposite, he again answers: 'Not so! I appeal from the intellect, which is detected as incompetent, to the higher court of the moral consciousness. And there I find the ignorance to be justified: for it is the instrument of **a** higher purpose, a means whereby what is best is gained, namely, Love.'

> **"My curls were crowned**
> **In youth with** knowledge,—off, alas, crown slipped
> Next moment, pushed by better knowledge still
> Which nowise proved more constant: gain, to-day,
> Was toppling loss to morrow, lay at last
> —Knowledge, the golden?—lacquered ignorance!
> **As** gain—mistrust it! Not as means to gain:
> Lacquer **we learn by:** . . . .
> The prize is in the process: knowledge means
> **Ever-renewed** assurance by defeat
> **That victory is** somehow still to reach,
> **But love is victory, the** prize itself:
> Love—trust to! Be rewarded for the trust
> In trust's mere act."[2]

Now, in order to complete our examination of this theory, we must follow the poet in his attempt

---

[1] *Reverie—Asolando.*   [2] *A Pillar at Sebzevar*

to escape from the testimony of the intellect to that of the heart. In order to make the most of the latter we find that Browning, especially in his last work, tends to withdraw his accusation of utter incompetence on the part of the intellect. He only tends to do so, it is true. He is tolerably consistent in asserting that we know our own emotions and the phenomena of our own consciousness; but he is not consistent in his account of our knowledge, or ignorance, of external things. On the whole, he asserts that we know nothing of them. But in *Asolando* he seems to imply that the evidence of a loveless power in the world, permitting evil, is irresistible.[1] To say the least, the testimony of the intellect, such as it is, is more clear and convincing with regard to evil than it is with regard to good. Within the sphere of phenomena, to which the intellect is confined, there seems to be, instead of a benevolent purpose, a world ruled by a power indifferent to the triumph of evil over good, and either 'loveless' or unintelligent.

> "Life from birth to death,
> Means—either looking back on harm escaped,
> Or looking forward to that harm's return
> With tenfold power of harming."[2]

And it is not possible for man to contravene this evidence of faults and omissions: for, in doing so, he would remove the facts in reaction against which his moral nature becomes active. What proof is there, then, that the universal love is

---

[1] *See passage just quoted.*   [2] *A Bean-Stripe.*

also no mere dream? None! from the side of
the intellect, answers the poet. Man, who has the
will to remove the ills of life,

> "Stop change, avert decay,
>   Fix life fast, banish death,"[1]

has not the power to effect his will; while the
Power, whose limitlessness he recognizes everywhere around him, merely maintains the world in
its remorseless course, and puts forth no helping
hand when good is prone and evil triumphant.
'God does nothing.'

> "'No sign,'—groaned he,—
> 'No stirring of God's finger to denote
>   He wills that right should have supremacy
>   On earth, not wrong! How helpful could we quote
>   But one poor instance when He interposed
>   Promptly and surely and beyond mistake
>   Between oppression and its victim, closed
>   Accounts with sin for once, and bade us wake
>   From our long dream that justice bears no sword,
>   Or else forgets whereto its sharpness serves.'"[2]

But he tells us in his later poems, that there is no
answer vouchsafed to man's cry to the Power, that
it should reveal

> "What heals all harm,
>   Nay, hinders the harm at first,
>   Saves earth."[3]

And yet, so far as man can see, there were no
bar to the remedy, if 'God's all-mercy' did really
'mate his all-potency.'

---

[1] *Reverie—Asolando.*   [2] *Bernard de Mandeville.*
        [3] *Reverie—Asolando.*

> " How **easy** it seems,—to sense
>   Like man's—if somehow met
> Power with its match—immense
>   **Love,** limitless, unbeset
> By hindrance on every side." [1]

But that love nowhere makes itself evident. "Power," we recognize,

> " Finds nought too hard,
>   Fulfilling itself all ways,
> Unchecked, unchanged ; while barred,
>   Baffled, what good began,
> Ends evil on every side." [2]

Thus, the conclusion to which knowledge inevitably leads us is that mere power rules.

> " No more than **the** passive clay
>   Disputes the potter's act,
> Could the whelmed mind disobey
>   Knowledge, the cataract." [3]

But if the intellect is thus overwhelmed, so as to be almost passive to the pessimistic conclusion borne in upon it by 'resistless fact,' the heart of man is made of another mould. It revolts against the conclusion of the intellect, and climbs

> " Through turbidity all between,
>   From the known to the unknown **here,**
> Heaven's ' Shall be,' from earth's ' Has **been.**' " [4]

It grasps a fact beyond the reach of knowledge, namely, the possibility, or even the certainty, that 'power is love.' At present there is no substantiating by knowledge the testimony of the heart ; and man has no better anchorage for his

[1] *Reverie—Asolando* [2] *Ibid.* [3] *Ibid.* [4] *Ibid.*

optimism than faith. But the closer view will come, when even our life on earth will be seen to have within it the working of love, no less manifest than that of power.

> "When see? When there dawns a day,
>   If not on the homely earth,
> Then, yonder, worlds away,
>   Where the strange and new have birth,
> And Power comes full in play."[1]

Now, what is this evidence of the heart, which is sufficiently cogent and valid to counterpoise that of the mind ; and which gives to 'faith,' or 'hope,' a firm foothold in the very face of the opposing 'resistless' testimony of knowledge?

Within our experience, to which the poet knows we are entirely confined, there is a fact, the significance of which we have not as yet examined. For, plain and irresistible as is the evidence of evil, so plain and constant is man's recognition of it as evil, and his desire to annul it. If man's mind is made to acknowledge evil, his moral nature is made so as to revolt against it.

> "Man's heart *is made* to judge
> Pain deserved no-where by the common flesh
> Our birth-right—bad and good deserve alike
> No pain to human apprehension."[2]

Owing to the limitation of our intelligence, we cannot deny but that

> "In the eye of God
> Pain may have purpose and be justified."

---

[1] *Reverie—Asolando.*
[2] *Mihrab Shah—Ferishtah's Fancies.*

But whether it has its purpose for the supreme intelligence or not,

> "Man's sense avails to only see, in pain,
>   A hateful chance no man but would avert
>   Or, failing, needs must pity."[1]

Man must condemn evil; he cannot acquiesce in its permanence, but is, spite of his consciousness of ignorance and powerlessness, roused into constant revolt against it.

> "True, he makes nothing, understands no whit:
>   Had the initiator-spasm seen fit
>   Thus doubly to endow him, none the worse
>   And much the better were the universe.
>   What does Man see or feel or apprehend
>   Here, there, and everywhere, but faults to mend,
>   Omissions to supply,—one wide disease
>   Of things that are, which Man at once would ease
>   Had will but power and knowledge?"[2]

But the moral worth of man does not suffer the least detraction from his inability to effect his benevolent purpose. "Things must take will for deed," as Browning tells us. David is not at all distressed by the consciousness of his weakness.

> "Why is it I dare
>   Think but lightly of such impuissance? What stops my
>   despair?
>   This;—'tis not what man Does which exalts him, but what
>   man Would do."[3]

The fact that 'his wishes fall through,' that he cannot, although willing, help Saul, "grow poor to

---

[1] *Mihrab Shah—Ferishtah's Fancies.*
[2] *Francis Furini.*   [3] *Saul.*

enrich him, fill up his life by starving his own,' does not prevent him from regarding his 'service as perfect.' The will was there, although it lacked power to effect itself. The moral worth of an action is complete, if it is willed, and is in nowise affected by its outer consequences—as both Browning and Kant teach. The loving will, the inner act of loving, though it can bear no outward fruit, being debarred by outward impediment, is still a complete and highest good.

> "But Love is victory, the prize itself:
> Love—trust to! Be rewarded for the trust
> In trust's mere act. In love success is sure
> Attainment—no delusion, whatsoe'er
> The prize be: apprehended as a prize,
> A prize it is."[1]

Whatever the evil in the world and the impotence of man, his duty and his dignity in willing to perform it, are ever the same. Though God neglect the world

> "Man's part
> Is plain—to send love forth,—astray, perhaps:
> No matter, he has done his part."[2]

Now, this fact of inner experience, which the poet thinks incontrovertible—the fact that man, every man, necessarily regards evil, whether natural or moral, as something to be annulled, were it only possible—is an immediate proof of the indwelling of that which is highest in man. On this basis, Browning is able to re-establish the optimism which, from the side of knowledge, he had utterly abandoned.

---

[1] *A Pillar at Sebzevar.*   [2] *The Sun.*

The very fact that the world is condemned by man is proof that there dwells in man something better than the world, whose evidence the pessimist himself cannot escape. All is not wrong, as long as wrong *seems* wrong. The pessimist, in condemning the world, must except himself. In his very charge against God of having made man in His anger, there lies a contradiction ; for he himself fronts and defies the outrage. There is no depth of despair which this good cannot illumine with joyous light, for the despair is itself the reflex of the good.

> "Were earth and all it holds illusions mere,
> Only a machine for teaching love and hate, and hope and fear,
>
> "If this life's conception new life fail to realize—
> Though earth burst and proved a bubble glassing hues of
> hell, one huge
> Reflex of the devil's doings—God's work by no subterfuge,"[1]

still, good is good, and love is its own exceeding great reward. Alone, in a world abandoned to chaos and infinite night, man is still not without God, if he loves. In virtue of his love, he himself would be crowned as God, as the poet often argues, were there no higher love elsewhere.

> "If he believes
> Might can exist with neither will nor love,
> In God's case—what he names now Nature's Law—
> While in himself he recognizes love
> No less than might and will,"[2]

man takes, and rightly takes, the title of being 'First, last, and best of things.'

[1] *La Saisiaz.*　　　　[2] *A Death in the Desert.*

" Since if man prove the sole existent thing
  Where these combine, whatever their degree,
  However weak the might or will or love,
  So they be found there, put in evidence—
  He is as surely higher in the scale
  Than any might with neither love nor will,
  As life, apparent in the poorest midge,
  Is marvellous beyond dead Atlas' self,
  Given to the nobler midge for resting-place !
  Thus, man proves best and highest—God, in fine." [1]

To any one capable of spiritually discerning things, there can be no difficulty in regarding goodness, however limited and mated with weakness, as infinitely above all natural power. Divinity will be known to consist, not in any senseless might, however majestic and miraculous, but in moral or spiritual perfection. If God were indifferent to the evil of the world, acquiesced in it without reason, and let it ripen into all manner of wretchedness, then man, in condemning the world, though without power to remove the least of its miseries, would be higher than God. But we have still to account for the possibility of man's assuming an attitude implied both in the opinion that, while he himself is without power, God is without pity, and also in the despair which springs from his hate of evil. How comes it that human nature rises above its origin, and is able—nay, obliged—to condemn the evil which God permits ? Is man finite in power, a mere implement of a mocking will, so far as knowledge goes ; is he the plaything of remorseless forces, and yet author and first source of

<hr>

[1] *A Death in the Desert.*

something in himself which invests him with a dignity that God Himself cannot share? Is the moral consciousness which, by its very nature, must bear witness against the Power, although it cannot arrest its pitiless course, or remove the least evil,

> "Man's own work, his birth of heart and brain,
>   His native grace, no alien gift at all?"

We are thus caught between the horns of a final dilemma. Either the pity and love, which make man revolt against all suffering, are man's own creation; or else God, who made man's heart to love, has given to man something higher than He owns Himself. But both of these alternatives are impossible.

> "Here's the touch that breaks the bubble."

The first alternative is impossible, because man is by definition powerless, a mere link in the endless chain of causes, incapable of changing the least part of the scheme of things which he condemns, and therefore much more unable to initiate, or to bring into a loveless world abandoned to blind power, the noble might of love.

> "Will of man create?
> No more than this my hand, which strewed the beans,
>   Produced them also from its finger-tips."[1]

All that man is and has is a mere loan; his love, no less than his finite intellect and limited power, has had its origin elsewhere.

> "Back goes creation to its source, source prime
>   And ultimate, the single and the sole."[2]

[1] *A Bean-Stripe.*   [2] *Ibid.*

The argument ends by bringing us back

> "To the starting-point,—
> Man's impotency, God's omnipotence,
> These stop my answer."[1]

I shall not pause at present to examine the value of this new form of the old argument, "*Ex contingentia mundi*." But I may point out in passing, that the reference of human love to a divine creative source is accomplished by means of the idea of cause, one of the categories of that thought which Browning has aspersed. And it is a little difficult to show why, if we are constrained to doubt our thought, when by the aid of causality it establishes a connection between finite and finite, we should regard it as worthy of trust when it connects the finite and the infinite. In fact, it is all too evident that the poet assumes or denies the possibility of knowledge, according as it helps or hinders his ethical doctrine.

But, if we grant the ascent from the finite to the infinite, and regard man's love as a divine gift—which it may well be, although the poet's argument is invalid—then a new light is thrown upon the Being who gave man this power to love. The 'necessity,' 'the mere power,' which alone could be discerned by observation of the irresistible movement of the world's events, acquires a new character. Prior to this discovery of love in man as the work of God—

> "Head praises, but heart refrains
> From loving's acknowledgment.

[1] *A Bean-Stripe.*

> Whole losses outweigh half-gains :
> Earth's good is with evil blent :
> God struggles, but evil reigns."[1]

But love in man is a suggestion of a love without; a proof in fact, that God is love, for man's love is God's love in man. The source of the pity that man shows, and of the apparent evils in the world which excite it, is the same. The Power which called man into being, itself rises up in man against the wrongs in the world. The voice of the moral consciousness, approving the good, condemning evil, and striving to annul it, is the voice of God, and has therefore supreme authority. We err, therefore, in thinking that it is the weakness of man which is matched against the might of evil in the world, and that we are fighting a losing battle. It is an incomplete, abstract, untrue view of the facts of life which puts God as irresistible Power in the outer world, and forgets that the same irresistible Power works under the higher form of love, in the human heart.

> "Is not God now i' the world His power first made?
> Is not His love at issue still with sin,
> Visibly when a wrong is done on earth?
> Love, wrong, and pain, what see I else around?"[2]

In this way, therefore, the poet argues back from the moral consciousness of man to the goodness of God. And he finds the ultimate proof of this goodness in the very pessimism and scepticism and despair that come with the view of the apparently infinite waste in the world and the endless miseries

[1] *Reverie—Asolando.*   [2] *A Death in the Desert.*

of humanity. The source of this despair, namely, the recognition of evil and wrong, is just the God-hood in man. There is no way of accounting for the fact that 'Man hates what is and loves what should be,' except by 'blending the quality of man with the quality of God.' And 'the quality of God' is the fundamental fact in man's history. Love is the last reality the poet always reaches. Beneath the pessimism is love : without love of the good there were no recognition of evil, no condemnation of it, and no despair.

But the difficulty still remains as to the permission of evil, even though it should prove in the end to be merely apparent.

> "Wherefore should any evil hap to man—
> From ache of flesh to agony of soul—
> Since God's All-mercy mates All-potency?
> Nay, why permits He evil to Himself—
> Man's sin accounted such? Suppose a world
> Purged of all pain, with fit inhabitant—
> Man pure of evil in thought, word, and deed—
> Were it not well? Then, wherefore otherwise?"[1]

The poet finds an answer to this difficulty in the very nature of moral goodness, which, as we have seen, he regards as a progressive realization of an infinitely high ideal. The demand for a world purged of all pain and sin is really, he teaches us, a demand for a sphere where

> "Time brings
> No hope, no fear: as to-day, shall be
> To-morrow: advance or retreat need we
> At our stand-still through eternity?"[2]

[1] *Mihrab Shah.*   [2] *Rephan—Asolando.*

What were there to 'bless or curse, in such a
uniform universe,'

> "Where weak and strong,
> The wise and the foolish, right and wrong,
> Are merged alike in a neutral Best." [1]

There is a better way of life, thinks Browning, than
such a state of stagnation.

> "Why should I speak? You divine the test.
> When the trouble grew in my pregnant breast
> A voice said, So would'st thou strive, not rest,
>
> "Burn and not smoulder, win by worth,
> Not rest content with a wealth that's dearth,
> Thou art past Rephan, thy place be Earth." [2]

The discontent of man, the consciousness of sin,
evil, pain, is a symbol of promotion. The peace
of the state of nature has been broken for him ;
and, although the first consequence be

> "Brow-furrowed old age, youth's hollow cheek,—
> Diseased in the body, sick in soul,
> Pinched poverty, satiate wealth,—your whole
> Array of despairs," [3]

still, without them, the best is impossible. They
are the conditions of the moral life, which is
essentially progressive. They are the consequences
of the fact that man has been "startled up"

> "by an Infinite
> Discovered above and below me—height
> And depth alike to attract my flight,
>
> "Repel my descent : by hate taught love.
> Oh, gain were indeed to see above
> Supremacy ever—to move, remove,

[1] *Rephan—Asolando.* [2] *Ibid.* [3] *Ibid.*

> "Not reach—aspire yet never attain
> To the object aimed at."[1]

He who places rest above effort, Rephan above the earth, places a natural good above a moral good, stagnation above progress. The demand for the absolute extinction of evil betrays ignorance of the nature of the highest good. For right and wrong are relative. "Type needs antitype." The fact that goodness is best, and that goodness is not a stagnant state but a progress, a gradual realization, though never complete, of an infinite ideal, of the perfection of God by a finite being, necessarily implies the consciousness of sin and evil. As a moral agent man must set what should be above what is. If he is to aspire and attain, the actual present must seem to him inadequate, imperfect, wrong—a state to be abolished in favour of a better. And therefore it follows that

> "Though wrong were right
> Could we but know—still wrong must needs seem wrong
> To do right's service, prove men weak or strong,
> Choosers of evil or good."[2]

The apparent existence of evil is the condition of goodness. And yet it must only be apparent. For if evil be regarded as veritably evil, it must remain so for all that man can do; he cannot annihilate any fact or change its nature, and all effort would, therefore, be futile. And, on the other hand, if evil were known as unreal, then there were no need of moral effort, no quarrel with the present, and therefore no aspiration and no achievement. That

---

[1] *Rephan—Asolando.*   [2] *Francis Furini.*

which is man's highest and best—namely, a moral life, which is a progress—would thus be impossible, and his existence would be bereft of all meaning and purpose. And if the highest is impossible then all is wrong, 'the goal being a ruin, so is all the rest.'

The hypothesis of the moral life as progressive is essential to Browning.

But if this hypothesis be granted, then all difficulties disappear. The conception of the endless acquirement of goodness at once postulates the consciousness of evil, and the consciousness of it as existing in order to be overcome. Hence the consciousness of it as illusion comes nearest to the truth. And such a conception is essentially implied in the idea of morality. To speculative reason, however, it is impossible, as the poet believes, that evil should thus be at the same time regarded as both real and unreal. Knowledge leads to despair on every side; for, whether it takes the evil in the world as seeming or actual, it stultifies effort, and proves that moral progress, which is best of all things, is impossible. But the moral consciousness derives its vitality from this contradiction. It is the meeting point and conflict of actual and ideal; and its testimony is indisputable, however inconsistent it may be with that of knowledge. Acknowledging absolute ignorance of the outer world, the poet has still a retreat within himself, safe from all doubt. He has in his own inner experience irrefragable proof.

> "How things outside, fact or feigning, teach
> What good is and what evil—just the same,
> Be feigning or be fact the teacher."[1]

[1] *Francis Furini.*

The consciousness of being taught goodness by interaction with the outside unknown is sufficient; it is 'a point of vantage' whence he will not be moved by any contradictions that the intellect may conjure up against it. And this process of learning goodness, this gradual realization by man of an ideal infinitely high and absolute in worth, throws back a light which illumines all the pain and strife and despair, and shows them all to be steps in the endless 'love-way.' The consciousness of evil is thus at once the effect and the condition of goodness. The unrealized, though ever realizing good, which brings despair, is the best fact in man's history; and rightly it should bring, not despair, but endless joy.

CHAPTER IX

A CRITICISM OF BROWNING'S VIEW OF THE FAILURE OF KNOWLEDGE

"Der Mensch, da er Geist ist, darf und soll sich selbst des höchsten würdig achten, von der Grösse und Macht seines Geistes kann er nicht gross genug denken ; und mit diesem Glauben wird nichts so spröde und hart seyn, das sich ihm nicht eröffnete. Das zuerst verborgene und verschlossene Wesen des Universums hat keine Kraft, die dem Muthe des Erkennens Widerstand leisten könnte: es muss sich vor ihm aufthun, und seinen Reichtbum und seine Tiefen ihm vor Augen legen und zum Genusse geben."[1]

BEFORE entering upon a criticism of Browning's theory, as represented in the last chapter, it may be well to give a brief summary of it.

The most interesting feature of Browning's proof of his optimistic faith is his appeal from the intelligence to the moral consciousness. To show theoretically that evil is merely phenomenal is, in his view, both impossible and undesirable. It is impossible, because the human intellect is incapable of knowing anything as it really is, or of pronouncing

[1] *Hegel's Inaugural Address at Heidelberg.*

upon the ultimate nature of any phenomenon. It is undesirable, because a theoretical proof of the evanescence of evil would itself give rise to the greatest of all evils. The best thing in the world is moral character. Man exists in order to grow better, and the world exists in order to help him. But moral growth is possible only through conflict against evil, or what seems to be evil ; hence, to disprove the existence of evil would be to take away the possibility of learning goodness, to stultify all human effort, and to deprive the world of its meaning.

But, if an optimistic doctrine cannot be reached by way of speculative thought, if the intellect of man cannot see the good in things evil, his moral consciousness guarantees that all is for the best, and that " the good is all in all." For, in distinguishing between good and evil, the moral consciousness sets up an ideal over against the actual. It conceives of a scheme of goodness which is not realized in the world, and it condemns the world as it is. Man, as moral being, is so constituted that he cannot but regard the evil in the world as something to be annulled. If he had only the power, there would be no pain, no sorrow, no weakness, no failure, no death. Is man, then, better than the Power which made the world and let woe gain entrance into it ? No ! answers the poet ; for man himself is part of that world and the product of that Power. The Power that made the world also made the moral consciousness which condemns the world ; if it is the source of the evil in the world, it is also the source of that love in man, which, by self-expenditure, seeks to remedy it. If the external world is merely an expression of a remorseless Power, whence comes the love which is the principle of the moral life in man? The same Power brings the antidote as well as the bane. And, further, the bane exists for the sake of the antidote, the wrong for the sake of the remedy. The evil in the world is means to a higher good, and the only means possible; for it calls into activity the divine element in man, and thereby contributes to its realization in his character. It gives the necessary opportunity for the exercise of love.

Hence, evil cannot be regarded as ultimately real. It is real only as a stage in growth, as means to an end; and the means necessarily perishes, or is absorbed in, the attainment of the end. It has no significance except by reference to that end. From this point of view, evil is the resistance which makes progress possible, the negative which gives meaning to the positive, the darkness that makes day beautiful. This must not, however, be taken to mean that evil is nothing. It *is* resistance; it *is* a negative; it does oppose the good, although its opposition is finally overcome. If it did not, if evil were unreal, there would be no possibility of calling forth the moral potency of man, and the moral life would be a figment. But these two conditions of the moral life—on the one hand, that the evil of the world must be capable of being overcome, and is there for the purpose of being overcome, and that it is unreal except as a means to the good; and, on the other hand, that evil must be actually opposed to the good, if the good is to have any meaning,—cannot, Browning thinks, be reconciled with each other. It is manifest that the intellect of man cannot, at the same time, regard evil as both real and unreal. It must assert the one and deny the other ; or else we must regard its testimony as altogether untrustworthy. But the first alternative is destructive of the moral consciousness. Moral life is alike impossible whether we deny or assert the real existence of evil. The latter alternative stultifies knowledge, and leaves all the deeper concerns of life—the existence of good and evil, the reality of the distinction between them, the existence of God, the moral governance of the world, the destiny of man—in a state of absolute uncertainty. We must reject the testimony either of the heart or of the head.

Browning, as we have seen, unhesitatingly adopts the latter alternative. He remains loyal to the deliverances of his moral consciousness, and accepts as equally valid, beliefs which the intellect finds to be self-contradictory : holding that knowledge on such matters is impossible. And he rejects this knowledge, not only because our thoughts are self-contradictory in themselves, but because the failure of a speculative solution of these problems is necessary to morality. Clear, convincing, demonstrative knowledge would destroy morality ; and the fact that the power to attain such knowledge has been withheld from us is to be regarded rather as an indication of the beneficence of God, who has not held even ignorance to be too great a price for man to pay for goodness.

Knowledge is not the fit atmosphere for morality.

R

It is faith and not reason, hope and trust but not
certainty, that lend **vigour** to the good life. We
may believe, and **rejoice in the** belief, that the
absolute good is fulfilling itself in all things, and
that even the miseries of life are really its refracted
rays—the light that gains in splendour by being
broken. But we must not, and, indeed, cannot
ascend from faith to knowledge. **The heart** may
trust, and must trust, if it faithfully listens to its
own natural voice ; but reason must not demonstrate.
Ignorance on the side of intellect, faith on the
side of the emotions ; distrust of knowledge, absolute
confidence in love ; such is the condition of man's
highest welfare : it is only thus that the purpose
of his life, and of the world which is his instrument,
can be achieved.

No final estimate of the value of this theory of
morals and religion can be made, without examining
its philosophical presuppositions. Nor is **such an**
examination in any way unfair ; for it is obvious
that Browning explicitly offers to us a philosophical
doctrine. He appeals to argument and not **to**
artistic intuition ; he offers a definite theory to
which **he** claims attention, not on account of any
poetic beauty that may lie within it, but on the
ground that it is **a true** exposition of the moral
nature of man. Kant's *Metaphysic of Ethics* is not
more metaphysical in intention than the poet's
later utterances on the problems of morality. In
La Saisiaz, in *Ferishtah's Fancies*, in the *Parleyings*,
and, though less explicitly, in *Asolando*, *Fifine at the
Fair*, and *Red Cotton Nightcap Country*, Browning
definitely states, and endeavours to demonstrate a

theory of knowledge, a theory of the relation of knowledge to morality, and a theory of the nature of evil ; and he discusses the arguments for the immortality of the soul. In these poems his artistic instinct avails him, not as in his earlier ones, for the discovery of truth by way of intuition, but for the adornment of doctrines already derived from a metaphysical repository. His art is no longer free, no longer its own end, but coerced into an alien service. It has become illustrative and argument-ative, and in being made to subserve speculative purposes, it has ceased to be creative. Browning has appealed to philosophy, and philosophy must try his cause.

Such, then, is Browning's theory ; and I need make no further apology for discussing at some length the validity of the division which it involves between the intellectual and the moral life of man. Is it possible to combine the weakness of man's intelligence with the strength of his moral and religious life, and to find in the former the con-dition of the latter? Does human knowledge fail, as the poet considers it to fail? Is the intelli-gence of man absolutely incapable of arriving at knowledge of things as they are? If it does, if man cannot know the truth, can he attain good-ness? These are the questions that must now be answered.

It is one of the characteristics of recent thought that it distrusts its own activity: the ancient philosophical ' Scepticism ' has been revived and strengthened. Side by side with the sense of the triumphant progress of natural science, there is a conviction, shared even by scientific investigators themselves, as well as by religious teachers and by many students of philosophy, that our knowledge has only limited and relative value, and that it always stops short of the true nature of things. The reason of this general conviction lies in the fact that thought has become aware of its own activity. Men realize more clearly than they did in former times that the apparent constitution of things depends directly on the character of the intelligence which apprehends them.

This relativity of things to thought has—not unnaturally—suggested the idea that the objects of our knowledge are different from objects as they are. 'That the real nature of things is very different from what we make of them, that thought and thing are divorced, that there is a fundamental antithesis between them,' is, as Hegel said, "the hinge on which modern philosophy turns." Educated opinion in our day has lost its naïve trust in itself. "The natural belief of man, it is true, ever gives the lie" to the doctrine that we do not know things. "In common life," adds Hegel, "we reflect without particularly noting that this is the process of arriving at the truth, and we think without hesitation and in the firm belief that thought coincides with things."[1] But, as soon as attention is directed to the process of thinking, and to the way in which the process affects our consciousness of the object, it is at once concluded that thought will never reach reality, that things

[1] Wallace's *Translation of Hegel's Logic*, p. 36.

are not **given to us** as they are, but distorted by the media—by the sense and the intelligence—through which they pass. The doctrine of the relativity of knowledge **is** thus **very** generally regarded as equivalent to the doctrine that there is no true knowledge whatsoever. We know only phenomena, **or** appearances ; and **it is these**, and not veritable facts, that we systematize **into sciences.** "We can arrange the appearances—the shadows **of our** cave—and that, for the practical purposes **of the cave, is** all that we require." [1]   **Not** even 'earth's least atom' can **ever** be known **to us as it** really is; it is for us at the best,

> "An atom with some certain properties
> Known about, thought of as occasion needs." [2]

In this general distrust of knowledge, however, there are, **as** might **be** expected, many different degrees. Its origin in modern times was, no doubt, the doctrine of Kant. "This divorce of thing and thought," says Hegel, "is mainly the work of the critical philosophy and runs counter to the conviction of all previous ages." And the completeness of the divorce corresponds, with tolerable **accuracy, to** the degree in which the critical philosophy has been understood ; for Kant's writings, like those of all great thinkers, are capable of many interpretations, varying in depth with the intelligence of the interpreters.

The most common and general form of this view of the limitation of the human intelligence is that which places the objects of religious faith

---

[1] Caird's *Comte.*   [2] *A Bean-Stripe.*

beyond the reach of human knowledge. We find traces of it in much of the popular theology of our day. The great facts of religion are often spoken of as lying in an extra-natural sphere, beyond experience, into which men cannot enter by the native right of reason. It is asserted that the finite cannot know the infinite, that the nature of God is unknowable—except by means of a supernatural interference, which gives to men a new power of spiritual discernment, and 'reveals' to them things which are 'above reason,' although not contrary to it. The theologian often shields certain of his doctrines from criticism, on the ground, as he contends, that there are facts which we must believe, but which it would be presumptuous for us to pretend to understand or to demonstrate. These are the proper objects of 'faith.'

But this view of the weakness of the intelligence when applied to supersensuous facts, is held along with an undisturbed conviction of the validity of our knowledge of ordinary objects. It is believed, in a word, that there are two kinds of realities,—natural and supernatural; and that the former are knowable and the latter not.

It requires, however, no great degree of intellectual acumen to discover that this denial of the validity of our thought in these matters involves its denial in all its applications. The ordinary knowledge of natural objects, which we begin by regarding as valid, or, rather, whose validity is taken for granted without being questioned, depends upon our ideas of these supersensible objects. In other words, those fundamental difficulties which pious opinion discovers in the region of theology, and which—as is supposed—fling the human intellect back upon itself into a consciousness of frailty and finitude, are found to lurk beneath our ordinary knowledge. Whenever, for instance, we endeavour to know any object, we find that we are led back along the line of its conditions to that which unconditionally determines it. For we cannot find the reason for a particular object in a particular object. We are driven back endlessly from one fact to another along the chain of causes; and we can neither discover the first link nor do without it. The first link must be a 'cause of itself,' and experience yields none such. Such a cause would be the unconditioned, and the unconditioned we cannot know. The final result of thinking is thus to lead us to an unknown; and, in consequence, all our seeming knowledge is seen to have no intelligible basis, and, therefore, to be merely hypothetical. If we cannot know God, we cannot know anything.

This view is held by the Positivists, and the most popular English exponent of it is, perhaps, Mr. Herbert Spencer. Its characteristics are its repudiation of both theology and metaphysics as pseudo-sciences, and its high esteem for science. That esteem is not disturbed by the confession that 'noumenal causes,'—that is, the actual reality of things,—are unknown; for we can still lay claim to valid knowledge of the laws of phenomena. And positivism, having acknowledged that natural things as known are merely phenomena, treats them in all respects as if they were realities; and it rejoices in the triumphant progress of the natural sciences as if it were a veritable growth of knowledge. It does not take to heart the phenomenal nature of known objects. But, having paid its formal compliments to the doctrine of the relativity of all knowledge, it neglects it altogether.

Those who understand Kant better carry his scepticism further, and *complete* the divorce between man's knowledge and reality. The process of knowing, they hold, instead of leading us towards facts, as it was so long supposed to do, takes us away from them : *i.e.* if either 'towards' or 'away from' can have any meaning when applied to two realms which are absolutely severed from one another. Knowledge is always concerned with the relations between things ; with their likeness, or unlikeness, their laws, or connections ; but these are universals, and things are individuals. Science knows the laws of things, but not the things; it reveals how one object affects another, how it is connected with it ; but what are the things themselves, which are connected, it does not know. The laws are mere forms of thought, 'bloodless categories,' and not facts. They may somehow be regarded as explaining facts, but they must not be identified with the facts. Knowledge is the sphere of man's thoughts, and is made up of ideas ; real things are in another sphere, which man's thoughts cannot reach. We must distinguish more clearly than has hitherto been done, between logic as the science of knowledge, and metaphysics as a science which pretends to reveal the real nature of things. In a word, we can know thoughts or universals, but not things or particular existences. " When existence is in question it is the individual, not the universal, that is real ; and the real individual is not a composite of species and accidents, but is individual to the inmost fibre of its being." Each object keeps its own real being to itself. Its inmost secret, its reality, is something that cannot appear in knowledge. We can only know its manifestations ; but these manifestations are not its reality, nor connected with it. These belong to the sphere of knowledge, they are parts in a system of abstract thoughts ; they do not exist in that system, or no-system, of individual realities, each of which, in its veritable being, is itself only, and connected with nought beside.

Now, this view of the absolute impossibility of knowing any reality, on account of the fundamental difference between things and our thoughts about things, contains a better promise of a true view both of reality and of knowledge, than any of the previously mentioned half-hearted theories. It forces us explicitly either to regard every effort to know as futile, or else to regard it as futile *on this theory of it*. In other words, we must either give up knowledge, or else give up the account of knowledge advanced by these philosophers. Hitherto, however, every philosophy that has set itself against the possibility of the knowledge of reality has had to give way. It has failed to shake the faith of mankind in its own intellectual endowment, or to arrest, even for a moment, the attempt by thinking to know things as they are. The view held by Berkeley, that knowledge is merely subjective, because the essence of things consists in their being perceived by the individual, and that they are nothing but his ideas, was refuted by Kant, when he showed that the very illusion of seeming knowledge was impossible on that theory. And this later view, which represents knowledge as merely subjective on the ground that it is the product of the activity of the thought of mankind, working according to universal laws, is capable of being refuted in the same manner. The only difference between the Berkeleian and this modern speculative theory is that, on the former view, each individual constructed his own subjective entities or illusions; while, on the latter, all men, by reason of the universality of the laws of thought governing their minds, create the same illusion, the same subjective scheme of ideas. Instead of each having his own private unreality, as the product of his perceiving activity, they have all the same, or at least a similar, phantom-world of ideas, as the result of their thinking. But, in both cases alike, the reality of the world without is beyond reach, and knowledge is a purely subjective apprehension of a world within. Thoughts are quite different from things, and no effort of human reason can reveal any community between them.

Now, there are certain difficulties which, so far as I know, those who hold this view have scarcely attempted to meet. The first of these lies in the obvious fact, that all men at all times consider that this very process of thinking, which the theory condemns as futile, is the only way we have of finding out what the **reality of** things is. Why do we reflect **and** think, except in order to pass beyond the illusions of sensuous appearances to the knowledge of things as they are? Nay, why do these philosophers themselves reflect, when reflection, instead of leading to truth, which is knowledge of reality, leads only to ideas, which, being universal, cannot represent the realities that are said to be 'individual'?

The second is, that the knowledge of 'the laws' of things gives to us practical command over them ; although, according to this view, laws are not things, nor any part of the reality of things, nor even true representations of things. Our authority over things seems to grow *pari passu* with our knowledge. The natural sciences seem to prove by their practical efficiency, that they **are** not building up a world of apparitions, similar to the real world ; but gradually getting inside nature, learning more and more to wield her powers, and to make them the instruments of the purposes of man, and the means of his welfare. To common-sense,—which frequently 'divines' truths **that it** cannot prove, and, like ballast in a ship, has often given steadiness to human progress although it is only a dead weight—the assertion that man knows **nothing is as** incredible as that he knows all things. If it **is** replied, that the 'things' which we seem to dominate by the means of knowledge **are** themselves only phenomena, the question arises, what then are the real things to which they are opposed?

What right has any philosophy to say that there is any reality which no one can in any sense know? The knowledge that such reality is, is surely a relation between that reality and consciousness, and, if so, the assertion of an unknowable reality is self-contradictory. For the conception of it is the conception of something that is, and at the same time is not, out of relation to consciousness.

To say what kind of thing reality is, is a still more remarkable feat, if reality is unknowable. Being beyond knowledge, why is reality called particular or individual, rather than universal? How is it known that the true being of things is different from ideas? Surely both of the terms must be regarded as known to some extent, if they are called like or unlike, contrasted or compared, opposed or identified.

But, lastly, this theory has to account for the fact that it constitutes what is not only unreal, but impossible, into the criterion of what is actual. If knowledge of reality is altogether different from human knowledge, how does it come to be its criterion? That knowledge is inadequate or imperfect can be known only by contrasting it with its own proper ideal, whatever that may be. A criticism by reference to a foreign or irrelevant criterion, or the condemnation of a theory as imperfect because it does not realize an impossible end, is unreasonable. All true criticism of an object implies a reference to a more perfect state of itself.

We must, then, regard the knowledge of objects as they are, which is opposed to human knowledge, as only a completer and fuller form of that knowledge ; or else **we** must cease **to contrast it with** our human knowledge, as valid with invalid, true with phenomenal. Either knowledge of reality is complete knowledge, **or else it is a chimera.** And, .in either case, the sharp distinction **between** the real and the phenomenal vanishes ; and what remains, is not a reality outside of consciousness, or different from ideas, but a reality related to consciousness, or, in other words, a knowable reality. " The **distinction of objects into** phenomena and noumena, *i.e.* into things that for us exist, and things that for us do not exist, is an Irish bull in philosophy," **said Heine. To** speak of **reality** as unknowable, **or** to speak of anything as unknowable, is to utter a direct self-contradiction ; it **is to** negate in the predicate what is asserted in the subject. It is a still more strange perversion to erect this knowable emptiness into a criterion of knowledge, and **to call** the latter phenomenal by reference **to it.**

These difficulties **are** so fundamental **and so** obvious, **that** the theory of the phenomenal nature of human knowledge, which, being interpreted, means that we know nothing, could scarcely maintain its **hold, were** it not confused with another **fact of** human experience, which is apparently inconsistent with the doctrine that man can know **the truth.** Side by side with the faith of ordinary consciousness,—that in order to know anything we must think, in other words, that knowledge shows us what things really are,—there is a conviction, strengthened by constant experience, **that** we never know things fully. Every investigation into the nature of an object **soon** brings us to an enigma, a something more **we do not** know. Failing to know this something more, we generally consider that we have fallen short of reaching the reality of the object. **We** recognize, as it has been ex-pressed, that we have been brought to a stand, and we therefore conclude that we are also brought to the end. We arrive at what we do not know, and **we pronounce** that unknown to be unknowable ; that is, we regard it as something different in **nature** from what we do know.

So far as I can see, the attitude of ordinary thought in regard to this matter might be fairly represented by saying, that it always begins by considering objects as capable of being known in their reality, or as they are, and that experience always proves the attempt to know them as they are, to be a failure. The effort is continued although failure is the result, and even although that failure be exaggerated and universalized into that despair of knowledge which we have described. We are thus confronted with what seems **to be a contra-**diction ; a trust and distrust in knowledge. It **can** only be solved by doing full justice to both of the conflicting elements ; and then, if possible, by showing that they **are** elements, and not the complete, concrete fact, except when held together.

From one point of view, it is undeniable that in every object of perception, we come upon problems that we cannot solve. Science at its best, and even when dealing **with the** simplest of things, is forced to stop short of its final secret. Even when it **has** discovered its law, there is still apparently something over and above which science cannot grasp, and which seems to give to the object its reality. All the natural sciences concentrated on a bit of iron ore fail to exhaust the truth in it : there is always a 'beyond' in it, something still more fundamental which is not yet understood. And that something beyond, that inner essence, that point in which the laws meet and which the sciences fail to lift into knowledge, is regarded as just the reality of the thing. Thus the reality is supposed, at the close of every investigation, to lie outside of knowledge ; and conversely, all that we do know, seeing that it lacks this last element, seems to be only apparent knowledge, or knowledge of phenomena.

In this way the process of knowing seems always to stop short at the critical moment, when the truth is just about to be reached. And those who dwell on this aspect alone are apt to conclude that man's intellect is touched with a kind of impotence, which makes it useless when it gets near the reality. It is like a weapon that snaps at the hilt just when the battle is hottest. For we seem to be able to know everything but the reality, and yet apart from this reality all knowledge seems to be merely apparent. Physical science penetrates through the outer appearances of things to their laws, analyzes them into forms of energy, calculates their action and predicts their effects with certainty. Its practical power over the forces of nature is so great that it seems to have got inside her secrets. And yet science will itself acknowledge that in every simplest object there is an unknown. Its triumphant course of explaining seems to be always arrested at the threshold of reality. It has no theory, scarcely an hypothesis, of the **actual** nature of things, or of what that is in each object which constitutes it a real existence. Natural science, with a scarcely concealed sneer, hands over to the metaphysician all questions as to the real being of things : and itself makes the more modest pretension of **showing how** things behave, not what they are ; what effects follow the original noumenal causes, but not the veritable nature of these causes. Nor **can the** metaphysician, in his turn, do more than suggest an hypothesis as to the nature of the ultimate reality in things. He cannot detect or demonstrate it in any particular fact. In a word, every minutest object in the world baffles the combined powers of all forms of human thought, and holds back its essence or true being from them. And so long **as** this true being, or reality, is not known, the knowledge which we seem to have cannot be held as ultimately true. It is demonstrably a makeshift.

Having made this confession, there seems to be **no** alternative but to postulate an utter discrepancy **between** human thought and real existence, or between human knowledge and truth, which is the correspondence of thing and thought. For, at no point is knowledge found to be in touch with real being ; it is everywhere demonstrably conditioned and relative, and inadequate to express the true reality of its objects. What remains, then, except to regard human knowledge as completely untrustworthy, as merely of phenomena ? If we cannot know *any* reality, does not knowledge completely fail ?

Now, in dealing with the moral life of man, we saw that the method of hard alternatives was invalid. The moral life, being progressive, was shown to be the meeting point of the ideal and the actual ; and the ideal of perfect goodness was regarded as manifesting itself in actions which, nevertheless, were never adequate to express it. The good when achieved was ever condemned as unworthy, and the ideal when attained ever pressed for more adequate expression in a better character. The ideal was present as potency, as realizing itself, but it was never completely realized. The absolute good was never reached in the best action, and never completely missed in the worst.

The same conflict of real and unreal was shown to be essential to every natural life. So long as anything grows it neither completely attains, nor completely falls away from its ideal. The growing acorn is not an oak tree, and yet it is not a mere acorn. The child is not the man ; and yet the man is in the child, and only needs to be evolved by interaction with circumstances. The process of growth is one wherein the ideal is always present, as a reconstructive power gradually changing its whole vehicle, or organism, into a more perfect expression of itself. The ideal is reached in the end just because it is present in the beginning ; and there is no end so long as growth continues.

Now, it is evident that knowledge, whether it be that of the individual man or of the human race, is a thing which grows. The process by means of which natural science makes progress, or that whereby the consciousness of the child expands and

deepens into the consciousness of the man, is best
made intelligible from the point of view of evolution.   It is like an organic process, in which
each new acquirement finds its place in an old
order, each new fact is brought under the permanent principles of experience, and absorbed into
an intellectual life, which itself, in turn, grows
richer and fuller with every new acquisition.   No
knowledge worthy of the name is an aggregation
of facts.   Wisdom comes by growth.

Hence, the assertion that knowledge never attains
reality, does not imply that it always misses it.
In morals we do not say that a man is entirely
evil, although he never, even in his best actions,
attains the true good.   And if the process of
knowing is one that presses onward towards an
ideal, that ideal is never completely missed even
in the poorest knowledge.   If it grows, the method
of fixed alternatives must be inapplicable to it.
The ideal, whatever it may be, must be considered
as active in the present, guiding the whole movement, and gradually manifesting itself in each of
the passing forms, which are used up as the raw
material of new acquirement ; and yet no passing
form completely expresses the ideal.

Nor is it difficult to say what that ideal of
knowledge is, although we cannot define it in any
adequate manner.   We know that the end of
morality is the *summum bonum*, although we cannot,
so long as we are progressive, define its whole
content, or find it fully realized in any action.
Every failure brings new truth, every higher grade
of moral character reveals some new height of

goodness to be scaled ; the moral ideal acquires definiteness and content as humanity moves upwards. And yet the ideal is not entirely unknown even at the first ; even to the most ignorant it presents itself in a form sufficiently definite to serve as a criterion whereby he is able to distinguish between right and wrong, evil and goodness, and to guide his practical life.

The same truth holds with regard to knowledge. Its growth receives its impulse from, and is directed and determined by, that which is conceived as the real world of facts. This truth, namely, that the ideal knowledge is knowledge of reality. the most subjective philosopher cannot but acknowledge. That there is possible a knowledge of real being is implied in his condemnation of knowledge as merely phenomenal. That thought and reality can be brought together, or, rather, that they *are* always together, is presupposed in all knowledge and in all experience. The effort to know is the effort to *explain* the relation of thought and reality, not to create it. The ideal of perfect knowledge is present from the first ; it generates the effort to know, directs it, and distinguishes between truth and error. And that which man ever aims at, whether in the ordinary activities of daily thought, or through the patient labour of scientific investigation, or in the reflective self-torture of philosophic thought, is to know the world as it is. No failure damps the ardour of this endeavour. Relativists pheno-menalists, agnostics, sceptics, Kantians or Neo-Kantians—all the crowd of thinkers who cry down the human intellect, and draw a charmed circle around reality so as to make it unapproachable to the mind of man—ply this labour which they pronounce useless. They are seeking to penetrate beneath the shows of sense and the outer husk of phenomena to the truth, which is the meeting-point of knowledge and reality; they are endeavouring to translate into an intellectual possession the powers that play within and around them; or, in other words, to make these powers express themselves in their thoughts, and supply the content of their spiritual life. The irony, latent in their endeavour, gives them no pause; they are in some way content to pursue what they call phantoms, and to try and satisfy their thirst with the waters of a mirage. This comes from the presence of the ideal within them, that is, of the implicit unity of reality and thought, which seeks for explicit and complete manifestation in knowledge. The reality is present in them as thinking activity, working towards complete revelation of itself by means of knowledge. And its presence is real, although the process is never complete.

In knowledge, as in morals, it is necessary to remember both the truths implied in the pursuit of an ideal—that a growing thing not only always fails to attain, but also always succeeds. The distinction between truth and error in knowledge is present at every stage of the effort to attain truth, as the distinction between right and wrong is present in every phase of the moral life. It is the source of the intellectual effort. But that distinction cannot be drawn except by reference to a criterion of truth which condemns our actual knowledge;

just as it is the absolute good which condemns the present character. The ideal may be indefinite, and its content confused and poor ; but it is always sufficient for its purpose, always better than the actual achievement. And, in this sense, reality, the truth, the veritable being of things, is always reached by the poorest knowledge. As there is no starved and distorted sapling which is not the embodiment of the principle of natural life, so the meanest character is the product of an ideal of goodness, and the most confused opinion of ignorant mankind is an expression of the reality of things. Without it there would not be even the semblance of knowledge, not even error and untruth.

Those who, like Browning, make a division between man's thought and real things, and regard the sphere of knowledge as, at no point, touching the sphere of actual existence, are attributing to the bare human intellect much more power than it has. They regard mind as creating its phenomenal knowledge, that is, the apparent world. For, having separated mind from reality, it is evident that they cannot avail themselves of any doctrine of sensations or impressions as a medium between them, or postulate any other form of connection or means of communication. Connection of any kind must, in the end, imply some community of nature, and must put the unity of thought and being—here denied—beneath their difference. Hence the world of phenomena which we know, and which, as known, does not seem to consist of realities, must be the product of the unaided human mind. The intellect, isolated from all real being, has manufactured the apparent universe, in all its endless wealth. It is a creative intellect, although it can only create illusions. It evolves all its products from itself.

But thought, set to revolve upon its own axis in an empty region, can produce nothing, not even illusions. And, indeed, those who deny that it is possible for thought and reality to meet in a unity, have, notwithstanding, to bring over 'something' to the aid of thought. There must be some effluence from the world of reality, some manifestations of the thing (though they are not the reality of the thing, nor any part of the reality, nor connected with the reality!) to assist the mind and supply it with data. In fact, the 'phenomenal world' is a hybrid, generated by thought and 'something' which yet is not reality; for the real world is a world of things in themselves, altogether beyond thought. By bringing in these data, it is virtually admitted that the human mind reaches down into itself in vain for a world, even for a phenomenal one.

Thought apart from things is quite empty, just as things apart from thought are blind. But such thought and such reality are mere abstractions, hypostasized by false metaphysics; they are elements of truth rent asunder, and destroyed in the rending. The dependence of the intelligence of man upon reality is direct and complete. The foolishest dream, that ever played out its panorama beneath a nightcap, came through the gates of the senses from the actual world. Man is limited to his material in all that he knows, just as he is ruled by the laws of thought. He cannot go one step beyond it. To transcend 'experience' is impossible. We have no wings to sustain us in an empty region, and no need of any. It is as impossible for man to create new ideas, as it is for him to create new atoms. Our thought is essentially connected with reality. There is no *mauvais pas* from thought to things. We do not need to leap out of ourselves in order to get into the world. We are in it from the first, both as physical and moral agents, and as thinking beings. Our thoughts are expressions of the real nature of things, so far as they go. They may be and are imperfect; they may be and are confused and inadequate, and express only the superficial aspects and not 'the inmost fibres'; still, they are what they are, in virtue of 'the reality,' which finds itself interpreted in them. Severed from that reality, they would be nothing.

Thus, the distinction between thought and reality is a distinction within a deeper unity. And that unity must not be regarded as something additional to both, or as a third something. It *is* their unity. It is both reality and thought: it is existing thought, or reality knowing itself and existing through its knowledge of self; it is self-consciousness. The distinguished elements have no existence or meaning except in their unity. Like the actual and ideal, they have significance and being only in their reference to each other.

There is one more difficulty connected with this matter which I must touch upon, although the discussion may already be regarded as prolix. It

is acknowledged by every one that the knowledge of the individual, and his apparent world
of realities, grow *pari passu.* Beyond his sphere
of knowledge there is no reality *for him*, not even
apparent reality.   But, on the other hand, it is
rightly argued, the real world of existing things
exists all the same whether he knows it or not.
It did not begin to be with any knowledge he
may have of it, it does not cease to be with his
extinction, and it is not in any way affected by
his valid, or invalid, reconstruction of it in thought.
The world which depends on his thought is his
world, and not the world of really existing things.
And this is true alike of every individual.   The
world is independent of all human minds.   It
existed before them, and will, very possibly, exist
after them.   Can we not, therefore, conclude that
the real world is independent of thought, and that
it exists without relation to it ?

A short reference to the moral consciousness
may suggest the answer to this difficulty.   In
morality (as also is the case in knowledge) the
moral ideal, or the objective law of goodness, grows
in richness and fulness of content with the individual who apprehends it.   *His* moral world is
the counterpart of *his* moral growth as a character.
Goodness *for him* directly depends upon his
recognition of it.   Animals, presumably, have no
moral ideal, because they have not the power to
constitute it.   In morals, as in knowledge, the
mind of man constructs its own world.   And yet,
both alike, the world of truth and the world of
goodness exist all the same whether the individual

knows **them or not.** He does not call the moral law **into** being, but finds it without, and then **realizes it in** his own life. The moral law does not vanish and reappear with its recognition by mankind. It is not subject to the chances and changes of its life, but **it is a** good in itself that is eternal.

Being independent of man, **can it** therefore be independent of **all** intelligence? Can goodness be anything **but the** law of a self-conscious being? Is it the quality or motive or ideal of a mere thing? Manifestly not. Its relation to self-consciousness **is essential.** With the extinction of self-consciousness all moral goodness **is** extinguished.

The same holds true of reality. The question **of** the reality or unreality of things **cannot arise** except in an intelligence. Animals have neither illusions nor truths—unless they are self-conscious. The reality, which man sets over against his own inadequate knowledge, is assumed by him ; and it has no meaning whatsoever except in this contrast. And to endeavour to conceive a reality which no one knows, is to assert a relative term **without its** correlative, which is absurd; it is to assert an ideal which is opposed to nothing actual.

In this view, so commonly held in our day, namely, that knowledge is subjective and reality unknowable, we have another example of the falseness and inconsistency of abstract thinking. If this error be committed, there is no fundamental gain in saying with Kant, that things are relative to the thought of all, instead of asserting, with

Berkeley or Browning, that they are relative to the thought of each. The final result is the same. Things as known, are **reduced** into mere creations of thought; things as they are, are regarded as **not** thoughts, and as partaking in **no** way of the nature **of** thought. And yet 'reality' is virtually **assumed to** be given at the beginning of knowledge; for the sensations are supposed to be emanations from it, or roused in consciousness by it. These sensations, it is said, man does **not** make, but receives, and receives from the concealed reality. They flow from it, and are the manifestations **of its activity.** Then, in the next moment, reality is regarded as not given in any way, but as something to be discovered by **the effort of** thought; for **we** always strive to know things, and not phantoms. Lastly, the knowledge thus acquired being regarded as imperfect, and experience showing to us continually that every object has **more in** it than **we** know, the reality is pronounced to be unknowable, and all knowledge is regarded as failure—as acquaintance with mere phantoms. Thus, in thought, as in morality, the ideal is present **at the beginning**—it is an effort after explicit realization, and its process is never complete.

Now, all **these** aspects of the ideal of knowledge, **that** is, of reality, are held by the unsophisticated intelligence of man; and abstract philosophy is **not** capable of finally getting rid of any one of **them.** It too holds them *alternately.* Its denial of the possibility of knowing reality is refuted by its own starting-point; for it begins with a given something, regarded as real, and its very effort to know is an attempt to know that reality by thinking. But it forgets these facts, when it is discovered that knowledge at the best is incomplete. It is thus tossed from assertion to denial, and from denial to assertion ; from one abstract or one-sided view of reality, to the other.

When, however, these different aspects of truth are grasped together from the point of view of evolution, there seems to be a way of escaping the difficulties to which they give rise. For the ideal must be present at the beginning, and yet it cannot be present in its fulness till the process is complete. What is here required is to lift our theory of man's knowledge to the level of our theory of his moral life, and to treat it frankly as the process whereby reality manifests itself in the mind of man. In that way, we shall avoid the absurdities of both of the abstract schools of philosophy, to both of which alike the native intelligence of man gives the lie. We shall say neither that man knows nothing, nor that he knows all ; we shall regard his knowledge, neither as purely phenomenal and out of all contact with reality, nor as an actual identification with the real being of things in all their complex variety. For, in morality, we do not say either that the individual is absolutely evil, because his actions never realize the supreme ideal of goodness ; nor that he is at the last term of development, and 'taking the place of God,' because he lives as 'ever in his great Taskmaster's eye.' Just as every moral action, however good, leaves something still to be desiderated, something that may become a stepping-stone for new movement towards the ideal which it has failed to actualize ; so all our knowledge of an object leaves something over that we have not apprehended, which is truer and more real than anything we know, and which in all future effort we strive to master.   And, just as the very effort to be good derives its impulse and direction from the ideal of goodness which is present, and striving for realization ; so the effort to know derives its impulse and direction from the reality which is present, and striving for complete realization in the thought of man.   We know reality confusedly from the first ; and it is because we have attained so much knowledge that we strive for greater clearness and fulness.   It is by planting his foot on the world that man travels.   It is by opposing his power to the given which is actual that his knowledge grows.

When once we recognize that reality is the ideal of knowledge, we are able to acknowledge all the truth that is in the doctrine of the phenomenalists, without falling into their errors and contradictions.   We may go as far as the poet in confessing intellectual impotence, and roundly call man's knowledge " lacquered ignorance." " Earth's least atom " does veritably remain an enigma to him.   He is actually flung back into his circumscribed sphere by every fact ; and he will continue to be so flung to the end of time.   He will never know reality, nor be able to hold in his hand the very heart of the simplest thing in the world.   For the world is an organic totality, and its simplest thing will not be seen, through and through, till everything is known, till every fact and event is related to every other under principles which are universal; just as goodness cannot be fully achieved in any act, till the agent is in all ways lifted to the level of absolute goodness. Physics cannot reveal the forces which keep a stone in its place on the earth, till it has traced the forces that maintain the starry systems in their course. No fact can be thoroughly known, *i.e.* known in its reality, till the light of the whole universe has been focussed upon it: and, on the other hand, to know any subject through and through would be to explain all being. The highest law and the essence of the simple fact, the universal and the particular, can only be known together, in and through one another. 'Reality' in 'the least atom' will be known, only when knowledge has completed its work, and the universe has become a transparent sphere, penetrated in every direction by the shafts of intelligence.

But this is only half the truth. If knowledge is never complete, it is always *completing*; if reality is never known, it is ever *being known*; if the ideal is never actual, it is always *being actualized*. The complete failure of knowledge is as impossible as its complete success. It is at no time severed from reality; it is never its mere adumbration, nor are its contents mere phenomena. On the contrary, it is reality partially revealed, the ideal incompletely actualized. Our very errors are the working of reality within us, and apart from it they would be impossible. The process towards truth by man is the process of truth *in* man; the movement of knowledge towards reality is the movement of reality into knowledge. A purely subjective consciousness which knows, such as the poet tried to describe, is a self-contradiction : it would be a consciousness at once related, and not related, to the actual world. But man has no need to relate himself to the world. He is already related, and his task is to understand that relation, or, in other words, to make both its terms intelligible. Man has no need to go out from himself to facts ; his relation to facts is prior to his distinction from them. The truth is that he cannot entirely lift himself away from them, nor suspend his thoughts in the void. In his inmost being he is creation's voice, and in his knowledge he confusedly murmurs its deep thoughts.

Browning was aware of this truth in its application to man's moral nature. In speaking of the principle of love, he was not tempted to apply fixed alternatives. On the contrary, he detected in the 'poorest love that was ever offered' the veritable presence of that which is perfect and complete, though never completely actualized in man. His interest in the moral development of man, and his penetrative moral insight, acting upon, and guided by the truths of the Christian religion, warned him, on this side, against the absolute separation of the ideal and actual, the divine and human. Human love, however poor in quality and limited in range, was to him God's love in man. It was a wave, breaking in the individual, of that First Love which is ever flowing back through the life of humanity to its primal source. To him all moral endeavour is the process of this Primal Love ; and every man, as he consciously identifies himself with it, may use the language of Scripture, and say, " It is not I that live, but Christ lives in me."

But, on the side of knowledge, Browning was neither so deeply interested, nor had he so good a guide to lean upon. Ignorant, according to all appearances, of the philosophy which has made the Christian maxim, " Die to live "—primarily only a principle of morality—the basis of its theory of knowledge, he exaggerated the failure of science to reach the whole truth as to any particular object, into a qualitative discrepancy between knowledge and truth. Because knowledge is never complete, it is always mere lacquered ignorance ; and man's apparent intellectual victories are only conquests in a land of unrealities, or mere phenomena. Browning occupies, in regard to knowledge, a position strictly analogous to that of Carlyle, in regard to morality ; his intellectual pessimism is the counterpart of the moral pessimism of his predecessor, and it springs from the same error. He forgot that the ideal without is also the power within, which makes for its own manifestation in the mind of man.

He opposed the intellect to the world, as Carlyle opposed the moral frailty of man to the law of duty; and he neglected the fact that the world was there for him only because he knew it, just as Carlyle neglected the fact that the duty was without only because it was recognized within. He strained the difference between the ideal and actual into an absolute distinction ; and, as Carlyle condemned man to strive for a goodness which he could never achieve, so Browning condemns him to pursue a truth which he can never attain. In both, the failure is regarded as absolute. "There is no good in us," has for its counterpart, "There is no truth in us." Both the poet and the moralist dwell on the *negative* relation of the ideal and actual, and forget that the negative has no meaning, except as the expression of a deeper affirmative. Carlyle had to learn that we know our moral imperfection, only because we are conscious of a better within us; and Browning had to learn that we are aware of our ignorance, only because we have the consciousness of fuller truth with which we contrast our knowledge. Browning, indeed, knew that the consciousness of evil was itself evidence of the presence of good, that perfection means death, and progress is life, on the side of morals; but he has missed the corresponding truth on the side of knowledge. If he acknowledges that the highest revealed itself to man, on the practical side, as love; he does not see that it has also manifested itself to man on the theoretical side, as reason. The self-communication of the Infinite is incomplete; love is a quality of God, intelligence a quality of man; hence, on one side, there is no limit to achievement, but on the other there is impotence. Human nature is absolutely divided against itself; and the division, as we have already seen, is not between flesh and spirit, but between a love which is God's own and perfect, and an intelligence which is merely man's and altogether weak and deceptive.

This is what makes Browning think it impossible

to re-establish faith in God, except by turning his back on knowledge. Whether, having denied the validity of knowledge, it is possible for him to appeal to the moral consciousness, we shall inquire in the next chapter.

CHAPTER X

THE HEART AND THE HEAD—LOVE AND REASON

"And though all the winds of doctrine were let loose to play upon the earth, so truth be in the field, we do injuriously by licensing and prohibiting to misdoubt her strength. Let her and falsehood grapple ; who ever knew truth put to the worse, in a free and open encounter?"[1]

IT has been shown that Browning appeals, in defence of his optimistic faith, from the intellect to the heart. His theory rests on three main assumptions :—namely, (1) that knowledge of the true nature of things is impossible to man, and that, therefore, it is necessary to find other and better evidence than the intellect can give for the victory of good over evil, (2) that the failure of knowledge is a necessary condition of the moral life, inasmuch as certain knowledge would render all moral effort either futile or needless ; (3) that after the failure of knowledge there still remains possible a faith of the heart, which can furnish a sufficient objective basis to morality and religion.

[1] Milton's *Areopagitica.*

The first of these assumptions I endeavoured to deal with in the last chapter. I now turn to the remaining two.

Demonstrative, or certain, or absolute knowledge of the actual nature of things would, Browning asserts, destroy the very possibility of a moral life.[1] For such knowledge would show either that evil is evil, or that evil is good ; and, in both cases alike, the benevolent activity of love would be futile. In the first case, it would be thwarted and arrested by despair ; for, if evil be evil, it must remain evil for aught that man can do. Man cannot effect a change in the nature of things, nor create a good in a world dominated by evil. In the second case, the saving effect of moral love would be unnecessary; for, if evil be only seeming, then all things are perfect and complete, and there is no need of interference. It is necessary, therefore, that man should be in a permanent state of doubt as to the real existence of evil ; and, whether evil does exist or not, it must seem, and only seem to exist to man, in order that he may devote himself to the service of good.[2]

Now, if this view of the poet be taken in the strict sense in which he uses it in this argument, it admits of a very easy refutation. It takes us beyond the bounds of all possible human experience, into an imaginary region, as to which all assertions are equally valueless. It is impossible to conceive how the conduct of a being who is moral would be affected by absolute knowledge ; or, indeed, to conceive the existence of such a being. For

[1] See Chapter VIII., p. 250.   [2] *Ibid.*

morality, as the poet insists, is a process in which an ideal is gradually realized through conflict with the actual—an actual which it both produces and transmutes at every stage of the progress. But complete knowledge would be above all process. Hence we should have, on Browning's hypothesis, to conceive of a being in whom perfect knowledge was combined with an undeveloped will. A being so constituted would be an agglomerate of utterly disparate elements, the interaction of which, in a single character, it would be impossible to make intelligible.

But, setting aside this point, there is a curious flaw in Browning's argument, which indicates that he had not distinguished between two forms of optimism which are essentially different from each other,—namely, the pantheistic and the Christian.

To know that evil is only apparent, that pain is only pleasure's mask, that all forms of wickedness and misery are only illusions of an incomplete intelligence, would, he argues, arrest all moral action and stultify love. For love—which necessarily implies need in its object—is the principle of all right action. In this he argues justly, for the moral life is essentially a conflict and progress; and, in a world in which "white ruled unchecked along the line," there would be neither the need of conflict nor the possibility of progress. And, on the other hand, if the good were merely a phantom, and evil the reality, the same destruction of moral activity would follow. "White may not triumph" in this absolute manner, nor may we "clean abolish, once and evermore, white's faintest trace." There must be "the constant shade cast on life's shine."

All this is true; but the admission of it in no way militates against the conception of absolutely valid knowledge; nor is it any proof that we need live in the twilight of perpetual doubt in order to be moral. For the knowledge of which Browning speaks would be knowledge of a state of things in which morality would be really impossible; that is, it would be knowledge of a world in which all was evil or all was good. On the other hand, valid knowledge of a world in which good and evil are in conflict, and in which the former is realized through victory over the latter, would not destroy morality. What is inconsistent with the moral life is the conception of a world where there is no movement from evil to good, no evolution of character, but merely the stand-still life of "Rephan." But absolutely certain knowledge that the good is at issue with sin in the world, that there is no way of attaining goodness except through conflict with evil, and that moral life, as the poet so frequently insists, is a process which converts all actual attainment into a dead self, from which we can rise to higher things—a self, therefore, which is relatively evil—would, and does, inspire morality. It is the deification of evil not negated or overcome, of evil as it is in itself and apart from all process, which destroys morality.

And the same is equally true of a pantheistic optimism, which asserts that all things *are* good. But it is not true of a Christian optimism, which asserts that all things are *working together for* good.

For such optimism implies that the process of negating or overcoming evil is essential to the attainment of goodness; it does not imply that evil, as evil, is ever good. Evil is unreal, only in the sense that it cannot withstand the power which is set against it. It is not *mere* semblance, a mere negation or absence of being; it *is* opposed to the good, and its opposition can be overcome only by the moral effort which it calls forth. An optimistic faith of this kind can find room for morality; and, indeed, it furnishes it with the religious basis it needs. Browning, however, has confused these two forms of optimism; and, therefore, he has been driven to condemn knowledge, because he knew no alternative but that of either making evil eternally real, or making it absolutely unreal. A third alternative, however, is supplied by the conception of moral evolution. Knowledge of the conditions on which good can be attained —a knowledge that amounts to conviction—is the spring of all moral effort; whereas an attitude of permanent doubt as to the distinction between good and evil would paralyze it. Such a doubt must be solved before man can act at all, or choose one end rather than another. All action implies belief, and the ardour and vigour of moral action can only come from a belief which is whole-hearted.

The further assertion, which the poet makes in *La Saisiaz* and repeats elsewhere, that sure knowledge of the consequences that follow good and evil actions would necessarily lead to the choice of good and the avoidance of evil, and destroy morality by destroying liberty of choice, raises the whole question of the relation of knowledge and conduct, and cannot be adequately discussed here. It may be said, however, that it rests upon a confusion between two forms of necessity : namely, natural and spiritual necessity. In asserting that knowledge of the consequences of evil would determine human action in a necessary way, the poet virtually treats man as if he were a natural being. But the assumption that man is responsible and liable to punishment, involves that he is capable of withstanding all such determination. And knowledge does not and cannot lead to such necessary determination. Reason brings freedom ; for reason constitutes the ends of action.

It is the constant desire of the good to attain to such a convincing knowledge of the worth and dignity of the moral law that they shall be able to make themselves its devoted instruments. Their desire is that 'the good' shall supplant in them all motives that conflict against it, and be the inner principle, or necessity, of all their actions. Such complete devotion to the good is expressed, for instance, in the words of the Hebrew Psalmist : "Thy testimonies have I taken as an heritage for ever ; for they are the rejoicing of my heart. I have inclined mine heart to perform Thy statutes alway, even unto the end. I hate vain thoughts, but Thy law do I love." "Nevertheless I live," said the Christian apostle, "yet not I, but Christ liveth in me ; and the life which I now live in the flesh I live by the faith of the Son of God." In these words there is expressed that highest form of the moral life, in which the individual is so identified in desire with his ideal, that he lives only to actualize it in his character. The natural self is represented as dead, and the victory of the new principle is viewed as complete. This full obedience to the ideal is the service of a necessity; but the necessity is within, and the service is, therefore, perfect freedom. The authority of the law is absolute, but the law is self-imposed. The whole man is convinced of its goodness. He has acquired something even fuller than a mere intellectual demonstration of it; for his knowledge has ripened into wisdom, possessed his sympathies, and become a disposition of his heart. And the fulness and certainty of his knowledge, so far from rendering morality impossible, is its very perfection. To bring about such a knowledge of the good of goodness and the evil of evil, as will engender love of the former and hatred of the latter, is the aim of all moral education. Thus, the history of human life, in so far as it is progressive, may be concentrated in the saying that it is the ascent from the power of a necessity which is natural, to the power of a necessity which is moral. And this latter necessity can come only through fuller and more convincing knowledge of the law that rules the world, and is also the inner principle of man's nature.

There remains now the third element in Browning's view,—namely, that the faith in the good implied in morality and religion, can be firmly established, after knowledge has turned out deceptive, upon the individual's consciousness of the power of love within himself. In other words, I must now try to estimate the value of Browning's appeal from the intellect to the heart.

Before doing so, however, it may be well to repeat once more that Browning's condemnation of knowledge, in his philosophical poems, is not partial or hesitating. On the contrary, he definitely confines knowledge to the individual's consciousness of his own inner states.

> "Myself I solely recognize.
> They, too, may recognize themselves, not me,
> For aught I know or care."[1]

Nor does Browning endeavour to correct this limited testimony of the intellect as to its own states, by bringing in the miraculous aid of revelation, or by postulating an unerring moral faculty. He does not assume an intuitive power of knowing right from wrong; but he maintains that ignorance enwraps man's moral sense.[2]

And, not only are we unable to know the rule of right and wrong in details, but we cannot know whether there *is* right or wrong. At times the poet seems inclined to say that evil is a phenomenon conjured up by the frail intelligence of man.

> "Man's fancy makes the fault!
> Man, with the narrow mind, must cram inside
> His finite God's infinitude,—earth's vault
> He bids comprise the heavenly far and wide,
> Since Man may claim a right to understand
> What passes understanding."[3]

God's ways are past finding out. Nay, God Himself is unknown. At times, indeed, the power to love within man seems to the poet to be a clue

---

[1] *A Bean-Stripe.* See also *La Saisiaz.*
[2] See Chapter VIII.   [3] *Bernard de Mandeville.*

to the nature of the Power without, and God is all but revealed in this surpassing emotion of the human heart. But, when philosophizing, he withdraws even this amount of knowledge. He is

> "Assured that, whatsoe'er the quality
>   Of love's cause, save that love was caused thereby,
>   This—nigh upon revealment as it seemed
>   A minute since—defies thy longing looks,
>   Withdrawn into the unknowable once more."[1]

Thus—to sum up Browning's view of knowledge—we are ignorant of the world, we do not know even whether it is good, or evil, or only their semblance, that is presented to us in human life; and we know nothing of God, except that He is the cause of love in man. What greater depth of agnosticism is possible?

When the doctrine is put in this bald form, the moral and religious consciousness of man, on behalf of which the theory was invented, revolts against it. Nevertheless, the distinction made by Browning between the intellectual and emotional elements of human life is very common in religious thought. It is not often, indeed, that either the worth of love, or the weakness of knowledge, receives such emphatic expression as that which is given to them by the poet; but the same general idea of their relation is often expressed, and still more often implied. Browning differs from our ordinary teachers mainly in the boldness of his affirmatives and negatives. They, too, regard the intellect as merely human, and the emotion of love as divine.

[1] *A Pillar at Sebzevar.*

They, too, shrink from identifying the reason of man with the reason of God; even though they may recognize that morality and religion must postulate some kind of unity between God and man. They, too, conceive that human knowledge differs *in nature* from that of God, while they maintain that human goodness is the same in nature with that of God, though different in degree and fulness. There are two *kinds* of knowledge, but there is only one kind of justice, or mercy, or loving-kindness. Man must be content with a semblance of a knowledge of truth; but a semblance of goodness would be intolerable. God really reveals Himself to man in morality and religion, and He communicates to man nothing less than 'the divine love.' But there is no such close connection on the side of reason. The religious life of man is a divine principle, the indwelling of God in him; but there is a final and fatal defect in man's knowledge. The divine love's manifestation of itself is ever incomplete, it is true, even in the best of men; but there is no defect in its nature.

As a consequence of this doctrine, few religious opinions are more common at the present day, than that it is necessary to appeal, on all the high concerns of man's moral and religious life, from the intellect to the heart. Where we cannot know, we may still feel; and the religious man may have, in his own feeling of the divine, a more intimate conviction of the reality of that in which he trusts, than could be produced by any intellectual process.

> " Enough to say, ' I feel
> Love's sure effect, and, being loved, must love
> The love its cause behind,—I can and do.'" [1]

Reason, in trying to scale the heights of truth, falls back, impotent and broken, into doubt and despair : not by the path of reason can we come to that which is best and highest.

> " I found Him not in world or sun,
>   Or eagle's wing, or insect's eye ;
>   Nor thro' the questions men may try,
> The petty cobwebs we have spun." [2]

But there is another way to find God and to conquer doubt.

> " If e'er when faith had fall'n asleep,
>   I heard a voice ' believe no more,'
>   And heard an ever-breaking shore
> That tumbled in the Godless deep ;
>
> " A warmth within the breast would melt
>   The freezing reason's colder part,
>   And like a man in wrath the heart
> Stood up and answer'd ' I have felt.' " [3]

What, then, I have now to ask, is the meaning and value of this appeal to emotion? Can love, or emotion in any of its forms, reveal truths to man which his intellect cannot discover? If so, how? If not, how shall we account for the general conviction of good men that it can? We have, in a word, either to justify the appeal to the heart, by explaining how the heart may utter truths that are

---

[1] *A Pillar at Sebzevar.*
[2] *In Memoriam.*   [3] *Ibid.*

hidden from reason ; or else to account for the illusion, by which religious emotion seems to reveal such truths.

The first requirement is shown to be unreasonable by the very terms in which it is made. The intuitive insight of faith, the immediate conviction of the heart, cannot render, and must not try to render, any account of itself. Proof is a process ; but there is no process in this direct conviction of truth. Its assertion is just the denial of process ; it is a repudiation of all connections; in such a faith of feeling there are no cobweb lines relating fact to fact, which doubt could break. Feeling is the immediate unity of the subject and object. I am pained, because I cannot rid myself of an element which is already within me ; I am lifted into the emotion of pleasure, or happiness, or bliss, by the consciousness that I am already at one with an object that fulfils my longings and satisfies my needs. Hence, there seems to be ground for saying that, in this instance, the witness cannot lie ; for it cannot go before the fact, as it is itself the effect of the fact. If the emotion is pleasurable it is the consciousness of the unity within ; if it is painful, of the disunity. In feeling, I am absolutely with myself; and there seems, therefore, to be no need of attempting to justify, by means of reason, a faith in God which manifests itself in emotion. The emotion itself is its own sufficient witness, a direct result of the intimate union of man with the object of devotion. Nay, we may go further, and say that the demand is an unjust one, and that it betrays ignorance of

the true nature of moral intuition and religious
feeling.

I am not concerned to deny the truth that
lies in the view here stated ; and no advocate of
the dignity of human reason, or of the worth of
human knowledge, is called upon to deny it.   There
is a sense in which the conviction of 'faith,' or
'feeling,' is more intimate and strong than any
process of proof.   But this does not in any wise
justify the contention of those who maintain that
we can feel what we do not in any sense know, or
that the heart can testify to that of which the
intellect is absolutely silent.

> "So let us say—not 'Since we know, we love,'
> But rather, 'Since we love, we know enough.'"[1]

In these two lines there are combined the truth I
would acknowledge, and the error I would confute.
Love is, in one way, sufficient knowledge ; or,
rather, it is the direct testimony of that completest
knowledge, in which subject and object interpenetrate.   For where love is, all foreign elements have
been eliminated.   There is not 'one and one with
a shadowy third'; but the object is brought within
the self as constituting part of its very life.   This
is involved in all the great forms of human thought—
in science and art, no less than in morality and religion.   It is the truth which we love, and it only, that
is altogether ours.   By means of love the poet is

> "Made one with Nature.   There is heard
> His voice in all her music, from the moan
> Of thunder to the song of night's sweet bird";

[1] *A Pillar at Sebzevar.*

and it is because he is made one with her that he is able to reveal her inmost secrets. "Man," said Fichte, "can will nothing but what he loves; his love is the sole and at the same time the infallible spring of his volition, and of all his life's striving and movement." It is only when we have identified ourselves with an ideal, and made its realization our own interest, that we strive to attain it. Love is revelation in knowledge, inspiration in art, motive in morality, and the fulness of religious joy.

But, although in this sense love is greater than knowledge, it is a grave error to separate it from knowledge. In the life of man, at least, the separation of the emotional and intellectual elements extinguishes both. We cannot know that in which we have no interest. The very effort to comprehend an object rests on interest, or the feeling of ourselves in it; so that knowledge, as well as morality, may be said to begin in love. We cannot know unless we love; but, on the other hand, we cannot love that which we do not in some degree know. Wherever the frontiers of knowledge may be, it is certain that there is nothing beyond them which can either arouse feeling, or be a steadying centre for it. Emotion is like a climbing plant. It clings to the tree of knowledge, adding beauty to its strength. But, without knowledge, emotion is impossible for man. There is no feeling which is not also incipient knowledge; for feeling is only the subjective side of knowledge—that face of the known fact which is turned inwards.

If, therefore, the poet's agnosticism were taken literally, and, in his philosophical poems he obviously means it to be taken literally, it would lead to a denial of the very principles of religion and morality which it was meant to support. His appeal to love would then, strictly speaking, be an appeal to the love of nothing known or knowable ; and such love is impossible. For love, if it is to be distinguished from the organic impulse of beast towards beast, must have an object. A mere instinctive activity of benevolence in man by means of which he lightened the sorrows of his brethren, if not informed with knowledge, would have no more moral worth than the grateful warmth of the sun. Such love as this there may be in the animal creation. If the bird is not rational, we may say that it builds its nest and lines it for its brood, pines for its partner and loves it, at the bidding of the returning spring, in much the same way as the meadows burst into flower. Without knowledge, the whole process is merely a natural one ; or, if it be more, it is so only in so far as the life of emotion can be regarded as a foretaste of the life of thought. But such a natural process is not possible to man. Every activity in him is relative to his self-consciousness, and takes a new character from that relation. His love at the best and worst is the love of something that he knows, and in which he seeks to find himself made rich with new sufficiency. Thus love can not 'ally' itself with ignorance. It is rather an impulse pressing for the closer communion of the lover with the object of his love.

"Like two meteors of expanding flame,
Those spheres instinct with it become the same,
Touch, mingle, are transfigured ; ever still
Burning, yet ever inconsumable ;
In one another's substance finding food."[1]

But, for a being incapable of knowledge, such
as Browning describes, who is shut up within
the blind walls of his own self, the self-tran-
scending impulse of love would be impossible. If
man's inner consciousness is to be conceived as
a dark room shutting out the world, upon whose
shadowy phenomena the candle of introspection
throws a dim and uncertain light, then he can
have no interest outside of himself ; nor can he
ever take that first step in goodness, which carries
him beyond his narrow individuality to seek and
find a larger self in others. Morality, even in
its lowest form, implies knowledge, and knowledge of something better than 'those *apparent*
other mortals.' With the first dawn of the moral
life comes the consciousness of an ideal, which is
not actual ; and such a break with the natural
is not possible except to him who has known a
better and desired it. The ethical endeavour of
man is the attempt to convert ideas into actuality ;
and all his activity as moral agent takes place
within the sphere that is illumined by the light
of knowledge. If knowledge breaks down, there
is no law of action which he can obey. The
moral law that must be apprehended, and whose
authority must be recognized by man, either sinks
out of being or becomes an illusive phantom, if

[1] Shelley's *Epipsychidion.*

U

man is doomed to ignorance or false knowledge.
To extinguish truth is to extinguish goodness.
Morality is impossible if knowledge of reality is
impossible.

In like manner religion, which the poet would
fain defend for man by means of agnosticism,
becomes impossible, if knowledge be denied. Religion is not blind emotion ; nor can mere feeling,
however ecstatic, ascend to God. Animals can
feel, but they are not, and cannot be, religious—
unless they can also know. The love of God
implies knowledge. " I know Him whom I have
believed " is the language of religion. For what
is religion but a conscious indentification of the
self with One who is known to fulfil its needs
and satisfy its aspirations? And if so, agnosticism
is directly destructive of it. We cannot, indeed,
prove God as the conclusion of a syllogism. He
is rather the primary hypothesis of all proof.
But, nevertheless, we cannot reach Him without
knowledge. Emotion reveals no object, but is
consequent upon the revelation of it ; feeling
yields no truth, but is the witness of the worth
of a truth for the individual. If man were shut
up to mere feeling, even the awe of the devout
agnostic would be impossible. For the Unknowable cannot generate any emotion. It appears
to do so, only because the Unknowable of the
agnostic is not altogether unknown to him ; but
is a vast, abysmal 'Something,' that has occupied
with its shadowy presence the field of his imagination. It is paganism stricken with the plague,
and philosophy afflicted with blindness, that build

altars to an unknown **God.** The highest and the **strongest** faith, the deepest trust and the most loving, come with the fullest knowledge. Indeed, the distinction between **the awe of** the agnostic, which is the lowest form of **religion, and that** highest form in which **perfect love casteth out** fear, springs **from the fuller knowledge of the** nature of the object of worship, which the latter implies. **Thus,** religion and morality grow **with** the growth of knowledge ; and neither has **a** worse enemy **than ignorance.** The human spirit cannot grow in **a one-sided manner.** Devotion to great moral ends is possible only through the deepening **and** widening of man's knowledge of the nature of the world. Those who know God best, render **unto** Him the purest service.

So evident is this, that it seems at first sight to be difficult to account for that antagonism **to the** intellect **and distrust of** its deliverances, **which are** so emphatically expressed in the writings of Browning, and which **are marked characteristics** of the ordinary religious opinion of our day. On closer examination, however, we shall discover **that it is not pure** emotion, or mere feeling, whose authority is **set** above that of reason, but rather the emotion which is *the result of knowledge.* The appeal of **the** religious man from the doubts and **difficulties,** which reason levels against 'the faith,' is really an appeal to the character that lies behind the emotion. The conviction of the heart, **that** refuses to yield **to** the arguments of the understanding, is not **mere** feeling ; but, rather, **the complex experience of the** past life, that manifests itself in feeling. When an individual, clinging to his moral or religious faith, says, "I have felt it," he opposes to the doubt, not his feeling as such, but his personality in all the wealth of its experience. The appeal to the heart is the appeal to the unproved, but not, therefore, unauthorized, testimony of the best men at their best moments, when their vision of truth is clearest. No one pretends that "the loud and empty voice of untrained passion and prejudice" has any authority in matters of moral and religious faith; though, in such cases, 'feeling' may lack neither depth nor intensity. If the 'feelings' of the good man were dissociated from his character, and stripped bare of all the significance they obtain therefrom, their worthlessness would become apparent. The profound error of condemning knowledge in order to honour feeling, is hidden only by the fact that the feeling is already informed and inspired with knowledge. Religious agnosticism, like all other forms of the theory of nescience, derives its plausibility from the adventitious help it purloins from the knowledge which it condemns.

That it is to such feeling that Browning really appeals against knowledge becomes abundantly evident, when we bear in mind that he always calls it 'love.' For love in man is never ignorant. It knows its object, and is a conscious identification of the self with it. And to Browning, the object of love, when love is at its best—of that love by means of which he refutes intellectual pessimism—is mankind. The revolt of the heart against all evil is a desire for the good of all men.   In other words, his refuge against the assailing doubts which spring from the intellect, is in the moral consciousness.   But that consciousness is no mere emotion; it is a consciousness which *knows* the highest good, and moves in sympathy with it.   It is our maturest wisdom; for it is the manifestation of the presence and activity of the ideal, the fullest knowledge and the surest.   Compared with this, the emotion linked to ignorance, of which the poet speaks in his philosophic theory, is a very poor thing.   It is poorer than the lowest human love.

Now, if this higher interpretation of the term 'heart' be accepted, it is easily seen why its authority should seem higher than that of reason; and particularly, if it be remembered that, while the heart is thus widened to take in all direct consciousness of the ideal, 'the reason' is reduced to the power of reflection, or mental analysis.   'The heart,' in this sense, is the intensest unity of the complex experiences of a whole life, while 'the reason' is taken merely as a faculty which invents arguments, and provides grounds and evidences : it is what is called, in the language of German philosophy, the 'understanding.'   Now, in this sense, the understanding has, at best, only a borrowed authority.   It is the faculty of rules rather than of principles.   It is ever dogmatic, assertive, repellent, hard; and it always advances its forces in single line.   Its logic never convinced any one of truth or error, unless, beneath the arguments which it advanced, there lay some deeper principle of concord.   Thus, the opposition between 'faith and reason,' rightly interpreted, is that between a concrete experience, instinct with life and conviction, and a mechanical arrangement of abstract arguments. The quarrel of the heart is **not** with reason, but with reasons. "Evidences of Christianity?", said Coleridge ; "I am weary of the word." **It is this** weariness of evidence, of the endless arguments *pro* and *con*, which has caused so many to distrust reason and knowledge, and which has sometimes driven believers to the dangerous expedient of making their faith dogmatic and absolute.

Nor have the opponents of 'the faith' been slow **to seize** the opportunity thus offered them. " From **the** moment that a religion solicits the aid **of** philosophy, its ruin is inevitable," said Heine. " In the attempt at defence, it prates itself into destruction. Religion, like every absolutism, must not seek to justify itself. Prometheus is bound **to** the rock by a silent force. Yea, Æschylus permits not personified power to utter a single word. It must remain mute. The moment that a religion ventures to print a catechism supported by arguments, the moment that a political absolutism publishes an official newspaper, both are near their end. But therein consists our triumph : we have brought our adversaries to speech, and they must reckon with us."[1] But we may answer, religion is *not* an absolutism ; and, therefore, it is *not* near its end when it ventures to justify itself. On the contrary, no spiritual power, be it moral or religious, can maintain its authority, **if it assumes a** despotic attitude ; for the human spirit inevitably moves towards freedom, and that movement is the deepest

[1] *Religion and Philosophy in Germany.*

necessity of its nature, which it cannot escape. "Religion on the ground of its sanctity, and law on the ground of its majesty, often resist the sifting of their claims. But in so doing, they inevitably awake a not unjust suspicion that their claims are ill-founded. They can command the unfeigned homage of man, only when they have shown themselves able to stand the test of free inquiry."

And if it is an error to suppose with Browning, that the primary truths of the moral and religious consciousness belong to a region which is higher than knowledge, and can, from that side, be neither assailed nor defended; it is also an error to suppose that reason is essentially antagonistic to them. The facts of morality and religion are precisely the richest facts of knowledge; and that faith is the most secure which is most completely illumined by reason. Religion at its best is not a dogmatic despotism, nor is reason a merely critical and destructive faculty. If reason is loyal to the truth of religion on which it is exercised, it will reach beneath all the conflict and clamour of disputation, to the principle of unity, on which, as we have seen, both reason and religion rest.

The 'faith' to which religious spirits appeal against all the attacks of doubt, 'the love' of Browning, is really implicit reason; it is 'abbreviated' or concentrated knowledge; it is the manifold experiences of life focussed into an intense unity. And, on the other hand, the 'reason' which they condemn is what Carlyle calls the logic-chopping faculty. In taking the side of faith when troubled with difficulties which they cannot lay, they are really defending the cause of reason against that of the understanding. For it is quite true that the understanding, that is, the reason as reflective or critical, can never bring about either a moral or religious life. It cannot create a religion, any more than physiology can produce men. The reflection which brings doubt is always secondary; it can only exercise itself on a given material. As Hegel frequently pointed out, it is not the function of moral philosophy to create or to institute a morality or religion, but to understand them. The facts must first be given; they must be actual experiences of the human spirit. Moral philosophy and theology differ from the moral or religious life, in the same way as geology differs from the earth, or astronomy from the heavenly bodies. The latter are facts; the former are theories about the facts. Religion is an attitude of the human spirit towards the highest; morality is the realization of character; and these are not to be confused with their reflective interpretations, that is, with ethics or theology. Much of the difficulty in these matters comes from the lack of a clear distinction between *beliefs* and *creeds*.

Further, not only are the utterances of the heart prior to the deliverances of the intellect in this sense, but it may also be admitted that the latter can never do full justice to the contents of the former. So rich is character in content and so complex is spiritual life, that we can never, by means of reflection, lift into clear consciousness all the elements that enter into them. Into the organism of our experience, which is our faith, there is continually absorbed the subtle influences of our complex natural and social environment. We grow by means of them, as the plant grows by feeding on the soil and the sunshine and dew. It is as impossible for us to set forth, one by one, the truths and errors which we have thus worked into our mental and moral life, as it is to keep a reckoning of the physical atoms with which the natural life builds up the body. Hence, every attempt to justify these truths seems inadequate ; and the defence which the understanding sets up for the faith, always seems partial and cold. Who ever fully expressed his deepest convictions ? The consciousness of the dignity of the moral law affected Kant like the view of the starry firmament, and generated a feeling of the sublime which words could not express; and the religious ecstasy of the saints cannot be confined within the channels of speech, but floods the soul with overmastering power, possessing all its faculties. In this respect, it will always remain true that the greatest facts of human experience reach beyond all knowledge. Nay, we may add further, that in this respect the very simplest of these facts passes all understanding. Still, as we have already seen, it is reason that constitutes them ; that which is presented to reason for explanation, in knowledge and morality and religion, is itself the product of reason. Reason is the power which, by interaction with our environment, has generated the whole of our experience. And, just as natural science interprets the phenomena given to it by ordinary opinion, *i.e.* interprets and purifies a lower form of knowledge by con-

verting it into a higher; so the task of reason,
when it is exercised upon morality and religion, is
simply to evolve, and amplify the meaning of its
own products. The movement from morality and
religion to moral philosophy and the philosophy
of religion, is thus a movement from reason to
reason, from the implicit to the explicit, from the
germ to the developed fulness of life and structure.
In this matter, as in all others wherein the human
spirit is concerned, that which is first by nature is
last in genesis—νικᾷ δ' ὁ πρῶτος καὶ τελευταῖος
δραμών. The whole history of the moral and
religious experience of mankind is comprised in
the statement, that the implicit reason which we
call 'faith' is ever developing towards full consciousness of itself: and that at its first beginning, and
throughout the whole ascending process of this
development, the highest is present in it as a self-
manifesting power.

But this process from the almost instinctive
intuitions of the heart towards the morality and
religion of freedom, being a process of evolution,
necessarily involves conflict. There are men, it is
true, the unity of whose moral and religious faith
is never completely broken by doubt; just as there
are men who are not forced by the contradictions
in the first interpretation of the world by ordinary
experience, to attempt to re-interpret it by means
of science and philosophy. Throughout their lives
they may say like Pompilia—

> "I know the right place by foot's feel,
> took it and tread firm there; wherefore change?"[1]

[1] *The Ring and the Book—The Pope*, 1886-1887.

Jean Paul Richter said that he knew another way of being happy, beside that of soaring away so far above the clouds of life, that its miseries looked small, and the whole external world shrunk into a little child's garden. It was, " Simply to sink down into this little garden ; and there to nestle yourself so snugly, so homewise, in some furrow, that in looking out from your warm lark-nest, you likewise can discern no wolf-dens, charnel-houses, or thunder-rods, but only blades and ears, every one of which for the nest-birds, is a tree, and a sun-screen, and rain-screen." There is a similar way of being good, with a goodness which, though limited, is pure and perfect in nature. Nay, we may even admit that such lives are frequently the most complete and beautiful ; just as the fairest flowers grow, not on the tallest trees, but on the fragile plants at their foot. Nevertheless, even in the case of those persons who have never broken from the traditional faith of the past, or felt it to be inadequate, that faith has been silently reconstructed in a new synthesis of knowledge. Spiritual life cannot come by inheritance ; but every individual must acquire a faith for himself, and turn his spiritual environment into personal experience. " A man may be a heretic in the truth," said Milton, " and if he believe things only because his pastor says so, or the assembly so determines, without knowing other reason, though his belief be true, yet the very truth he holds becomes his heresy." It is truth to another but tradition to him ; it is a creed and not a conviction.

Browning fully recognizes the need of this conflict—

> " Is it not this ignoble confidence,
>   Cowardly hardihood, that dulls and damps,
>   Makes the old heroism impossible ?"[1]

asks the Pope. The stream of truth when it
ceases to flow onward, becomes a malarious swamp.
Movement is the law of life; and knowledge of the
principles of morality and religion, as of all other
principles, must, in order to grow, be felt from time
to time as inadequate and untrue. There are men
and ages whose mission is—

> **"to shake**
> This torpor of assurance from **our creed,**
>   Re-introduce the doubt discarded, bring
>   That formidable danger back, we drove
>   Long ago to the distance and the dark."[2]

Such a spirit of criticism seems to many to exercise a merely destructive power, and those who
have not felt the inadequacy of the inherited faith
defend themselves against it, as the enemy of their
lives. But no logic, or assailing doubt, could have
power against the testimony of 'the heart,' unless
it was rooted in deeper and truer principles than
those which it attacked. Nothing can overpower
truth except a larger truth; and, in such a conflict,
the truth in the old view will ultimately take the
side of the new, and find its subordinate position
within it. It has happened, not infrequently, as in
the case of the Encyclopædists, that the explicit
truths of reason were more abstract, that is, less
true, than the implicit 'faith' which they assailed.
The central truths of religion have often proved

---

[1] *The Ring and the Book—The Pope,* 1848-1850.
[2] *Ibid.* 1853-1856

themselves to possess some stubborn, though semi-articulate power, which could ultimately overcome or subordinate the more partial and explicit truths of abstract science. It is this that gives plausibility to the idea, that the testimony of the heart is more reliable than that of the intellect. But, in this case also, it was really reason that triumphed. It was the truth which proved itself to be immortal, and not any mere emotion. The insurrection of the intellect against the heart is quelled, only when the untruth, or abstract character, of the principle of the assailants has been made manifest, and when the old faith has yielded up its unjust gains, and proved its vitality and strength by absorbing the truth that gave vigour to the attack. Just as in morality it is the ideal, or the unity of the whole moral life, that breaks up into differences, so also here it is the implicit faith which, as it grows, breaks forth into doubts. In both cases alike, the negative movement which induces despair is only a phase of a positive process—the process of reason towards a fuller, a more articulate and complex realization of itself.

Hence it follows that the value and strength of a faith corresponds accurately to the doubts it has overcome. Those who never went forth to battle cannot come home heroes. It is only when the earthquake has tried the towers, and destroyed the sense of security, that

> "Man stands out again, pale, resolute,
> Prepared to die,—that is, alive at last.
> As we broke up that old faith of the world,
> Have we, next age, to break up this the new—

> Faith, in the thing, grown faith in the report—
> Whence need to bravely disbelieve report
> Through increased faith i' the thing reports belie?"[1]

"Well knows he who uses to consider, that our faith and knowledge thrive by exercise, as well as our limbs and complexion.[2]

It was thus, I conclude, a deep speculative error into which Browning fell, when, in order to substantiate his optimistic faith, he stigmatized human knowledge as merely apparent. Knowledge does not fail, except in the sense in which morality also fails; it does not at any time attain to the ultimate truth, any more than the moral life is in any of its activities[3] a complete embodiment of the absolute good. It is not given to man, who is essentially progressive, to reach the ultimate term of development. For there is no ultimate term: life never stands still. But, for the same reason, there is no ultimate failure. The whole history of man is a history of growth. If, however, knowledge did fail, then morality too must fail; and the appeal which the poet makes from the intellect to the heart would be an appeal to mere emotion. Finally, even if we take a generous view of the poet's meaning, and put out of consideration the theory he expresses when he is deliberately philosophizing, there is still no appeal from the reason to an alien and higher authority. The appeal to 'the heart' is, at best, only an appeal from the understanding to the reason, from a conscious logic

---

[1] *The Ring and the Book—The Pope*, 1862-1868.
[2] Milton's *Areopagitica*.   [3] See Chapter IX., p. 288.

to the more concrete fact constituted by reason which reflection has failed to comprehend in all its completeness ; at its worst, it is an appeal from truth to prejudice, from belief to dogma.

And in both cases alike, the appeal is futile ; for, whether 'the heart be wiser than the head,' or not, whether the faith which is assailed be richer or poorer, truer or more false, than the logic which is directed against it, an appeal to the heart cannot any longer restore the unity of the broken life. Once reflection has set in, there is no way of turning away its destructive might, except by deeper reflection. The implicit faith of the heart must become the explicit faith of reason. "There is no final and satisfactory issue from such an endless internal debate and conflict, until the 'heart' has learnt to speak the language of the head—*i.e.* until the permanent principles, which underlay and gave strength to faith, have been brought into the light of distinct consciousness."[1]

I conclude, therefore, that the poet was right in saying that, in order to comprehend human character,

> "I needs must blend the quality of man
> With quality of God, and so assist
> Mere human sight to understand my Life."[2]

But it was a profound error, which contained in it the destruction of morality and religion, as well as of knowledge, to make 'the quality of God' a love that excludes reason, and the quality of man an intellect incapable of knowing truth. Such incongruous elements could never be combined into

---

[1] Caird's *Comte.*   [2] *A Bean-Stripe—Ferishtah's Fancies.*

the unity of a character. A love that was mere emotion could not yield a motive for morality, or a principle of religion. A philosophy of life which is based on agnosticism is an explicit self-contradiction, which can help no one. We must appeal from Browning the philosopher to Browning the poet.

CHAPTER XI

CONCLUSION

> " Well, I can fancy how he did it all,
>   Pouring his soul, with kings and popes to see
>   Reaching, that heaven might so replenish him,
>   Above and through his art—for it gives way ;
>   That arm is wrongly put—and there again—
>   A fault to pardon in the drawing's lines,
>   Its body, so to speak : its soul is right,
>   He means right—that, a child may understand."[1]

I HAVE tried to show that Browning's theory of life, in so far as it is expressed in his philosophical poems, rests on agnosticism; and that such a theory is inconsistent with the moral and religious interests of man. The idea that truth is unattainable was represented by Browning as a bulwark of the faith, but it proved on examination to be treacherous. His optimism was found to have no better foundation than personal conviction, which any one was free to deny, and which the poet could in no wise prove. The evidence of the heart, to which he appealed, was the evidence of an emotion severed from intelligence,

[1] *Andrea del Sarto.*

x

and, therefore, without **any** content whatsoever. 'The faith,' which he professed, was not the faith **that anticipates and** invites proof, **but a** faith which **is incapable of proof.** In **casting** doubt upon the validity of knowledge, he degraded the whole spiritual nature of man; **for** a love **that** is ignorant of its **object is a** blind impulse, and **a moral con**sciousness that does not know the law **is an impossible** phantom—a self-contradiction.

But, although Browning's explicitly philosophical **theory** of life fails, there appears **in his earlier poems,** where his poetical freedom was not yet trammelled, nor his moral enthusiasm restrained **by the** stubborn difficulties of reflective thought, **a far truer** and richer view. In this period of **pure** poetry, **his** conception of man was less abstract than in **his** later **works, and his inspiration was more** direct and full. The poet's dialectical ingenuity increased with the **growth of his reflective** tendencies; but his relation to the great principles of spiritual life seemed to become **less** intimate, and his expression of them more halting. What we find in his earlier works are vigorous ethical convictions, a glowing optimistic faith, achieving **their** fitting expression in impassioned poetry; **what we** find in his later works are arguments, **which, however** richly adorned with poetic metaphors, have **lost** the completeness and energy of **life.** His poetic fancies are like chaplets which crown the dead. **Lovers** of the poet, who seek in **his** poems for inspiring expressions **of** their hope and faith, will always do well **in** turning from his militant **metaphysics to his art.**

In his case, as in that of many others, spiritual experience was far richer than the theory which professed to explain it. The task of lifting his moral convictions into the clear light of conscious philosophy was beyond his power. The theory of the failure of knowledge, which he seems to have adopted far too easily from the current doctrine of the schools, was fundamentally inconsistent with his generous belief in the moral progress of man ; and it maimed the expression of that belief. The result of his work as a philosopher is a confession of complete ignorance and the helpless asseveration of a purely dogmatic faith.

The fundamental error of the poet's philosophy lies, I believe, in that severance of feeling and intelligence, love and reason, which finds expression in *La Saisiaz, Ferishtah's Fancies, The Parleyings*, and *Asolando.* Such an absolute division is not to be found in *Christmas-Eve and Easter-Day, Rabbi Ben Ezra, A Death in the Desert*, or in *The Ring and the Book* ; nor even in *Fifine at the Fair.* In these works we are not perplexed by the strange combination of a nature whose principle is love, and which is capable of infinite progress, with an intelligence whose best efforts end in ignorance. Rather, the spirit of man is regarded as one, in all its manifestations; and, therefore, as progressive on all sides of its activity. The widening of his knowledge, which is brought about by increasing experience, is parallel with the deepening and purifying of his moral life. In all Browning's works, indeed, with the possible exception of *Paracelsus*, love is conceived as having a place and function of supreme importance in the development of the soul. Its divine origin and destiny are never obscured ; **but** knowledge is regarded as merely human, and, therefore, as falling short of the truth. In *Easter-Day* it is definitely contrasted with love, and shown **to be** incapable of satisfying the deepest wants of **man**. It is, at the **best**, only a means to the higher purposes of **moral** activity, and, except in the *Grammarian's Funeral*, it is nowhere regarded as in itself **a worthy end**.

> "'Tis one thing to know, and another to practise.
>   And thence I conclude that the real God-function
>   Is to furnish a motive and injunction
>   For practising what we know already."[1]

Even here, there is implied that the motive comes otherwise than by knowledge ; still taking these earlier poems as a whole, we may say that in them knowledge is regarded **as** means to morality and not as in any sense contrasted with or destructive of it. Man's motives are rational motives ; the ends he seeks are ends conceived and even constituted by his intelligence, and not purposes blindly followed **as** by instinct and impulse.

> "Why live,
> **Except for** love—how love, unless **they know** ?"[2]

asks the Pope. Moral progress is not secured apart from, or in spite of knowledge. We are not exhorted to reject the verdict of the latter as

---

[1] *Christmas-Eve and Easter-Day.*
[2] *The Ring and the Book—The Pope,* 1327, 1328.

illusive, in order to confide in a faith which not only fails to receive support from the defective intelligence, but maintains its own integrity only by repudiating the testimony of the reason. In the distinction between knowledge as means and love as end, it is easy, indeed, to detect a tendency to degrade the former into a mere temporary expedient, whereby moral ends may be served. The poet speaks of "such knowledge as is possible to man." The attitude he assumes towards it is apologetic, and betrays a keen consciousness of its limitation, and particularly of its utter inadequacy to represent the infinite. In the speech of the Pope—which can scarcely be regarded otherwise than as the poet's own maturest utterance on the great moral and religious questions raised by the tragedy of Pompilia's death—we find this view vividly expressed :—

> "O Thou—as represented here to me
> In such conception as my soul allow,—
> Under Thy measureless, my atom width !—
> Man's mind, what is it but a convex glass
> Wherein are gathered all the scattered points
> Picked out of the immensity of sky,
> To reunite there, be our heaven for earth,
> Our known unknown our God revealed to man ?"[1]

God is "appreciable in His absolute immensity solely by Himself," while, "by the little mind of man, He is reduced to littleness that suits man's faculty." In these words, and others that might be quoted, the poet shows that he is profoundly impressed with the distinction between human

[1] *The Ring and the Book—The Pope,* 1308-1315.

knowledge, and that knowledge which is adequate to the whole nature and extent of being. And in *Christmas-Eve* he repudiates, with a touch of scorn, the absolute idealism which is supposed to identify altogether human reason with divine reason ; and he commends the German critic for not making

> "The important stumble
> Of adding, he, the sage and humble,
> Was also one with the Creator." [1]

Nowhere in Browning, unless we except *Paracelsus*, is there any sign of an inclination to treat man's knowledge in the same spirit as he deals with man's love,—namely, as a direct emanation from the inmost nature of God, a divine element that completes and crowns man's life on earth. On the contrary, he shows a persistent tendency to treat love as a power higher in nature than reason, and to give to it a supreme place in the formation of character ; and, as he grows older, that tendency grows in strength. The philosophical poems, in which love is made all in all, and knowledge is reduced to nescience, follow by logical evolution from principles, the influence of which we can detect even in his earlier works. Still, in the latter, these principles are only latent, and are far from holding undisputed sway. Browning was, at first, restrained from exclusive devotion to abstract views, by the suggestions which the artistic spirit receives through its immediate contact with the facts of life. That contact is very difficult for philosophy to maintain as it pursues its effort

[1] *Christmas-Eve.*

after universal truth. Philosophy is obliged to analyze in order to define, and, in that process, it is apt to lose something of that completeness of representation, which belongs to art. For art is always engaged in presenting the universal in the form of a particular object of beauty. Its product is a 'known unknown,' but the unknown is the unexhausted reality of a fact of intuition. Nor can analysis ever exhaust it; theory can never catch up art, or explain all that is in it. On similar grounds, it may be shown that it is impossible for reason to lay bare all the elements that enter into its first complex product, which we call faith. In religion, as in art, man is aware of more than he knows; his articulate logic cannot do justice to all the truths of the 'heart.' "The supplementary reflux of light" of philosophy cannot "illustrate all the inferior grades" of knowledge. Man will never completely understand himself.

> "I knew, I felt, (perfection unexpressed,
>   Uncomprehended by our narrow thought,
>   But somehow felt and known in every shift
>   And change in the spirit,—nay, in every pore
>   Of the body, even,)—what God is, what we are
>   What life is—how God tastes an infinite joy
>   In infinite ways—one everlasting bliss,
>   From whom all being emanates, all power
>   Proceeds."[1]

I believe that it is possible, by the help of the intuitions of Browning's highest artistic period, to bring together again the elements of his broken faith, and to find in them suggestions of a truer

[1] *Paracelsus.*

philosophy of life than anything which the poet himself achieved. Perhaps, indeed, it is not easy, nor altogether fair, to press the passionate utterances of his religious rapture into the service of metaphysics, and to treat the unmeasured language of emotion as the expression of a definite doctrine. Nevertheless, rather than set forth a new defence of the faith, which his agnosticism left exposed to the assaults of doubt and denial, it is better to make Browning correct his own errors, and to appeal from the metaphysician to the poet, from the sobriety of the logical understanding to the inspiration of poetry.

I have already indicated what seems to me to be the defective element in the poet's philosophy of life. His theory of knowledge is in need of revision; and what he asserts of human love should be applied point by point to human reason. As man is ideally united with the absolute on the side of moral emotion (if the phrase may be pardoned), so he is ideally united with the absolute on the side of the intellect. As there is no difference of *nature* between God's goodness and man's goodness, so there is no difference of nature between God's truth and man's truth. There are not two kinds of righteousness or mercy; there are not two kinds of truth. Human nature is not 'cut in two with a hatchet,' as the poet implies that it is. There is in man a lower and a higher element, ever at war with each other; still he is not a mixture, or an agglomerate, of the finite and the infinite. A love perfect in nature cannot be linked to an intelligence imperfect in nature;

if it were, the love would be either a blind impulse or an erring one. Both morality and religion demand the presence in man of a perfect ideal, which is at war with his imperfections; but an ideal is possible only to a being endowed with a capacity for knowing the truth. In degrading human knowledge, the poet was disloyal to the fundamental principle of the Christian faith which he professed—that God can and does manifest Himself in man.

On the other hand, we are not to take the unity of man with God, of man's moral ideal with the All-perfect, as implying, on the moral side, an absolute indentification of the finite with the infinite; nor can we do so on the side of knowledge. Man's moral life and rational activity in knowledge are the process of the highest. But man is neither first, nor last; he is not the original author of his love, any more than of his reason; he is not the divine principle of the whole to which he belongs although he is potentially in harmony with it. Both sides of his being are equally touched with imperfection— his love, no less than his reason. Perfect love would imply perfect wisdom, as perfect wisdom, perfect love. But absolute terms are not applicable to man, who is ever *on the way* to goodness and truth, progressively manifesting the power of the ideal that dwells in him, and whose very life is conflict and acquirement.

> "Ah, but a man's reach should exceed his grasp,
> Or what's a heaven for? All is silver-grey
> Placid and perfect with my art : the worse."[1]

[1] *Andrea del Sarto.*

Hardly any conception is more prominent in Browning's writing than this, of endless progress towards an infinite ideal ; although he occasionally manifests a desire to have done with effort.

> "When a soul has seen
>   By the means of Evil that Good is best,
> And, through earth and its noise, what is heaven's serene,—
>   When our faith in the same has stood the test—
> Why, the child grown man, you burn the rod,
>   The uses of labour are surely done,
> There remaineth a rest for the people of God,
>   And I have had troubles enough, for one."[1]

It is the sense of endless onward movement, the outlook towards an immortal course, 'the life after life in unlimited series,' which is so inspiring in his early poetry. He conceives that we are here, on this lower earth, just to learn one form, the elementary lesson and alphabet of goodness, namely, 'the uses of the flesh': in other lives, other achievements. The separation of the soul from its instrument has very little significance to the poet ; for it does not arrest the course of moral development.

> "No work begun shall ever pause for death."

The spirit pursues its lone way, on other 'adventures brave and new,' but ever towards a good which is complete.

> "Delayed it may be for more lives yet,
>   Through worlds I shall traverse, not a few:
> Much is to learn, much to forget
>   Ere the time be come for taking you."[2]

[1] *Old Pictures in Florence.*   [2] *Evelyn Hope.*

Still the time will come when the awakened need shall be satisfied ; for the need was created in order to be satisfied.

> "Wherefore did I contrive for thee that ear
>   Hungry for music, and direct thine eye
>   To where I hold a seven-stringed instrument,
>   Unless I meant thee to beseech me play?"[1]

The movement onward is thus a movement in knowledge, as well as in every other form of good. The lover of Evelyn Hope, looking back in imagination on the course he has travelled on earth and after, exclaims—

> "I have lived (I shall say) so much since then,
>   Given up myself so many times,
> Gained me the gains of various men,
>   Ransacked the ages, spoiled the climes."[2]

In these earlier poems, there is not, as in the later ones, a maimed, or one-sided, evolution—a progress towards perfect love on the side of the heart, and towards an illusive ideal on the side of the intellect. Knowledge, too, has its value, and he who lived to settle "*Hoti's* business, properly based *Oun*," and who "gave us the doctrine of the enclitic *De*," was, to the poet,

> "Still loftier than the world suspects,
>   Living and dying.

> "Here's the top-peak ; the multitude below
>   Live, for they can, there :
> This man decided not to Live but Know—
>   Bury this man there?

---

[1] *Two Camels.*   [2] *Evelyn Hope.*

> Here—here's his place, where meteors shoot, clouds form,
>   Lightnings are loosened,
> Stars come and go."[1]

No human effort goes to waste, no gift is delusive ; but every gift and every effort has its proper place as a stage in the endless process. The soul bears in it *all* its conquests.

> "There shall never be one lost good ! What was, shall live
>   as before ;
>   The evil is null, is nought, is silence implying sound ;
>   What was good, shall be good, with, for evil, so much good
>   more ;
>   On the earth the broken arcs ; in the heaven, a perfect
>   round."[2]

The 'apparent failure' of knowledge, like every apparent failure, is 'a triumph's evidence for the fulness of the days.' The doubts that knowledge brings, instead of implying a defective intelligence doomed to spend itself on phantom phenomena, sting to progress towards the truth. He bids us "Learn, nor account the pang ; dare, never grudge the throe."

> "Rather I prize the doubt
> Low kinds exist without,
> Finished and finite clods, untroubled by a spark."[3]

Similarly, defects in art, like defects in character, contain the promise of further achievement.

> "Are they perfect of lineament, perfect of stature?
>   In both, of such lower types are we

[1] *A Grammarian's Funeral.*   [2] *Abt Vogler.*
[3] *Rabbi Ben Ezra.*

Precisely because of our wider nature ;
  For time, their's—ours, for eternity.

"To-day's brief passion limits their range ;
  It seethes with the morrow for us and more.
They are perfect—how else? They shall never change :
  We are faulty—why not? We have time in store."[1]

Prior to the period when a sceptical philosophy came down like a blight, and destroyed the bloom of his art and faith, he thus recognized that growing knowledge was an essential condition of growing goodness. Pompilia shone with a glory that mere knowledge could not give (if there were such a thing as *mere* knowledge).

"Everywhere
I see in the world the intellect of man,
That sword, the energy his subtle spear,
The knowledge which defends him like a shield—
Everywhere; but they make not up, I think,
The marvel of a soul like thine, earth's flower
She holds up to the softened gaze of God."[2]

But yet she recognized with patient pain the loss she had sustained for want of knowledge.

"The saints must bear with me, impute the fault
  To a soul i' the bud, so starved by ignorance,
Stinted of warmth, it will not blow this year
Nor recognize the orb which Spring-flowers know."[3]

Further on in the Pope's soliloquy, the poet shows that, at that time, he fully recognized the risk of entrusting the spiritual interests of man, either to

---

[1] *Old Pictures in Florence.*
[2] *The Ring and the Book—The Pope*, 1013-1019.
[3] *The Ring and the Book—Pompilia*, 1515-1518.

the enthusiasm of elevated feeling, or to the mere
intuitions of a noble heart.   Such intuitions will
sometimes guide a man happily, as in the case of
Caponsacchi :

> "Since ourselves allow
> He has danced, in gaiety of heart, i' the main
> The right step through the maze we bade him foot."[1]

But, on the other hand, such impulses, not
instructed by knowledge of the truth, and made
steadfast to the laws of the higher life by a
reasoned conviction, lead man rightly only by accident.   In such a career there is no guarantee of
constancy ; other impulses might lead to other
ways of life.

> "But if his heart had prompted to break loose
> And mar the measure? Why, we must submit,
> And thank the chance that brought him safe so far.
> Will he repeat the prodigy? Perhaps.
> Can he teach others how to quit themselves,
> Show why this step was right while that were wrong?
> How should he? 'Ask your hearts as I asked mine,
> And get discreetly through the morrice too ;
> If your hearts misdirect you,—quit the stage,
> And make amends,—be there amends to make.'"[2]

If the heart proved to Caponsacchi a guide to
all that is good and glorious, 'the Abate, second
in the suite,' puts in the testimony of another
experience : 'His heart answered to another tune.'

> "I have my taste too, and tread no such step !
> You choose the glorious life, and may for me !

[1] *The Ring and the Book—The Pope,* 1915-1917.
[2] *Ibid.* 1916-1927

> I like the lowest of life's appetites,—
> So you judge—but the very truth of joy
> To my own apprehension which decides." [1]

Mere emotion is thus an insecure guide to conduct, for its authority can be equally cited in support of every course of life. No one can say to his neighbour, " Thou art wrong." Every impulse is right to the individual who has it, and so long as he has it. *De gustibus non disputandum.* Without a universal criterion there is no praise or blame.

> " Call me knave and you get yourself called fool !
> I live for greed, ambition, lust, revenge ;
> Attain these ends by force, guile   hypocrite,
> To-day, perchance to-morrow recognized
> The rational man, the type of common-sense." [2]

This poem which, both in its moral wisdom and artistic worth, marks the high tide of Browning's poetic insight, while he is not as yet concerned with the defence of any theory or the discussion of any abstract question, contrasts strongly with the later poems, where knowledge is dissembling ignorance, faith is blind trust, and love is a mere impulse of the heart. Having failed to meet the difficulties of reflection, the poet turned upon the intellect. Knowledge becomes to him an offence, and to save his faith he plucked out his right eye and entered into the kingdom maimed. In *Rabbi Ben Ezra* the ascent into another life is triumphant, like that of a conqueror bearing with him the

---

[1] *The Ring and the Book—The Pope*, 1932-1936.
[2] *Ibid.* 1937-1941.

spoils of earth ; but in the later poems he escapes
with a bare belief, and the loss of all his rich
possessions of knowledge, like a shipwrecked
mariner whose goods have been thrown overboard.
Browning's philosophy was a treacherous ally to his
faith.

But there is another consideration which shows
that the poet, as artist, recognized the need of
giving to reason a larger function than seems to be
possible according to the theory in his later
works. In the early poems there is no hint of the
doctrine that demonstrative knowledge of the
good, and of the necessity of its law, would
destroy freedom. On the contrary, there are
suggestions which point to the opposite doctrine,
according to which knowledge is the condition of
freedom.

While in his later poems the poet speaks of love
as an impulse—either blind or bound to erring
knowledge—and of the heart as made to love, in
his earlier ones he seems to treat man as free to
work out his own purposes, and to act out his
own ideals. Browning there finds himself able to
maintain the dependence of man upon God
without destroying morality. He regards man's
impulses not as blind instincts, but as falling
within his rational nature, and constituting the
forms of its activity. He recognizes the distinction
between a mere impulse, in the sense of a tendency
to act, which is directed by a foreign power, and
an impulse informed, that is, directed by reason.
According to this view, it is reason which at once
gives man the independence of foreign authority that

is implied in morality, and constitutes that affinity between man and God which is implied in religion. No doubt, the impulse to know, like the impulse to love, was put into man ; his whole nature is a gift, and he is therefore, in this sense, completely dependent upon God—" God's all, man's nought." But, on the other hand, it *is* a rational nature which has been put into him, and not an irrational impulse. Or, rather, the impulse that constitutes his life as man, is the self-evolving activity of reason.

> " Who speaks of man, then, must not sever
> Man's very elements from man."[1]

However the rational nature of man has come to be, whether by emanation or creation, it necessarily brings freedom with it, and all its risks and possibilities. It is of the very essence of reason that it should find its law within itself.

> " God's all, man's nought :
> But also, God, whose pleasure brought
> Man into being, stands away
> As it were a hand-breadth off, to give
> Room for the newly-made to live,
> And look at him from a place apart,
> And use his gifts of brain and heart,
> Given, indeed, but to keep for ever."[2]

Thus, while insisting on the absolute priority of God and the original receptivity of man ; while recognizing that love, reason, and every inner power and outer opportunity are lent to man, Browning does not forget what these powers are. Man can

[1] *Christmas Eve.* [2] *Ibid.*

only act as man ; he must obey his nature, as the
stock or stone or plant obeys its nature. But to
act as man is to act freely, and man's nature is not
that of a stock or stone.   He is rational, and cannot
but be rational.   Hence he can neither be ruled, as
dead matter is ruled, by natural law; nor live, like
a bird, the life of innocent impulse or instinct.   He
is placed, from the very first, on " the table land
whence life upsprings aspiring to be immortality."
He is a spirit,—responsible because he is free, and
free because he is rational.

> " Man, therefore stands on his own stock
> Of love and power as a pin-point rock,
> And, looks to God who ordained divorce
> Of the rock from His boundless continent." [1]

The divorce is real, although ordained, but it is
possible only in so far as man, by means of reason,
constitutes his own ends of action.   Impulse cannot
bring it about.   It is reason that enables man to
free himself from the despotic authority of outer law,
to relate himself to an inner law, and by reconciling
inner and outer to attain to goodness.   Thus reason
is the source of all morality.   And it also is the
principle of religion, for it implies the highest and
fullest manifestation of the absolute.

Although the first aspect of self-consciousness is
its independence, which is, in turn, the first condition
of morality, still this is only the first aspect.   The
rational being plants himself on his own individuality, stands aloof and alone in the rights of his
freedom, *in order that* he may set out from thence

----

[1] *Christmas-Eve.*

to take possession, by means of knowledge and action, of the world in which he is placed. Reason is potentially absolute, capable of finding itself everywhere. So that in it man is " honour-clothed and glory-crowned."

> " This is the honour,—that no thing I know,
> Feel or conceive, but I can make my own
> Somehow, by use of hand, or head, or heart." [1]

Man, by his knowledge, overcomes the resistance and hostility of the world without him, or rather, discovers that there is not hostility, but affinity between it and himself.

> " This is the glory,—that in all conceived,
> Or felt or known, I recognize a mind
> Not mine but like mine,—for the double joy,—
> Making all things for me and me for Him." [2]

That which is finite is hemmed in by other things, as well as determined by them ; but the infinite is all-inclusive. There exists for it no other thing to limit or determine it. There is nothing finally alien or foreign to reason. Freedom and infinitude, self-determination and absoluteness, imply each other. In so far as man is free, he is lifted above the finite. It was God's plan to make man on His own image :—

> " To create man and then leave him
> Able, His own word saith, to grieve Him,
> But able to glorify Him too,
> As a mere machine could never do,
> That prayed or praised, all unaware

[1] *Prince Hohenstiel-Schwangau.*   [2] *Ibid.*

> Of its fitness for aught but praise or prayer,
> Made perfect as a thing of course." [1]

Man must find his law within himself, be the source of his own activity, not passive or receptive, but outgoing and effective.

> " Rejoice we are allied
> To that which doth provide
> And not partake, effect and not receive !
> A spark disturbs our clod ;
> Nearer we hold of God
> Who gives, than of His tribes that take, I must
> believe." [2]

This near affinity between the divine and human is just what Browning seems to repudiate in his later poems, when he speaks as if the absolute, in order to maintain its own supremacy over man, had to stint its gifts and endow him only with a defective reason. In the earlier period of the poet there is far less timidity. He then saw that the greater the gift, the greater the Giver ; that only spirit can reveal spirit ; that ' God is glorified in man,' and that love is at its fullest only when it gives itself.

In insisting on such identity of the human spirit with the divine, our poet does not at any time run the risk of forgetting that the identity is not absolute. Absolute identity would be pantheism, which leaves God lonely and loveless, and extinguishes man, as well as his morality.

> " Man is not God, but hath God's end to serve,
> A Master to obey, a course to take,
> Somewhat to cast off, somewhat to become." [3]

[1] *Christmas-Eve.* [2] *Rabbi Ben Ezra.* [3] *A Death in the Desert.*

Man, at best, only moves *towards* his ideal : God is conceived as the ever-existing ideal. God, in short, is the term which signifies for us the Being who is eternally all in all, and who, therefore, is hidden from us who are only moving *towards* perfection, in the excess of the brightness of His own glory. Nevertheless, as Browning recognizes, the grandeur of God's perfection is just His outflowing love. And that love is never complete in its manifestation, till it has given itself. Man's life, as spirit, is thus one in nature with that of the absolute. But the unity is not complete, because man is only potentially perfect. He is the process *of* the ideal ; his life is the divine activity within him. Still, it is also man's activity. For the process, being the process of spirit, is a *free* process—one in which man himself energizes ; so that, in doing God's will, he is doing his own highest will, and, in obeying the law of his own deepest nature, he is obeying God. The unity of divine and human within the spiritual life of man is a real unity, just because man is free ; the identity manifests itself through the difference, and the difference is possible through the unity.

Thus, in the light of an ideal which is moral, and therefore perfect—an ideal gradually realizing itself in a process which is endless—the poet is able to maintain at once the community between man and God, which is necessary to religion, and their independence, which is necessary to morality. The conception of God as giving, which is the main doctrine of Christianity, and of man as akin with God, is applied by him to the whole spiritual nature of man, and not merely to his emotion. The process of evolution is thus a process towards truth, as well as goodness; in fact, goodness and truth are known as inseparable. Knowledge, too, is a divine endowment. "What gift of man is not from God descended?" What gift of God can be deceptive?

> "Take all in a word: the truth in God's breast
> Lies trace for trace upon ours impressed:
> Though He is so bright and we so dim,
> We are made in His image to witness Him."[1]

The Pope recognizes clearly the inadequacy of human knowledge; but he also recognizes that it has a divine source.

> "Yet my poor spark had for its source, the sun;
> Thither I sent the great looks which compel
> Light from its fount: all that I do and am
> Comes from the truth, or seen or else surmised,
> Remembered or divined, as mere man may."[2]

The last words indicate a suspicion of a certain defect in knowledge, which is not recognized in human love; nevertheless, in these earlier poems, the poet does not analyze human nature into a finite and infinite, or seek to dispose of his difficulties by the deceptive solvent of a dualistic agnosticism. He treats spirit as a unity, and refuses to set love and reason against each other. Man's *life*, for the poet, and not merely man's love, begins with God, and returns back to God in the rapt recognition of God's perfect being by reason, and in the identi-

---

[1] *Christmas-Eve.*

[2] *The Ring and the Book—The Pope*, 1285-1289.

fication of **man's** purposes **with** His by means **of**
will and love.

> " What is left for us, save, **in** growth
> Of soul, to rise up, far past both,
> From the gift looking to the giver,
> And from the cistern to the river,
> And from the finite to infinity,
> And from man's dust to God's divinity?"[1]

It is this movement of the absolute in man, this
aspiration towards the full knowledge and perfect
goodness which can never be completely attained,
that constitutes man.

> " **Man**, therefore, thus conditioned, **must expect**
> **He** could not, what he knows now, know at first :
> What he considers that he knows to-day,
> Come but to-morrow, he will find mis-known ;
> Getting increase of knowledge, since he learns
> Because he lives, which is to be **a man,**
> **Set** to instruct himself by his **past self** :
> **First,** like the brute, obliged by **facts** to learn,
> Next, as man may, obliged by his own mind,
> Bent, habit, nature, knowledge turned to law.
> God's gift was that man shall conceive of truth
> And yearn to gain it, catching at mistake,
> As midway help till he reach fact indeed?"[2]

" Progress," the poet **says, is** " man's distinctive
mark alone." The endlessness of the progress, the
fact that every truth known to-day seems mis-
known to-morrow, that every ideal once achieved
only points to another and becomes itself a stepping-
stone, does not, as in his later days, bring despair
to him. For the consciousness of failure is possible

---

[1] *Christmas-Eve.*　　　　[2] *A Death in the Desert.*

in knowledge, as in morality, only because there has come fuller light. Browning does not, as yet, dwell exclusively on the negative element in progress, or forget that it is possible only through a deeper positive. He does not think that, because we turn our backs on what we have gained, we are therefore not going forward ; nay, he asserts the contrary. Failure, even the failure of knowledge, is triumph's evidence in these earlier days ; and complete failure, the unchecked rule of evil in any form, is therefore impossible. We deny

> " Recognized truths, obedient to some truth
> Unrecognized yet, but perceptible,—
> Correct the portrait by the living face,
> Man's God, by God's God in the mind of man."[1]

Thus the poet ever returns to the conception of God in the mind of man. God is the beginning and the end ; and man is the self-conscious worker of God's will, the free process whereby the last which is first, returns to itself. The process, the growth, is man's life and being ; and it falls within the ideal, which is eternal and all in all. The spiritual life of man, which is both intellectual and moral, is a dying into the eternal, not to cease to be in it, but to live in it more fully ; for spirits necessarily commune. He dies to the temporal interests and narrow ends of the exclusive self, and lives an ever-expanding life in the life of others, manifesting more and more that spiritual principle which is the life of God, who lives and loves in all things. " God is a being in whom we exist ; with

---

[1] *The Ring and the Book—The Pope*, 1871-1874.

whom we are in principle one ; with whom the human spirit is identical, in the sense that He *is* all which the human spirit is capable of becoming."[1]

From this point of view, and in so far as Browning is loyal to the conception of the community of the divine and human, he is able to maintain his faith in God, not in spite of knowledge, but through the very movement of knowledge within him. He is not obliged, as in his later works, to look for proofs, either in nature, or elsewhere ; nor to argue from the emotion of love in man, to a cause of that emotion. He needs no syllogistic process to arrive at God ; for the very activity of his own spirit as intelligence, as the reason which thinks and acts, is the activity of God within him. Scepticism is impossible, for the very act of doubting is the activity of reason, and a profession of the knowledge of the truth.

> "I
> Put no such dreadful question to myself,
> Within whose circle of experience burns
> The central truth, Power, Wisdom, **Goodness,—God :**
> I must outlive a thing ere know it dead :
> When I outlive the faith there is a sun,
> When I lie, ashes to the very soul,—
> Someone not I, must wail above the heap,
> 'He died in dark whence never morn arose.'"[2]

And this view of God as immanent in man's experience also forecloses all possibility of failure. Beneath the failure, the possibility of which is involved in a moral life, lies the divine element,

---

[1] Green's *Prolegomena to Ethics*, p. 198.
[2] *The Ring and the Book—The Pope*, 1631-1639.

working through contradiction to its own fulfilment. Failure is necessary for man, because he grows: but, for the same reason, the failure is not final. Thus, the poet, instead of denying the evidence of his intellect as to the existence of evil, or casting doubt on the distinction between right and wrong, or reducing the chequered course of human history into a phantasmagoria of mere mental appearances, can regard the conflict between good and evil as real and earnest. He can look evil in the face, recognize its stubborn resistance to the good, and still regard the victory of the latter as sure and complete. He has not to reduce it into a phantom, or mere appearance, in order to give it a place within the divine order. He sees the night, but he also sees the day succeed it. Man falls into sin, but he cannot rest in it. It is contradictory to his nature, he cannot content himself with it, and he is driven through it. Mephistopheles promised more than he could perform, when he undertook to make Faust declare himself satisfied. There is not within the kingdom of evil what will satisfy the spirit of man whose last law is goodness, whose nature, however obscured, is God's gift of Himself.

> " While I see day succeed the deepest night—
> How can I speak but as I know?—my speech
> Must be, throughout the darkness ' It will end :
> The light that did burn, will burn !' Clouds obscure—
> But for which obscuration all were bright?
> Too hastily concluded ! Sun-suffused,
> A cloud may soothe the eye made blind by blaze,—
> Better the very clarity of heaven :
> The soft streaks are the beautiful and dear.

What but the weakness in a faith supplies
The incentive to humanity, no strength
Absolute, irresistible, comports?
How can man love but what he yearns to help?
And that which men think weakness within strength,
But angels know for strength and stronger yet—
What were it else but the first things made new,
But repetition of the miracle,
The divine instance of self-sacrifice
That never ends and aye begins for man?
So, never I miss footing in the maze,
No,—I have light nor fear the dark at all." [1]

[1] *The Ring and the Book—The Pope*, 1640-1660.

INDEX TO BROWNING'S POEMS

REFERRED TO IN THE TEXT.

GLASGOW : PRINTED AT THE UNIVERSITY PRESS BY ROBERT MACLEHOSE AND CO. LTD.

WORKS BY
SIR HENRY JONES

Idealism as a Practical Creed

Being the Lectures on Philosophy and Modern Life delivered before the University of Sydney. By HENRY JONES, M.A., LL.D., D.Litt., F.B.A., Professor of Moral Philosophy in the University of Glasgow. Crown 8vo. Second Edition. 6s. nett.

"He is always lucid ; he is always candid. While he is stimulating, he is also persuasive."—*Spectator*.

A Critical Account of the Philosophy of Lotze

The Doctrine of Thought. Crown 8vo. 6s. nett.

"This is a genuine contribution to philosophy. It amounts to a destructive criticism of the half-hearted attitude adopted by Lotze towards the problem of thought and reality."—Mr. BERNARD BOSANQUET in the *Pall Mall Gazette*.

Social Responsibilities

Lectures to Business Men. Demy 8vo. 1s. nett.

GLASGOW: JAMES MACLEHOSE AND SONS
PUBLISHERS TO THE UNIVERSITY

www.ingramcontent.com/pod-product-compliance
Lightning Source LLC
Chambersburg PA
CBHW051221120726
47905CB00004B/1208